P9-BZM-068

m T

HIS CHISELED FACE
WAS A MASK
OF NAKED DESIRE

Kaylene took a slow step away from Fire Thunder. She was aware of the keen silence in the cabin. She wondered if Fire Thunder might even hear the pounding of her heart.

She said nothing, only watched him as he came closer. She could go no farther. She could feel the heat of the fireplace on her back and knew that she couldn't step away from him.

She gasped when suddenly his hands were on her cheeks, his thumbs gently stroking them. Closing her eyes, she shuddered with ecstasy when he suddenly surrounded her with his hard, strong arms, pressing her against him.

As his lips claimed hers, and he held her so tenderly to him, she was no longer afraid. It was as though his lips were drugging her, speaking to her, telling her that the only thing alive tonight in this cabin was passion, sweet, wonderful, undying passion.

This passion was them; how they felt for one another; how they finally allowed themselves to feel.

Fire Thunder's mouth slipped away from Kaylene's lips. He whispered against her cheek. "Say you want me."

ALSO BY CASSIE EDWARDS

Wild Thunder
Wild Bliss
Wild Abandon
Wild Desire
Wild Splendor
Wild Embrace
Wild Rapture
Wild Ecstasy

WILD WHISPERS

by

Cassie Edwards

A TOPAZ BOOK

TOPAZ
Published by the Penguin Group
Penguin Books USA Inc., 375 Hudson Street,
New York, New York 10014, U.S.A.
Penguin Books Ltd, 27 Wrights Lane,
London W8 5TZ, England
Penguin Books Australia Ltd, Ringwood,
Victoria, Australia
Penguin Books Canada Ltd, 10 Alcorn Avenue,
Toronto, Ontario, Canada M4V 3B2
Penguin Books (N.Z.) Ltd, 182–190 Wairau Road,
Auckland 10, New Zealand

Penguin Books Ltd, Registered Offices:
Harmondsworth, Middlesex, England

First published by Topaz, an imprint of Dutton Signet,
a division of Penguin Books USA Inc.

First Printing, May, 1996
10   9   8   7   6   5   4   3   2   1

Copyright © Cassie Edwards, 1996
All rights reserved
Topaz Man photo © Charles William Bush

 REGISTERED TRADEMARK—MARCA REGISTRADA

Printed in the United States of America

Without limiting the rights under copyright reserved above, no part of
this publication may be reproduced, stored in or introduced into a
retrieval system, or transmitted, in any form, or by any means (electronic,
mechanical, photocopying, recording, or otherwise), without the prior written
permission of both the copyright owner and the above publisher of this
book.

BOOKS ARE AVAILABLE AT QUANTITY DISCOUNTS WHEN USED TO PROMOTE
PRODUCTS OR SERVICES. FOR INFORMATION PLEASE WRITE TO PREMIUM
MARKETING DIVISION, PENGUIN BOOKS USA INC., 375 HUDSON STREET, NEW
YORK, NEW YORK 10014.

If you purchased this book without a cover you should be aware that this
book is stolen property. It was reported as "unsold and destroyed"
to the publisher and neither the author nor the publisher has received
any payment for this "stripped book."

With much affection, I dedicate *Wild Whispers* to the following special friends:

Lillian Aiello	Stella Alexander
Nancy Applegate	Deborah Abrams
Lori Ann Adkison	Cindy Arquette
Marcella Burris	Aera Bryant
Clara Ann Bentley	Rae Berlove
Cheryl Betancourt	Myrtle Barben
Dee Bockes	Vivian Castrodale
Ann Clough	Doris Denardo
Rena Esposito	Carol Kita
Cindy Strothers	Marion Campbell

WILD AND FREE

In my heart I am Indian, wild and free.
But in this world, it was not meant to be.
Sun Father, Moon Woman, Earth Mother,
Guiding me through my day,
But, somehow, in this world I lost my way.
Great Spirits, far and wide,
Please come to me and be my guide.
Take me as your daughter and you'll be proud of me,
And then I shall become an Indian on the land that's
Wild and free,
Where for me happiness shall always be.

—Brandy Reidnauer,
Poet and reader of
Indian romances.

1

At night, when gazing
On the gay hearth blazing,
O, still remember me!
—THOMAS MOORE

1854, Texas

In continuing, brilliant zigzags, lightning raced against
the dark, stormy sky. Chief Fire Thunder, of the Coahuila Thunder clan of the Kickapoo, held tight to his
reins as his white stallion became uneasy over the omi-
nous play of lightning, and the great claps of thunder
that rumbled through the ground beneath his hooves.

Fire Thunder leaned low over his stallion and spoke
soothingly to him. As Fire Thunder looked nervously
at the herd of longhorn steers, he stroked his steed's
thick neck.

When Fire Thunder saw a familiar glow that appeared on the horn tips of one of the steers at the
head of the herd, he stiffened. He had seen it before.
He braced himself for the worst, when sparks raced
along the horns, danced along the steer's back, then
rolled off its tail into the ground.

Fire Thunder straightened his back and sucked in a

wild, nervous breath when, deep in the center of the packed mass of steers, the lightning appeared in many other places. As though it were a living thing, it leapt from steer to steer. It bounced off horn tips and tails in a frightening phosphorescent display. The steers snorted and trumpeted as the air crackled and popped around them.

Black Hair, Fire Thunder's best *nekanaki,* friend, sidled his horse closer to his. "They are going to stampede!" he shouted above the howling wind and the rain that suddenly fell from the sky in torrents. "Cry to the heavens, Fire Thunder. Tell Grandfather to stop!"

Fire Thunder looked guardedly around him, at his other warriors who were too close to him for him to perform his magic, his special powers that were known only to him and his friend Black Hair.

"This is not the time or the place for me to do that," Fire Thunder shouted back at Black Hair. He gave his friend a steady gaze. "You know as well as I that my powers are reserved for times when I am alone. We will battle the elements today with the strength bestowed upon us by *Kitzihiat,* our Great Spirit!"

No sooner was that said than the leaders of the longhorn herd whirled and balked. Dazzled by the play of lightning, the animals churned in confusion.

Suddenly they turned and reversed their direction.

The wet ground was pounded by more than a hundred hooves as the animals began their crazed flight.

"Stampede!" Fire Thunder shouted, grabbing his lariat from his saddle. His eyes blurred from the rain as he rode in a hard gallop toward an old moss-horned bull that was in the lead.

"Let's head him off together!" Black Hair said as

he rode after the same longhorn. "If we can get him stopped, the rest will follow suit."

Fire Thunder nodded and looked over his shoulder at the rest of his warriors, who were attempting to head off the bulk of the herd, and, lead them back in the direction of the Rio Grande.

Fire Thunder's gaze turned back to the old bull. Gaining on him, he whirled his lariat in the air over his head.

Black Hair was riding side by side with the bull. He swung his lariat and cut the air in front of the bull's nose.

Fire Thunder reined his horse off to the side, his animal skidding to a halt and spewing mud. Fire Thunder watched, smiling, as Black Hair brought his coiled rope down over the old bull's nose.

The rope landed with a whack. The old bull snorted and turned, his horn tips barely missing Black Hair and his feisty mustang.

Fire Thunder swung his rope in the air in a wide circle, then slung it over the old bull's head and tightened it.

The longhorn yanked and jerked against both ropes, then snorted and stood quiet.

Breathing hard, Fire Thunder watched his warriors round up the rest of the herd, the storm finally floating on past them overhead.

The herd's panic evaporated, with only a few continuing in wild plunging lopes.

The warriors cut in front of the longhorns, moved them into a mill, then turned the mill into a controlled drive toward the Rio Grande once again.

"I thought we had lost them," Black Hair said as he rode beside Fire Thunder toward the river.

"Longhorns are a stubborn lot, that is for sure,"

Fire Thunder said, smiling at Black Hair. "But not as stubborn as you or I, my friend."

Black Hair laughed and nodded.

Fire Thunder yanked his water-soaked, red cotton bandanna from around his brow and used it to wipe the rain from his face. He flung his wet, waist-length, coal-black hair back from his shoulders as he stuck the bandanna into the pocket of his buckskin shirt. His fringed buckskin outfit clung to him like a second skin. The leather chaps he wore, to give good protection against rope burns, were now wet, tight, and abrasive.

"We will cross the border with the steers at the Rio Grande under the cover of darkness, go on until we reach the foot of our mountain, then make camp for the night," Fire Thunder said. He looked upward. The moon was only a tiny sliver in the sky.

"Yes, that is best," Black Hair said, nodding. "The steers are tired after their run. They would move too slowly tonight to get them safely up the mountain pass."

"Even I move too slowly," Fire Thunder said, chuckling. "But it has been a good day for us, my friend. We have retrieved a good portion of the longhorns stolen from us by the Texans many moons ago when we lived in Texas. Now that we live in Mexico, we have enough land to take back the steers that were stolen from us. And we shall, until the number we steal matches that which was stolen from us."

Reins slack in his hands, Fire Thunder let his steed pick its own way through the darkness. It was now a night of scudding clouds, which intermittently shrouded the moon, making the dark seem blacker in sudden contrast.

The air was motionless, full of the lowing of the longhorns.

As they rode on in silence, Fire Thunder became lost in thought—about how he came to be here, instead of his home in Wisconsin. He had grown tired of the white people taking land from his people. He had broken away from the other Kickapoo people and had led his own here, where he had found freedom for them in Mexico.

His request to migrate into Mexico had been granted by the Mexican Ministry of War. The permission had been given to Fire Thunder as long as he agreed to help keep marauding Comanche renegades out of Mexico, and also white men who came with their promises that they always broke.

Although the Kickapoo had to subject themselves to the laws of the land of Mexico, it was not demanded of them to change their habits and customs.

The Mexican government allowed the Kickapoo to form a loose confederacy and permitted them to establish a village where they would be free to farm their own land, and raise large herds of livestock. To the Kickapoo, this was a paradise, without the cunning white government always interfering.

Fire Thunder was called "Captain" by the Mexican leaders. He had many privileges not enjoyed by the others. He was recognized as the head of his clan by the Mexican authorities, and received a small salary from the local municipality.

In the white world, Fire Thunder would be called a cattle baron because he owned vast tracts of grazing land.

He was honored and respected by all who knew him, and feared by his enemies.

When the Rio Grande was reached, Fire Thunder's thoughts came back to the present. He watched carefully and saw that his herd made it safely across the river, near to Eagle Pass. Thus far the Texans hadn't suspected the Kickapoo of stealing their cattle. The Comanche renegades, who were well known for such thievery, were always blamed.

Once the foot of Fire Thunder's mountain was reached, the herd was checked over. Fire Thunder's blood boiled when he saw how the Texans had changed the Kickapoo brand to one of theirs that was similar.

But he placed this aside too until he reached home, and his warriors could renew their own brand on the animals over the Texans'.

The camp was readied for the night. Bathed and wearing dried buckskins, Fire Thunder and Black Hair sat away from the others, before their own campfire. They were stretched out comfortably on blankets that were spread atop chestgrass that was plush as velvet.

They each chewed on a piece of jerky and a mixture of seeds and dried fruit, while a coffeepot spurted a trailing wisp of steam heavenward.

Not far from them, some of the longhorns were grazing on high, thick, dew-wet grass. Here and there one of the animals was dust-scratching, rolling on its back like a cat in a patch of clear ground, sharp polished hooves waving in the air while it twisted.

The cool breeze was full of longhorn talk, a drawn-out tympanic rattling of throaty noises.

"My friend, you are more quiet tonight than usual," Black Hair said. "Is it the Texans you are thinking about?" He lifted a tin cup to his mouth and slowly sipped his coffee.

"You know that all Texans opposed the presence of we Kickapoo in their country when we lived *there,*" Fire Thunder said sullenly. "They despised us. Some even called us marauders. They were glad when we moved into Mexican territory."

"Yes, and the Mexicans want us to stay," Black

Hair said, setting his empty coffee cup aside. "They see us as protectors."

"I wonder how those who only *pass* through Texas see us," Fire Thunder said, casting Black Hair a quick, questioning glance.

"Is there anyone particular in mind when you wonder about such a thing as that?" Black Hair said, raising an inquisitive eyebrow. "You have not ever mentioned such a worry to me before."

"I have not had cause to wonder about it before," Fire Thunder said, raking his long, lean fingers through his thick, black hair.

"Why do you now?" Black Hair said, straightening his back. "Or should I say *who* . . . brings such a question to your mind?"

"You are astute to all my thoughts, my friend," Fire Thunder said, reaching a hand over to Black Hair, clasping it on his shoulder. "There *is* someone lingering in my mind tonight."

Black Hair saw the sparkle in his friend's blue eyes, his blue eyes supporting Fire Thunder's claim to his mixture of French and Indian ancestry. Only a woman could cause such a look; such wonder.

"What woman, my friend?" Black Hair prodded. "Have I looked upon her, myself, with pleasure?"

"You have seen her, yes, and if you did not feel a stirring in your loins as you gazed upon her loveliness, you are not a man of passion," Fire Thunder said, laughing softly.

"*Who,* Fire Thunder?" Black Hair said, leaning his face closer. "Who intrigues you so much you torment your best friend with talk of him being passionless?"

"I was only jesting," Fire Thunder said, patting Black Hair's shoulder. "About your being *passionless,* that is. There *is* a certain woman who fills my thoughts tonight, who makes my heart feel as though it is thumping like Kickapoo warriors are playing a million drums inside my chest."

"Are you going to keep me guessing all night?" Black Hair said, impatience showing in the clipped tone of his voice.

"You cannot help but recall the long caravan of wagons we saw earlier in the day before we reached the Texan's ranch from whom we stole the longhorns," Fire Thunder said, watching the slow knowing appear in his friend's eyes. "Being a skilled reader, I read 'THE SHELTON FAMILY CARNIVAL' on the side of the wagons. In one of those wagons do you not recall seeing this beautiful young woman whose black hair was as sleek as a raven's, and whose eyes were as green and crisp as a panther's? She was delicate and pale skinned, almost fragile and doll-like in appearance."

"Yes, I remember her well," Black Hair said, nodding.

"She was, ah, *muy bonito,* very pretty," Fire Thunder said. "I surmise that she is at least eighteen winters of age. I wonder if she is yet married?"

"You, who avoid speaking of marriage to a woman like it is the plague, speak of it now when you have only seen this woman once?" Black Hair said incredulously.

"I have only avoided women because none have yet stirred my soul with such longings as I . . . feel . . . now for *this* woman," Fire Thunder said. He cleared his throat as he gave Black Hair an awkward glance. "This goes no farther, Black Hair. This is something spoken between you and myself only. I am my people's chief. I do not want to look weak in their eyes because I have been intrigued by a woman."

"A *white* woman . . . a *stranger* . . . a *carnival* person," Black Hair did not hesitate to say.

Fire Thunder ignored Black Hair's thoughts on the subject. And Black Hair knew that this was only a fleeting thing, for Fire Thunder would never see the woman again.

"I do wonder what goes on inside the carnival's mystery tents," Fire Thunder blurted out.

"Perhaps you would not want to know," Black Hair said, then lay down to sleep.

Fire Thunder stayed musing by the fire for a while. Then he spread his blankets out, and snuggled into his bedroll.

But he couldn't go to sleep. He kept seeing those green eyes and the soft smile of the woman.

Finally he drifted off into a restless sleep.

Yet even then he could not escape the green eyes and smile.

He dreamed of the woman.

She was in his arms.

She was so delicate, so sweet, so loving.

Their lips met in a trembling kiss.

He filled his hands with her breasts, their touch like silk against his palms.

Slowly she lowered her dress past her thighs.

He grew hot all over when she allowed him to touch her between her thighs, where she was wet with need of him.

He caressed her there until she cried out with soft pleasure.

She, in turn, caressed him, until he spilled his juices into the tiny palm of one of her hands.

Then their bodies met.

He plunged himself deep inside her.

They tangled and sank into a chasm of pure rapture. . . .

His heart pounding, his body aching with need, Fire

Thunder awakened in a fever. His eyes were wide. His breathing was rapid.

"It was a dream," he whispered huskily to himself.

The Kickapoo believed that the reason a person dreamed was because, while they slept, their spirit left the body and wandered, observing, watching what was occurring.

At other times, the spirit had personal experiences. It was of the utmost importance that a sleeping person never be brusquely awakened. The spirit had to have time to re-enter the body; otherwise, the spirit may become frightened and remain out of the body.

Not all dreams had significance, but certain ones had special meanings.

Fire Thunder knew that this dream tonight had *much* meaning.

He looked toward the heavens. "Grandfather, I must find a way to make it real! I ... must ... find her!"

Kaylene Shelton's head bobbed as she sat beside her mother and father on the seat of the covered wagon. They had passed through a storm and had gone safely onward. The carnival was headed now across the border, toward San Carlos, Mexico.

"Kaylene, sweetie, why not go to the back of the wagon and stretch out? You will be able to sleep more comfortably," Kaylene's mother said, as she placed a soft hand on Kaylene's arm. "I'm sure Midnight would love to have your company. The storm gave him quite a start, you know."

Kaylene rubbed the sleep from her eyes and nodded. "Wake me up, Mother, when we reach San Carlos," she said. "We've not performed in Mexico before. I'm anxious to see the town, how large it is, and what the people seem like."

"Yes, Kaylene, I'll awaken you," her mother said. "I, too, am anxious to see how we are received. We could come back more often if the people like us."

"How could they not like us?" Kaylene's father boasted. "We are the best carnival performing today in *and* out of Mexico." His pitch-black eyes narrowed. His thick mustache twitched nervously. "We'll show 'em. They'll not think of us just as 'carnie' people. They'll see us as special."

"Yes, Father, they'll see us as special," Kaylene said, sighing. She had grown tired of worrying long ago about what anyone thought of her.

She, in truth, was tired of the whole thing; performing at each stop, watching people ogle her as though she were, herself, a sideshow.

She wanted a real life, with a real house, with a husband and children.

She wanted roots.

Before she reached the back of the wagon, she could see the glowing, green eyes of her pet panther as it watched her approaching.

"Midnight, did you miss me?" Kaylene asked, reaching out to stroke her panther's sleek, black fur.

She curled up next to Midnight, welcoming the warmth of his body next to hers. She smiled when Midnight began to purr contentedly as he settled in more comfortably against her.

"Oh, Midnight, I thought sitting outside with Mother and Father would keep me awake.... Would keep me from thinking and dreaming about that handsome Indian I saw today," Kaylene murmured. She laughed softly as the rough-textured tongue of her pet licked her face, tickling it. "But nothing helps. I can't get him off my mind."

She squeezed her eyes tightly shut. "I must get some

sleep," she whispered. "We have several performances to give tomorrow, Midnight. I must look my best."

Sighing, again she drifted off to sleep. The Indian was there, his blue eyes touching her as though they were his hands. His smile sent a radiant glow throughout her.

"Who ... are ... you?" she whispered in her sleep to the Indian. "Ah, but your eyes! How they sparkle so blue against your dark, coppery skin. Can ... I ... touch your skin? Do you want to touch mine?"

In her dream, he was standing before her, so tall and lean, so very handsome. His dark, waist-length hair was blowing gently in the breeze, lifting from his bare, muscular shoulders.

"Yes, I wish to touch you, to hold you, to kiss you," the Indian said, making Kaylene tremble in response.

"Please do all those things," she whispered, her head swimming with desire as he grabbed her in his arms and kissed her.

She clung to him.

She reveled in the kiss and the way he held her.

Then Kaylene's insides melted when the Indian reached inside her blouse and cupped her breasts with his hands, his thumbs tweaking her nipples.

Then he drew his hands away and lifted her and carried her toward a campfire. Kaylene lay her head against his massive bare chest and let the sensual feelings inside her take over.

She had never made love with a man before.

She had never loved a man.

And now she was ready to give herself to an Indian, the one she had seen pass by with several warriors on horseback earlier in the day.

Even then, their eyes had revealed their sudden attraction to each other.

She had not wanted him to pass by. She had wanted to at least know his name.

"What is your name?" she asked in her dream as he lay her on a blanket and removed the rest of her clothes.

As he covered her with his body, she reached a hand to his lips. "Please tell me your name," she whispered.

His only response was to kiss her.

Then his lips trailed downward, along the vulnerable, sensitive line of her throat, and then to her breasts.

One by one he tasted her nipples with his tongue.

She thrilled with intense, rapturous feelings. But when his lips moved lower and his tongue flicked out and touched that part of her at the juncture of her thighs that was private, she jerked away . . . and awakened.

"It . . . seemed . . . so real," she whispered, shimmering with ecstasy as she relived the dream in her mind. She placed a finger to her lips. "I can even taste the kiss."

She ran a hand inside her blouse and touched a breast. She shivered with pleasure as she ran her fingers over its sensitive nipple. "It's his hands, not mine," she said, closing her eyes, envisioning him there, loving her.

"Kaylene, darling, did you say something?" her mother shouted back at her.

Her face hot with a blush, and shame of touching herself so intimately, Kaylene jerked her hand from inside her blouse and promptly answered her mother.

"I h-had a d-dream," she stammered. "That's all."

"You'd best get back to sleep," her mother said. "Tomorrow you can't perform with dark circles under your eyes."

"Yes, Mother," Kaylene said, sighing.

Again she settled in against Midnight. She felt a dejection come over her. So often she felt that her parents thought more of her performances than of her.

She too often felt used, not . . . loved.

Sullenly, she drifted off to sleep, to the rhythm of the wagon wheels, and the night sounds of crickets and frogs croaking in the distance. Not so far away a coyote howled at the moon.

"You have returned to me," the male voice said, giving Kaylene a start. The dream had returned, as though she had never awakened from it.

She was still nude.

She was still lying within the Indian's muscled arms.

"Yes, and I would love to stay forever, if you would have me," she murmured, accepting the bold thrust of his body as he entered her and showed her what, until now, had been a mystery to her.

She smiled in her sleep and trembled sensually.

In the dark, two shadows on horseback moved along a small trail. "White Wolf, I see a light up ahead," Dawnmarie said, as she squinted in the darkness toward the lamplight flaring from the window of a ranch house. Her gaze shifted. "And I see a barn. Surely the rancher and his wife will allow us to sleep in the barn tonight. Darling, a bed of straw would feel much better than the ground."

"Then that is what you will have," White Wolf said, reaching over to gently touch his wife's ashen face. "Dawnmarie, I fear for you so much. We should not have made this long journey from Wisconsin. It has worn you out."

"White Wolf, this is something I promised Mother I would do," Dawnmarie said with a stubborn lift of her chin. "Long ago, I promised her, before she died, that I would find my true people, the Kickapoo. I am a half-breed, bridging two worlds. I must make peace with the Kickapoo side of my heritage before my time comes to enter the afterworld. I must have the permission of the Kickapoo to enter their world. I must prove to my Kickapoo people that, although I had a white father, I *am* Kickapoo, heart and soul."

"And I understand and will continue to seek ways to get you to them," White Wolf said, sighing heavily. "We know they are in Mexico. We draw closer and closer each day. Surely, before long, you will be among your people."

"Thank you, darling, for being so understanding," Dawnmarie said, then became quiet as they passed through a wide gate and they rode onward toward the ranch house.

When they arrived, they did not have to knock on the door. The sound of their horses was enough to bring a man and woman to the porch. The man held high a lit lantern, the light spreading out toward Dawnmarie and White Wolf.

"And who are you? What do you want here?" the man asked, his free hand resting on a holstered pistol.

"Only lodging for the night in your barn if you will be so kind," White Wolf said. He gestured with a hand toward Dawnmarie. "My wife. She needs a good night of rest. At dawn tomorrow we shall be on our way."

"I don't deal much with Indians," the man said, his eyes narrowing at White Wolf. "You ain't Comanche, are you?"

"No, I am from the Lac du Flambeau clan of Chippewa," White Wolf said. "My wife is part white and Kickapoo. We are looking for her people. We have been told they are in Mexico. That is where we are headed."

"Chippewa? Kickapoo, huh?" the man said, kneading his chin. "I ain't never had no trouble with either tribe." He nodded toward the barn. "Go ahead. Take the barn for the night. But be on with you tomorrow before I come out to tend to my cows and chickens."

"We will be gone," White Wolf said. "Thank you. May the Great Spirit bless you for your kindness to strangers."

"You don't have to leave before breakfast, now do you?" the woman blurted out, getting a frown from her husband. "I'll bring you biscuits and gravy early in the morning. And hot coffee. My conscience wouldn't rest if I didn't feed you before you headed out again."

"Thank you," Dawnmarie said. "That would be most kind of you. We would be glad to share biscuits and gravy with you in the morning."

White Wolf and Dawnmarie wheeled their horses around and rode to the barn.

After the horses were turned out to eat in the pasture, and White Wolf had made a bed of straw for his wife, they stretched out together beneath a blanket.

"Violet Eyes, you seem unsettled," White Wolf said, drawing Dawnmarie closer to him.

"I so miss our children," she murmured. "Wisconsin is so far away now."

"Our children are all right," White Wolf reassured her. "Now go to sleep. You need your rest. I need mine."

Dawnmarie snuggled closer to her husband, always finding solace in his powerful arms.

2

She yet more pure, sweet, straight, and fair,
Than gardens, woods, meads, rivers are.
                                    —ANDREW MARVELL

Fire Thunder sank his heels into his horse's flanks and sent it into a lope ahead of the longhorn steers. The trail was rough up the mountainside, especially with a large herd of longhorns, their hooves occasionally slipping and sliding on the rocky path.

Determined to keep his people together at all costs, Fire Thunder had chosen to build his village on land that was many miles into the mountains. It was well hidden from those who might try and intrude on his people's privacy.

His village was strategically located several miles from the United States border, close enough to San Carlos so that it would not be inconvenient for his clan to go there and sell their wares, and to trade with the Mexican people.

Above him on his right, the rimrock glowed like stirred coals in the early morning sunrise.

Somewhere in the pines that spread out on both

sides of him, a meadowlark gave the morning its first song.

A chickenlike bird strutted from a thicket, onto a cropped dome. Another bird fluttered in, and soon there were a dozen.

A pair of cowbirds squeaked like rusty hinges.

Then he rode onto a flat stretch of land carpeted with pungent sagebrush giving off a bittersweet scent.

Fire Thunder edged his horse aside to watch the longhorns pass by, quickly now, the pastureland in view. He then rode on, Black Hair beside him on his mustang.

When they reached a shallow creek, the Kickapoo point men gave little crooning yells, encouraging the steers to cross. Their throaty cries were barely audible over the thudding hooves and the splash of the roiled waters as the longhorns dove into the stream.

The longhorns streamed past in a flurry of bobbing backs and tossing horns. Shades of tan predominated in their hides—ranging from a creamy-yellow to a rich chocolate-brown that was so dark, it looked more black than brown.

After the longhorns were on dry land again, and moving peacefully along the trail toward the Kickapoo pastures, Fire Thunder and Black Hair broke away from them and rode into their village.

It was just in time for Fire Thunder to discover that the women and children of his village were ready to leave on their burros, to sell the wild *chilepiqiquin,* chili peppers, they had harvested.

They had also harvested much wild oregano and pennyroyal, which they preferred to sell from door to door, rather than on the town square, since this method always brought them a better price.

Fire Thunder's eight-year-old deaf-mute sister, Little Sparrow, was among those who were going to the town of San Carlos.

Fire Thunder dismounted and went to her.

Little Sparrow's eyes gleamed with love as Fire Thunder reached up and took her from her burro. He hugged her, then placed her on the ground and knelt before her. Gently he framed her copper face between his hands. She could read lips well, and she watched his lips as he spoke to her.

"Is your cousin Good Bear going with you, to keep watch on you?" Fire Thunder asked. His gaze moved over his sister, to see if she wore the proper clothes for the adventure that lay ahead of her.

For going into town to sell their wares, the women and young girls wore a special dress. It consisted of a bodice sewn to a full skirt that had no flounces. The skirt was pulled up toward the body and secured on each side, thus forming an ample bag in which the chilies, stems, and leaves were carried.

Since his sister was still a child, she wore a hairdo which young girls wore until they reached their *menarche*, maturity. Her hair was braided in three sections, one on either side of the head, and another in the center. Three braids were brought to the top of the head to form a little topknot, secured with a ribbon.

"Yes, Fire Thunder, Good Bear is accompanying me to San Carlos," Little Sparrow related to him in her form of sign language. "And I am so excited."

She hugged her brother, her dark eyes dancing as she looked past Fire Thunder's shoulder and saw her fifteen-year-old cousin approaching. He was a thin lad whose voice was in the process of changing, proving to everyone that he was becoming a man. He wore his long hair past his waist. His jaw was square. His nose was wide on his copper face, and his lips were thick. He was dressed in a fringed outfit and buck-skin moccasins.

Fire Thunder held Little Sparrow close, his hands caressing her tiny back. Their parents having died at the hand of a Comanche raid when they lived in Texas, he had become his sister's guardian. And he had quite a task in hand, for being unable to hear or speak, she was more vulnerable than the rest of the Kickapoo children.

But Fire Thunder had always tried to make his sister not feel different. He had never wanted her affliction to get in the way of living a normal life. He made certain that Little Sparrow participated in everything the other girls did. She harvested as the other girls and women harvested. She sold her harvests as the others sold theirs. She entered into the dancing ceremonies as the others danced. She didn't hear the music, but she felt it deeply within her heart as she watched the others.

With most who knew her, she communicated by way of sign language, or by reading their lips. She was a sweet, innocent child who trusted everyone, and who never saw an enemy.

That troubled Fire Thunder more than the affliction she had been born with. She might trust the wrong person some day and he might not be there to protect her.

With the worries for his sister deep inside his heart and mind, Fire Thunder rose to his feet, and turned, and faced Good Bear as the lad came and stood beside him.

"Good Bear, you must stay with my sister at all times while on your journey to San Carlos," Fire Thunder said, laying a heavy hand on the young boy's shoulder. "And once there, do not take your eyes off her. Do you understand? You will be her voice when those she tries to sell her chilies to do not understand what she is trying to say to them. You will make sure she is not cheated when she receives payment for her chilies. Do you understand the importance of staying close to my sister?"

"Have not I earned your trust?" Good Bear asked, glancing over at Little Sparrow, who sent him a trustingly sweet smile. He turned his eyes back up to Fire Thunder. "I have always brought her home safely, have I not?"

"This is *today* that I am speaking of," Fire Thunder said seriously. "Not yesterday, or the day before that. Prove to me again today that your trust is earned."

"Yes, sir," Good Bear said, squaring his shoulders. "Thank you for entrusting her into my care. That alone is an honor, when there are so many others you could ask besides me, your mere cousin."

Fire Thunder patted the boy's shoulder, then drew him into his arms. "I do trust you, Good Bear," he said, hugging him. "Go to San Carlos. Enjoy the outing."

"Thank you, my chief," Good Bear said. He helped Little Sparrow onto her mule.

Strained voices turned Fire Thunder around. His eyes wavered when he saw his friend Black Hair having trouble again with his daughter, Running Fawn. Her mother had died in the same raid as Fire Thunder's parents. Running Fawn had never accepted the death of her mother. She had never gotten over the trauma of that day, when many died, and when many were wounded as the village was set to flames by the Comanches.

Without a mother's guidance, Running Fawn had become rebellious, too strong-willed for her own good.

Fire Thunder stood back and listened to father and daughter, as did the rest of the village. People were silent in the wave of the rage building in Black Hair's voice.

Fire Thunder never interfered in any of his people's personal affairs. That was not the duty of a chief.

"Get off the burro, Running Fawn," Black Hair said as he glared at his daughter. "You are not going with the others this time to San Carlos." He hated to even think about the gossip about his daughter—that she was suspected of having trysts with young Mexican men her age.

Running Fawn, her black hair loose and flowing around her shoulders, her face beautiful, but twisted now in a stubborn glare, folded her arms defiantly and refused to budge from the burro.

"Do as you are told, Running Fawn," Black Hair said, trying to speak in a softer tone so that the others might not hear. He tried to invoke the sternness that was necessary to make his daughter realize just how angry he was at her insolence.

Still she did not stir from the burro.

Black Hair's face flamed with anger. He placed his hands at his daughter's waist and lifted her bodily from the burro and placed her feet on the ground before him.

"You shame me among our people by not only gossip that is ugly about you, but also now, when you refuse to do as you are told," Black Hair said, his jaw tight, his nostrils flaring. "Tell me, daughter, are your pockets filled with chilies? Or is your reason for going to San Carlos today to see a young man? Running Fawn, do you not see the wrong in being so loose with yourself? You should remain a virgin to the day of your marriage. Until you have spoken vows, you should be completely innocent of men."

Running Fawn's lips parted in a gasp. She paled and looked shyly from person to person as they stared back at her. Tears crept from her eyes as she looked quickly up at her father. "How could you?" she cried, then ran to her lodge, sobbing.

There was another moment of strained silence, then Fire Thunder went to his sister and gave her another hug and a kiss. In sign language he told her good-bye, and that he loved her, and to be safe while away from him.

She nodded, her eyes wide and shining.

Fire Thunder gave Good Bear a nod, then stepped back as the slow procession of burros started down the mountainside on a separate path from that which was used to bring the longhorns to safe pasture.

Black Hair went to Fire Thunder. "My daughter, she is such a worry," he said, his head bowed.

"You will in time work things out," Fire Thunder said, taking the reins of his horse. He swung himself into his saddle. "Let us go and see to our longhorns." He laughed throatily. "We have some changes to make, do you not agree?"

Black Hair eased into his saddle and grabbed his reins. "I find it hard to concentrate now that I am back at home, where my daughter disappoints me over and over again," he said thickly as he rode off with Fire Thunder through the village.

At first sight, when anyone came to call on the Kickapoo, the village of wigwams, with an occasional Mexican *jacal,* hut, seemed to sprawl randomly through the valley.

But upon closer examination, one perceived that it was laid out according to a plan. The village had been built at the site of eleven crystal-clear springs, protected by a sharply rising hill.

Fire Thunder and Black Hair passed across a large cleared plot of land where ceremonial ballgames took place, then rode onward to where great seas of grass provided food for their cattle.

"How can you let your worries about your daughter linger in your mind when you have this to please your eyes and your heart?" Fire Thunder said. He swung his hand in a wide arc before him toward the great herd of longhorns grazing peacefully on the tall, thick, sweet grass.

"Can you tell me that you do not have a woman still bothering your heart?" Black Hair said, giving Fire Thunder a lingering stare. "Or have you forgotten the woman with the green eyes and raven-black hair?"

Fire Thunder's heart skipped a sensual beat at the very mention of the woman that he had seen with the carnival caravan. He gave Black Hair a slow smile. "Thinking of that woman is much different than thinking of a daughter," he said, laughing huskily. "And, yes, she is still on my mind."

"Is it not a waste of time to keep thinking about her?" Black Hair taunted. "You will never see her again."

"Perhaps yes, perhaps no," Fire Thunder said, shrugging.

When they reached the other warriors, who were heating branding irons in a small fire, they both drew tight rein and dismounted.

Women, daughters, and otherwise were soon forgotten in their anger as they checked the blotched attempt of the Texans to change the Kickapoo brand.

"The fools," Fire Thunder grumbled. "Yet they surely sold many at the market before we came and claimed the rest as ours again. Those who bought the steers looked the other way."

"Yes, the penalty for stealing cattle seems to depend, in large part, on who you are, and how you did it," Black Hair said, placing his fists on his hips.

"Longhorns are comparable to the nuggets of gold that miners find in creek beds. If a white man brings a steer to market for another white man to buy, and it is known, without actually saying it, that the steer came from Indian stock, nothing is done about the theft."

"That is for certain, for any man who knows our brand would have seen it on these longhorns, that the brands have obviously been changed," Fire Thunder grumbled. "And who is to say where the longhorns were finally sold? At which marketplace? Texas long-horns can be driven one thousand miles to market with almost no ill effects."

He went and stood over a steed as one of his men held it with his lasso, while another prepared a red-hot branding iron. The Kickapoo, as a tribe, used the same brand on all of their cattle—a circle with a hook. This circle might be placed in various positions. The hook might be upright, downward, to the left, to the right, or in the four other positions between them.

The brand could be placed on the animal's jaw, shoulder, rump, or leg. This ingenious scheme gave the Kickapoo thirty different versions of this one brand.

As Fire Thunder watched the brand sizzle while being placed on the rump of the longhorn, he grew even more somber. "We were forced to leave our land in Wisconsin because of the extinction of fur-bearing animals by not only whites, but also the Iroquois," he said, his voice low. "We Kickapoo have been victims of battles, treaties made and broken by the white man, and encroachment on our lands. Then, too, came those who stole our cattle."

He turned glaring eyes to Black Hair. "But never again," he hissed. "We, the Coahuila Kickapoo, have now amassed a herd of some three thousand cattle. No one will be allowed to take even one head of that cattle from us again. We have worked hard to improve the stock, importing expensive blooded bulls, breeding them to choice native cows. No one will get near them, except for those men at the markets we choose to take them to."

He swung himself into his saddle and rode away.

Alone, he rode his horse to a prominent shelf jutting out to the east of the ridge, and surveyed the surrounding land. He looked at the grasses and pines, absorbing the panorama that belonged to his people.

He could see the reddish-brown *wapiti,* the elk.

In the valley below stood many elk, all ages, both male and female. Two elks were grazing in a stream bed.

Then he saw two elks mating, and his mind returned to the beautiful, alluring white woman. He wondered where she was; how faraway she was from his home in Mexico.

He felt this strange longing, as though she might be near.

He did not feel foolish thinking that even she might have similar longings, and that she might be thinking of him. The moment their gaze had met and had held, something *had* been exchanged between them. It was as though their destinies had intertwined at that moment into one destiny charted in the heavens.

"I have never experienced this before," Fire Thunder cried as he stared up at the blue sky. "Why do I now? Why?"

3

She's loveliest of the festal throng,
In delicate form and Grecian face—
A beautiful, incarnate song,
A marvel of harmonious grace.
　　　　　—PAUL HAMILTON HAYNE

San Carlos was crowded with shoppers. Outdoor markets lined the streets. They displayed beautiful, colorful shawls, jewelry, and vegetables and fruits.

The carnival tents had been pitched at the edge of town. People were crowding in and around the tents, the smell of popcorn and sawdust filling the air with their competing aromas.

The carnival sideshows drew the most attention as the performers on small platforms just outside their tents tempted people with a portion of their shows. After enough tickets were sold, they would perform their entire show within the private confines of their tents.

Some men, young and old alike, tasted the forbidden view of a naked woman who was tattooed from head to toe, a large, winding snake wrapping itself around her body.

Kaylene was in her own private tent. The audience crowded in and stood around the roped-off area where she was performing. She was petite and beautiful. Her green eyes were sparkling. She wore a short skirt that shamelessly showed a good portion of her legs above her knees. The deep cleavage of her breasts was revealed where her drawstring blouse swept low in front.

Kaylene held her head back and laughed as she rode her large and stately black panther around the circle, a sparkling, gold-sequined rein gripped in her dainty, tapering fingers.

When Good Bear saw the carnival tents, and the crowd of people rushing toward them, he was not able to hold back his excitement of possibly seeing, for the first time in his life, what a carnival truly offered.

Gripping onto Little Sparrow's hand, he sneaked away from the other Kickapoo women and children and rushed toward the tents with the crowd. Little Sparrow was as intrigued and willingly went with him.

Elbowing his way through the crowd, Good Bear's eyes widened as he went from tent to tent to see what sideshows were being offered in each. The smell of the popped corn made his stomach ache with hunger, yet something else that quickly drew his attention made him forget that he, nor Little Sparrow, had taken time to eat, as they had gone from house to house, selling the chilies.

His heart beat like wild thunder within his chest as he pushed his way to the front of the crowd and gasped at what he saw. The tattooed, naked lady, with the monstrous snake coiled around her body, was gesturing toward the crowd with her hands, trying to lure them into buying a ticket, to see her private show.

When the lady's eyes met Good Bear's, and she smiled seductively at him, he experienced the first stirrings of a man. His gaze lowered. He gulped hard and felt his face heating up with a blush as he stared at the woman's large, thick breasts. He was so intently staring at them, he was not aware of anything but the hungry ache inside his loins.

He did not feel Little Sparrow slip her hand free.

He did not see her turn away from him and push her way through the crowd of people.

Excited and intrigued, Little Sparrow moved slowly from tent to tent, then went from stand to stand, to see the beautiful ceramics that were for sale. One in particular caught her eye. It was a horse with small, sparkling sequins glued all over its body.

She tilted her head one way and then the other, taken by how the sun reflected on the sequins, sending off rainbow colors.

"You like the horse?"

When Little Sparrow did not respond to John's question, he placed a hand on her shoulder.

Feeling the hand made Little Sparrow jump with alarm. She turned wide and questioning eyes up at the man, then watched his lips as he spoke to her.

"Do you like the horse?" John Shelton asked, an evil gleam in his eyes.

Little Sparrow did not respond right away. She stared at the man, studying him. He was tall, with thick, dark eyebrows over severe, unfriendly dark eyes. He wore colorful clothes, his red satin shirt casting a sheen on his pockmarked face. She stared at his thick, black mustache, and then looked again into his eyes. Their coldness caused a shiver to race through her flesh.

Having always been taught not to befriend strangers, especially men, Little Sparrow ran away from the man and past a ticket stand and ducked quickly into a tent. The crowd of people were applauding as they stood in a circle around the tent.

Intrigued anew, the man forgotten, Little Sparrow pushed her way to the front of the crowd.

She stopped and stared as she stood at the roped-off area. She had never seen anything as wonderful, as intriguing, as the lovely lady riding the beautiful panther. Little Sparrow had always loved animals.

She was unaware of eyes on her, and didn't realize that she was being stalked, until a large hand suddenly grabbed her arm and whisked her away.

When she looked up and saw that it was the same man who had spoken to her earlier, she tried to wriggle free of his grip.

But his hand was too large. His hold was too tight. There was no way she could get free.

Her eyes wild, Little Sparrow scanned the crowd for Good Bear. She had been foolish to slip away from him. She was afraid, more afraid than she had ever been in her entire life.

She was taken to a dark and dreary tent.

John Shelton stood her on a chair and clasped hard onto her arms.

"Don't be afraid," John said, his eyes imploring her. "I'm not going to harm you." He held her with one hand, while with his other he caressed her soft, copper face with his thumb. "Now tell me your name. Friends should know each other's names. Mine is John. Yours is . . . ?"

Although the lamplight was dim, Little Sparrow managed to read his lips.

When she tried to speak and couldn't, he realized that she was a "mute." He felt even more fortunate to have found her wandering alone, without parents to look after her.

Being a mute, she would never be able to tell anyone who was responsible for her abduction, or where, or when.

In her he had found himself a new "sideshow." He would present this child to the public as a "savage" who was uncivilized, who had never learned how to talk.

He was extremely excited about having her; the many prospects of how he could use her.

There were so many ways to use her.

Yes, so ... many ...!

Knowing the importance of getting far away from San Carlos as quickly as possible, so that no one could come and claim this little "jewel" of a child, John took Little Sparrow to a tent where a middle-aged colored lady sat in a rocker, mending socks.

"Magnolia Jane, keep an eye on this girl until I return," John said, releasing Little Sparrow.

So glad to be away from the man, Little Sparrow ran to the woman and clung to her, her eyes wild as she watched John leave.

Magnolia Jane Blankenship, long past being pretty and shapely enough to draw a crowd with her unique style of belly dancing, sensed the child's fear. She had learned long ago never to question John's motives for anything he did. She feared him more than she had ever feared anyone. His cruel streak ran long and deep. She bore scars on her back that had been placed there by the tongue of John Shelton's whip.

Magnolia Jane laid her sewing aside and picked up Little Sparrow and sat her on her lap. Slowly she rocked her back and forth.

"Child, it's going to be all right," Magnolia Jane said, trying to reassure Little Sparrow, yet fearing, herself, the fate of the child. She was there to stay, that was for sure.

But for what? What cruel task would John give her?

Little Sparrow snuggled against Magnolia's large bosom as tears streamed across her tiny copper cheeks. She watched the tent entrance, hoping and praying that she would be rescued.

In her heart she cried out for her brother Fire Thunder.

John hurried from tent to tent and told everyone they were leaving. Even if they had to return money for tickets already paid for, do it. It was imperative that they leave this town. They weren't that far from their next stop. They would just stay a day longer there.

Kaylene rushed to her father. "Why are we leaving?" she asked, breathless as she followed him as he yanked stakes from the ground so the tents could be dismantled.

When her father did not respond, Kaylene placed a hand on one of his, stopping him from taking up another stake. "Father, please tell me what's happened," she asked, finally getting his attention. "We've never left so quickly from a town. Especially not this one. Didn't you see the crowd of people? And to give money back? That isn't like you, Father, to give back any money."

Kaylene's mother came and stood beside her, her eyes filled with worry. "John, what's happened?" she asked, wringing her hands.

John took Kaylene and her mother each by an elbow and led them aside, away from the commotion, and the others. "We're leaving because we have a runaway child that came to me, begging to stay with our carnival," he said, looking constantly over his shoulder. "I took pity on the child and gave her permission to stay. Who is to say whether or not she is an abused child, fleeing the clutches of some evil relative?"

"Did she tell you that?" Kaylene asked, her heart going out to any child in trouble.

"Well, not exactly. She can't talk," John said stiffly. "She's a deaf mute."

"A deaf mute?" Kaylene said, her voice drawn. Her spine stiffened. "Father, if she is deaf, and she can't speak, how could she beg you to let her stay with us?"

John's eyes became two points of angry fire. "Do you doubt my word?" he asked tightly.

"Well, n-no, but—" Kaylene stammered out.

"Then don't ask any more questions," John said, glancing over at his wife whose eyes were wavering on his. "Now let's get to work. Let's get the carnival out of this town. I cannot allow anyone to find the child with the carnival. I ... might be accused of having abducted her. And that isn't how it was at all. The child absolutely doesn't want to be found."

"Where is she now?" Kaylene asked, looking slowly around her.

"She's with Magnolia Jane," John said thickly. "The poor child. She's scared to death. Magnolia Jane has ways to make her feel better."

Kaylene broke into a mad run and hurried to Magnolia Jane's tent. There she found the small child curled up on Magnolia's lap, sound asleep.

"Why, she's so tiny, and ... and ... she's an *Indian*," Kaylene gasped out.

Kaylene's mother and father had followed her. "John, why?" Anna asked, giving him a despairing stare. "Why did you have to steal another child?"

He turned an angry glare at her. "Just keep your mouth shut," he growled out. "If you know what's best for you, you'll not interfere."

Good Bear was icy cold inside as he watched the carnival tents being dismantled. He was frantic because he hadn't been able to find Little Sparrow. She was missing and it was all his fault. He shouldn't have separated himself from the others. He shouldn't have allowed Little Sparrow to leave his side.

Good Bear hung his head. He had let his chief down. He couldn't face Fire Thunder.

His heart aching, feeling so ashamed for being such a disappointment to his people, Good Bear broke into a run and left the carnival and San Carlos behind him.

Fire Thunder had bathed after having been assured that all of the longhorns' brands had been changed, and was dressed in a fresh, fringed buckskin outfit. His horse had been brought to him and he was ready to mount it when one of his warriors, who had left for San Carlos to trade his wares many days ago before the women and children, rode up to him.

"Did you make good trade?" Fire Thunder asked as he looked at the burro attached to a rope behind the warriors' horse. It was loaded down with supplies beneath a leather covering.

"Very good," Big Left Hand said, smiling. "My trade was good for my *wife,* I should instead say."

"That is why she smiles and is so good to you," Fire Thunder said, returning the smile. "You bring her more than is required from a husband."

"She pleases me in many ways," Big Left Hand said, his eyes gleaming with silent meaning. "I never want to be disappointed. What I bring her today will assure me that I will not be."

Black Hair rode up, a troubled look on his face as he glanced over his shoulder at his daughter, who stood at the door of his lodge, pouting.

"More trouble with Running Fawn?" Fire Thunder asked, giving Running Fawn a quick glance.

"She will be the death of me," Black Hair said sullenly. "I just discovered a tattoo on one of my daughter's legs, put there with the juice from a poison ivy plant. Three of her friends have the same tattoo."

He hung his head, then looked slowly up at Fire Thunder. "I cannot understand this daughter who has turned wild and rebellious," he murmured.

"Perhaps she is rebellious, yet not as much as I am sure those daughters are, who are forced to live in carnivals with their parents," Big Left Hand blurted out.

The mention of "carnival" sent Fire Thunder's eyes to Big Left Hand, and his heart to racing. "Why do you speak of carnivals now?" he asked, lifting an eyebrow.

"While in San Carlos, I saw many pitched tents, and was told it was a carnival," Big Left Hand said matter-of-factly. "I walked through the carnival. I saw beautiful women dressed up in scanty clothing. I assumed they were daughters of those men who own the carnival. Do you think they enjoy living such a life? I would think they feel ashamed."

His heart pounding harder, his throat dry, Fire Thunder reached a hand to Big Left Hand's shoulder. "My friend, your knowledge of reading and writing matches my own," he said thickly. "Did you see the writing on the sides of the wagons that belong to the carnival people?"

"Yes, and the name Shelton was there," Big Left Hand said, taken aback by the sudden look of wonder in his chief's eyes. "Why ... do ... you ask?"

Black Hair and Fire Thunder exchanged quick glances.

Then, trying to control his anxiousness to get to San Carlos, to possibly get another look at the beautiful white woman, perhaps even one of those that Big Left Hand had referred to, Fire Thunder gave Big Left Hand a forced, easy smile.

"I have seen that particular carnival caravan and wondered if it might be the same, that is all," Fire Thunder said.

He was relieved when Big Left Hand's wife discovered that he was there with all of the wonderful gifts on the burro. All smiles, she ran up to Big Left Hand. She giggled when he reached down and pulled her onto his lap on his horse.

He cast Fire Thunder a mischievous smile over his shoulder as he rode away toward his lodge, his wife clinging to him.

"Black Hair, I am going into San Carlos to see the woman again," Fire Thunder said as he grabbed up his reins. He looked over at Black Hair. "Perhaps you should come, also. You might find you as intriguing a lady."

"One woman in my lodge is enough," Black Hair grumbled. "But I will ride with you. It might be interesting to see the woman's reaction to seeing *you*."

"While in San Carlos, we can also see if our women and children's chilies are selling," Fire Thunder said to Black Hair. "We can later escort them home."

As they made their way down the mountainside on the rocky, uneven path, their hearts were happy ... until they came upon their women and children returning from San Carlos way too soon. One look at their faces told Fire Thunder that things weren't right. Everyone was quiet and troubled. They lowered their eyes as Fire Thunder and Black Hair drew tight rein before them.

His blood pumping cold through his veins, sensing something terribly wrong here, Fire Thunder looked hurriedly among the crowd for his sister, and Good Bear.

His stomach tightened with fear when he saw neither of them.

"Where is my sister?" he finally asked, his voice trembling as fear mounted within him. "Where is Good Bear?"

There was a prolonged silence, and then one of the women stepped forth. "Both are gone," she said, her voice quaking.

Feeling as though someone was squeezing his gut, Fire Thunder couldn't speak for a moment.

Then words came to him so quickly, hardly anyone could understand him.

He demanded answers. He demanded their attention. He ordered them not to be cowards now when his sister had disappeared.

The same woman explained that they had been peddling their chilies when suddenly they realized that Good Bear and Little Sparrow were not among them. They had immediately searched for them.

When they could not find them, they had gone to the Mexican authorities. They had searched then with them. The search stopped where the carnival had been pitched. It had disappeared, it seemed, right before their eyes.

The blame then seemed cast on the carnival people, but the Mexican authorities said it was not their duty to go farther than their town to search for Indian children. They told them to go to their chief and tell him. It was his job to see that his children were all right, not the Mexicans'.

An instant rage filled Fire Thunder. He was beside himself with anger and grief over his sister's disappearance. "The carnival," he shouted. "I must find the carnival!"

He turned to his people. "Go to the village," he ordered. "Tell many warriors to come quickly to my aid. Black Hair and I will head for San Carlos, and then we will be on our way to find the carnival once we find their trail out of San Carlos."

He rode off with Black Hair.

When they reached San Carlos, they went to the site where the carnival had been pitched.

Fire Thunder saw tracks made by the many wagons, and the direction in which they were headed. He and Black Hair followed the tracks.

Fire Thunder's mind went to the beautiful lady whom he had seen with the carnival caravan. If Little Sparrow and Good Bear had been forced to travel with the carnival, did that mean that the beautiful woman approved of kidnapping innocent children?

His very soul burned with the need for revenge, even if it was against the lady whose petiteness and pantherish eyes had touched his heart.

Fire Thunder vowed to himself that he would kill her as easy as looking at her if she was, in part, responsible for the abduction of his beloved sister!

Kaylene was glad when the caravan stopped for the night. She had already bathed, eaten, and was ready to go to bed beside the outdoor fire, but had not been able to get the small Indian girl off her mind. She hadn't seen her since that one time in Magnolia's tent. Everytime she asked about her, her father told her that the child was being cared for by Magnolia. The child was bringing something to Magnolia's life. Leave her be. Let her enjoy it.

Wanting to check on her welfare before retiring for the night, Kaylene, in her cotton nightgown, slipped away from the others and ran to Magnolia's wagon. It was dark. She had to guess that Magnolia was already asleep.

But that would not stop Kaylene.

"Magnolia?" she said, sticking her head through the opening at the back of the wagon. "It's me. Kaylene. I've come to see the child. Please let me."

"She ain't here," Magnolia said, her voice thick with alarm. "Go away, child. Leave me be."

"I thought ..." Kaylene said, then stiffened when she heard a soft whimpering coming from somewhere close by.

She turned and peered into the darkness, the campfire giving off just enough light for Kaylene to make out something in the dark. . . .

She felt faint at what she saw. But she had no chance to do anything about it. Her father loomed suddenly tall and threatening before her as he stepped in the line of her vision.

"Get back to your bedroll," he grumbled. "This ain't none of your affair."

"But, Father, you ... have ... the child in a cage, like some ... predatory *animal*," Kaylene said, stupefied that her father would do such a thing.

"You'd have found out soon enough, anyhow, so's I see no choice but to tell you now," John said coldly. "Kaylene, this child is going to be used as a sideshow. She'll be the cause of us makin' lots of money. So now get on back to the fire. Pretend you didn't see nothin' if it's somethin' you find hard to live with."

Kaylene tore past her father and stared wide-eyed at Little Sparrow as the small child stood in the cage, gripping the bars, begging Kaylene with her wild eyes.

"It'll be good for us, Kaylene," John tried to reassure her. "I will say she's been raised by a pack of wolves. I'll say she can't speak, read, or write, full proof of how she's been raised."

"I'm sure she was raised by loving parents," Kaylene cried. "She can't help it if she was born without the ability to hear or speak. Let her out, Father. Oh, God, set her free."

John grabbed Kaylene by the shoulders and gave her a rough shake. "You shut up, do you hear?" he shouted. "With you gettin' older has come a more bolder tongue. Never forget who makes the decisions around here. Never forget the importance of me finding new ways to lure people to our carnival. If not, all those who work for us will have to cut down on their food rations." He leaned down into her face. "I might even be forced to set your panther free, for Midnight eats almost as much as we humans."

This shut Kaylene up. Her panther was her only true friend. The other women of the carnival had always been jealous of her because of how beautiful she was, and because her father owned the carnival. She had learned to find comfort in her pet.

She nodded and went back to the fire.

Out of the corner of her eye, she watched her father until he was asleep. And although she knew that she must accept the fate of the small Indian child, she went and sneaked Little Sparrow extra food and blankets and talked slowly to her so that she could read her lips.

As Little Sparrow emitted a strange, forlorn cry from the depths of her throat, Kaylene's insides grew cold. She knew now that she had to find a way to make her father understand just how wrong it was to treat the child in such a way.

But for now, afraid that her father may have been awakened by the child's cry, Kaylene rushed back to her bedroll.

But she didn't get the chance to climb inside.

A sudden commotion drew Kaylene back to her feet.

She stumbled backward and paled when she discovered the arrival of many Indian warriors on horseback, surrounding the campsite. The handsome, blue-eyed Indian of her midnight dreams was at the lead.

Fire Thunder moved away from the other warriors and drew a tight rein only a few feet from where Kaylene stood. Slowly he slid out of his saddle, a rifle clasped in his right hand.

So taken by him so suddenly being there, after having thought and dreamed of him so often, Kaylene was not frightened of Fire Thunder. Noble in his bearing, he was a tall, straight-backed man. He was great in physique, and surely as great in prowess, purpose, and in intelligence. His blue eyes were large and vivacious.

Seeing him made Kaylene's heart thud strangely. Even her knees were somewhat weak.

Fire Thunder quickly recognized Kaylene. His gaze roamed over her. In the light of the fire, he saw the deep cleavage of her youthful breasts where the cotton nightgown gaped open. He saw her delicate, dewy white, pale skin, and glossy, waist-length deep black hair. As he remembered, she *did* have a fragile, doll-like appearance.

He couldn't deny the heat that grew within his loins at being near her, so captivated by her sheer loveliness. His eyes locked with hers and again, as the other time when they had seen each other, he saw in their depths something that made him realize that she was as intrigued by him.

For certain there was no fear in her crisp, green eyes. Only a keen interest.

But a shrill cry came from somewhere behind Kaylene. Recognizing the efforts of his sister to speak made Fire Thunder's heart leap.

He had not only found the woman of his midnight dreams—he had found his sister!

4

Eyes full of starlight, moist over fire,
Full of young wonder, touch my desire!
—MAX EASTMAN

Fire Thunder's whole insides turned into cold, icy shreds when he saw the moonlight reflecting upon his sister in the cage.

Then a fiery hate grabbed him at the pit of his stomach when a man stepped in front of the cage, blocking the way.

Seeing red, Fire Thunder tensed, his long muscles knotted in his anger.

Lithe as a panther, he rushed so quickly to place his hands around John Shelton's neck, half lifting him from the ground, there was a ripple of startled gasps from those who had come out to see what the commotion was all about.

That was followed then by a guarded silence as the Kickapoo warriors moved in closer on their horses, their weapons drawn.

"You must be the leader of this caravan or you would not take it upon yourself to step between this

Kickapoo chief and his sister," Fire Thunder snarled out, his nostrils flaring. "Order someone to release my sister at once, or my fingers will tighten around your neck. Slowly, I will squeeze your breath away."

Panic filled John's eyes. "Your ... sister ... ?" he managed to gasp out between choking breaths.

"Yes, and who do you think you are to treat her as less than an animal?" Fire Thunder hissed into John's face. "Do you have no respect for children? Our Kickapoo children are a gift of *Kitzihiat,* the Kickapoo Great Spirit. We treat them gently. We cherish them."

Fire Thunder leaned even more closely into John's face. "Have her released at once or you will die with Chief Fire Thunder's name on your last breath," he said with stiff resolve. He tightened his fingers, causing John's eyes to bulge and his tongue to partially protrude from between his lips.

Black Hair dismounted and came to stand beside Fire Thunder. He glared at John. "You must listen to my chief," he said coldly. "When Fire Thunder *el manda,* commands, it must be done ... or else."

Seeing that he had no choice but to do as he was ordered, John looked past the two Kickapoo warriors. "Someone, *any*one, come and let the little wench out," John managed to gasp out.

One of John's men ran to the cage. "I'll release the child," he said, his hands trembling as he removed the lock.

Kaylene rushed forth and opened the door and reached inside for Little Sparrow. "Come to me," she murmured. "Let me help you. Please forgive me for not doing this sooner. I feared my father's wrath. I was wrong."

Little Sparrow looked up at Kaylene and recalled how Kaylene had brought her food and blankets. A bond had quickly formed between them.

And she understood how Kaylene could be afraid to go against her father's wishes. John Shelton was an evil-hearted man, who could put the fear of god into anyone's heart. Surely even his daughter's.

Little Sparrow flung herself into Kaylene's arms and hugged her. Then she ran to Fire Thunder and jumped into his arms. Sobbing, her legs straddled his waist as she clung desperately to him.

Fire Thunder hugged Little Sparrow to him and gave her the comfort she so badly needed, reassuring her that she was now safe. He told her that nothing like this would be allowed to ever happen again. He would now guard her as though he were her shadow.

Fire Thunder's gaze went to Kaylene, filled with wonder at how she had gone to help Little Sparrow from the cage.

Yet surely she did this only to fool him into believing she cared about the child, he argued to himself.

But in her eyes he *could* see a softness and gentleness. It was hard to imagine her as anything but genuinely sweet and compassionate.

Then another thought came to him that washed all of his wonder at this woman away. "The boy," he said, glaring at John. "Where is the boy who was with Little Sparrow? Is he also in a cage?"

"There was no boy, only the little girl," John said, rubbing his raw throat. He laughed mockingly. "And I'm glad to be free of this little wench. She was becoming more trouble than she's worth."

The man's words about his sister stung Fire Thunder's insides. Shelton would pay for them, and everything else he was guilty of. But first, Fire Thunder had to find out about Good Bear.

Placing a gentle hand beneath Little Sparrow's chin, he lifted her eyes to meet the question in his. "Where is Good Bear?" he asked, the moon giving enough light for her to read his lips.

Little Sparrow, recalling how she had sneaked away from Good Bear while he had been watching the naked lady, hung her head.

Again Fire Thunder raised her eyes to his. "Little Sparrow, where . . . is . . . Good Bear?" he persisted.

Tears flooded Little Sparrow's eyes. She shook her head, then gestured with her shoulders and spoke in sign language to her brother, explaining that she did not know where Good Bear was.

"Do you think he is here, hidden somewhere in a cage like the one you were in?" Fire Thunder asked. He squinted his eyes as he surveyed the shadows around the campsite, seeing no more cages.

Little Sparrow shook her head.

"Then why wasn't he with the others who returned from San Carlos?" he asked, fear entering his heart over the welfare of the young brave.

Again Little Sparrow gave him a soft shrug.

"We will search for him later," Fire Thunder said, again focusing his attention on John Shelton. "Your name. Tell me your name."

"That's none of your damn business," John said, squaring his shoulders.

Black Hair slapped John across the face. "Do not continue being insolent to my chief," he said darkly. "Answer him. What is your name?"

Blood was trickling from the corner of John's mouth and from his nose.

Anna ran to John and cowered beside him. She gave Fire Thunder a soft, pleading look. "His name is John. John Shelton. I am his wife," she said meekly, as though it were unusual for her to speak up. "Let us go. John made a mistake. I apologize for him. Please let us be on our way."

"Shelton," Fire Thunder said, recalling the name Shelton written in bold letters on the covered wagons that belonged to the caravan. "So you *are* the owner of this carnival?"

Fire Thunder's gaze slid slowly over to Kaylene. "What is *she* to you?" he asked, trying to hate her.

"She . . . is . . . Kaylene," Anna said, giving Kaylene a warning look. "She is our daughter." Anna then looked wildly up at Fire Thunder. "She isn't to blame for any of this," she blurted out. "Please don't harm her."

Fire Thunder and Kaylene's eyes locked for a moment longer, causing Kaylene's knees to weaken beneath his steady stare. Her heart throbbed and her face grew hot with a blush when his eyes lowered and she could feel his gaze hot on the cleavage of her breasts.

But when Fire Thunder jerked his eyes away and seemed to quickly forget her, Kaylene was torn with how to feel. A part of her was afraid of what he had planned for her and her family. A part of her wanted so badly to be liked by him.

No, not liked—she thought to herself. *Loved.*

For the first time in her life she had found a man who touched her deeply. From her head to her toes she felt a hungry desire . . . a strange yearning.

And she knew those feelings were foolish. Obviously she was nothing but an enemy to this man, someone he surely detested, for she was the daughter of the man guilty of having caged his sister.

Fire Thunder ignored the heat of his loins, the need to have this woman as his own threatening to overwhelm him. He forced himself to think of only one thing—revenge. He must make this man pay for what he did to his sister.

The fact that this evil man had even touched his

sister's flesh, dirtying her pureness, made Fire Thunder's insides boil with a renewed rage. Surely, this evil man had further degradation planned for Little Sparrow. Fire Thunder quickly made his decision of how to make John pay for his dirty deed.

Fire Thunder looked over his shoulder at his men. "Little Beak! Many Horses! Come and take this man away!" he shouted. "Many Horses, tie him up. Take him on your horse. You know what we do with our enemies!"

His warriors dismounted and went to John.

Pale, Anna watched her husband taken away, half dragged to Many Horses's mount and tied onto it behind the saddle. A part of her wanted to reach out and beg again for his release, for she was helpless without him. But a part of her was glad that he was being treated in such a way. For having treated her so unjustly for so many years, he deserved what he was getting now at the hands of the Indians.

Fire Thunder felt Anna's eyes on him. He turned to her. "Woman, be thankful you are not included in this vengeance," he said, as he placed Little Sparrow on his horse. "As for your husband, he must pay for the humiliation he has brought upon my sister. You know, deep in your heart, that he deserves being reprimanded for what he has done to an innocent child."

Anna backed away from Fire Thunder, cowering even more.

Fire Thunder looked over at Kaylene. Again his heart leaped at the mere sight of her, and at her nearness. "Black Hair, seize the woman named Kaylene!" he suddenly blurted out.

Kaylene sucked in a wild breath and backed away from Fire Thunder. Every fiber of her being cried out in alarm as to what his intentions for her might be. But deep inside her, where her desires were formed, she only wanted one thing from him: To be loved! Not hated!

But it looked as though he was including her in his vengeance and she saw her future as bleak. She might even die before she saw another sunrise.

Kaylene started to turn and run away, but something held her there, as though something willed her not to be afraid, not to look foolish by trying to take flight when she knew that she could not possibly get far. There were too many warriors on horseback, and too many rifles pointed her way.

Black Hair questioned Fire Thunder with his eyes about the white woman. But not wanting to look insolent in front of the other warriors, he hurried to Kaylene and grabbed her by an arm and shoved her toward Fire Thunder's horse.

Kaylene's mother went wild. She found the courage to run to Black Hair and pound on his back as he lifted Kaylene to the front of the saddle.

Fire Thunder went to Anna and grabbed her around the waist and lifted her from the ground. He carried her over to stand among the other white people. He gave one of the men a cold stare. "Keep her here with you or she will die," he said icily.

Then he shot warning glances all around him. "None of you follow with thoughts of freeing the man and woman," he shouted. He lifted a fist into the air. "Or the man will be the first to die, and then the . . . woman."

He smiled demonically. "And then I shall take delight in seeing you die a slow death for interfering with the vengeance of a mighty Kickapoo chief," he snarled out.

Frightened by her brother's anger, Little Sparrow slid quickly from Black Hair's horse and ran to him. She stood before him and pleaded with him with wide, tearful eyes as she signed to him. She relayed to him with quick movement of her fingers that Kaylene was good, that she did not deserve to be harmed over the wrongful deeds of an evil father. She pleaded with her brother not to harm the beautiful, sweet, white woman.

Touched by Little Sparrow's vouching for Kaylene, knowing that the woman must have been kind to her. Little Sparrow was cautious to whom she offered friendship. Fire Thunder bent on a knee before his sister.

Speaking in sign language, which he hoped Kaylene could not understand, Fire Thunder explained to Little Sparrow that he had no intention, whatsoever, of harming the white woman. He told Little Sparrow that he had feelings for the white woman that he had to sort out.

No, no matter what happened, he was not going to harm her.

But for now, he *was* going to use her as a pawn.

Little Sparrow gazed up at her brother with wonder. She was confused as to how her brother could have feelings for a woman that he had only met moments ago.

But relieved that he meant Kaylene no harm, Little Sparrow gave Fire Thunder a tender hug, then went back to Black Hair. She smiled at Black Hair as he lifted her on his horse with him. Fire Thunder swung himself into his saddle behind Kaylene.

A sensual thrill swept through Kaylene when Fire Thunder slipped his muscled arm around her waist and held her in place before him in his saddle. The toes of her bare feet curled with delight, and she sighed as he bent down close to her, his breath hot on her cheek.

"Behave," he whispered as the sweet fragrant smell of her hair caused his insides to warm with need.

Kaylene flashed him a frown over her shoulder. But she didn't speak, for fear of her voice giving away her feelings, feelings that confused her. She wanted to hate him. She wanted to fear him. But neither emotion plagued her.

She must remember that the fate of both her and her father lay in the hands of this powerful Kickapoo chief. She must do nothing to stir his wrath any more. For now she would cooperate. Hopefully, somehow, she could find a way to release her father later. They both would flee into the dark, even though she wanted nothing more than to be held in the arms of this handsome Indian.

When sensual thoughts would creep into her consciousness, she would keep reminding herself that he was her enemy.

Fire Thunder gazed into Kaylene's green eyes, glad when she turned them away from him. He must fight this pulsing need for this woman. For now, family came first. His sister's vengeance must be dealt with!

Sinking his moccasined heels into the flanks of his proud steed, Fire Thunder rode away from the campsite, his warriors following dutifully.

Kaylene took one last look over her shoulder, to see how her mother was faring. She stiffened and tears spilled from her eyes when she discovered that her mother had fainted.

Fighting back the tears, feeling helpless, Kaylene turned her eyes back around and focused them on her father. She was confused about him. It looked like he may have purposely abducted the small Indian child, yet he had said that she had come to him, asking to stay with the carnival.

Yet Little Sparrow's behavior toward Kaylene's father made Kaylene believe that, yes, he may have abducted her and made up the story to make himself look less the rogue.

And to have caged her!

Did that not prove that his intentions were evil . . . that he thought only of his own selfish needs, not the child's?

Yet, she just would not allow herself to believe that her father could be this evil. Yes, while growing up, at times she had feared her father. She had felt that something was missing that should be there between a father and daughter. And she would never forget the times she had witnessed him physically abusing her mother!

Was her father just basically cold and evil?

No. She would not think that about him at this time, when he lay tied so helplessly to an Indian's horse.

She wanted to think the best of him. She wanted to believe that the child *had* come to him, perhaps having fled from the Kickapoo village for another purpose.

But again, there was the missing boy. What had happened to him?

Had this small Indian girl fled with the young boy, both running from something in their lives that was not pleasant? Had the young girl had a change of heart after seeing that the world could be cruel to her everywhere? No. Kaylene would not think the worst of her father. Not until there was absolute proof that he was evil through and through, and that he *had* abducted the girl.

Kaylene could not help but wonder, though, just how many lies her father might have told her through the years. Was that dark side of him that she had grown to know even worse than she ever imagined?

She shivered at the thought of him possibly having abducted the child. If he was this evil, was there something about herself that might one day prove that she was just as evil? As sinister? Because her father's blood ran through her veins!

They rode awhile longer, then Fire Thunder drew a tight rein and stopped his horse at the border of Mexico and Texas, at the Rio Grande. He wheeled his horse around and faced his men.

"Many Horses and Black Hair, dig a pit in the ground!" Fire Thunder shouted. "You know what sort I mean. Leave the center unexcavated and higher than the ground around it."

"What . . . ?" Kaylene gasped, paling at the thought of what this pit might be for.

Fire Thunder dismounted and placed his hands at Kaylene's waist and helped her to the ground.

He turned her back to him and yanked her against him. One arm went around her waist and held her in a steely like grip.

Kaylene's heart thudded as she watched her father being taken from Many Horses' steed. She feared that it meant nothing good when the rope was untied from around him and thrown to the ground.

Kaylene scarcely breathed as she waited and watched. When the pit was soon completed, she flinched and stifled a gasp behind her hand when her father was shoved in.

Kaylene stiffened as she watched the rest of the proceedings. She could hardly believe what she was witnessing. How could they . . . ? Were they . . . ?

Then she knew. God, she knew!

She never felt as helpless in her entire life as now.

Black Hair took strips of buckskin to the river and soaked them. Four other warriors pounded stakes into the ground on the edge of the pit.

Kaylene screamed when her father was forced to stretch out across the pit, his arms and wrists tied to the stakes with the wet buckskin thongs, while his body, humped in the middle, lay facedown.

One of Fire Thunder's warriors took a buckskin bag to the pit and shook a rattlesnake from its depths into the pit.

Kaylene could take no more. She shoved and yanked at Fire Thunder's arm in an effort to get free. She dug her nails into the buckskin fabric of his shirt, hoping he could feel their sharpness through it.

But Fire Thunder didn't wince. Nor did he budge. He continued to hold her tightly against him.

"Please don't do this to my father!" Kaylene cried as she looked up at Fire Thunder. "Please! Set him free! He ... will ... die!"

Fire Thunder gazed down at her, his blue eyes gleaming. "That is exactly what I have in mind," he said, smiling smugly down at her.

Kaylene turned her eyes away from him and spat at his feet. "You are a dark and sinister man," she cried. "You are heartless!"

Fire Thunder yanked her around to face him.

His fingers dug into the flesh of her arms as he held her at arm's length. He glowered down at her.

"Your father is the darkest-hearted man of all," he said tightly. "He preys on innocent, small children. Our Kickapoo children are revered! Never defiled! Your father will never defile children again!"

Limp and exhausted from trying to get away from Fire Thunder, Kaylene gave in as he took her to his horse and lifted her into the saddle.

She hung her head as they left her father behind in the pit just as the sun rose along the horizon.

Soon it would be hot. Soon the wet thongs tied to her father's wrists and ankles would dry and shrink.

His circulation would be cut off.

And the snake would want to leave the hot pit. It would slither up the sides of the pit. . . .

White Wolf and Dawnmarie traveled onward on horseback. They had not stopped to rest. They had traveled at night instead of during the long, hot days of sunshine.

Dawnmarie cast White Wolf a forlorn look. "I doubt I will ever find my people," she said, limp with exhaustion. "If not soon, I will be tempted to turn back and return to Wisconsin. I am weary of the long days of travel. I miss our children more and more as each day passes."

"We have come this far, please do not give up now," White Wolf said. He reached over and placed a gentle hand to her cheek. "I love you and know you better than anyone. If you do not find your Kickapoo people, your heart . . . your longing . . . will never truly rest. We are close. You know it. We know the Kickapoo are in Mexico. We soon will be there."

"But, darling, I—"

She stopped in midsentence when she saw a ranch house just ahead, along the horizon. They had judged that they would soon be at the Mexican border. This would be a perfect place to find shelter and, hopefully, food, before they traveled onward.

They went to the ranch. They didn't even get off their horses before the rancher came outside, leveling a shotgun at them with a dog at his side, its teeth bared as it growled.

"Get on with you," the man shouted, motioning with his shotgun toward them. "I've had my bellyful of Injuns lately. You're all nothing but thieving renegades. I only recently lost almost every head of longhorns that I owned. I know that one tribe or another took them."

"We are not responsible," White Wolf said. He gestured toward his wife. "My wife. She needs rest. Surely you can offer shelter in your barn. My wife is hungry. Perhaps you can spare a biscuit or two."

"You deaf or somethin'?" the man said, taking a step closer, his dog at his heels. "Get outta here. Go and beg somewheres else."

White Wolf inhaled deeply to keep from saying things that came swiftly to his mind. He knew that Fort Duncan couldn't be that faraway. The fort sat on the Rio Grande at Eagle Pass.

"Come, Violet Eyes," White Wolf said, wheeling his horse around. "We don't have far to go until I am sure we will be offered refuge."

Dawnmarie hung her head, nodded, and followed him away from the threat of the shotgun and barking dog.

"I . . . am . . . so weary," Dawnmarie whispered. She trembled. She felt so weak, so dispirited.

Back at the campsite, where the carnival people stood in stunned silence around the fire, Kaylene's black panther strained at his leash.

The large, muscular beast had watched Kaylene being taken away. He sensed the danger that she was in.

Midnight strained one last time and he broke his leash and sprang from the campsite into the purple haze of morning.

5

Open the door of thy heart.
—BAYARD TAYLOR

Kaylene was stunned by what had happened to her father. Although she, for the most part, never understood him, and hated that dark side of him that she had seen too often, sometimes even taking a whip to those workers who did not work at the speed he demanded of them, she did not hate *him,* the *person.*

He was her father.

He had never harmed her in any way, except with mind games; games of control.

Disillusioned over this Kickapoo Indian chief, the man she had felt such sensual stirrings for, Kaylene was torn now with what to do with those feelings. When she had not known that he was a heartless, cruel man, it had been easy to envision herself with him—that *he* might be the man to take her away from the drudgery of carnival life. Even if she had to live in a tepee or wigwam, she would have finally had roots.

Now she doubted she would live long enough to ever have a solid footing anywhere and be *anyone's* wife. Because of her father's greed, so deeply entrenched in his soul that he had to put children into what would be considered slavery, her life might soon be over.

She closed her eyes and tried to will herself into that wonderful land of sleep, where nothing could harm her—where sweet dreams usually erased the ugliness of her life.

But sleep would not come. The steady rhythmic beat of the horse's hooves, multiplied by the sounds of those other horses following them, kept her awake.

She glanced down at Fire Thunder's arm that held her in an ironlike grip around her waist. He had not let up on his possessive hold. In the chill wind of night, she could feel the warmth of his breath stirring her hair as he would sometimes lean lower, perhaps fighting off the urge to sleep himself.

Bone tired, she turned a sour glance his way over her shoulder. "When will we stop?" she asked, her voice drawn. "We left the Rio Grande behind us a long time ago. How far into Mexico *is* your village? That *is* where you are taking me, isn't it?"

Fire Thunder gazed into her defiant green eyes, wishing that he could have found a different way to bring them together than this. Now, since he had been forced to make her father pay for what he had done to Little Sparrow, he doubted she would ever feel anything for him but loathing. . . .

Not unless he could somehow prove to her just how evil her father was, and that he deserved to die.

It was hard for Fire Thunder to understand why that had to be proved to this woman. It already had been. And he knew that she had not approved of what her father had done, for she had befriended his sister. Little Sparrow had even grown fond of her in the short time they had been thrown together.

"We will camp at the foot of my mountain," Fire Thunder said gently, trying to make her trust him by being gentle and caring with her. "If you or my sister were not with us, my warriors and I would travel onward up the mountain. But I can see that you are weary. And not only from being tired from the journey. You are having to accept many things tonight that surely tear at your heart."

"And you call that fair?" Kaylene argued. "*I* am not responsible for anything. Why punish me?"

"You are my guarantee that the carnival people will not come after us, causing much blood to spill on the ground tonight," Fire Thunder said.

He rode onward, working his way into the dark shadows of his mountain. "Do you not recall? I warned them not to follow. I told them that if they did, your blood would be the first to be spilled."

Kaylene paled and swallowed hard. "Would you truly do that ... ?" she asked, her voice breaking. "Would you kill me in cold blood, knowing that I am innocent of any wrongdoing?"

"Do you truly think that I would?" Fire Thunder said, his eyes softening into hers. "That I could?"

The look in his eyes and the way he spoke to Kaylene made her eyes widen in wonder.

Did he mean what she thought? she marveled to herself.

Had he truly had no intention of killing her?

Had he used her only as a ploy to ensure his escape into the dark with her and her father?

Did he plan to release her once he had returned his warriors home, safely among their people—their wives ... their children?

Not wanting to let her guard down and be taken in by soft, alluring talk, which surely was lies, Kaylene again turned her eyes quickly away from him.

Fire Thunder understood. Trust had to be earned. Having taken her captive would make her trust come slowly, if ever.

It was a chance that he had to take. Now that he had her, he would never let her go. In time, his dreams of her in his arms would become a reality.

He smiled and his eyes warmly gleamed, having learned the art of patience long ago. Patience had been learned through the years of having to deal with white people.

Finally arriving at where he wanted to make camp, beneath a sprawl-branched tree where there were windfall branches for firewood, Fire Thunder drew a tight rein and slid from his saddle.

Black Hair dismounted beside him and helped Little Sparrow to the ground.

Little Sparrow ran over and watched Fire Thunder lift Kaylene to the ground, then took Kaylene's hand and held it as she smiled up at her.

They stood together, their hands clinging, until a warm campfire was built, its coals glowing a deep red under a steaming coffeepot.

"Come, little sister," Fire Thunder said, placing a gentle hand on Little Sparrow's shoulder. "Bring your friend. Sit by the fire. We will eat a few bites, then get some sleep before heading on to our village tomorrow."

Little Sparrow gave Kaylene's hand a tug, to encourage her to go with her and sit down with the others who had circled around the fire, sitting on blankets, and taking food from their parfleche bags.

Kaylene stood stiffly, her jaw tight, as she glared at Fire Thunder. She had seen the warriors take their bedrolls from their horses. She had seen Fire Thunder remove his own.

She had to wonder if he was going to force her to sleep with him.

If he tried, she would fight him every inch of the way. For certain she would not allow him to fool her with his gentle voice and sweet talk. She would never trust him.

Never!

After Little Sparrow yanked on Kaylene's hand enough times, and Kaylene finally looked at her, Little Sparrow gazed up at her with pleading in her dark eyes.

Touched by the child's sweetness and innocence, Kaylene found it hard to refuse her anything. She went with her and sat down on a blanket before the fire, truthfully wishing she had not waited so long. Her bare feet stung from the cold. Her cotton nightgown was not enough to ward off the chill wind.

She placed her feet next to the fire and sighed as the warmth bled into the soles.

Fire Thunder sat down and watched Kaylene, thinking that he had been lax in not realizing how cold she must be. The way she was soaking up the warmth of the fire was proof of that.

He went back to his horse and grabbed another blanket from his supplies and took it back to Kaylene.

She started when his hand grazed against her cheek as he bent and gently placed his blanket around her shoulders.

Loving the feel of the wool blanket, Kaylene grabbed the ends and drew it more snugly around her shoulders. She smiled a weak thank-you up at Fire Thunder, then looked quickly away from him when, as before, she felt his mystical blue eyes troubling her sensually.

It was as though they caressed her.

And his smile seemed genuine enough.

Kaylene's heart thumped wildly within her chest. She was finding it harder and harder to fight off her attraction to Fire Thunder—his handsomeness, his noble presence, his demeanor.

She had never been as attracted to a man as now, and she had been approached by many men. Dressed in her seductive outfits while performing on her panther at the carnival, many men became intrigued by her and had approached her with invitations—some to sleep with them; others to marry them.

She had not found any of them to her liking and had turned them all down flat.

Until now, no man had caused her heart to become crazed with a need she did not understand. It seemed like a sexual longing that started at the tip of her toes, languorously working its way throughout her.

She trembled even now at Fire Thunder's closeness.

"All I can give you to eat now is beef jerky and black medicine," Fire Thunder said as he offered her a piece of the jerky in one hand, and held out to her a steaming cup of coffee in his other.

Wanting to fight her feelings, Kaylene glared up at him and slapped the jerky out of his hand, and then the coffee, spilling it. "Keep your food ... and ... your so-called black medicine, which you so dumbly call coffee," she hissed out. "I'd as soon starve to death as be your prisoner."

"You are foolish if you do not eat and drink," Fire Thunder said as he glared at the spilled coffee. He sat the empty cup aside and settled down next to his sister. "In time, you will get hungry enough to eat anything I offer you. I will wait now, until you ask. I do not force many things on women."

"Hah!" Kaylene retorted angrily. "How can you say that? Aren't I your captive? Would you not say that was forced on me?"

"Not by choice I took you in such a way," Fire Thunder said sullenly. "I would prefer being with you under much different circumstances. Your father caused me to go about knowing you better in a much different fashion than I had hoped for, should we have ever met by chance."

"You ... wished ... to know me better?" Kaylene asked, her voice trailing off in her wonder at his words. "You remembered that one time we chanced to see one another?"

"Yes, that is so," Fire Thunder said softly.

He held a piece of jerky out toward her again. "Eat, we will talk later," he said, going back on what he had said he would not do.

Feeling as though he was drawing her into something she still could not trust, thinking that he might be a skilled liar, Kaylene turned her eyes from him and folded her arms across her chest, again refusing the food.

Enjoying her own piece of beef, Little Sparrow had sat watching what was transpiring between her brother and the beautiful woman. She had not managed to read their lips. All that she could tell was that Fire Thunder was trying to make friends and Kaylene would not trust him enough to allow it.

And Little Sparrow understood. If Little Sparrow's brother had been left staked to the ground, would not she hate the very one who did it?

But why could not Kaylene see how evil her father was, and that he deserved to be left to die? Surely if Little Sparrow's brother had been as cruel, surely *she* would have understood the vengeance of those whom he had wronged.

Wanting to persuade Kaylene into loving both herself and her brother, hoping that her brother had finally found a woman he desired, Little Sparrow took the beef from her brother's hand and scooted closer to Kaylene.

She placed a gentle hand on Kaylene's cheek, drawing her eyes around to see her. With sign language, Little Sparrow asked Kaylene to eat. She even formed the word "eat" with her lips as she handed the beef jerky to Kaylene.

Nervously, Kaylene glanced over at Fire Thunder. When she saw that he was not watching, she took the beef jerky and gobbled it down.

Afterward, she hugged Little Sparrow and kissed her softly on the cheek.

Little Sparrow placed her hands together and leaned her face sideways into them to show Kaylene that she was sleepy.

Kaylene nodded, smiled, and watched Little Sparrow go to Fire Thunder's bedroll and get comfortably between the blankets.

She nervously watched the other warriors as they retired for the night.

Before long, she saw dark lumps made by the bedrolls of the sleeping men, scattered at random around the fire.

"You must also have your rest before we venture up the mountain to my village at daybreak," Fire Thunder said, taking one of Kaylene's wrists as he attempted to bring her to her feet. "Come. We will make a pallet in a more private place for you. I have seen you look uneasy in the presence of so many men."

Kaylene jerked her wrist away from him and refused to stand. "The men are all asleep. I'll do just fine here," she murmured. "That is, if *you* will sleep elsewhere."

"You will sleep where I tell you to sleep," Fire Thunder said, again grabbing her wrist. "Why do you

fight me every inch of the way? I do not plan to harm
you. So do you not see how much easier it would be
for you if you just go along with what I ask of you?''

"And just what else are you going to ask of me?"
Kaylene said, glaring into his blue eyes. "Aren't I at
your mercy? You are a man who has shown interest
in . . . in . . . possibly seducing me. Everyone is asleep.
No one would be the wiser if you forced yourself on
me sexually."

Tired of bantering with her, especially now since
she had brought something into the conversation that
incensed him, that she actually thought him capable
of raping her, Fire Thunder yanked her to him.

"Is that what you want?" he hissed between
clenched teeth. "To be seduced? Surely you must, or
you would not have mentioned it for, woman, *I* have
not made any wrongful advances toward you to give
you even an inkling of an idea that I will take advantage of you sexually."

"You . . . are . . . hurting my wrist," Kaylene was
only able to say as their eyes locked in silent battle.
"Please unhand me."

"If I do, will you behave?" Fire Thunder spat out.
"Will you quit sparring wrongfully with me? I have
no intentions of forcing myself on you. If we ever
come together in that way, I would hope that it would
be something desired by both of us at that moment. I
cannot lie. I have dreamed of kissing you, of holding
you. But not this way. Not while we are facing one
another as enemies."

Kaylene was at a loss for words at his confession of
feelings toward her. They matched her own, how she
felt about *him*. She saw even more danger in that. She
had to hate him for what he did. And she could never
forget that he was holding her hostage.

How on earth could he ever believe that she could

show him how she truly felt while he was holding her against her will?

She saw no future for them whatsoever, for it had all begun between them in the wrong way. What she had dreamed of, their being together in ways that men and women come together when they loved one another, was doomed.

And she could not altogether blame him. They could never be together as lovers because of her father's greedy, evil ways. Her father had forced Fire Thunder's hand so that Fire Thunder had had no choice but to react in the way that anyone would, should their sisters have been held captive in a dreadful cage.

Fire Thunder released his hold on Kaylene. He took the blanket from around her shoulders, grabbed up the one that he had spread beside the fire, then gave her an angry stare. "Come with me," he said sternly.

"No," Kaylene said stubbornly, not budging. The chill wind swept around her. Missing the warmth of the blanket around her shoulders, she hugged herself. "I refuse to sleep anywhere near you, the murdering vile man that you are."

At his wit's end, finding this situation with Kaylene hopeless, Fire Thunder slung the blankets over his left shoulder and with his right hand grabbed Kaylene by the arm. "If that is what you truly want, to sleep totally alone, especially away from me, I think that can be arranged. I will see to it that you are far enough away to satisfy you. I will take you far from the campsite and tie you to a tree."

Kaylene gasped as she stared up at him. "You wouldn't," she said, her voice trembling with shock.

Fire Thunder ignored her. In angry, determined steps, he yanked her along with him, Kaylene struggling against his hold.

In truth, Fire Thunder had no intentions of leaving her tied to a tree. He was hoping that by making her think that, it might force her to say that she would cooperate with him after all.

He was anxiously waiting for her to say that she would cooperate with him; that she *would* sleep *anywhere* he told her to, if only she wasn't left tied to a tree.

But the farther they walked, the moon lighting their path, the more doubtful he became of her begging him for anything. She was proving to be a stubborn woman. He just might be forced to leave her out there alone, tied to a tree, or look like a fool in her eyes from having backed down from something he had said he would do.

"You *would* leave me alone like that," Kaylene cried. "I know it. Did you not leave my father to die in a horrible way? You are capable of anything."

She laughed throatily. "And look at you," she taunted. "You say you are an Indian, yet you have the eyes of a white man! And you speak English as well as a white man! I would say you are only half Indian! You are a 'breed.' Does my saying so insult you?"

"Nothing you can say insults Fire Thunder," he said, giving her a smug smile. "*I* am proud of my heritage, having French kin somewhere in my background. As for my speech, my ability to speak your language? I am proud of my excellent command of English. It has come in handy when I have been forced to deal with cheating, lying white men!"

Before Kaylene could think of another way to rile him, hopefully enough to have him release his tight hold on her so that she could try to escape into the darkness, she noticed a hint of movement in the shadows of the trees; something she sensed, rather than saw.

When they stepped out more into the open, where the trees had thinned and the moon had a chance to illuminate things around them, the moonbeams outlined the tawny body of a panther traveling directly toward them in their path. The big cat stopped in midstep, the gleam of green eyes staring at Fire Thunder, white fangs quickly showing as the animal hissed a snarling growl and crouched, ready to spring.

Kaylene quickly recognized Midnight. But before she could explain to Fire Thunder that this panther was her pet, Fire Thunder released his hold on her and drew his knife from his sheath at his right side, his rifle having been left at the camp.

Knowing that she had no time to stop her panther from leaping onto Fire Thunder, Midnight surely having sensed that Fire Thunder was Kaylene's enemy, Kaylene now wanted to protect her panther—the same as he wanted to protect her. Kaylene stepped quickly between Fire Thunder and Midnight just as the panther leaped and Fire Thunder threw his knife. Midnight twisted sideways to avoid landing on Kaylene just as Fire Thunder brought the knife down.

Instead of hitting his target, the panther, Fire Thunder's knife plunged into Kaylene's left shoulder.

Kaylene screamed with pain. She gazed pleadingly up at Fire Thunder, then collapsed in a dead faint at his feet.

Fire Thunder stared disbelievingly down at Kaylene, and then at the panther as the animal went to Kaylene and licked her face.

He was in awe of how the panther, in an effort to stop the blood flow, lapped up the blood with his tongue as it poured from Kaylene's wound.

*   *   *

Running Fawn had taken advantage of her father's absence. She had sneaked away with three other friends and had met the young Mexican men at their secret trysting place in the forest, many miles from their village.

Running Fawn and Pedro Rocendo, the son of the powerful Mexican general who ruled from his villa in San Carlos, had slipped away from the others and had spent the night making maddening love.

It was coming close to the time when they would have to return to their own villages.

Suddenly Running Fawn's friends and their three young Mexican lovers sneaked up on Running Fawn and Pedro and jumped out from behind the bushes, laughing and joking.

"Running Fawn, my beautiful *señorita,* you must have some tequila before you return to papa," Miguel teased as he staggered over to Running Fawn and Pedro and fell clumsily down beside them.

Starshine, one of Running Fawn's friends, tripped and fell on the other side of Running Fawn, her face flushed from the tequila she had already consumed. "Come on, Running Fawn," she said, yanking the jug of tequila from Miguel.

He shoved it into Running Fawn's hand after she had managed to quickly lower her skirt, her face flushed from having been discovered making love so openly with Pedro.

"I must not drink any," Running Fawn said, shoving the jug away. "And I must return home now. If my father returns home before me and finds me gone, he will never forgive me."

"*Señorita,* you have stayed this long. It shouldn't hurt to stay longer," Miguel said, grabbing the bottle from Starshine and shoving it forcefully into Running Fawn's hands.

She had no choice but to take it, else drop it and spill the stinking stench of tequila all over her skirt.

"Do not be, eh, what is it you say, Miguel, when I do not do as you ask?" Starshine said, giggling as she leaned her face into his, running her tongue across his thick lips.

"Do not be a prude," Miguel said, yanking Starshine closer, his hands cupping her newly budded breasts through the cotton fabric of her blouse. He yanked her closer and kissed her, their tongues flicking between each other's lips.

"It might steady your nerves," Pedro urged. "It might ease your fear of your father."

"I do not fear him," running Fawn spat out. "I ... just ... don't want to antagonize him."

And to prove that she could do anything her friends could do, Running Fawn tipped the jug to her lips and choked down several swallows.

"There, now don't you feel better, sweet *señorita*?" Pedro asked, placing an arm around her waist, drawing her close. She held the jug away from her as he licked the tequila from her lips, then kissed her.

Giggling, the tequila lethal to a young maiden who never touched the stuff, Running Fawn soon felt giddy and lightheaded. She pushed Pedro away and took another long, deep swallow.

"That's enough," Pedro said, grabbing the jug away from her.

He had waited too long to take it from her. Dizzy, and feeling her stomach doing flip-flops, Running Fawn ran behind a bush and retched.

When she stepped back into view, swaying, she smiled awkwardly at Pedro, then fell in a dead faint on the ground.

Pedro panicked. He was afraid that there was no

way that Running Fawn's father would *not* discover
where she had been tonight, and with whom.

"I must get her home," he said thickly. He looked
at the others.

The girls scrambled to their feet and, wild eyed with
worry, ran off into the forest toward home.

"Cowardly *señoritas*!" Pedro shouted after them.

He watched his friends run away also.

Alone with Running Fawn, he sighed, then picked
her up in his arms and carried her toward home.

When he came to the outside edge of the Kickapoo
village, he stopped and laid her gently on the ground.

Bending low over her, Pedro gently shook her by
the shoulders. "Running Fawn, wake up," he whispered. "You must get home. Now! Oh, pretty *señorita*,
wake up, or we shall never be able to meet like this
again. Your father will guard you. I . . . don't . . . think
I can live without your loving now that I have tasted
of it!"

Running Fawn groaned and rolled over on her side.

Afraid to wait any longer, Pedro took one long last
look at her, then rose to his feet and ran into the
shadows.

6

Oh, love more real than though
  such dreams were true,
If you but knew.
                              —ANONYMOUS

Stunned at the sight of the panther with Kaylene, and realizing that it must be her pet, Fire Thunder stared a moment longer.

He came out of his trance when Black Hair ran up to him, a rifle in his hand.

When Black Hair saw the panther he aimed at it.

"No!" Fire Thunder said, shoving Black Hair's rifle aside. "Do not shoot it!"

"Why would I not?" Black Hair said, his eyebrows raised inquisitively.

"Shoot your rifle, but not *at* the animal," Fire Thunder said. "Fire one shot into the air to frighten it away. That is all."

Black Hair stared disbelievingly at Fire Thunder for a moment longer, then did as he was told.

Fire Thunder watched the animal lurch with fright, and then lope away into the dark shadows of night.

He paid no heed to his warriors who had been awakened by the gunfire and were now there, relieved when they saw that their chief was not in danger.

"What happened?" Black Hair asked, staring down at Kaylene and the blood-soaked sleeve of her gown.

Then his eyes widened when he saw the knife in Fire Thunder's hand.

"It was the panther," Fire Thunder said, his gaze shifting, to look at his knife. "It came out of nowhere. When Kaylene saw that it was ready to pounce on me, she stepped in the way." He gave Black Hair a quick glance. "The panther means something to her. It must be her pet. It somehow knew to come to her rescue."

Fire Thunder stared at the bloody knife again. He shivered, knowing whose blood. Then he leaned over and wiped the knife clean on a thick stand of grass, and slid it back inside its sheath.

Again he looked at Kaylene. The pooling of blood beneath her arm, and the way she lay, so helpless and unconscious on the ground, made Fire Thunder move quickly. He knelt down beside her and ripped the sleeve of her gown open and peered intently at the knife wound. He was relieved to see that he had missed the bone.

"You carry medicinal herbs with you at all times," Fire Thunder said, looking at Black Hair. "I will carry Kaylene to the camp. You ready the herbs. We shall apply them to her wound."

Black Hair nodded and turned and pushed his way through the milling warriors.

With a gentleness, Fire Thunder slipped his arms beneath Kaylene and lifted her.

When she groaned and her eyes fluttered slowly open, Fire Thunder waited for her to look up at him, guilt washing through him.

Through a pain-induced haze, Kaylene gazed at Fire Thunder. "What ... happened ... ?" she whispered, her one arm lying limp across her stomach.

"I am glad that you are awake, but now is not the time to talk," Fire Thunder said, holding her closer. "I must take you back to the warmth of the campfire. I must see to your wound."

Pain spread through Kaylene in great hot waves. "My wound?" she whispered. Her eyes drifted slowly closed, then flew open again. "What ... wound ... ?"

Not wanting to explain just yet, nor wanting to alarm her into worrying her about her panther, Fire Thunder ignored her question.

Instead, he ran toward the campsite, his warriors moving aside to make a path for him.

"Oh, no," Kaylene cried, suddenly recalling everything. "Midnight! Where is Midnight?" She gathered a fistful of Fire Thunder's buckskin shirt in her free hand and yanked at it. Wild-eyed, she looked up at him. "Tell me you didn't shoot my panther! Tell me!"

"Your panther is all right," Fire Thunder said, his eyes wavering on hers. "It ran into the brush. I realized, by how it came so gently to you after ... after ... I plunged the knife into your shoulder, that it meant something to you. I did not shoot it. I did not allow Black Hair to shoot it."

Kaylene exhaled a quavering sigh of relief, then closed her eyes as the waves of pain swept through her shoulder again. "Thank you," she whispered, barely audible. "Midnight . . . is . . . everything to me. Everything."

Stunned to know that she would have such a connection with an animal, Fire Thunder stared down at her. He started to speak to her, to apologize for all the trauma that he had brought upon her, but she had drifted back to sleep.

For now he knew that was best. He was not sure just how much he should say to her when he apologized. Should he take advantage of this moment, when she was vulnerable, to tell her that he intended to keep her, to make her love him so that she would stay willingly? Or should he allow things to develop slowly between them? Surely she still held much resentment deep within her heart for what he had done to her father.

Could she ever truly forgive him?

Or would she someday understand why it had to happen that way?

Such a man as her father could not be allowed to continue abusing children. If Fire Thunder had not stopped him, then who would have ... ?

Back at the camp, where the fire was still burning high, Fire Thunder laid Kaylene on a blanket beside it.

Then he saw Little Sparrow being held by another warrior. She was wriggling to get free, wanting to see what had happened. Fire Thunder had always ordered his men to, at all costs, keep his sister from harm.

As at all other times, tonight they had obeyed him. When they heard gunfire they had not known the cause, and did not know if their chief was hurt or not. So they had not wanted to take his sister there, possibly to see her beloved brother injured.

"Set her free," Fire Thunder said as he gave Little Sparrow a nod and a smile. Then he spoke to her slowly, telling her that he was all right.

She watched his lips carefully, understanding each word.

He could see her look of shock as she turned and went to kneel beside Kaylene. She clutched frantically to Fire Thunder's arm as she pleaded up at him with her eyes.

"She will be fine," Fire Thunder explained. He

clasped her shoulders. "Little sister, you just sit down now and be calm. I have to see to Kaylene's wound."

A warrior brought Little Sparrow a blanket and slipped it around her shoulders.

Eyes wide, Little Sparrow clutched the blanket and watched Fire Thunder as he tended Kaylene's wound. A part of her heart ached from seeing her newly found friend injured. Why did Kaylene lie so quiet? Why did she sleep so soundly?

Was Kaylene dying? Little Sparrow thought in fear.

But she did not disturb her brother with any more questions. He had to fix Kaylene's wound. And it was obvious to Little Sparrow that he had deep feelings for the white woman by his gentleness with her, and by the way he would occasionally gaze at Kaylene's face, as though he adored her.

This made Little Sparrow feel somewhat better. A hope blossomed inside her that just perhaps her brother *did* love this woman. Although Little Sparrow was only eight, she had been told in sign language by her older friends about love, and how it sometimes happened between two people. Some said that it happened at first sight! Had it happened this way for her brother?

She smiled at the thought, then winced and turned her eyes away when Fire Thunder took a dampened buckskin cloth and began bathing the blood from Kaylene's wound.

Black Hair came and knelt beside Fire Thunder. He opened his small buckskin pouch.

Fire Thunder nodded to him and watched as Black Hair slowly sprinkled the medicinal herbs on the knife wound. The wound soaked up the herbs like a sponge, the blood quickly disappearing.

"It will heal well now," Black Hair said.

He tightened the drawstring and slipped the tiny

pouch in his rear pocket as Fire Thunder wrapped Kaylene's wound with soft buckskin.

Black Hair stood up and ushered the warriors away from Fire Thunder, giving his chief privacy.

His assistance no longer needed, he himself went back to his bedroll and stretched out under the blankets. He watched for a while how his chief tended to the white woman. He knew without a doubt that this woman was in his chief's blood, in his life, *forever*.

Sighing heavily, wishing it were not so, Black Hair turned his back to Fire Thunder, and closed his eyes. His thoughts drifted to his daughter. He hoped that she was asleep in her bed. He wished that she would find a Kickapoo warrior with whom to share her love instead of wasting it on someone not of their beliefs and customs.

Hopefully, in time, he could turn his daughter's life around. He did not want to see it wasted. She was his life, for he had sworn never to marry again. Losing one wife in a lifetime was enough. If he also lost his daughter ...? He was not sure if he could bear it. Life would surely lose its meaning.

Fire Thunder gently drew a blanket over Kaylene, up to her chin, then sat down beside her and looked at her at length.

But when he heard the cry of the panther in the distance, and felt the danger, he reached for his rifle and placed it close beside him.

Little Sparrow sat with her gaze on Kaylene, waiting for her to awaken.

Kaylene's eyes slowly opened, and she found Little Sparrow there. Little Sparrow was so glad to see her friend awake, she hurried to Kaylene and softly kissed her cheek.

She then turned to her brother. In sign language she asked Fire Thunder to return Kaylene to her mother, that although Little Sparrow wanted to have Kaylene as a friend for always, it was not fair to keep her from her family. It wasn't right to hold her captive.

Fire Thunder explained to his sister that this was something a small child must not interfere with. He asked her if she did not trust her brother's judgment in all things?

Little Sparrow lowered her eyes, then looked up at Fire Thunder. She nodded, saying that yes, she had never doubted him.

She would not doubt him now.

Feeling tired, and hardly able to keep her eyes open, she stretched out beside her brother. Forcing her eyes to stay open, she watched Fire Thunder and Kaylene as they began to talk.

She wished that she could hear. She wished that she could talk—she had so much to say!

She so badly wanted to hear the words spoken between the white woman and her brother, to see what kind of relationship was forming. But she had to settle for watching their lips and trying to see by that how things were between them.

And she could also watch their eyes. Eyes said so much to someone like Little Sparrow, who had learned to observe people way more closely than those who took hearing and speaking for granted.

She badly wanted to continue watching, but her eyelids grew heavier . . . heavier. She curled up in a fetal position and allowed sleep to possess her.

Fire Thunder reached over and covered Little Sparrow with a blanket, then turned back to Kaylene when she continued to talk.

"My shoulder feels much better," Kaylene said, reaching her hand beneath the blanket, feeling the bandage. "It is painful, yet not searing. What did you do to take away the pain?"

"Black Hair placed medicinal herbs directly on the wound after I bathed it," Fire Thunder said, realizing that they were actually speaking civilly to one another. For the moment, Kaylene was not challenging his each and every word.

This enabled him to see the sweetness of her personality that he knew was there, hidden beneath the surface.

But he did not expect it to last for long. After she was stronger, he knew she would become as belligerent as before.

But in time, that would pass again, and her true self would always be there for him to marvel over.

"Had I not stepped in the way, you would have killed my panther," Kaylene said, her voice suddenly drawn. "I gladly took the knife that was meant for Midnight."

"Midnight?" Fire Thunder said. He stretched out beside her and leaned up on an elbow, facing her. "That is what you call the panther?"

"Yes, because he is the color of the darkest of midnights," Kaylene said, closing her eyes for a moment when sleep fought to claim her.

"How is it that you have a panther for a pet?" Fire Thunder asked. He watched her eyes open again, mesmerized anew by their green color.

"It happened a long time ago," Kaylene murmured. "I found the panther when it was quite small. Its mother had been killed. I took it in and cared for it. Midnight and I have a close bond."

She paused and lowered her eyes. Fire Thunder could tell that what she had to tell him next might be painful ... might be regretful.

"My father took advantage of my friendship with the panther," Kaylene said, looking up at him again.

"He ... he ... turned us into a carnival act. We became his favorite sideshow."

"Sideshow?" Fire Thunder said, lifting an eyebrow. "I am not familiar with that word. What does it mean? What did your father force upon you and the panther?"

"Force is the right word," Kaylene said bitterly. "I never wanted to do it. But he insisted."

"Insisted?" Fire Thunder prodded. "What did he make you do?"

"A sideshow means an exhibition," Kaylene said, recalling that first time she had slipped onto the back of her panther. She had been only ten. Although she had not wanted to be stared at, and she had not wanted to make her pet into something gawked at, she *had* felt a certain excitement in riding the panther around the roped-off area inside the tent. There had been a thrill in the applause.

She explained to Fire Thunder how she had performed with her panther, and how obedient he had been to her every wish.

"You see, my panther is special," she murmured. "Please never harm him, for I am certain that he will come to me again. Our hearts are one and the same. Our bond can never be broken."

"As long as your panther poses no threat to me or my people, he will not be harmed," Fire Thunder said softly.

Tears sprang to Kaylene's eyes when she suddenly thought of her father. Surely he was dead now. "What do you plan to do with *me*?" she blurted out.

When he did not answer her, Kaylene tried to rise on an elbow to move closer to him, to demand answers.

But the pain was too intense. She closed her eyes

and breathed hard, then gazed over at Fire Thunder again.

"Surely what you think about my father is all a misunderstanding," she said, in her voice a soft pleading. "Surely my father truly thought your sister was a runaway and took pity on her."

Fire Thunder could not help but laugh sarcastically at that. "Yes, your father took pity on her and then locked her in a cage like an animal," he retorted, his eyes blazing.

The memory of Little Sparrow in the cage made Kaylene ashamed and uncomfortable. She would always be ashamed for her father having done this terrible thing to the small child.

She turned her back to Fire Thunder. Weary over so many things, she closed her eyes, and soon drifted off into a restless sleep.

Fire Thunder sat up and stared at Kaylene. When she groaned with pain in her sleep, he eased over next to her. Gently he lifted her, and the blankets that she was wrapped in, onto his lap. While she slept, he rocked her, slowly. Back and forth he rocked her as his eyes devoured the loveliness of her face; the innocence.

He nestled her cheek close to his chest and kissed the waves of her hair at the back of her head, inhaling the perfumed sweet fragrance of it.

When she snuggled more comfortably against him, the fires of desire raging through him spoke to him in wild whispers, saying that this woman was his, *forever* his.

He would do whatever was necessary to make it so.

7

I want you when the shades of eve are falling,
And purpling shadows drift across the land.
                                    —ARTHUR I. GILLOM

A soft hand on Fire Thunder's cheek awakened him
with a start. He looked over and found Little Sparrow
on her knees beside him.

He then followed the path of her eyes and discovered that he still held Kaylene on his lap, his arm on
which her body rested numb from not having moved
it for several hours. He had fallen asleep and Kaylene
had not awakened yet to find herself there.

Fire Thunder looked awkwardly around him in the
morning twilight, glad that none of his warriors had
yet awakened. For certain he did not want to be
caught in such a compromising position, showing that
he cared so much for the white woman.

At least not yet. He had to secure her feelings for
him before allowing anyone but Black Hair to know
that he had plans that would bind their futures together as one.

Little Sparrow moved her hand to Fire Thunder's

free arm and shook it slightly, to draw his attention back to her.

He then watched her hands as, in sign language, she asked how Kaylene was this morning.

His hands not free to respond in sign language, he moved his lips in unspoken words that would tell his sister that it seemed that the white woman was all right. It was apparent that she had enjoyed a restful night of sleep.

He slipped the blanket down from Kaylene's shoulder and gazed at the bandaged wound. No blood had seeped through it. That had to mean that the herbs were working well. The wound was healing.

As the sun peeked over the horizon in a great ball of orange fire, which would surely awaken everyone else, Fire Thunder anxiously, but gently and slowly, placed Kaylene back on the blanket beside the glowing embers of the campfire.

He watched her as she blinked her eyes open, being shifted from his lap and arms having awakened her.

Kaylene opened her eyes wildly and widely, at first disoriented as to where she was, and with whom.

Then she found two sets of eyes on her. One set, the child's, smiled down at her. The other, Fire Thunder's, studied her guardedly.

Kaylene gazed up at him, everything that had happened the prior day returning to her in flashes, causing her heart to ache to think about the fate of her father, and making the anger return against this man who was responsible.

Words failing her, to describe her feelings to her captor, Kaylene turned her eyes away.

She then looked slowly around again when she felt a tiny, soft hand on her face. She gazed at Little Sparrow as the child spoke in sign language to her.

Not familiar with sign language, Kaylene felt at a

loss as to what to say in return. It was obvious the child was asking her something.

Just as Little Sparrow started to form the words of her question on her lips, Fire Thunder intervened.

"My sister is inquiring as to your welfare this morning," he said. He reached for Little Sparrow and swung her around to sit on his lap. Beyond the campfire he saw the men rising one by one from their bedrolls.

Fire Thunder's eyes met and held with Kaylene's. "And what do I tell my sister?" he asked, his voice soft as he was caught up in the sight of this beautiful, green-eyed woman.

But he reminded himself once again that he must control his urges—his desires. Time lay ahead of them where he would prove to her that he set the rules between them. She was the captive, he the captor.

He must never be caught off guard with her, to allow her to know that if she played her cards right, she would be able to get more from him than she would ever imagine!

Yes, he had to watch his actions and his emotions well, or be made to look a fool, not only in the eyes of this woman, but also his people's.

"And how should I be this morning after having been stabbed yesterday, after losing my father, after being forced to leave my mother?" Kaylene spat out.

She trembled from the anger that rose in her insides like hot coals. "I have no idea what your plans are for me," she said, her voice breaking emotionally. "I'm not sure if I am to live or die the sort of death forced upon my father. So, tell me, Fire Thunder, how would you feel if you were in *my* position?"

He wanted to tell her that her anger was understandable, and that, in time, he would be so kind and gentle to her, she would wonder why she had ever felt this way about him.

Even about her father's death. In time she would accept, even admit, that her father was a fiend who preyed on children. She would know that the world was a better place without him.

But each day as she drew closer to Little Sparrow as a friend, she would think back to when the girl was caged like an animal. She would feel a deep, cold dread inside her heart, that if Fire Thunder had not come and rescued his sister, and made the evil man pay for having treated her so unjustly, Little Sparrow would even now be caged.

Little Sparrow would have become nothing more to people than a novelty—something to gawk at. Kaylene would have been witness to Little Sparrow dying a slow death inside, eventually becoming only a shell of the sweet little girl she had always been.

Black Hair came to Fire Thunder.

Fire Thunder was glad to have someone interrupt the awkward moment with Kaylene.

"Should I send warriors out to find food for the morning meal? Or do you wish to go on to our village and eat when we arrive?" Black Hair asked, giving Kaylene a wondering stare, finding her glare cold and pitiless.

Fire Thunder rose to his feet. "We have been gone too long from our people," he said. He combed his long powerful fingers through his thick, black hair, then lifted it back across his shoulders. "We will return home now. Once we are there, we will eat."

Black Hair nodded and spread the word.

The campfire was covered with dirt, putting out any embers that might flare up again in the morning's brisk wind. The blankets and bedrolls were tied to the horses.

Fire Thunder went to Kaylene and started to lift her to carry her to his horse, but she took a step away from him, refusing to allow it.

"You are still stubborn, I see," Fire Thunder said, placing his fists on his hips. "You force me to give you two choices. You either come willingly with me on my horse, or you can walk the rest of the way to my village."

Kaylene's cheeks grew hot with a blush. She lowered her eyes, then looked up at Fire Thunder again as she shifted nervously from one foot to the other. She had to relieve herself in the worst way, yet how could she with all of these men around her? How could she even tell Fire Thunder what the true problem was? Never had she been in such an embarrassing, precarious position.

Little Sparrow came and took her by the hand and gently yanked on it.

Kaylene glanced down at her, touched deeply again by the child's sweet, innocent smile.

Then an idea came to her. She moaned as she bent to her knees before Little Sparrow, the sudden searing pain in her shoulder a reminder that it was far from well.

She started to mouth the words slowly to Little Sparrow, that she needed to go to the bathroom, so that Little Sparrow could read her lips.

But Kaylene was keenly aware of eyes on her, watching her, knowing that Fire Thunder could read her lips just as easily as Little Sparrow.

Kaylene turned anger-filled eyes up at Fire Thunder. She sighed with impatience. "Please turn your eyes from me," she said, her voice drawn. "I have something I wish to tell Little Sparrow." Another blush rushed up from her neck to her cheeks. She smiled awkwardly at Fire Thunder. "Please? What I have to say is quite private."

Glad at least that Kaylene and Little Sparrow had this growing bond, Fire Thunder turned his back to them.

Kaylene spoke the words slowly and distinctly to Little Sparrow, making sure to form them exactly on her lips so that she would not have to repeat them. The need was getting urgent.

Oh, how on earth was she going to manage to do this embarrassing thing without the world knowing and watching? She despaired as she waited to see if Little Sparrow had understood her.

Little Sparrow giggled, took Kaylene's hand, and walked toward the thick stand of oak trees beside the meandering creek a short distance away.

Hearing the patter of feet moving away made Fire Thunder turn with a start. His eyebrows lifted when he saw his sister leading Kaylene to the stand of trees.

He started to go after them, then smiled slowly when suddenly it came to him what Kaylene had not wanted to tell him, yet confided freely in his sister.

He went to his horse and waited as the others mounted and gave him questioning stares. "Go on," he said, gesturing with his hand toward the mountain pass. "Black Hair and I will catch up to you later."

The horses' hooves thundered off, leaving Fire Thunder and Black Hair alone as they waited for Kaylene and Little Sparrow to return.

"You are still determined to keep her?" Black Hair asked, fidgeting nervously with his reins as he waited on horseback.

"Forever," Fire Thunder said.

Fire Thunder's insides warmed at the sight of Kaylene as she walked toward him alongside Little

Sparrow. Even with a wounded shoulder, she walked with such dignity, with such beautiful grace and ease.

Her raven-black hair fluttered around her face and shoulders in the breeze. Her face reflected the color of the rising sun in her cheeks. In her eyes, he saw a lessening of defiance.

Yet he feared that was just for the moment. He did not know what to expect from her in the coming hours or the coming days.

"I see that you are ready to travel now," Fire Thunder said as Kaylene stopped and stood before him. His eyes danced before hers. "Have you decided whether or not you wish to travel by horse? Or by foot?" he teased.

Kaylene's eyes narrowed and her jaw tightened as she glared at him.

He saw that his jesting had gone awry. It had brought out the antagonism in her again.

Shrugging slightly, he placed his hands at her waist and lifted her into his saddle.

He then went to Little Sparrow and lifted her up for Black Hair to put her in his saddle before him.

Fire Thunder swung himself up behind Kaylene. He grabbed the reins with one hand and slid his free arm around Kaylene's waist, feeling her stiffening against his hold.

"Your ride will be much more comfortable if you will relax," Fire Thunder said as he snapped the reins and rode off beside Black Hair.

"How am I to relax while I am still some crazed chief's captive?" Kaylene spat out.

She gave him a venomous stare over her shoulder.

When she saw an angry fire leap into his eyes, she smiled smugly, then turned her eyes away from him and decided to make this easier on herself.

She inhaled a deep breath and forced herself to

relax against his hard, powerful body. In time, when she was stronger, she would show him just how stubborn she could be.

She would escape. She would go back to where her father had been left tied to stakes. She would give him a proper burial.

She hoped that Midnight would stay close by so that she could escape with him. They both would return to the carnival. She would talk her mother into disbanding it to go and try and find some sort of semblance of a normal life elsewhere.

Roots. Kaylene longed for roots.

She gave Fire Thunder a sly glance. Her heart throbbed. While he was not aware of it, she was attracted to his handsomeness again. She could have loved him so much had he not proved to be such a fiend! She would have willingly lived with him in his lodge. She could have made such a perfect, contented wife for him. Even the thought of one day possibly having his children thrilled her clean to the very core of her being.

Lowering her eyes, and sighing with regret, she looked away from him, for that dream was no longer possible. Even if she did love him deep down, he could never know it, for that would mean that she condoned what he had done to her father.

Not wanting to think about such things any longer, Kaylene tried to focus her thoughts on the scene around her. Except for the rough travel up the mountainside on a bone-rattling dirt road, everything was beautiful in the early morning. They rode past a tangle of mountain streams, a vivid carpet of purple verbena, and yellow globe mallow, which snaked its way up the hillside.

She admired the prickly pear plants. They looked

to her like they were going to devour their own flower, their brilliant yellow blooms like pieces of sunshine.

Not far from the road, she spied several sharp-tailed grouse, undisturbed by the passing horses. They were obviously too absorbed in staking out territory on the side of the mountain. A single male walked to the most prominent point, lifted his wings until they made an arc from the ground on one side of its body to the other. Small purple air sacs emerged from his breast, the feathers behind his head standing erect, his tail going stiff and upright.

The bird lowered his head, whined, and started moving his feet rapidly, pounding a throbbing rhythm on the ground.

He moved forward quickly as a second male moved toward him and began his dance. They met, leaped into the air, and thrashed the space in between them with their feet.

The hens clucked while the males determined their squares of territory.

A whining filled the air again, followed by the dancing males. The air vibrated with their constant challenges.

Kaylene smiled as the horse traveled up the mountainside, feeling strangely serene, and at peace with her surroundings.

In the foothills there were quail and coyotes. Ponderosa pine had the shy mule deer and sly bobcat. Some of the flat valleys were covered with soft, graygreen sagebrush.

Kaylene had never seen anything as beautiful as this mountain and its offerings.

It was all like one big magnificent painting.

It was as though she were entering another world, one which had never included her mother, the carnival, and perhaps never would again!

8

Let those love now who never loved,
Let those who have loved, love again.
—COVENTRY PATMORE

Kaylene's spine stiffened as the mountain spread out
and Fire Thunder took her across an extensive valley,
where nestled under great-grandfatherly trees was a
mixture of glistening wigwams, Mexican *jacals*, which
were small huts, and cabins.

She gazed at the wigwams. Instead of being covered
with birch bark, as she knew they were in the northern
states she had traveled with the carnival, they were
covered with something else. The absence of birch
trees in Mexico, had apparently forced the Kickapoo
to seek a new material for their lodge coverings.

Soon she recognized that the coverings were cattail
mats. She knew them well, because her mother had
acquired several cattail mats from an Indian tribe to
make traveling in a covered wagon more comfortable.

At the far end of the village, stood a lodge which
she knew must be the medicine lodge. It was distinct
from the others, painted with the symbols of the sha-

man's particular dream-giving powers—two huge grizzly bears in black, below which were red circles of moons.

Way beyond the village, in the farther reaches of the valley, Kaylene saw vast herds of longhorns grazing. On the far side of the pasture, she saw many beautiful horses fenced off from the longhorns.

In another section of the valley, away from the animals, crops were growing in extensive fields.

She assumed from these sights that the Kickapoo were a rich tribe, far richer than the Indians who lived across the border in the States.

She had heard tell of the Mexicans having been generous to an Indian tribe, in order to get them to come to Mexico, to help ward off Comanche renegades.

Now she knew which tribe. She knew which chief led this tribe, and silently admired his prowess and power, now more than before.

If only she had not been given cause to hate him, she thought sadly to herself. This man, this powerful Kickapoo chief, had the means to give her all that she had ever hungered and dreamed for. Roots.

It was obvious that he and his people had deeply entrenched roots in this mountain land. She doubted anyone could ever wrench it away from them. She silently envied them, wishing she could, somehow, become a part of it.

As they entered the village, people came from their lodges to stare. When they saw Kaylene on the horse with Fire Thunder, they held their children back so that they could not come to greet their chief as they usually did.

It was obvious to Kaylene that these people did not trust all that easily.

When they shifted their gazes and saw Little Sparrow on Black Hair's horse with him, they broke into relieved smiles to know that she was safe and unharmed.

Then Kaylene started when a man and woman ran from their lodge and met Fire Thunder's approach.

Fire Thunder drew a tight rein as they came to the right side of his horse, their anxious eyes on him.

"I do not see Good Bear with you," Gentle Song said worriedly. "You found your sister. Where is my son?"

Fire Thunder's gaze wavered. "I hoped that he would be here," he said thickly. "I hoped that he would return home. You have not seen him?"

Tears sprang from Gentle Song's eyes. She placed a hand over her mouth in despair. "He is lost!" she cried. "I know he must be dead!"

White Foot gathered his wife into his arms. He gazed up at Fire Thunder. "You will send many warriors out to look for my son?" he asked, his voice breaking. "Or do you blame him still for what happened to your sister?"

White Foot looked over at Little Sparrow, then up at Fire Thunder again. "You have your sister with you again," he said, holding his wife more closely when sobs racked her frail body. "Do not forget what our son means to *us*."

"Your son neglected his duties to my sister," Fire Thunder said, his voice gentle, yet firm. "But, no, I do not blame him to the extent that I do not still care for his welfare. I shall soon get a search party together. We shall try and find Good Bear."

Gentle Song wrenched herself free of her husband's embrace and reached for Fire Thunder's hand. "Thank you," she murmured, clasping it. "I knew that you would not want the worst for our son." Her gaze went to Kaylene.

Kaylene looked back at her, then turned her eyes

away when she saw the anguish in the depths of the woman's eyes. She had seen it many times before when parents had come to the carnival to look for their runaway children. She recalled that her father had hid the children from these parents.

At the time, she had thought that the children had come willingly to him, to be a part of the excitement of the carnival.

She now began to wonder how wrong she might have been. Could this Kickapoo boy who was missing be back at the carnival even now, forever a part of their long journeys?

She brushed this thought aside. She did not want to believe that her father *had* forced the carnival life upon *any* children.

No, to think that would be the worst thing to think about her father, a father who was now surely dead and alone, without anyone there to bury him ... to say words from the Bible over him....

Fire Thunder eased his hand from Gentle Song's and rode onward through the village until he came to a larger log cabin at the far end, where a stream wove like a white snake behind it.

Kaylene's heart skipped a beat as she stared at it, thinking that in her dreams, since she was a child, she had seen herself in such a cabin as a wife, a mother, ah, with the stability she had so hungered for all of her life.

She was impressed by its size in comparison to the other lodges in the village.

But she had to remember that this man was chief and *would* have the best.

Again she longed not to hold a grudge against this man. He had so much to offer a woman. If only she could be that woman, she thought unhappily to herself.

Out of the corner of her eye, she saw a young woman rush between the lodges, her eyes wide as she took quick glances at Kaylene.

Running Fawn had entered the village just in time, after having awakened and found herself in a half-drunken stupor at the far edge of the village.

Pedro must have left her there.

She felt lucky that she had awakened before her father had arrived and found her gone. Her father would have known that she had been gone the long night through.

Her tongue felt thick, and her head ached. But she did not want to go immediately to her lodge.

She was intrigued by the white woman on Fire Thunder's horse.

She was young and beautiful. She was *ravishing*.

But there was something quite peculiar about her being with Fire Thunder. Was she his captive?

But surely not. Fire Thunder had not brought captives home, ever. And the woman was wounded.

Running Fawn stood in the shadows of a lodge and watched as Fire Thunder lifted Kaylene from the horse.

She shifted her gaze and watched her father take Little Sparrow from his saddle.

Her eyebrow lifted when Running Fawn saw Little Sparrow run to Kaylene, take her hand, and look up at her as though she adored her.

Then Running Fawn frowned when Fire Thunder ushered both the stranger and his sister into his lodge, Running Fawn's father taking the horses to the corral.

Running Fawn turned around and ran to her lodge. She quickly slipped her soiled dress over her head, and dressed quickly in a flounced skirt and a loose overblouse of printed cotton.

She stepped outside and was brushing her hair just as her father came toward her.

Black Hair sighed when he caught sight of his daughter standing there so innocent, so lovely. Perhaps she had obeyed him this time, he thought to himself, and had not sneaked off to be with the young Mexican men.

When he reached her, she faked a bout of coughing, to keep him from hugging her. If he got too close, she knew for certain that he would smell the stench of the tequila that she had consumed the previous night.

Black Hair walked past her, into the lodge. He laid sticks on the fire in the fireplace.

He glanced over his shoulder when Running Fawn came back inside the lodge, her black hair glistening.

"Father, who was with our chief?" she asked, busying herself preparing breakfast.

"She is his captive," Black Hair said, yanking his buckskin shirt off.

"A ... captive ... ?" Running Fawn gasped. "Why, Father? Why did he bring a captive to our village?"

Black Hair took the time, before his morning bath, to explain everything to her.

Afterward, a gleam rose in Running Fawn's dark eyes at the thought of her chief being interested in the white woman for more than her being a captive. Running Fawn saw an opportunity that might work to *her* advantage.

"Father, can I offer my services at Fire Thunder's lodge?" she asked, thinking that if she could get close to this white woman, she might be able to get closer to Fire Thunder and win his favor, so that Fire Thunder would speak favorably of her to her father.

In the end, her father might grow to trust her more so she could be more free with her adventures.

If her chief spoke favorably of her, yes, surely her

father would not punish her, which might alienate himself from Fire Thunder.

"What favors do you speak of?" Black Hair asked, giving his daughter an inquisitive, untrusting stare.

"I noticed that the white woman wears only night clothes and she has no shoes," Running Fawn said as she placed a skillet over the flames. "I could offer her one of my dresses and a pair of my moccasins. I could offer her my friendship. Would not all those things please our chief?"

"And why would you be so kind to a stranger?" Black Hair asked, removing the headband from around his brow.

"For our chief, that is all," Running Fawn said, shrugging idly.

"Perhaps it would be good for you to have something besides household duties for a father to busy your hands with," Black Hair said, nodding. "Yes. Offer your services to our chief. I am sure he will welcome it."

"Thank you, Father," Running Fawn said, smiling mischievously as he left the lodge.

Kaylene was stunned that Fire Thunder would take her into his lodge and leave her there so quickly, to go with the search party to look for Good Bear.

He had left Little Sparrow there to look after her, but only because he knew that Kaylene was in no shape to travel.

He knew that she could not even attempt to escape, much less get far if she did. She was weak from the loss of blood. Too weak to even get up from the pallet of blankets by the great stone fireplace that he had set her upon before he left.

As she lay there, Kaylene looked around her to familiarize herself with the house before Fire Thunder returned. It was a three-room log cabin, the cracks between the logs "chinked," or "daubed," with a mixture of clay, grass, and mud.

There was a bedroom at the back of the house, and one at the front, the two rooms separated by one large room which served as a kitchen and a living room.

Each room had a window, with animal skins drawn open over them.

The central fireplace, where a roaring fire burned on the grate, seemed to be the focal point of the house, where perhaps everything but sleeping took place.

Along the walls were low benches, four inches above the ground. Several brightly dyed mats of cattail were neatly arranged on the benches.

Above them, on the walls, were beautiful hides.

Several crudely made, unpainted chairs sat around a table in the kitchen. Cupboards lined one wall above a cook stove. Under them was a lone shelf where food could be kept warm.

The stove had six plates for cooking, and beside it stood a tank in which water could be taken from earthenware water jugs and heated.

On the table, she saw wire baskets containing eggs, vegetables, and fruit.

A few ears of dried ceremonial corn hung from the rafters overhead.

Kaylene further noticed that the earthen floor of the cabin was tamped almost to the consistency of cement.

Wood was stacked at the right side of the fireplace.

Kaylene stiffened and looked toward the door when the young woman, whom she had seen earlier in the shadows of the other lodges, came into the cabin. She carried a basin of water and clothes slung over one of her arms, with moccasins held between her fingers of her right hand.

Running Fawn knelt down beside Kaylene. "I have come to bathe you and to give you clothes and moccasins to wear," she said.

This close, Running Fawn saw just how beautiful the white woman was. Her eyes were as green as grass. Her hair matched the color of Running Fawn's, as though she might herself be part Indian.

"Go away," Kaylene said, trying to scoot back from Running Fawn. "I don't want a bath. I don't want your *clothes*. I don't want to be here."

Then Kaylene reached suddenly and grabbed Running Fawn by an arm. "Help me to escape," she blurted out. "I am not strong enough to do it alone. Please get me a horse. Help me mount it."

Running Fawn set the moccasins and the water basin down on the floor, then gently eased Kaylene's hand from her arm. "You are here because my chief wants you here," she murmured. She lifted the skirt and blouse from her arm and lay them beside Kaylene. "I would never go against my chief's wishes."

She reached a hand to Kaylene's hair. "So beautiful," she said, then flinched when Kaylene slapped her hand away.

Running Fawn then stared at the bandage. "How did you become injured?" she asked, her eyes innocently wide, as though she truly did not know. Her father had explained everything to her, even how Fire Thunder's knife had mistakenly sank into this woman's shoulder.

"That's none of your business," Kaylene said, turning on her side away from Running Fawn. "Go away. I don't want to talk to you. I don't want anything from you if you can't help me escape."

"I want to be your friend," Running Fawn said, her voice low and sympathetic. "Allow it, please? It will benefit you to have a friend in our village."

"I need no one," Kaylene said, though knowing that she cherished Little Sparrow's friendship. Theirs was a bond that no one would sever, even if Kaylene managed to escape. She would always remember the sweet goodness of the small deaf-mute Kickapoo child.

"I saw how you and Little Sparrow showed friendship toward one another," Running Fawn said, watching for Kaylene's reaction. "If you would have a small child's friendship, why not mine?"

Kaylene began to see an advantage in the friendship that the pretty woman offered. Perhaps the woman had no other friends if she needed Kaylene's friendship so desperately. Such a friendship *could* work to her advantage. If she gave her friendship and then threatened to take it away from the woman, perhaps the woman would do anything to keep from losing it.

Kaylene turned slowly over and faced Running Fawn. "What is your name?" she asked softly.

"I am Running Fawn, the daughter of Black Hair," Running Fawn said, her eyes suddenly dancing when she realized that perhaps this white woman was going to be receptive to her after all.

"Black Hair?" Kaylene said, eyes widening. "Fire Thunder's warrior friend?"

"Yes, he is my father," Running Fawn said, lowering a cloth in the basin of warm water. She smiled at Kaylene. "It would so please my chief, if when he returned, you were freshly bathed and clothed. It would please me if I could tell him that I am responsible."

Kaylene looked down at herself, at her soiled gown, and then at the ripped sleeve where blood was caked to it.

She felt itchy from not having a bath. And she knew that she might even feel better, mentally, if she smelled and looked clean.

"I do need bathing," she conceded, smiling awkwardly at Running Fawn. "But I would rather do it myself."

"You cannot, not with your injured shoulder," Running Fawn said, staring at the bandage. Then she gazed at Kaylene's face as she managed to move into a sitting position. "We are both women," she murmured. "What would it matter if I saw you unclothed?"

"I have never made it a practice to undress in front of anyone, even my mother," Kaylene said. She sighed with pain as she tried to lift her arm to prove that she could care for herself.

"Do you see?" Running Fawn said softly. "You are not well enough to bathe yourself. Let me remove your soiled gown. Let me wash you. Then I will help you put on my blouse and skirt. You may want to wait until later to put on the moccasins, when you are able to get up and walk around. It is warm enough in the cabin for you to go without shoes. Fire Thunder's fire is kept burning both day and night, even when he is not here to see to it. There are those of my people who see to his needs. After he has a wife, then things will change somewhat."

The mention of a wife sent Kaylene's eyes quickly to Running Fawn. "He has never had a wife?" she asked warily.

"No, never," Running Fawn said, dropping the wet cloth into the water again. She placed her fingers at the hem of Kaylene's gown and slowly lifted it up over her head. "He has been too busy with the duties of chief. No woman has interested him enough."

Running Fawn lay the gown aside and gazed intently into Kaylene's eyes. "But perhaps that has changed?" she murmured. "He would not bring a captive into his private lodge unless ... unless he has feelings for her."

Kaylene's face heated with a blush. She looked away from Running Fawn.

She sat quietly as Running Fawn bathed her, then stiffened when Running Fawn placed a finger to her chin and turned her eyes to meet hers.

"You did not tell me your name," she said.

"Kaylene," she said, not offering her last name.

"That is a pretty name," Running Fawn said, placing the cloth back into the water.

"Thank you," Kaylene said softly, glad to have her nudity covered with a skirt and blouse. The skirt was made with four flounces. The blouse was a loose over-blouse of solid blue cotton. Both the skirt and blouse were embellished with rickrack of a contrasting color.

"You feel better now?" Running Fawn said, rising to carry the basin of water toward the door.

"Yes, much," Kaylene said, her fingers going to her hair. She shuddered when she felt how tangled it was. "But I would feel much better if I had a brush for my hair."

She felt that it was strange that Running Fawn gave her a strained sort of look at that request. Then she went to the door and pitched the water outside, as though Kaylene hadn't asked for anything.

"Truly, I would love to have a brush for my hair," Kaylene said as Running Fawn came back to her and knelt down behind her. She could feel Running Fawn stroking her fingers through her long, waist-length hair. "That won't be enough, Running Fawn. Please go and get me a brush."

Still the request was ignored.

"I am arranging your hair in one long braid down your back," Running Fawn said softly. "I shall take the ribbon from my hair and tie it around your braid.

That will make you lovely enough. Do you not think so?"

"I doubt anyone would say that I look lovely right now, with my shoulder bandaged and my hair in need of a brushing," Kaylene argued.

Running Fawn leaned around, closer to Kaylene's face than before. "You are beautiful even without a bath or pretty clothes," she said, giving Kaylene a friendly, sincere smile.

Kaylene looked quickly at Running Fawn, quite aware of the stench of tequila on the young woman's breath. Running Fawn had not gotten close enough until now for her to smell it.

No one could fool Kaylene where the stench of alcohol of any kind was concerned. Her father had been drunk way too often these past *several* years.

"Do your people accept the practice of drinking alcohol?" Kaylene asked guardedly.

She wished she hadn't said anything when she saw the instant fear leap into Running Fawn's dark eyes.

"Why . . . do . . . you ask?" Running Fawn said, leaning slowly away from Kaylene, after securing the bow at the end of her braid.

"Oh, nothing," Kaylene said, not wanting to pursue this any further.

"You smell it on my breath, do you not?" Running Fawn said, covering her mouth with a hand.

"Well, yes," Kaylene answered.

Running Fawn moved around in front of Kaylene. "Oh, I beg you not to tell," she cried. Kneeling, she clutched at one of Kaylene's hands. "It is not the practice of my people to drink freely of firewater. I . . . was . . . with friends last night. I . . . should not have followed their lead as they consumed way too much tequila. But I did. I may have even consumed more than they."

"I won't tell," Kaylene said softly.

"It will be our secret as friends?" Running Fawn begged.

"Yes, our secret," Kaylene said.

Running Fawn gently hugged her. "Thank you," she whispered. "Anytime you wish to share a secret with me, I shall listen and not tell a soul."

Little Sparrow came suddenly into the cabin, carrying a black pot.

She stopped, startled, when she found Running Fawn and Kaylene in an embrace. She was stunned to see that Kaylene made friends this easily, especially with someone like Running Fawn. That seemed to make the friendship Little Sparrow had found with Kaylene less important—perhaps less sincere.

Running Fawn rushed to her feet. Her eyes locked momentarily with Little Sparrow's, then she brushed past her and left.

Little Sparrow went and placed the pot of food on the hearth close to Kaylene. She turned and stared at Kaylene, then bent to her knees and hugged her.

Kaylene felt a strange sort of desperation in Little Sparrow's hug. She knew it had to do with her having seen Running Fawn hugging her.

Kaylene returned the hug. Then with her free hand, she eased Little Sparrow away from her. Slowly she spoke the word "friends" to Little Sparrow so that she could read her lips. She placed her hand over her heart and then placed the same hand over Little Sparrow's heart.

Little Sparrow broke into a wide grin and nodded. She mouthed the word "friend."

She then frowned toward the door, and looked at Kaylene once again. She mouthed the words "ugly person" to Kaylene, and Kaylene knew those words were meant to describe Running Fawn.

Kaylene was stunned to know that Little Sparrow felt such contempt toward Running Fawn, since Running Fawn was the daughter of Fire Thunder's best friend.

The smell of the food wafted through the air, made Kaylene hungry. As Little Sparrow ladled some corn gruel into a bowl and handed it to her, Kaylene forgot Running Fawn and her wonder about what sort of person she truly was. Although the corn gruel was tasteless, even somewhat horrible, she ate ravenously.

Footsteps outside the lodge made Kaylene turn with a start. She almost dropped the empty bowl when she found Fire Thunder standing in the shadows, his eyes on her.

She felt the pit of her stomach grow warm with desire, when she realized that his gaze was raking over her, observing her clothes, her braided hair.

It was as though he were branding her as his.

9

Alter? When the hills do.
Falter? When the sun
Question if his glory
Be the perfect one.
—EMILY DICKINSON

Kaylene was torn with how to feel as Fire Thunder strode through the doorway into the lodge. Part of her was glad to see him. The other part could not help but fear him.

She still was not sure what her final fate was going to be at the hands of the Kickapoo chief.

She recalled how his people had stared at her as she had entered the village on his horse.

She had felt their mistrust. She had to wonder how they felt about her being in his lodge?

She was glad to have at least two Kickapoo friendly with her, and she felt that the proffered friendships had been genuine.

Except there was some doubt in her heart about Running Fawn. Little Sparrow had even referred to her as . . .

Her thoughts were brought back to Fire Thunder as he knelt down on his haunches before her.

Still he stared at her, but more so in her eyes now.

Little Sparrow broke the silence as she went to Fire Thunder and knelt between him and Kaylene, giving Fire Thunder cause to stare at her instead of Kaylene. She asked in quick sign language if Fire Thunder had found Good Bear.

Fire Thunder framed her tiny, copper face between his powerful hands. He slowly shook his head, then spoke the word "no" distinctly.

Little Sparrow emitted a soft sob as she lowered her eyes.

Then she looked slowly up at her brother again. Her tiny fingers signed as she finally confessed to Fire Thunder that she blamed herself for Good Bear's disappearance. It had been *she* who had slipped away from *him*.

Now she knew that she should have not done that. Surely when he discovered her gone, Good Bear had blamed himself. In shame, he probably ran away, not wanting to face Fire Thunder with the news that *she* was missing. But he had had no idea that she was a captive all along, right there in one of the carnival tents.

"What was Good Bear doing that he would even not realize your hand slipped from his?" Fire Thunder asked, forming the words on his lips carefully so that she had no trouble reading them.

When he saw an instant blush leap into her cheeks from the question, he forked an eyebrow.

Kaylene sat, scarcely breathing, as she watched the silent deliberation between brother and sister. She was glad that Fire Thunder had spoken the last question aloud, for she felt that she might have the answer. Many a curious little boy had slipped into the tent where the naked tattooed lady performed with her snake.

Kaylene suspected that was exactly where Good Bear had been, perhaps for the very first time in his life having seen a naked lady.

Little Sparrow kept her eyes lowered not wanting to reveal the naughtiness of Good Bear to her brother. All Kickapoo boys Good Bear's age were taught the dangers of bad women.

They were told many stories about them.

Little Sparrow knew that Good Bear had known better than to look at the naked lady at the carnival. That was why *she* had left his side so eagerly. She had been too embarrassed to watch the lady prance around with the snake coiled around her tattooed body.

"Little Sparrow, you know the answer to my question, but something keeps you from telling me," Fire Thunder prodded. He placed a finger beneath her chin and lifted it, so that their eyes could meet and hold.

Still Little Sparrow did not respond to his persistent questions. It was bad enough that Good Bear was missing, let alone tell Fire Thunder the worst about him.

"Little Sparrow, how can we find Good Bear if we do not know all truths about the afternoon that he disappeared?" Fire Thunder said.

Tears splashed from Little Sparrow's eyes. She flung herself into Fire Thunder's arms, sobbing.

"I think I know what the answer is," Kaylene murmured. She was glad that Little Sparrow's back was to her, unaware that she was going to tell Fire Thunder what Little Sparrow refused to tell. Kaylene did not want to risk destroying her friendship with the child by telling a secret that the child seemed to want to keep to herself. But for the good of the boy, Kaylene felt that she had no other choice.

Fire Thunder's gaze went to Kaylene. "You know where Good Bear was before he disappeared?" he asked guardedly.

"Yes, where most young men and adults alike were for a portion of the afternoon," Kaylene said. "He may have been in the tent where the naked tattooed lady performed with her snake. Wouldn't that prove why Little Sparrow doesn't want to talk about it? She doesn't want to tell on her friend."

"A naked tattooed lady?" Fire Thunder said, lifting an eyebrow. "So that is the type of performances that go on in carnival tents? It is best that I have never allowed my people to go to a carnival. The boys and young men would have an education they need not be taught."

"Not all performances are . . . are bad," Kaylene said, blushing. "Don't you recall what I said about mine? How I performed with my panther? There is nothing at all naughty or immoral about that."

"What is immoral is what happened to my sister, and the temptation that Good Bear could not say no to," Fire Thunder grumbled.

He eased Little Sparrow from his arms. Just speaking about what had happened to Little Sparrow and Good Bear gave him cause to be angry all over again.

And although he wanted Kaylene to love him, he still had a lesson to teach her so that she would understand just how badly her father had treated his sister. Once she truly understood the depths of the humiliation, surely she would accept that her father was a wicked man and she would begin to see the rightness of Fire Thunder's punishment.

Only then would she let down her guard and allow

herself to feel that which she was now denying, her true feelings for Fire Thunder.

He spoke in sign language to Little Sparrow. He told her to go and get more food and hot tea from the woman in charge of preparing their food and drink today.

Little Sparrow nodded and left at a run.

Fire Thunder stared at Kaylene for a moment longer, then added dry sticks to the fire until bright flames leapt forward. "I am unmarried," he murmured, going then to sit down beside her. "And since I am chief, the women of the village look after me and Little Sparrow. They not only feed us, they clean my lodge, sew our clothes, and bring fresh water and wood."

"All that is missing is a harem of women living with you, responding to your every whim and desire," Kaylene said sarcastically. "It's the same, though, isn't it? The women just don't live with you."

"These women do these things for me because they respect me as their chief," Fire Thunder said, defensively.

"Those women are nothing more than slaves," Kaylene said, lifting her chin. "But of course you wouldn't admit it."

Wishing that he could break down the spiteful wall that Kaylene again had built between them, Fire Thunder said nothing to this latest remark.

He gave her a quick, roaming glance, appreciating how beautiful she was in the clothes of his people. Even her hair. Although he most admired it when it was spread out fully across her shoulders, he liked the braid. It made her look as though she was part Indian.

He only wished that she were. But it was obvious that she was born of the white culture. Her sharp tongue was proof enough.

Little Sparrow came back to the cabin and Running Fawn was with her. Little Sparrow carried a pot of hot tea. Running Fawn carried a large black pot which she placed on the tripod in the fireplace.

Fire Thunder eyed Running Fawn curiously. "Running Fawn, it is good to see you involved in things other than causing your father heartbreak," he said sternly. "You have not often participated in bringing food to my lodge. Is my special guest the only reason you do this today? You are curious about her?"

"She is my friend," Running Fawn said, kneeling down beside Kaylene. She brushed a stray lock of hair back from Kaylene's eyes. "Are we not friends, Kaylene?"

Kaylene felt the angry eyes of Little Sparrow on her, and the inquisitive eyes of Fire Thunder. She hoped that in time Little Sparrow would accept that Kaylene wished to have Running Fawn's friendship because she felt it might be useful.

Perhaps Running Fawn could help her escape.

It was obvious that Running Fawn often went against what was expected of her. Kaylene saw this as an advantage. When Kaylene was stronger and she saw the opportune time, she would put Running Fawn's rebel personality to a true test ... to a good *use*.

"I am glad to have Running Fawn's friendship," Kaylene said, then smiled at Little Sparrow. "And also your sister's. I feel lucky that they wish to be my friends, when they could so easily see me as the enemy."

Fire Thunder did not respond. He gave Running Fawn a mistrustful stare, then nodded toward the kitchen. "Running Fawn, if you wish to make yourself useful, get three bowls from the shelves and ladle stew in them," he said flatly. "Make it four if you wish to

eat with us." He looked toward the door. "Would
your father wish to share the evening meal with us?"

"He is with Good Bear's people," Running Fawn
said, taking the bowls from the shelves. She grabbed
wooden spoons and went back to the fireplace. Soon
she had four bowls filled. Little Sparrow poured hot
tea into wooden mugs.

They all sat in silence as they ate. Kaylene had
eaten the corn gruel earlier, but only because she had
been hungry. She had found it horrible. The stew was
delicious in comparison.

"Fire Thunder, your *rancheria* is much larger than
I would have imagined," Kaylene said, between bites
of stew and sips of tea. "So many of your people live
the modern life of white people."

"Do not call my village a *rancheria*," Fire Thunder
scolded, setting his empty bowl aside. "That is a name
used by the Mexicans to denote our Indian village.
The Kickapoo resent this name. It connotes a small
group of humble Mexican *jacales*."

"But I thought you were friends with the Mexicans," Kaylene said, shoving her empty bowl away
from her. "Why would you resent what they call your
village? And I saw many *jacales*, Mexican huts, in your
village. So why use them if you resent their use?"

"I allow my people to use whatever form of lodge
they wish," Fire Thunder said, rising to go and take
a look outside when he heard a horse ride past his
lodge.

When he saw that it was no one of importance,
he returned and sat down again before the fire. "We
Kickapoo use the name *Colonia de los Kickapoo* to
designate our village. That is how you are to refer to
it when *you* speak of it from now on."

Feeling as though she had been reprimanded,
Kaylene said nothing for a moment. Then, wishing to

get on the good side of Fire Thunder so that she might be allowed to leave as soon as she was well, and not have to devise an escape, she tried to find something favorable to say about his way of life.

"Your cabin is quite nice," she murmured. "It is so nicely furnished."

"Our lodges are constructed well," Fire Thunder said. He looked slowly from the roof to the log walls. "Our houses must be made of virgin material. No nails or hardware are used. Every coupling is made of virgin material. Every coupling is made fast with *pita*."

"As I arrived, I noticed the fields filled with crops," Kaylene said. "I also saw horses and longhorn cattle. You appear to be a wealthy tribe of Indians."

"The fields *are* filled with food eaten by my people," Fire Thunder said. "And, yes, we are wealthy in many ways. But nothing was gained easily. It has been a struggle since the beginning of time for my people."

Black Hair came into the lodge without knocking. "Good Bear's parents are suffering deep inside their hearts for their son," he said thickly. He glowered at Kaylene. "If not for her people luring innocent people into the tents of the carnival, Good Bear would be here today."

Black Hair knelt before Kaylene. He glared at her. "Good Bear's mother can bear no more children," he growled. "To lose her son is the same as losing her life, her reason to live."

"You can't blame me for—" Kaylene began, but Black Hair interrupted her as he rose to his feet and stood over Fire Thunder and spoke.

"I have readied your horse," he said. "You will ride with us tonight to go for horses, will you not? The warriors who are not still searching for Good Bear await you, my chief."

Fire Thunder rose. He placed a gentle hand on

Black Hair's shoulder. "Yes, I will ride with you tonight," he said softly. "I need the time . . . the fresh
air . . . to think." He glanced down at Kaylene. "I
have decisions to make about many things."

"I know that I am such a bother to you," Kaylene
said. She tried to stand up, but fell back down to her
knees. Oh, how her shoulder pained her! And she was
so weak.

"Just let me go," she said, pleadingly. "You will
then have only the concerns and welfare of your people to see to. Please take me to my mother. I promise
the carnival will never return to these parts, ever
again."

Fire Thunder bent over Kaylene and swept her up
into his arms. "Accept your fate just as my sister was
forced to accept hers when she was abducted and
placed in a cage," he said.

"What . . . fate . . . ?" Kaylene murmured, her heart
hammering inside her chest. "What are you going to
do with me? Please let me go."

Fire Thunder gazed into her eyes for a moment
longer, then looked over his shoulder at his sister,
whom he knew would not readily accept what he was
about to do. He then carried Kaylene outside, where
the sun was bronzing the sky as it sank.

Kaylene's face paled as Fire Thunder carried her
toward a cage that sat not that far from his lodge. It
was not the same sort of cage that her father had used
at the carnival. This was much shorter—so small a
person could not stand in it, only huddle or sit.

"No, you're not going to put me in there!" Kaylene
cried, struggling to free herself. She went limp when
the pain shot through her shoulder. She grew cold
inside when Fire Thunder sat her in the cage and
locked it.

Kaylene cowered at the back of the cage as the Kickapoos came and stared at her through the bars.

"You can't do this to me!" Kaylene cried as Fire Thunder stalked toward his waiting horse. "How can you? I thought you said you weren't going to harm me. Lord, Fire Thunder, don't leave me. Please don't leave me!"

Fire Thunder stopped in midstep. He turned and gave Kaylene a steady gaze, his insides aching to see her humiliation, her hurting gaze as she stared back at him. "How does it feel to be treated like an animal?" he said, his voice steady. "My people own such a cage only to cage wild cats after they have become a threat to us. We take them faraway and set them free again, on the other side of our mountain. Perhaps that is where I shall also set you free when I return."

"No," Kaylene cried. "I don't want to be set free all alone, where only wild animals roam. Please take me out of here now, Fire Thunder. Take me to my mother!"

When Fire Thunder saw Little Sparrow moving slowly toward Kaylene, he went to her and placed his hands on her waist and turned her back toward their cabin.

He gave Running Fawn a frown, discouraging her interference. Running Fawn shied away from him and ran to her own lodge.

Fire Thunder ran to his horse and swung himself into his saddle. Tonight he was going to steal horses from another Texan who had given his people problems when they lived in Texas. It was good to finally be able to avenge those long years of degradation at the hands of whites.

But he sorely regretted having to cage Kaylene.

And as for taking her to the wild side of his mountain—no, never. He would never let her out of his sight, not now that he had her there, solely his.

Kaylene was in a state of shock as Fire Thunder rode away. She now knew that she was doomed to be in this cage for as long as he was gone. She gazed at the darkening sky. She shivered at the thought of him possibly being gone the whole night.

She huddled upon the cold floor of the cage. Slowly her eyes went from bar to bar, truly knowing now how Little Sparrow must have felt when she had been forced inside her cage.

Shame engulfed her in cold splashes that her own father could have forced such a thing upon a small child. She hung her head as tears swam in her eyes. Then chilled with fear, she sat stiff and silent.

Midnight hovered nervously at the edge of the forest, close to the village, his eyes reflecting the moon.

Slowly he paced back and forth as he watched the activity in the Kickapoo village wane, until Kaylene was the only one left outside. He started to leap out into the open, but stopped when he saw a small child come into view, her shadow slight beneath the rays of the moon as she crept toward the cage.

His impatience running thin, Midnight growled and showed his pearly white fangs as his eyes followed the child's movements.

10

What clasp, what kiss mine inmost
   heart can prove?
O lovely and beloved, O my love?
       —DANTE GABRIEL ROSSETTI

Shivering from fear and cold, and feeling the total aloneness now that everyone had gone to their lodges, Kaylene huddled in the cage. She still found it hard to believe that Fire Thunder could have done this to her. This had to mean that he hated her. Would his next move be to kill her, to be rid of her in his life forever?

Yet she found that almost as impossible to believe as her being in this dreadful cage. Although she was his captive, she had seen something in his eyes too often that told her that he felt something besides loathing for her. She had seen his silent appreciation of her, the silent need, as though he desired her as a man desires a woman.

"But if he feels anything at all for me besides hate, why would he do this to me?" Kaylene whispered, a sob escaping across her lips from the depths of her throat.

When she heard a twig break from somewhere close by, then heard the soft patter of feet moving toward her, Kaylene leaned forward and grabbed the bars. She watched and waited, hoping that it might be someone who would release her. The cold night air made the wound in her shoulder pain her even more severely.

She hoped that someone would take mercy on her and would not only release her from the cage, but would also take her away from this place, even if it meant never seeing Fire Thunder again.

She would force herself not to have feelings for a man who treated her like an animal. When thoughts of him entered her mind, she would force herself to hate him.

Her eyes widened when Little Sparrow came into view, a blanket draped across her arms.

"Little Sparrow!" Kaylene whispered, surprised to see her there, for it was in blatant disobedience of her brother.

But seeing that it was only Little Sparrow, who would not dare release her from the cage, Kaylene's hopes were dashed. Except, oh, Lord, how she welcomed the warmth of the blanket.

She watched anxiously as Little Sparrow shoved the blanket through the bars of the cage, made the sign of friendship, then turned and fled into the darkness again.

"Thank you," Kaylene whispered, although knowing that Little Sparrow could not hear her.

But Kaylene knew that Little Sparrow knew that she was grateful. Little Sparrow had been in a cage. She had known how cold it could get as darkness threw its mighty black shroud all around her.

As she wrapped it around her shoulders, Kaylene snuggled into the blanket. She sat against the bars at the back of the cage, then forked an eyebrow when she heard the sound of someone else approaching.

Her hopes soared again when she saw that it was Running Fawn. She knew that Running Fawn was capable of going against everyone's wishes and might be the one to set her free.

But she soon discovered how wrong she was to assume that. Running Fawn came only to thrust another blanket through the bars of the cage. She gave Kaylene a downtrodden gaze, then moved into the darkness again, leaving Kaylene as alone as before.

But this second blanket was all that Kaylene needed to ward off the total chill of the night. She wrapped it around her legs and feet, sighing as her body absorbed the warmth of the blankets into her flesh.

Bone weary, sad, and disillusioned about life in general, Kaylene hung her head.

She must sleep. She would sleep away the awkward hours that lay ahead of her. She would try and find escape in dreams.

"But I don't want to dream about Fire Thunder," she whispered to herself. "Never again! I hate him!"

A sound, the familiarity of it, caused Kaylene's eyes to fly open. She scarcely breathed as she squinted into the darkness. She understood the sound of the language of her panther's padded footsteps.

Her insides melted as Midnight's eyes gleamed back at her as he came toward her.

When he reached the cage and he discovered that Kaylene was not able to leave the cage and go to him, Midnight paced nervously back and forth.

He growled. He hissed. His head swung back and forth in his agitation at not being able to be with Kaylene totally.

"Midnight," Kaylene whispered, the blankets falling

from around her as she moved to her knees to reach a hand out for her panther.

Tears sprang to her eyes when he stopped pacing and went to her and fondly licked her hand.

"I'm so afraid," Kaylene whispered to her panther. "Not only for myself, but also *you*. Although I am so happy to see you, my sweet pet, by coming here, you have placed yourself in danger."

Her hand still warm from his tongue, Kaylene drew it away and gestured toward the dark shadows of the forest. "Go now, Midnight," she softly cried. "Hide. Be safe. Don't let the Kickapoo find you. If they can do this to me, what might they do to *you*?"

Midnight placed a paw through the bars of the cage and rested it on Kaylene's lap.

Kaylene stroked his sleek fur, then lifted the paw back through the bars. "Midnight, please go," she whispered, then tensed when from the far side of the village she heard the full roar of hooves approaching. Her eyes went wild.

"They're returning," she gasped.

She stared frightened at Midnight. "Oh, Lord, Midnight!"

She sighed with relief when it was obvious that Midnight also heard the thundering hoofbeats. He growled and leapt away from Kaylene, back into the dark shadows from which he had emerged.

Kaylene grabbed a blanket and tugged it around her shoulders as many horses came into view, many warriors herding them away from the village, toward the corrals on the far side.

A slight gasp rose from Kaylene when she caught sight of Fire Thunder as he broke away from the others and rode toward the cage, his eyes never leaving her.

Not knowing what to expect now that Fire Thunder

had returned, unsure of whether or not she wanted him to release her, not knowing what his plans were next for her, Kaylene again cowered at the back of the cage.

When Fire Thunder drew a tight rein before the cage and dismounted, Kaylene's eyes locked with his.

He could see her defiance in her angry stare. He smiled to himself, for he did not expect Kaylene to belittle herself by asking to be released.

Then his eyes widened when he noticed not only one blanket in the cage, but *two*.

"Who brought you the blankets?" Fire Thunder asked, gripping the bars with his powerful hands.

When she refused to answer him, and smiled a slow, smug smile as he again looked from blanket to blanket, he knew without pursuing the matter who had gone against his wishes. But he had no plans to punish his little sister for having done this. If anyone knew the hardships of a cage, it was she! *She* would sympathize with Kaylene.

Out of the corner of his eye he saw a movement. He turned a quick gaze and found Running Fawn standing in the shadows.

His eyebrows forked. Perhaps he had been wrong to think that his sister had taken mercy on the caged woman.

Disobedience was something more like Running Fawn's nature.

He started to go to her, to scold her, but Kaylene spoke suddenly, distracting him.

"I see you've been busy tonight," Kaylene said, her eyes blazing into Fire Thunder's as he turned her way again.

She had seen Running Fawn and she had noticed that Fire Thunder had seen her, too. She had to do something to distract him so that Running Fawn could run back to her lodge.

She forced a sarcastic laugh. "Now where on earth would you get so many horses this time of night?" she said mockingly. "I'd wager that you stole them from some Texan's ranch."

She glared at him. "Now I realize how you managed to have so many *longhorn* cattle," she continued, not giving him the chance to respond. "You also stole *them*."

She laughed bitterly. "And you took it upon yourself to condemn my father because of the life he led?" she said. "Why, you are no better. You are nothing but a horse thief and cattle rustler. You cage innocent, injured women. You have a dark heart. I loathe you. Do you hear? I loathe you."

Stunned by her berating of him, despite his full intention of releasing her from the cage, Fire Thunder took a nervous step away from it.

He had no time to think, or to speak, for Black Hair was suddenly there, with a travois attached to the back of his horse.

Kaylene's breath and words were stolen away when she saw the travois and could see that a small body lay in the blankets on it. She placed a hand over her mouth to stifle a gasp when she realized who the child must be.

Good Bear! They had found Good Bear. And . . . he . . . was dead!

She watched silently as Black Hair dismounted and went solemnly to Good Bear's parents' lodge.

Eyes wide, Kaylene was touched deeply when Fire Thunder's eyes filled with tears as he knelt down beside the travois and gently lifted the young man's body in his arms and held him for a while, rocking him slowly in his arms, whispering something to him that Kaylene couldn't hear.

Kaylene was taken aback by this side of Fire Thunder's personality, proving to her that he was a vulnerable, caring man, a man with feelings.

She moved to her knees, a blanket clutched around her shoulders as Good Bear's parents walked up to Fire Thunder and stared in disbelief at their dead son.

Kaylene jumped with alarm when Good Bear's mother began chanting and pulling at her hair.

Kaylene's eyes filled with tears as Fire Thunder ever so gently placed the young boy in his father's outstretched arms, then swept his arms around the child's mother, in an attempt to comfort her.

Gentle Song ceased pulling her hair and clung desperately to Fire Thunder for a moment longer, her body trembling as her tears wet Fire Thunder's shirt.

Kaylene felt herself softening toward Fire Thunder. Any man who showed such a kind gentleness could not be totally mean. For certain, this man's heart was not black. He was filled with goodness.

And although she did not wish to, Kaylene felt herself becoming intrigued with him anew, her heart blending into his as Gentle Song swept away from him and followed her husband to the large council house, where the child would be prepared for burial.

Fire Thunder stood for a moment with his face held within his hands. An involuntary shiver ran through him at the thought of the child having been found in such a way. It was apparent that the child had chosen the time of his own death, *and* the weapon that had taken his last breath away.

He had stolen a knife and he had plunged it deeply into his own heart.

"I am so sorry about the child," Kaylene murmured,

drawing Fire Thunder's eyes toward her. "Truly, Fire Thunder, I am so sorry."

Fire Thunder stared at her for a moment, then swallowed hard and turned his eyes away.

"Fire Thunder, you are not to blame," Kaylene heard herself saying, surprised that she could be sympathetic to this man who had changed her whole life the day he had abducted both her and her father. But she could not help but be moved by him and his feelings for Good Bear. She could not help but feel his hurt deeply inside herself, which proved to her that she could never truly hate him.

That she was in love with him.

She had loved him since that very first time she had seen him. And she knew that, in time, he would forget his anger and feel free to show his true feelings for her.

Wiping tears from his eyes, Fire Thunder turned toward Kaylene.

Their eyes met and held.

He felt a deep stirring of emotion within him, to know that even though he had caged this woman, she could speak to him so sympathetically, so gently.

In one quick movement he pulled the key to the cage from his front breeches' pocket and removed the lock. He reached inside and grabbed Kaylene into his arms and carried her gently to his lodge.

Once there, Fire Thunder walked through the living room into his bedroom, and lay Kaylene on his bed.

He then suddenly knelt down over her and again held her in his arms. Then he kissed her.

Dazed by the kiss, and the suddenness of it, Kaylene lay limp within Fire Thunder's arms.

But as his kiss deepened, and he placed a hand over one of her breasts, sensually caressing it, Kaylene became breathless with a rush of desire, and responded to his kiss and caresses with abandon.

Closing her eyes, Kaylene recalled the dream in which Fire Thunder had kissed and held her. It was as wonderful in real life. The feelings aroused in her were washing away her anger; even her reasons for being angry with him.

All that she felt was rapture—a sweet, spinning euphoria that made her lean up into his embrace, wanting more.

As though willed to, her body arched up to meet his as he moved over her and pressed himself against her.

She was not that familiar with the male anatomy, except what she had imagined it might be.

Yet she knew enough to realize that there was something long and hard pressing against the inside of Fire Thunder's breeches against her thighs, that she had not been aware of before.

"I need you," Fire Thunder whispered against her parted lips. "I am sorry that I placed you in the cage. I had hoped to teach you something by it. Now . . . I . . . regret it."

His words broke the spell that had begun to weave between him and Kaylene.

Kaylene slapped his hand away from her breast. She shoved him away from her.

"Teach?" she said, eyes wide. "You placed me in that hideous cage to teach me a lesson? Don't you know that I already knew the horrors of your sister having been placed in such a cage? Why would you think I needed to experience it to know the horrors *of* it?"

Stung by her words, and how easily she slipped into her hateful personality after she had been so sweet and gentle, Fire Thunder rose quickly from the bed and stared down at her.

"Don't look at me like it was *I* who committed a sin," Kaylene said, her breast still throbbing sensually from his touch, her lips still burning from his kiss.

She yanked the blanket up to her chin and sat up against the iron headboard of the bed. "*I* never placed your sister in the cage," she said bitterly. "I even fought for her release. So I was punished wrongly, wouldn't you say?"

"I wanted you to see the depths of the humiliation of it, so that you would see the evil of your father and not always speak up in his behalf as though he were a moral man," Fire Thunder said, sighing heavily. He hung his head. "But this is not the time for any of this. I feel responsible for Good Bear's death. The child killed himself over Little Sparrow. Had I not expected the young lad to be as strong willed and as responsible as an adult, he would be alive today."

His pain, his anguish, his torment, reached inside Kaylene's heart, mellowing her once again toward him. "He killed himself?" she murmured, ashen at the thought of a young child being that desperate.

Fire Thunder started to walk away.

Kaylene moved from the bed.

Even though her shoulder pained her miserably, she caught Fire Thunder and took him by the hand.

"You are not to blame," she murmured, as he turned and gazed down at her. "As I am not to blame for what happened to your sister. We are *both* blameless. Why can't you see that?"

She stood on tiptoe and kissed him, then recoiled when she saw an instant anger leap into his eyes.

She took a step away from him as he turned and left the room.

Kaylene's heart sank, thinking that now she may never reach him. He was a complex man with many moods.

But she was so glad that he was not a rogue, but instead, deep down, a caring, gentle man.

Fire Thunder went and stood over the fire. Resting his arm on the mantel, he stared at the dancing flames, his heart thumping.

He was torn with how to feel. He had wanted to teach Kaylene to love him, and felt that just perhaps he might have succeeded at doing that: by the way she had kissed him, by the way she had pleaded with him not to feel guilty.

Did that not prove that she did have warm, honest, sensual feelings for him?

But now, so close to possibly having her, he was afraid. He did not want to feel anything for this woman. She was no good for him. She was born of an evil father, which meant that she had bad blood running through her veins.

Then his eyes widened as a thought sprang into his mind.

Was she John Shelton's daughter?

Could *she* have been stolen as a child . . . ?

He turned and found Kaylene standing behind him, her eyes pleading up at him.

He placed a gentle hand to her cheek. He so badly wanted to find a way to allow himself to love her.

Perhaps he *had* found a way to make *her* want to stay with him forever.

He wanted her to be free—free to love him.

Yet he knew that he must enter into his questions about her past with care. He did not want to give her cause for hurt, if the discoveries proved that she had been living a lie with the man and woman she had always known as her parents. . . .

11

You loved me for an hour,
But only with your eyes;
Your lips I could not capture
By storm or by surprise.
—SYDNEY KING RUSSELL

"How can you approve of a father who steals children?" Fire Thunder blurted out as he gazed down at Kaylene.

"You are accusing my father of something you only think he is guilty of," Kaylene said in defense of her father. "My father surely took Little Sparrow in out of pity." She swallowed hard. "And all of the *others*."

"How much longer are you going to use that as a defense against not accepting the truth about your father? You have to know that Little Sparrow has told me how it truly happened, why she was there at your father's carnival in a cage," Fire Thunder said, placing a gentle hand on one of her shoulders. "My sister does not lie. Why should she?"

Knowing that he was right, that Little Sparrow wouldn't lie about anything like that, Kaylene lowered her eyes. "I so badly want to believe that my father could not do such a terrible thing," she murmured. She looked slowly up at him again. "Don't you understand? Knowing that he did that makes me ... feel ... unclean. He's my father. I am the daughter of a wicked man."

She paled. "Oh, Lord," she said, searching his face as she thought of something else that made her feel as though worms were crawling through her insides. "Good Bear. Please don't tell me that you found Good Bear at my father's carnival."

"No, he was not there," Fire Thunder said, lowering his hand to his side.

He turned and faced the fire, the flames leaping like his heartbeat, at being reminded of the small child, and his own part in his death. Would he ever feel less guilty for having laid so much responsibility on Good Bear's shoulders?

When the child discovered that he had let his chief down, it was a shame so intense, mixed with fear, that sent him to death that no proud warrior would ever lay claim to.

If only Good Bear could have lived longer. If only he had been given the chance to become a proud warrior, Fire Thunder despaired to himself. Good Bear would have then known the true evil of dying at one's own hand.

"Thank God," Kaylene said, moving to his side. She lay a hand on his arm. "Where did you find him? Or is it too painful to talk about?"

"His parents are living a nightmare," Fire Thunder said sullenly. "And, no. I do not wish to talk about it. I am also a part of that nightmare."

"Fire Thunder, you know how distraught Good Bear's parents were when they did not know where he had disappeared," Kaylene said guardedly. "Think about my mother and what she is going through, not knowing *my* fate. It isn't fair to her to let her believe that perhaps by now I am dead. Please take me to her. Let her know that I am alive. She is not guilty of anything. She should not have to pay for the sins of my father."

"She is as guilty as he," Fire Thunder grumbled, turning a frown down at Kaylene. "She stood aside and watched my sister being caged."

"She had no choice but to," Kaylene said softly. "As I, she feared my father too much to interfere in anything that he chose to do."

"You feared him?" Fire Thunder said, forking an eyebrow. "Did he abuse you?"

Kaylene swallowed hard.

She turned away from Fire Thunder.

He took one of her hands and turned her to face him. "Did . . . he . . . ever harm you?" he asked thickly.

"Not purposely, or should I say, not *physically,*" Kaylene said, her voice drawn. "He would lose his temper so quickly. When I found out that Little Sparrow was at the carnival, and I was told that she was taken in out of pity, I truly wanted to believe that. When I hinted at anything different, my father flew into a rage. He threatened me. That is why I did nothing to free her when I saw her in the cage."

"Think back, Kaylene," Fire Thunder said, his heart beating quickly, he so badly wanted to tell her what he truly suspected—that the man might not be her father. It was possible that she was one of those children taken so long ago, that she had blanked it out of her memory.

But he had to take this slow and easy or he might cause a hurt within her heart that would not ever heal. "Were there other children? Did other children suddenly appear at your carnival? Could your father have done this time and again?" he asked warily.

Kaylene did not want to remember, did not want to recapture the other times, the other children, when they had happened to suddenly be there as workers in the carnival. Each time her father had said they were runaways, there on their own accord.

But the longer she thought about it, the more she didn't want to remember the way the children shied away from her father—the way the others would suddenly run away, only to be caught and brought back.

She had never wanted to believe the worst.

She had forced herself not to see the way it truly might have been.

"Kaylene, were there other children?" Fire Thunder insisted, wanting to plant the small seed of doubt in her brain about who her true biological parents *weren't,* without actually coming out and saying it.

He wanted her to come to the conclusion alone, not to blame him for bringing to light that she may have been abducted those many years ago.

And if he was wrong about this, she would hate him with a passion for placing such doubts inside her mind.

Kaylene gulped hard. "Yes, there were," she whispered.

Fire Thunder came close to saying that might it not be true, then, that she was a stolen child?

But he felt it was too cruel.

In her startled eyes, he saw that she might be coming to that conclusion, herself.

He could not help but fear what he had begun here, yet he knew that it was best for Kaylene, should he be right. She had the right to know that this demonic man had no true blood ties to her, releasing her of any guilt she may have at being kin to him.

He hoped with all of his heart and being that it was the truth!

Kaylene was remembering many things about her past that caused a wonder to build within her heart. If so many other children had been stolen away, might she also have been?

Yet there had been a difference between her and the other children. She had lived separate from the others. She lived with the Sheltons as their daughter.

She closed her eyes and gritted her teeth when she recalled something else so vividly it might have happened only yesterday—the time when her father had said that it was time that she earn her keep like the other children in the carnival.

She had found the panther, and they had become close friends. Midnight had grown up muscular and strong. Her father had forced her to perform with him.

As at other times in the past, she now felt used, as though the only reason she had been born was to perform and make money for her parents.

And she knew that her mother couldn't have any more children.

Could she, in truth, have *never* been able to have any? Had her father abducted Kaylene as a baby, to fill that gap in their lives?

Fire Thunder watched Kaylene's expressions change as she stood there in deep thought before him.

Then his heart skipped a beat when she lifted tearful eyes to him. "Please take me to my mother," she softly cried.

Deep inside her heart, she despaired over this question of whether or not this woman named Anna was her mother. Why hadn't she thought of it until now? The many times she had wondered which parent she looked like, seeing no resemblance in herself to either of them.

Why not then?

Why did it take all of this to make her realize that things were not exactly as they should have been between herself and ... those who called themselves her parents.

The cruelties of her father should have made her wonder long ago, for it would have been a blessing to discover that he was not truly her father!

Fire Thunder felt himself weakening beneath Kaylene's pleading eyes, and started to tell her that, yes, soon, he would take her back to her mother, but only to question her. She would have to return with him, for he now knew that no matter what her background was, he loved her with every fiber of his being. He could never let her go.

But he stopped and stared at the blood seeping through the bandage on her shoulder. Her wound was not healing as he had thought. It had opened again. He feared infection. He had to do everything in his power to make sure that did not happen.

Ignoring Kaylene's question, and the heart-wrenching way she had asked him to take her to her mother, Fire Thunder swept her into his arms and started walking toward the door.

"What are you doing?" Kaylene asked, her eyes wide. "Where are you taking me?"

As he carried her outside, and the early rising sun cast lengthy shadows on the cage, Kaylene's heart sank.

Struggling against Fire Thunder's hold, she looked desperately up at him.

"Have I said too much?" she cried. "Have I begged too much to be set free, so much that you will place me in that dreadful cage again? Please, oh, please don't."

She wiped frightened tears from her eyes with the

back of her hand. "I thought that you cared for me," she sobbed. "And now you are going to punish me again. I . . . don't . . . understand. Never shall I understand."

"I will never cage you again," he said thickly. "As I told you before, I caged you only that once so that you could experience what my sister experienced. It is a lesson taught, learned, and surely never forgotten."

"Yes, I have learned many lessons while at your village," Kaylene said guardedly. "And I understand why you had the need to teach me. But now I wish to leave."

Fire Thunder's eyes met hers and held. "This is now your home," he said softly, yet with finality. "Accept it."

Kaylene felt suddenly weak.

She was too lethargic to argue anymore.

And she had to admit to herself that the thought of staying with Fire Thunder forever made her insides grow warm with the wonder of this possibly being the place that she had sought all of her life, where her roots could be planted.

She would make a good wife. She would make a good mother.

Yet there were too many unanswered questions!

She . . . had . . . to find the answers.

But later.

Right now, all she wanted to do was sleep. She was sorely tired. And there was a pounding ache in her shoulder. She could feel the blood as it seeped from the corners of the bandage.

Her head spun as she started drifting . . . drifting. . . .

"Where . . . are . . . you taking me?" she managed to whisper.

"Where I should have taken you earlier," Fire

Thunder said thickly as he saw her eyes close, her cheek resting against his chest.

Fire Thunder broke into a soft run and stopped when he reached a lodge at the far end of the village from where his lodge was. A spiral of smoke rose from the smoke hole. A faint chanting sound wafted from the wigwam.

Fire Thunder knew that his village shaman, Bull Shield, had other things on his mind, with his duties to Good Bear to tend to today before the burial rites. But Bull Shield was always there for his chief.

Carrying a limp Kaylene in his arms, Fire Thunder stepped inside Bull Shield's lodge, where a fire burned softly in the fire pit in the center of the floor.

Bull Shield was sitting with his legs crossed before the fire, his long, gray hair flowing down his bare, thin back. He wore only a breech clout and armlets and a necklace of animal teeth.

Bull Shield was elderly. His eyes sank into his cheeks. His shoulders were hunched. His legs and arms were bony.

"You have brought the white woman to my lodge for curing?" Bull Shield said as he turned pale, almost sightless eyes of wisdom up at Fire Thunder.

Bull Shield's gaze went to the blood-soaked bandage. He rose to his feet and motioned with a hand toward a pallet of furs beside the fire. "Place her there," he said softly. "I will do what I can to make her well."

"I would have brought her sooner, but she seemed to be healing well enough," Fire Thunder said as he gently lay Kaylene on the pallet. "And I did not want to startle her by bringing her to you. As you know, white people are hesitant to accept shamen. They do not see shamen in the same light as they see their white doctors."

"Yes, I know," Bull Shield said, bending beside Kaylene. "And the white men and woman are wrong not to see that we shamen can work wonders that white doctors are ignorant of."

Fire Thunder knelt down beside Bull Shield as the shaman slowly unwound the bloody bandage from around Kaylene's shoulder.

Fire Thunder winced when he saw the bright redness of Kaylene's wound, and how it was strangely puckered. "The herbs did not work their magic enough on the wound," he said, scarcely in a whisper.

"What I do today will begin the process of healing her," Bull Shield quickly reassured him. "But tomorrow a Buffalo Dance must be held in her honor to guarantee her full recovery."

"But tomorrow is Good Bear's burial," Fire Thunder said softly.

"Good Bear's burial will come first; this woman's healing ritual will come second," Bull Shield said.

He stepped to the back of his lodge to gather several tiny buckskin bags. Then he returned and peered into Fire Thunder's eyes. "The curing ceremony is the only way she will ever be totally healed," he said warningly.

Fire Thunder stood out of the way as Bull Shield placed his ointments and powders on Kaylene's wound. Then the shaman knelt over her and shook his rattles, made from gourds, as he chanted.

Fire Thunder was glad to have been able to give Bull Shield something in his life that made it worthwhile. He had appointed Bull Shield the village shaman, not out of pity, but out of admiration for a man who had been born partially blind.

Bull Shield had lived alone since his parents' deaths. No women had looked on him with favor, for no woman would marry a man who was unable to hunt.

Bull Shield had told Fire Thunder that being the village shaman had brought him much more recognition and admiration and worth than any woman ever could. He was happy. Bull Shield was at peace with himself, and Fire Thunder was proud to know the old man.

Kaylene stirred. She heard the drone of a voice and the shaking of a rattle closeby. It lured her slowly awake, feeling blessed that the pain in her shoulder was all but gone again.

When she was finally fully awake, she saw an elderly man leaning over her. His eyes were sunken, his hair gray and long over his shoulders as he chanted and shook his rattle. She gasped with alarm.

Then a gentle hand took one of her hands. The familiar voice of the man she could not help but love spoke to her. Quickly, Kaylene turned toward Fire Thunder. Alarm in her eyes, she started to speak.

But the words would not come to her when she saw how lovingly Fire Thunder was gazing at her. His fingers twined through hers in a way a man would hold a woman's hand only if he loved her.

Fire Thunder leaned closer to Kaylene. "Do not be afraid," he whispered, not wanting to disturb Bull Shield's trancelike chant. "This man, whose name is Bull Shield, is our village shaman. He is what a white man's doctor is to the white man. Only *his* skills surpass *any* white man's doctor I have ever become acquainted with. When I saw that your wound had worsened, I brought you to Bull Shield. You drifted off to sleep before we arrived."

Kaylene gazed from Fire Thunder back to Bull Shield, then looked down at her shoulder. Then she turned to Fire Thunder again. "I do feel better," she whispered back. "The pain is all but gone in my arm. The bleeding has stopped."

Bull Shield stopped chanting and lay his rattle aside.

He placed a gentle hand on Kaylene's brow, drawing her attention to him. "Your shoulder will soon be well and your strength will return, but first you must participate in the Buffalo Dance ceremony tomorrow," he said, his voice low and deep.

"Buffalo Dance ceremony?" Kaylene gasped, paling. She gave Fire Thunder a pleading, questioning look.

"It is a curing ceremony," Fire Thunder said.

"No," Kaylene said, trying to get up. Her weakness caused her to drop back to the pallet of furs. She looked wild-eyed up at Fire Thunder. "I don't want to be a part of any curing ceremony. Please don't force me to."

"It will be something that will intrigue, not frighten you once you see what it is all about," Fire Thunder said, gently lifting her into his arms. He rose to his full height. "Now I will take you to my lodge. You will get your rest. Soon all of this will be behind you. Then you can start life with renewed vigor."

Kaylene clung around his neck with one arm, and questioned him with her eyes again. Then she lay her cheek against his chest. She gave the shaman a sideways glance as he placed a hand on her injured shoulder, just above the bandage.

"Tomorrow we will meet again," he said, gently patting her.

She knew that she should thank the elderly man, but instead, she snuggled closer to Fire Thunder and clung harder to him. She feared tomorrow and what sort of hocus-pocus would be used on her.

Even though whatever the shaman had done today had made her feel much better, she did not want to be made a spectacle of, with ceremonies that included more chanting and more shaking of rattles over her.

Then another thought came to her: Fire Thunder's people! Would they accept a ceremony that would be held in her honor?

It was apparent that they saw her as an enemy. She would never forget the way they looked at her so loathingly when she had been in the cage.

Fire Thunder carried Kaylene from the lodge and through the village until he reached his own. When he took that first step inside he stopped, startled at what he saw.

Panic filled him when he saw Little Sparrow sitting with Kaylene's black panther beside the fire.

Little Sparrow was hugging it, and the cat was allowing it.

If Fire Thunder was not imagining things, he thought he might even be hearing the panther purring as Little Sparrow stroked her tiny fingers through his sleek black fur.

Sensing something was wrong by the way Fire Thunder had stiffened, Kaylene drew away from his chest and gazed around her.

Her eyes stopped, startled, at the sight of her panther with Little Sparrow. "Midnight!" she gasped out.

The sound of Kaylene's voice made Midnight leap away from Little Sparrow. He went and stood before Fire Thunder, his green eyes gleaming as he gazed up at Kaylene.

"Midnight, oh, Midnight," Kaylene said, as Fire Thunder slowly eased her feet on the floor. "What are you doing here? You just don't know the danger of being here, do you?"

She knelt and drew Midnight into her arms. She hugged him as he cuddled close to her.

Fire Thunder stepped gingerly away from Kaylene and Midnight and went to take Little Sparrow's hand. He urged her slowly to her feet.

Little Sparrow yanked on his hand to draw his attention.

In sign language she told him that she and the panther had made a fast, lasting friendship. She told Fire Thunder that she and the panther knew how to communicate. Midnight had told her that he was worried about Kaylene. He had come to be with her. Little Sparrow begged her brother to allow Midnight to stay.

Fire Thunder turned and watched Kaylene and the panther, absorbing what Little Sparrow had said to him.

When Kaylene looked up at him with a soft pleading in her eyes, he was lost to her and to what she wished. He saw no choice but to allow the panther to stay. It was apparent that it would mean a lot to both Kaylene and Little Sparrow.

He had always tried to find ways to make his sister's life more pleasant, more sweet. Now he wished to do the same for Kaylene.

"The panther can stay as long as it poses no threat to anyone," he said to Kaylene. Then he turned to Little Sparrow and told her the same in sign language.

His heart warmed when Little Sparrow flung herself into his arms and hugged him as Kaylene looked up at him, tears shining in her eyes.

"Thank you," Kaylene murmured. "And you will see what little bother Midnight is. He is as gentle as a baby bird, unless given cause to be otherwise."

Little Sparrow went to the panther and hugged him. Fire Thunder lifted Kaylene into his arms again and carried her to his bed and covered her to her chin with a soft blanket.

Little Sparrow and Midnight came into the room. Midnight leaped on the bed and snuggled next to Kaylene. Little Sparrow crawled onto the bed and snuggled next to the panther.

Fire Thunder listened to the panther purr contentedly as though it were no more than a mere house
cat. He saw the love the panther had for Kaylene, and
understood why. When Fire Thunder wasn't fighting
his decision to keep Kaylene there with him against
her will, she was everything sweet in this world. She
had stolen his heart.

And Fire Thunder could tell by the way he found
Kaylene looking at him even now, just how she felt
about him.

He did not think there was one ounce of her heart
now that loathed him!

When Kaylene looked down at the panther purring in her arms, no one was there to see that wild a
wished. There was no choice, but to allow the panther to
stay. If this panther, that it would take ??? left of
Kaylene and Little ???

He had always tried to find ways to make his wives
his were ??? ???. Now he wanted to do
this same ??? ???.

"The panther can stay as long as it pleases no harm
to anyone," he said at ??? ???. Then he turned to
Little Snow waited and ??? ??? in sign language
Distant ??? when Little Snow to him ??? ??
him. Fire Thunder ??? his ??? and Kaylene looked up
at him ???.

"Thank you, Kaylene murmured." And you will
see that the panther will digit ??? be safe provided
a ??? ??? ??? ??? ??? ???.

Fire ??? ??? the panther and indeed you,
the ??? ??? ??? ??? that the ??? ???
??? ??? ??? the ??? ??? ??? ??? ???
??? ??? ??? ???

Little Snow to and Kaylene ??? into the woods
Thunder ??? ??? the ??? ??? ??? ??? to
a wine, Little ??? ??? ??? ??? his ??? had
??? ??? ??? ???

12

My steps are nightly driven,
By the fever in my breast,
To hear from thy lattice breathed
The word that shall give me rest.
                    —BAYARD TAYLOR

Kaylene sat around the hearth of the fireplace on a blanket with Fire Thunder and Little Sparrow, eating a hearty breakfast of eggs and coffee, accompanied by tortillas.

But she was unnerved by what was going to happen today. She was going to be participating in the curing ceremony called the Buffalo Dance.

"Please, tell me what will happen today during the ceremony?" Kaylene asked as she gazed over at Fire Thunder, who seemed unusually withdrawn this morning.

She had to believe that his mood was more because of the burial rites for Good Bear than it had to do with her.

She placed her empty coffee mug on the floor beside her. "What will I be required to do?" she dared to ask.

Kaylene's panther was stretched out beside her, his head resting on her lap, asleep. "What of my panther while I am participating in the ceremony?" she asked. "I fear the reaction of your people when they see Midnight."

"I would suggest tying Midnight on a leash and leaving him here," Fire Thunder said, holding his cup out so that Little Sparrow could pour him some more coffee. "It will take time for my people to get used to the panther. I suggest you do it in small doses."

He nodded a thank-you to Little Sparrow, took a sip of his coffee, then set it down beside him. "As for what you will do today during the ceremony?" he said. "The ceremony will be held in the council house. Just sit there and let it happen all around you. When you are required to participate, you will be told."

"Then I *will* have to do something in the ceremony." Kaylene sighed. "And I may as well not ask you any more about it. It is obvious that you do not wish to tell me."

Kaylene stroked Midnight's head. "My sweet pet," she murmured, gazing down at the cat. "You cannot come with me today. I hope you will not get too restless."

Fire Thunder's eyebrows lifted at this comment, wondering what to expect of the panther if it did become restless?

But he trusted Kaylene's intuition about the panther. She knew that the animal could be trusted, or else she would not put him in danger by having him here. She knew that if the panther did anything that threatened his people, he would die.

A knock on the door drew Fire Thunder to his feet. When he opened the door, he found Running Fawn standing there, a towel and clothes draped over an arm.

"As you requested, I have come to take Kaylene to the river for a bath," Running Fawn said, looking past Fire Thunder at Kaylene.

Then she gazed up at Fire Thunder. "Is she truly able to walk to the river?" she asked. "Perhaps I should help her with her bath here in your lodge."

"She is strong enough to walk to the river," Fire Thunder said, knowing that Kaylene had to start moving around more in order to gain back her full strength. "But be careful not to get the bandage on her shoulder wet. She should walk only to her knees into the river. You enter with her and bathe her."

Kaylene could scarcely hear what was being said, except that she had heard the words "river" and "bath."

Surely they weren't discussing her. Her knees were still weak. How could she be expected to make it to the river? And there would be no privacy.

No, surely they weren't discussing her.

Fire Thunder turned to Kaylene. "Come," he said, gesturing to her. "You will go to the river with Running Fawn."

He looked toward his sister. In sign language he told her to get her clean clothes, towel, and soap, and to go to the river with Running Fawn and Kaylene.

Kaylene stared up in disbelief at him. They *had* been discussing her. She *would* have to go to the river.

And as she watched Little Sparrow scurrying around, gathering fresh clothes from a trunk that sat along the far wall, and then a towel and soap, she realized that Little Sparrow was also going to be a part of this excursion.

"Kaylene, it is best that you secure Midnight on a leash now, for you will go after your bath then to the council house for the curing ceremony," Fire Thunder explained. "I leave you now to go and say a final good-bye to Good Bear. While you bathe, he will be taken to the burial grounds. All of my people, except for my sister and Running Fawn, will be there. You will have total privacy while at the river."

As though in a daze, knowing it was useless to argue with Fire Thunder, Kaylene took a rope that Fire Thunder handed to her and tied it gently around Midnight's neck. She secured him to the iron bedpost of the bed, hugged him, then left the lodge with Running Fawn and Little Sparrow.

As she walked through the dim twilight of morning, she winced when she heard coming from the very council house where she would endure the curing ceremony, chants being said over Good Bear's body. She sucked in a wild breath when a woman's voice rose over the rest, shouting Good Bear's name, then hysterically crying.

"That is Good Bear's mother," Running Fawn said, shivering as the mourning cries rose into the air like white silver flashes. "If not for your bath, I would be there, a part of the mourning."

"Go on if you feel you must," Kaylene said, her knees trembling as she moved slowly toward the river. Her shoulder seemed heavier with each step she took, although thankfully it was not paining her.

"My duty is to you this morning," Running Fawn said, proudly lifting her chin. "It is something I wish to do, though, because you are my friend."

Little Sparrow took Kaylene by the hand as they came to the bank of the river. Little Sparrow smiled up at her, then unbashfully let go of Kaylene's hand and undressed.

Folding her arms over her tiny breasts, she ran into the river.

Kaylene watched as Little Sparrow began to swim.

She was so expert a swimmer, it was as though she had been born with the fins of a fish.

"Let me help you get your clothes off," Running Fawn said, laying the fresh, clean clothes for both her and Kaylene on the ground. She left the towels closer to the river, so that they could cover themselves when they left the water.

"I just don't know," Kaylene said, taking a slow step away from Running Fawn.

"You are not used to bathing with others?" Running Fawn asked.

"No, never," Kaylene said, taking a quick glance over at the council house, now silent.

Then she caught sight of a slow procession of people moving away from the village, toward a wooded area. She could see several men holding the body of Good Bear up in the air on a platform. She trembled when she recognized Fire Thunder at the head of the procession.

When she turned around, Running Fawn was undressed.

"We must move quickly now," Running Fawn said as she reached for the bottom of Kaylene's blouse, and slowly began pulling it over her head. "Once the burial is done, we are expected in the council house."

Casting aside her bashfulness, Kaylene sighed and helped Running Fawn take off the rest of her clothes.

Running Fawn held on to Kaylene around the waist as Kaylene walked gingerly into the water, expecting it to be cold. Her eyebrows shot up in surprise when she found the water pleasantly warm; in fact, warmer than the air around her.

"It is like bathwater," Kaylene said, glancing at Running Fawn as she helped her move more deeply into the current.

"The water is warmed from hot springs that shoot

up from the ground beneath the river," Running Fawn said. She handed Kaylene a bar of soap. "You bathe what you can. I then will bathe the rest for you."

Glad to at least have some control over her bath, Kaylene gladly took the tiny bar of soap. She sudsed herself, bent low and dipped her hair into the water and sudsed it. After the soap was rinsed from her hair, she stood still as Running Fawn bathed her wounded shoulder, and her back.

When they were through bathing and fully clothed, they walked solemnly back to the village, where they could see people sullenly entering the council house.

One ritual had been completed this morning. Another was yet to be performed.

"Your people do not like me, so why do they agree to join Fire Thunder and Bull Shield in my curing ceremony?" Kaylene asked, her heart pounding more erratically the closer she got to the council house.

"Fire Thunder is our chief," Running Fawn answered. "They would never disappoint him."

Little Sparrow took Kaylene's hand and gave it a soft yank.

Kaylene looked down, melting inside from the smile of assurance the small child gave her.

Then she swallowed hard as they walked into the council house, where in the center, on a flooring of packed earth, roared a great fire. Its smoke lifted in slow spirals to the smoke hole. Its flames cast eerie shadows on those who sat around it, their eyes now on Kaylene as she slowly approached.

Fire Thunder went to Kaylene.

Running Fawn and Little Sparrow stepped aside as Fire Thunder placed a gentle arm around Kaylene's waist and led her toward the fire, where he nodded at her and urged her to sit down on a thick pallet of furs.

Gulping hard, her heart racing fearfully, Kaylene

smiled awkwardly up at Fire Thunder. Then she followed him onto the pallet of furs as he pulled her down beside him.

Running Fawn and Little Sparrow sat down behind them, Black Hair waiting there for his daughter.

Suddenly Bull Shield, in a long and flowing robe, entered the room, his hands clasped together before him. His gray hair was loose and rippling down his back.

He wore a necklace of animal teeth.

His almost sightless eyes stared straight ahead as he walked among the people, everyone's gaze on him. There was a silence as he came and sat between Kaylene and Fire Thunder.

Music of a ceremonial nature began, the musicians somewhere in the darker part of the council lodge, away from the light of the fire.

Kaylene's back stiffened when she heard the rhythmic thumping of a drum, with gourd rattles accompanying the drum beats. She could hear brass bells and tinkling cones. The distinct sound of a flute rose above the music of the other instruments.

Fire Thunder listened intently to the music, always moved by its mystery. He closed his eyes and envisioned the drums, the most important instruments of all those being played. They were made from three-legged iron kettles, the handles removed, with buckskin stretched over the top of each and fastened with rope.

Under the skin and at the top edges of the kettle were placed several pieces of corncob, around which the rope was twisted to keep the skin taut when it was moistened.

The gourd rattles were extremely sacred objects. When they were not being played, they were always kept in bundles.

The flute alerted the *manitous* that a ceremony was about to take place.

The music continued for a while longer, then everything became quiet when Bull Shield rose to his feet and went to stand over the fire.

A young brave went to him and placed a bundle of tobacco in his right hand.

To the Kickapoo, tobacco was an effective solace. It erased pain and hate, and drove away evil thoughts.

The young brave stepped aside as another brave came to Bull Shield's side, carrying four white eagle feathers.

The brave with the eagle feathers stood back somewhat from Bull Shield while the shaman opened the bundle of tobacco and sprinkled some in his left hand.

Bull Shield nodded to the young brave, who took the bundle. Then the other one, who held the eagle feathers, stepped next to Bull Shield.

One by one, Bull Shield took the eagle feathers. He knelt down beside the fire and placed the feathers on the ground, one in each direction.

He then took the bundle from the other young brave and placed it on the ground beside the feathers.

Raising his eyes heavenward, he chanted for a while, then sprinkled tobacco into the fire, as an offering to the *manitou* of the fire.

Scarcely breathing, Kaylene watched this religious ritual. She listened to Bull Shield as he spoke in a drone over the fire. She could hear him talking, as though to the fire, saying that the fire *manitou* had been put there by the great *Manitou, Kitzihiat,* to help the people alert the *manitous* of the sky, and the winds to notify the *manitou* of the buffalo that a ceremony was being performed.

A few moments passed as Bull Shield said and did

nothing as he waited to be sure that rapport had been established with the *manitous*.

Then he spoke again, so that everyone could hear. He asked for blessings, health, and a long life for his people, and that Chief Fire Thunder be protected, that their enemies be destroyed, and that the Kickapoo live as mortals again in the hereafter.

He asked for Kaylene's recovery, and that the *manitous* look to her as though her skin was copper, not white, and as though her heart was Indian, not white.

The drums beat four times.

The flute blew four times, once in each direction.

Bull Shield chanted a song four times.

A woman brought a boiling kettle of food into the council house and set it down beside Bull Shield. Several women and men came and stood around the pot, chanting.

To Kaylene's surprise and horror, the chanters then dipped their hands and arms into the boiling kettle of food and extracted portions which they, one by one, offered to Kaylene.

Kaylene sat with eyes wide and mouth agape, aghast at how the men and women had plunged their hands in the boiling pot of food without any signs of having been burned.

She stared at the food that lay in their hands, horrorstricken to know that she must eat it.

Understanding her dismay and fears, Fire Thunder leaned close to Kaylene and whispered to her. "To avoid burning their hands and arms, the chanters rubbed them with the masticated root of Texas Hercules-club and prickly ash before coming to partake in the ritual. They offer the food to you as a part of the healing process. Take it. Eat it. If you do not, you will humiliate not only my people, but also the *manitous*."

Kaylene sighed heavily, gave Fire Thunder a nervous smile, then took the food and ate it. She recognized pieces of carrots, potatoes, and some sort of meat. It had a pleasant taste which made it easier to swallow under the circumstances she had just witnessed.

After the chanters left, and the pot of food had been carried away, Bull Shield came to Kaylene and knelt before her. In his hand he held out to her some sort of plant. She gave Fire Thunder a questioning stare.

He nodded toward her. "You must also eat that," he whispered. "It is the root of the Solomon's seal plant combined with the rhizome of the wild purple iris. Swallowing small bits of this curing component will ensure your good health."

Kaylene looked guardedly at Bull Shield, gazed into his blind eyes, then allowed him to place the healing plants in the palm of her hand.

Her fingers trembled as she slipped bits of the plants between her lips, relieved that even this was not bad tasting, except for a slight bitterness.

Bull Shield smiled at Kaylene, placed a comforting hand on her shoulder, and then sat down between her and Fire Thunder as dancers sheathed in buffalo robes appeared.

Both men and women danced to the rhythm of the music. It went on for some time and Kaylene found it harder and harder to sit there. The walk to the river had tired her, oh, so sorely tired her. The tension that had built up inside her as she had waited for the curing ceremony had taken its toll. And the heat of the council house was stifling as wood kept being fed into the already great, roaring fire.

As a lightheadedness seized her, Kaylene tried to clear her head by slightly shaking it.

But nothing could stop the spinning.

Not wanting to embarrass herself or Fire Thunder, she fought off the urge to faint.

But she could not help the way the music seemed to be swallowing her whole, nor the way the heat from the fire made her feel as though she were melting.

Nor could she stop herself from swaying slowly back and forth and crying out Fire Thunder's name before blacking out.

The crowd gasped. The music ceased.

Fire Thunder bent over Kaylene. His heart ached when he saw her helplessly sprawled on the platform of soft pelts.

He had to push Little Sparrow and Running Fawn aside as they rushed to Kaylene, crying her name.

He lifted Kaylene into his arms and pushed his way through the crowd as everyone stood and pressed forward to stare at her.

When he was finally outside, Fire Thunder broke into a run. He gazed down at Kaylene's flushed face. He saw her dry lips. He saw the rapid beat of her pulse at the base of her throat and knew that although the ceremony had been a success, she had not been strong enough to endure it any longer.

"I ask too much of you always," Fire Thunder whispered, his eyes taking in Kaylene's gentle loveliness, her innocence.

When Fire Thunder got Kaylene inside his lodge and into his bedroom, he ignored how seeing Kaylene lying so limply in his arms affected her panther. Midnight growled and strained at his leash as he stared with his luminous green eyes at Kaylene.

Fire Thunder placed Kaylene on the bed and sat down beside her. He caressed her hot brow, now knowing for almost certain what had caused her to faint.

The council house had been hot and they had sat too close to the fire.

The heat had doubled her weakness. She had not warned anyone that she had begun feeling faint.

And he saw that as brave, for he felt that she had kept it to herself so that she would not disrupt the ceremonies.

As he continued to gently caress Kaylene's brow, he took advantage of this moment of privacy to again devour her loveliness, for he knew that she was not harmed and that she would soon awaken.

Her night-black hair spilled over her shoulders in wavy strands over her breasts. She had flawless features. Her body was sinuous, with a slim, exquisite waist, and slender legs with long and tapering calves.

He knew without even touching them that her thighs must have the feel of silk.

The blouse that she wore revealed slightly the tantalizing cleavage of her full breasts. He had only chanced touching them through her blouse that one time and had found them perfectly rounded and full.

His heart thudding like the drums he had left behind, his thumbs lightly caressed her flushed cheeks. He bent low over her, his lips a feather's touch from hers.

Tracing the line of her jaw with his fingers, his pulse racing, he pressed his lips softly against hers and kissed her. The dark droop of her lashes on her cheeks fluttered ever so slightly.

Cradling her face in his hands, his kiss deepened, his hunger, his desire mounting within him.

But voices outside his lodge made him draw quickly away from Kaylene.

He tried to gain control of his erratic breathing. He swallowed hard as he started to push himself up from the bed.

But when he turned his eyes back to Kaylene again, he flinched as though he had been shot when he found her gazing up at him with wonder.

Kaylene's heart raced within her. It was his *kiss* that had awakened her. She had felt the sensuous stirrings within her as the kiss had deepened.

She so badly wished to reach her arms out to him, to beckon him to come again to her, to kiss her, to caress her.

But Running Fawn and Little Sparrow were suddenly there at the archway of the bedroom, gazing questioningly from Fire Thunder to Kaylene.

"She is awake now," Fire Thunder said, his eyes locking momentarily with Kaylene's.

He cleared his throat, gave Kaylene a knowing smile, then turned and brushed past Running Fawn and Little Sparrow and hurriedly left the lodge.

Running Fawn and Little Sparrow went to Kaylene's bedside.

"I was so worried about you," Running Fawn said, gently touching Kaylene on the cheek.

Little Sparrow loosened Midnight's rope and released him so that he could leap onto the bed beside Kaylene.

Then Little Sparrow crawled on the bed beside Kaylene. She leaned over and kissed her softly on the cheek.

"Kaylene, you *are* all right, are you not?" Running Fawn asked, seeing something in Kaylene's eyes that she had not seen before. And there seemed to be a sensuous glow on her cheeks, pink and soft, instead of flushed as she had been in the council house.

"What?" Kaylene said, suddenly brought out of the sensual trance in which she had become enveloped while alone with Fire Thunder. She had pretended she was still unconscious while he had kissed her, not wanting anything to break the spell by telling him that she was awake. She had wondered just what else he might do while he thought she was unaware of it?

Her two friends had poor timing. They had come just when she had hoped that his hand would wander and cup one of her breasts as he had done once before.

But she knew that not too much time would pass now when he would approach her again sexually, and she would not turn her back on him, or anything that he offered.

She now knew that she never wanted to leave him, except to find answers to questions that plagued her about her parents.

But after that was all settled inside her heart, she would stay with Fire Thunder . . . *if* he still truly wanted her!

"Yes, I am fine, just fine," Kaylene finally said, as she beamed from Little Sparrow to Running Fawn. "Even more than that, I feel wonderful."

"Our people's shaman has worked his magic again," Running Fawn said, leaning over Kaylene, softly hugging her. "Now are you not glad that you went to the curing ceremony? It was not all that bad was it? You only fainted because of the heat and exhaustion. Otherwise, Bull Shield has made you well and put a pleasant pink glow on your face. In your eyes there is such a happiness."

"Yes, the shaman worked a miracle today," Kaylene said, returning Running Fawn's hug.

She smiled to herself, knowing that the shaman had nothing at all to do with how she felt at this moment.

Fire Thunder, and *only* Fire Thunder, was the cause of her joyous bliss.

13

O were my Love yon lilac fair,
Wi' purple blossoms to the spring,
And I a bird to shelter there,
When wearied on my little wing.
—ROBERT BURNS

Several days had passed. Kaylene's wound was finally healed enough for her to take walks. But until she got her full strength back, she could take only short jaunts through the village.

The evening meal had been eaten. The sun was slowly sinking in the west as Kaylene wandered now through the village, her panther devotedly at her side.

Kaylene kept Midnight with her as often as possible, even though seeing him with her made the Kickapoo shy away. Kaylene even knew that some called her a witch because of her panther companion.

Some had even said that she was a sister to the big cat, that she was part cat, herself, with her green eyes, and her sleek, black mane of hair that was almost the identical bluish-black coloring of her panther's pelt.

None of these things bothered Kaylene.

And she had even stopped asking Fire Thunder to allow her to leave the village, to go to her mother.

In truth, the more Kaylene thought about things, the more she was hesitant to hear the answers that her mother might give her. Sometimes truths hurt too much.

For certain, her heart still ached over knowing that her father was responsible for so many cruel deeds to humanity.

Father? she thought despairingly to herself. *Was he?*

Or was she wrong to think that she had been raised by people who had wanted her for no better reason than her father had wanted the other children?

Yes, they had treated her special. They had even shared their personal wagon and tent with her.

But when she had grown old enough to perform, her father had not hesitated ordering her to. She had then become just another performer, nothing more, nothing less.

Yes, it was possible that she had other parents out there, somewhere. Oh, so very, very possible.

Shaking such thoughts from her mind, as she had forced herself to do many times these past few days, Kaylene walked around the village, the large outdoor fire casting a golden glow on her face.

She usually took these walks with either Running Fawn or Little Sparrow.

This evening, she only walked with her panther. Little Sparrow had joined other children, who even now sat around the outdoor fire, while the village story-teller told fascinating stories of Indian lore. Little Sparrow always sat more closely to the storyteller, her eyes closely watching his lips.

In Little Sparrow's sign language, that Kaylene was just learning how to interpret, Little Sparrow had explained to Kaylene that after the evening meal was the time when old legends of the Kickapoo were told. Little Sparrow had told Kaylene that she was always glad when the sun hung low in the west, knowing that soon she would be among the others, filled with anxiousness to know what the next story might be.

Little Sparrow had giggled when she had relayed to Kaylene that when the storyteller told stories during the winter months, when everyone was more lethargic and lazy than in the summer, the listeners must constantly say, "Hi," to show that they were awake and listening.

If any of them fell asleep, the storyteller would take a stick from the fire and touch them with it on one of their fingernails, to awaken them.

Kaylene could envision Little Sparrow with the others, her sweet face filled with wonder as she studied the storyteller's lips, taking in all that he told them in the early evening.

And as for Running Fawn, Kaylene thought unhappily to herself, she had been disappearing more than not these past days. When Kaylene asked Running Fawn where she had been, or was going, Running Fawn would not answer her, only look mischievously into Kaylene's eyes, smiling slowly.

Kaylene had surmised from this that Running Fawn was having trysts with young Mexican men. It was something that Running Fawn would not talk to Kaylene about.

Running Fawn had most definitely found something that she chose not to share with her new friend. And that satisfied Kaylene. She wanted no part in such secrets. If *she* knew, then she would also be a part of the deceit.

Making a slow turn, Kaylene moved back toward Fire Thunder's lodge. Just looking at it in the distance made her heart take on a strange sort of beating. Since

their last brief encounter, when Kaylene had pretended to be asleep when Fire Thunder had kissed
her, he had not approached her again in such a way.

But she had caught him looking at her many times
with that look in his eyes that told her that he hungered for her as much as she did him. It was something
now that she could not deny to herself, that she would
always love this man.

True, she was his prisoner, but more a prisoner of
the heart now than any other kind.

As Kaylene walked past the various lodges, she
smiled at the people who stepped to their doors to
stare at her.

She melted inside when some actually returned her
smile, as though just perhaps *they* were beginning to
accept her as someone who meant them no harm.

None that she knew of had blamed her for Good
Bear's death. They surely understood that she had had
no part in his being at the carnival just prior to him
having killed himself. She was innocent except that
she was her father's daughter, and she was white of
skin—to them, an enemy.

Strange, she thought to herself, how recently she
had been feeling things inside herself that were new
and confusing to her. The longer she was around these
people, the more she felt a strange yearning.

It was as though in another lifetime she may have
been an Indian.

She so hungered to know more of these people's
customs, to understand everything about them. She
had the strong desire to join them when they sat
around the evening fire and shared stories, songs,
and dances.

But as too troubling to her, she brushed these
thoughts aside.

She stared into the far distance, where the lowering

evening sun was bronzing everything in its path. She looked at the longhorns grazing peacefully on the tall, sweet grass in the valley. She could see horsemen there and knew that Fire Thunder was among them.

Word had been received that one of the herd had disappeared. Fire Thunder had left immediately to check on things, to see how, or where, the hoofprints might lead.

A "mossy horn" was what Fire Thunder had called the lost longhorn, an older longhorn that had moss growing on its horns.

She turned to her left and walked to the far edge of the village, away from the lodges, to take the long way back to Fire Thunder's lodge. While Midnight was with her, safely on his leash, she felt safe *and* strong enough to wander just a little bit farther than usual.

Her hair rustling around her shoulders in the gentle breeze, she walked casually through the blowing sea of knee-high grass. Thickly carpeted, it was endlessly abundant. She knew that this land was fertile beyond dreams. The grass itself was surely a treasure greater than gold to those who raised cattle.

Now close enough to see the longhorns better, Kaylene stared at them again. All of them seemed to show the same body contours—long legs with knobby knees, compact hindquarters below peaked, narrow hips, and high-standing shoulders. Some of them were six feet from the ground. They had bulging rib cages, tapering back to concave bellies.

And all bore the imposing horns which gave the breed its name, the span from tip to tip seldom less than three feet, and often exceeding that. Some horns looked as though they might measure more than six feet from tip to tip.

The horns were smooth and gleamed like varnished

wood. Some wrinkled at the base, like the trunk of a gnarled, old tree.

On the butte tops, coyotes wailed, giving cause for Midnight to growl and strain against the leash.

"Midnight, it's all right," Kaylene murmured.

She jumped with alarm when sage sparrows flew quickly from the thick grass just ahead of her, flying away from the threat of the large, green-eyed cat.

Kaylene gave Midnight a comforting pat, then walked onward, picking up her pace somewhat as twilight lengthened the surrounding shadows.

Not that faraway she saw mule deer does and two fawns scramble away into the density of trees that stretched away in a patch of green, away from the flat land of the valley.

She sighed when she looked farther still, gazing at the sun that danced between the sky-scratching peaks in the distance, where shadows formed, moved, and disappeared.

She took a step sideways and shuddered when she glanced down at the ground and saw pronghorn bones drying and fading in the sun.

Then she enjoyed one last view again before heading back toward the village, where she was now directly behind Fire Thunder's lodge.

The valley was not only grassy, but rich with prickly pear plants. She had been surprised when Little Sparrow had brought something unique for breakfast this morning—mush made from the prickly pear cactus plant.

An approaching horseman drew Kaylene's sudden attention.

When he drew closer, she recognized Fire Thunder.

As he drew rein beside her, she gazed up at him, her pulse racing just to be near him again.

"What are you doing this far from the village?" he

grumbled out, his eyes narrowing angrily into hers. "Do you not know the dangers? One stray longhorn could be the end of you."

"I was only enjoying my walk," Kaylene said, tightening her jaw under his continued angry stare. She stiffened her spine. "It was *you* who encouraged me to take walks so that I would get my strength back. And now you scold me for doing what you told me to do? You are a hard man to please."

"And is that what you wish to do?" Fire Thunder asked, leaning his face down closer to hers. "You wish to please me?"

"Well, I . . ." Kaylene stammered, feeling a rush of heat on her cheeks.

Fire Thunder's lips tugged into a smile. "I do believe you might be accepting being a part of my life," he said softly. "It has been a while since you have asked to be released of your captivity. Why is that, Kaylene?"

Frustrated, feeling somewhat trapped, still not wanting to give in that easily to him for fear of appearing as though he had beaten her down into obedience, Kaylene was at a loss for words.

"I see you do not wish to allow me to see inside your heart just yet," Fire Thunder said, straightening his back as he gripped his reins more tightly. "But words are not always required. I have learned much from my sister who cannot speak or hear. Like my sister, I have learned to sense many things that others cannot."

He gave her a long gaze, then flicked his reins and wheeled his horse around, away from her. "Go home!" he shouted. "Do not ever wander this far from our lodge again!"

Kaylene's eyebrows forked. Her lips parted in a gasp as she watched him ride away. *"Our lodge?"* she whispered, her heart skipping a beat at the reference to the lodge being hers as well as his.

She stared at him as he turned in the direction of the village and stopped at the horse corral and dismounted.

"He already sees me as his, and sees the lodge as equally mine," Kaylene murmured, still in a state of awe of what he had said.

She was torn with how to feel about that. Yes, she wished to stay forever with him. Yet it frayed at her nerves to know that he took her so much for granted!

"I'll show him," she said, stamping toward the lodge, Midnight dutifully following her. "He can't have control of me. I . . . just . . . won't allow it!"

Yet, she could not deny how thinking that he wanted her this much, perhaps truly loving her, made her knees grow weak with desire.

And her stomach. It seemed as weak, even mushy with a strange, rapturous warmth, at the thought of becoming his wife and staying with him forever.

"Forever," she whispered to herself, thrilling inside at the very thought of it.

Now she was not so certain that she wished to spar with him tonight over who possessed whom. She felt more inclined to give into anything he wished of her, in order to be held in his arms once again, and to be kissed by him.

"I just don't know," she whispered to herself. "I . . . just don't know . . . what I should do."

As she stepped in front of his lodge, she saw him headed toward the river for his evening bath.

She had bathed earlier. She could smell the sweetness of the river water in her hair, and the fragrance left on her skin from the tiny bar of soap, which Little Sparrow had explained had come from the shops in San Carlos.

She watched him until he stepped out of sight, then she went inside the lodge where a large pot of food hung on a tripod over the fire.

After Midnight was untied, giving him the opportunity to lie down before the fireplace, Kaylene went from room to room, looking for Little Sparrow.

Then she recalled what Little Sparrow had told her earlier in sign language. After listening to the storyteller by reading his lips, she was going to spend the night with a friend.

That made Kaylene's heart skip a sensual beat, for with Little Sparrow gone, that meant that she would be totally alone with Fire Thunder the entire night.

They had not been given this sort of privacy since she had arrived.

Was that what he had waited on before approaching her again, sexually? Had he even planned this?

Had he asked the family that Little Sparrow was staying the night with to do this, not so much for his sister, but for himself?

Her pulse racing, her head spinning with thoughts of what might transpire between her and Fire Thunder, made it impossible for her to relax.

She paced nervously.

When she felt Midnight's wondering eyes on her, she stopped and laughed softly.

She went to her panther and sat down beside him, then stared into the fire as she stroked his sleek fur.

She was so lost in thought, she didn't hear footsteps enter the cabin. She was not even aware that someone stood over her, studying her, wanting her.

Then, with a leap of her heart, she realized that Fire Thunder was behind her.

She turned with a start and gazed up at him.

Kaylene's face flooded with color when she recognized that same look in Fire Thunder's eyes that she had seen the day she had awakened after he had thought she was asleep and had kissed her.

She swallowed hard. "Your hair is wet," she blurted out, searching for anything to break the strained silence between them. "Did you enjoy your bath?"

"It was refreshing enough," Fire Thunder said, glad to have been drawn from his trance—a trance that made his heart swim with need of this woman.

He went to the kitchen and took down two wooden bowls, spoons, and mugs. He filled the mugs with cold tea that had been prepared by one of the village women and left there on the table in a pitcher.

He took all this to the fireplace hearth and set them down. "I have worked up an appetite," he said, ladling food into the bowls. He gave Kaylene a questioning look over his shoulder. "And you? Did your walk make you hungry?"

"Yes, quite," Kaylene said, taking the bowl and spoon. "Thank you." She glanced down at Midnight, whose eyes were on her as she started to eat.

Seeing that he was hungry, she excused herself and went and got another bowl.

After giving food to Midnight, she resumed eating and drinking.

"I found the stray longhorn," Fire Thunder said, between bites of stew. "It had wandered farther than the others. It was easy to find."

"That's nice," Kaylene said. Her heart pounded to realize that he seemed to be forcing small talk, surely because he was feeling the aloneness, the absence of Little Sparrow, as much as she.

It seemed strange to have the cabin all to themselves.

Strange, but nice, she thought to herself, as she glanced over at Fire Thunder. Being his captive, she

knew that she should be afraid of what might transpire
between them.

But she no longer thought of herself as a captive,
instead she was a woman in love with the man of her
desire, who just happened to be the one to have taken
her away from the life she had hated for so long she
could hardly remember!

If he only knew, Kaylene thought, smiling.

Although she had fought her captivity at first, he
had truly done her a favor. She had hated the carnival.

"Did you enjoy your outing?" Fire Thunder asked,
giving Kaylene a half glance as he shoved his empty
bowl aside.

"Very much," Kaylene said, turning to gaze at him.
His eyes locked with hers and held.

"Until you came and scolded me for taking the
walk," she quickly added.

"I was only thinking of your welfare," Fire Thunder
said, lifting a log and placing it on those that had
burned low on the grate.

"I've been wondering about something," Kaylene
said, wanting to lead them away from their strained
conversation.

"And that is?" Fire Thunder asked, settling down
beside her again. His eyes could not help but stray,
raking over her, taken anew by her loveliness.

Ah, her tiny waist. Her tempting breasts that
pressed against the inside of her cotton blouse. The
gentle taper of her slender ankles.

Oh, how he wished to place his fingers at her ankles
and slowly move them up her leg, venturing up past
her knees, to the inside, tender flesh of her thighs.

His loins burned with a fierce fire to think of what
lay beyond, where her secrets were hid behind tendrils
of hair.

He did not doubt that no man's hands had roamed there yet. She was surely virginal in every way.

He had thought that just perhaps he had been the first to kiss her. She had seemed so unpracticed in how to react to the kiss, except that he had heard the sharp intake of her breath. He knew by that, that his kiss had given her pleasure.

Kaylene became unnerved by the way he was looking at her. The way his gaze traveled over her, it was as though she might be some sweet morsel, food for his hungers to feed upon!

She cleared her throat nervously and placed the empty bowl beside her. "Where are you originally from?" she blurted out. "Few Indians are welcome in Mexico. Why are you here? Why did they allow it?"

She knew some of the answers to her questions, but she needed to speak of something, *anything,* to help calm herself.

"My people first lived in Wisconsin," Fire Thunder said, turning his gaze to watch the fire lick the logs on the grate. "Many are still there."

"But why then did you choose to live here in a land so different from your native Wisconsin?" Kaylene asked, seeing that she had touched a delicate chord within his heart by the way he gazed longingly into the fire, and spoke so emotionally.

"My Thunder clan of Kickapoo left there long ago," Fire Thunder said, turning a wistful gaze her way. "We tired of broken treaties, of the white man's constant intrusions on our lives. We are a private people. To find a measure of peace and privacy, we traveled to Indiana, Illinois, Texas, and then the Mexicans gave us much land and our freedom to do as we wished. We are happy here. We plan to stay."

"I'm happy for you," Kaylene said. "I'm glad the Mexicans have been kind to you."

"We have thanked the Mexicans time and time again so that they know for certain that we appreciate this that they have done for us," Fire Thunder said, amazed to see how Kaylene seemed so sincere in what she was saying, and in how she was acting.

He had *thought* that she had adapted to this change in her life. Now he knew for certain that she had.

It made his heart race to know that they were closer now than ever before to being able to embrace without antagonisms interfering.

"But," he quickly interjected. "We Kickapoo never forget who is truly responsible for our blessings. *Kitzihiat,* our Great Spirit, has guided us here, where life is finally good to my people. The Kickapoo, in appreciation for the bounty of *Kitzihiat,* dedicate their dances and ceremonial food to him and his *familiares,* relatives, to bring them pleasure."

"I only know of God, yet I have been kept from worshipping him," Kaylene said, her voice drawn. "My father never allowed me to enter a church. Not even once. I have hungered to know about God and His Goodness. Perhaps I can learn about your Great Spirit. Would you teach me?"

Stunned that Kaylene was this open and receptive to him tonight, Fire Thunder was for a moment at a loss for words.

Then he willingly told her what she seemed eager to know. "Religion is the principal force integrating all Kickapoo society," he said. "And although we Kickapoo guard religious information with the utmost secrecy, I shall share some of it with you because you are sincere in asking . . . and because you are now a part of our lives."

He moved in front of her. As he sat on his haunches before her, their eyes locked, their breaths mingling, he explained the mystery of his people to her.

He said, "Each aspect of the Kickapoo life is like the fingers, which are connected to the hand. Which means, Kaylene, that the Kickapoo culture is so integrated and so concerned with the holy, that it is impossible to separate facets of culture into strictly unrelated categories."

He paused, took her hands, then continued. "Our religion is essentially animistic, with the belief in *manitous* as its basic component," he murmured.

He sat down before her. "And most of the religious practices involve dealing with these spirits in order to keep life untroubled and serene," he said softly. "The Kickapoo believe that everything in this world has a spirit, life, and power. At the head of the order is *Kitzihiat,* who created everything but this world, which was made by *Wisaka.* In speaking of 'this world,' we do not mean the entire earth, but the world of Indians."

"I truly love knowing these things," Kaylene said softly, her pulse racing as Fire Thunder reached and placed his hands at her waist.

She sucked in a wild breath of surprise when he lifted her on his lap and urged her legs to straddle him around his waist.

Wearing no underthings, she was very aware of his hard body pressed up against her thighs and . . . and of that part of her that sensually throbbed as he kissed her endearingly.

Quickly, talk of religion waned and pleasures blossomed. She twined her arms around his neck and returned the kiss.

It was easy to forget her injured shoulder, her past hostility, her anger.

She moaned as one of his hands slowly began sliding up one of her legs, his fingers exploring tantalizingly.

Her head spinning, desire leaping through her veins,

Kaylene tried to find the senses required to say no to him.

But her needs overpowered her logic and she trembled when his hands finally found that secret place between her thighs and began a slow caress.

And she allowed it.

How could she not? she thought, with reeling senses. This need for him outweighed anything that she had ever felt in her life!

14

Keep, if thou wilt, thy maiden peace,
    still calm and fancy free,
For God forbid thy gladsome heart
    should grow less glad for me.
                                    —JOHN MOULTRIE

Hardly able to stand the ecstasy, weakened by it, Kaylene wrenched herself free from Fire Thunder, breathing hard. With a rapid heartbeat, she shoved her skirt down across her legs.

She gazed into Fire Thunder's blue eyes, startled by the intensity of her feelings for him.

Yet his feelings seemed the same for her. His eyes were charged with emotion. His chiseled face was a mask of naked desire. His jaw was tight, the muscles in his neck tightly corded.

Having never been rendered helpless so quickly by anything before, and afraid of it, Kaylene took a slow step away from Fire Thunder. She was aware of the keen silence in the cabin. She wondered if Fire Thunder could even hear the pounding of her heart.

Knowing that the first time for women was sometimes frightening, and wanting to reassure Kaylene that what they wanted of each other was beautiful and right, Fire Thunder moved slowly, cautiously toward her.

She said nothing, only watched him as he came closer. She could go no farther. She could feel the heat of the fire on her back. The fireplace kept her from stepping away from him.

She gasped when his hands were suddenly on her cheeks, his thumbs gently stroking them. Closing her eyes, she shuddered with ecstasy when he suddenly enfolded her in his hard, strong arms, pressing her against him.

As his lips claimed hers, and he held her so tenderly to him, she was no longer afraid. It was as though his lips were drugging her, speaking to her, telling her that the only thing alive tonight in this cabin was passion—sweet, wonderful, undying passion.

This passion was *them;* how they felt for one another; how they finally allowed themselves to feel.

Fire Thunder's mouth slipped away from Kaylene's lips to whisper against her cheek. "Say you want me," he said huskily.

One of his hands fell between them. He could feel the sensual shock of her body when he cupped one of her breasts into the heat of his palm. Softly, he stroked the breast through her blouse, hoping that within the next few, anxious minutes, he would finally be able to touch the silken flesh of the breast itself.

Through the material of her blouse, he could feel the nipple hardening against his palm. He knew for certain now that she sorely desired him.

Recalling how it had felt when his hand was beneath her skirt, caressing her where she still strangely ached, and, again, as before, feeling how wonderful it was to have his hand on one of her breasts, Kaylene wished for more, for the total fulfillment a woman could find with a man. Each moment with Fire Thunder brought her new awakenings.

Oh, Lord, just how much more was he going to arouse in her that was beautifully wonderful?

It made her tremble at the thought.

"Say . . . you . . . want me," Fire Thunder whispered against her lips.

"I . . . want . . . you," Kaylene whispered back, her voice trembling. "I do, oh, I do, Fire Thunder. I want you."

His mouth covered hers. Again he kissed her with exquisite tenderness.

He could feel her weaken within his arms. He could feel himself hard and throbbing beneath his buckskin breeches. He pressed himself more tightly against her.

When she gasped, he knew that she felt the hard length of himself that he now slightly ground against her.

He was taken aback, and gasped himself, when suddenly her left hand was between them, exploring, groping, stopping when she found what she sought.

When her fingers began stroking his swollen, aching member through the fabric of his breeches, Fire Thunder could hardly contain himself, the pleasure was so intense.

Kaylene was amazed at the length and fullness of this part of his anatomy. Strange how she did not fear it. Her fascination with it overpowered her fear.

And to dare touch him made her feel somewhat wicked.

But the way he responded to the touch, moaning even now with pleasure, she knew that surely her stroking him there was akin to him having stroked her where she knew she was meant to be touched only by the man she loved.

"Kaylene, no," Fire Thunder said, his voice deep with huskiness.

He slipped his hand down and gripped hers, slowly leading her fingers away from himself. He had wanted her for so long, he did not wish to find release only from being caressed. He wanted them to come together and jointly experience the final throes of ecstasy.

Kaylene's eyes widened when Fire Thunder placed his hands at the hem of her skirt and slowly lifted it upward. She closed her eyes, her heartbeats almost swallowing her whole.

She was actually allowing herself to be undressed by a man! He soon would see her naked. She could not help but feel embarrassed, even somewhat afraid. Yet she wanted him too much to deny him anything.

When he tossed her last garment aside, and she felt the heat of the fire on her backside, she slowly opened her eyes and gasped when she found that Fire Thunder had also quickly undressed himself and now stood totally, majestically, nude before her.

Sucking in a wild breath, her gaze moved slowly over him. Dressed, she had been mesmerized by him.

Unclothed, he was fascinating, and stirred, oh, so many strange feelings within her.

But it wasn't the wide, muscled shoulders, or his long, firm legs that caused her to be dizzy with desire.

It was that part of him that she had only moments ago caressed through his breeches.

Now she saw just how big, and how ready he was. Jutting out from his body, its purple head seeping a drop of juice from its very tip, his manhood caused such excitement, such eagerness stirring within her that she found it hard to control.

And when he circled his fingers around himself, and began slowly stroking himself right before her very eyes, she felt that she might faint dead away with the passion that this sight aroused.

As though something willed her to, as though puppet strings were attached to her, and the puppeteer was somewhere overhead, watching and guiding her, she went to Fire Thunder and splayed her hands across his hairless chest, while pressing her body into his so that his hand and that which he still held was there, touching her.

"Tell me again that you want me," Fire Thunder said huskily, slipping his hand from around his member, which ached unmercifully for this woman, whose shyness had been cast to the wind.

Kaylene stood on tiptoe, breathless, as he pressed the full length of himself against her abdomen.

"I want you," she whispered, then flung herself into his arms and kissed him, her lips softening into his.

Careful not to hurt her sore shoulder, Fire Thunder held her close. Her flesh was hot against his own as he moved his manhood slowly up and down against her silken nudity.

But no longer able to stand the waiting, and knowing that she was willing to go down that road with him into paradise, Fire Thunder swung her up into his arms and carried her from the living room into his bedroom.

As he lay her across his bed, he sent feathery kisses along her brow, across her cheeks, and then kissed the hollow of her throat as he moved over her and gently parted her thighs with the soft, slow nudge of one of his knees.

Kaylene felt the tip of his manhood probing where she ached, the heat and wetness there something new to her. Yet it gave her pleasure beyond words as she felt him shoving himself slowly into her.

And then he paused, leaving himself only a fraction inside her.

As he had wanted to for so long, he lifted both of her breasts into each of his hands. He knelt low over them, his heart racing as he squeezed the hardened nipples, his tongue flicking over one and then the other.

She sighed pleasurably and tossed her head back and forth, her hair flailing and trailing across her face.

A sensual ripple of desire raced through Fire Thunder to hear Kaylene's reaction to what he was doing. His fingers then ran down her body, touching and stroking all of her pleasure points. He watched her face and her expressions of rapture when he touched and stroked each place anew.

Her cheeks flushed, her insides so warmed with pleasure she felt as though she were on fire, Kaylene smiled up at Fire Thunder.

She reached a hand down to him and wove her fingers through his thick hair as he slowly kissed his way back up to her lips.

His mouth covered her lips in a fiery kiss. He held her close as his hips pressed quickly inward, sending his aching member into her clasping warmth. His senses reeled with pleasure.

He kissed her soft cry of pain away as he pierced that tiny strip of flesh inside her, her proof of having been a virgin.

Then he began his rhythmic strokes within her, knowing that the pain was turning into pleasure when she moaned and kissed him passionately.

Fire Thunder moved his hands beneath her and gently pressed his fingers into the flesh of her buttocks and lifted her closer.

She sensed what he wanted. She swung her legs around his waist, drawing him more deeply inside her, his bolder thrusts giving her even more wondrous pleasure.

Their bodies strained together hungrily.

Clinging, they rolled over, so that she was now on top, he on the bottom.

Then he turned her beneath him again, his hips moving in a wild, dizzying rhythm as he felt himself drawing closer to that peak of passion he sought.

He could tell by the way Kaylene trembled and moaned, that she soon would know the mystery of lovemaking, and its glories.

Kaylene had never imagined that a man and woman together like this could bring on such mindboggling pleasure. Her breathing was ragged. Her cheeks felt as though they were aflame, as did her heart.

She clung to Fire Thunder's shoulders as he kissed her urgently . . . eagerly.

Kaylene felt herself yearning for something more, something that she seemed to be moving toward as the pleasure mounted and spread throughout her.

Suddenly, so quickly it took her breath away, the spinning sensation, the rapture rose up and flooded her whole body, at the same moment that Fire Thunder's body quivered and shook against hers.

She arched her hips toward him as he thrust himself in maddening strokes deeply within her.

He held her tightly, their naked flesh seeming to fuse in sensual ecstasy.

The pleasure slowly subsided, as did Fire Thunder's strokes within her. He withdrew and moved lethargically to her side.

Lying there with his eyes closed, he became aware of her lips on him, nibbling at the flesh of his neck, then lower.

He sucked in a wild breath when he felt the heat of her breath on his manhood, then looked quickly down at her, in wonder, as she flicked her tongue

along the length of him, making him become
aroused anew.

Sighing, he closed his eyes. He stroked her hair as
she continued nibbling and kissing him until he knew
that it should not go any further than that.

Smiling at her as Kaylene gazed up at him, he
turned her so that she would be on her back, then
gave her the same sort of loving.

Her sighs of pleasure proved that his tongue, mouth,
and hands were having the same sensual affect on her
as hers had had on him.

He rolled over her. As he kissed her, he forced her
hips open with his, and shoved himself inside her and
again led her, stroke by stroke to paradise.

Afterward, after each had taken turns washing the
other, Fire Thunder pillowed Kaylene's head on his
lap. She nestled close.

The glow from the fire cast dancing shadows
through the door and onto the bedroom ceiling.

Midnight came sauntering into the room and lay
down on the floor beside the bed and went to sleep
again.

Perfectly content, feeling as though she belonged,
heart and soul, to this man, and glad of it, Kaylene
watched the shadows on the ceiling.

"I never knew that loving a man could be this beautiful," she murmured.

Fire Thunder leaned up on one elbow. "Do you
realize that you just admitted to loving me?" he said,
placing a finger to her chin, turning her eyes to him.

"Do you think I could have shared what we just
shared had I not?" Kaylene said, devouring his handsomeness with her eyes. "I fought my feelings until I
knew I could not fight them any longer."

"But you are still my captive," Fire Thunder said,

drawing her lips to his, brushing them with feathery touches of his tongue.

"If you say so," Kaylene said, giggling.

"I never want to let you go," Fire Thunder said huskily. He lowered his mouth to one of her breasts. She moaned when his tongue swept over her nipple, flicking against the swollen, pink nub.

"Keep on doing that and I wouldn't leave if you ordered me to," Kaylene said. Her insides swimming with pleasure, she sighed. She held her head back and closed her eyes.

"And so I have found a way to master you, have I?" Fire Thunder said, as he placed a hand to her waist and turned her to face him.

He drew her body next to his so that her breasts would be crushed into his chest.

"Perhaps," Kaylene said, then lay her cheek against his. "How can this be? How can I love you? Why do you love me? There are many beautiful Kickapoo women in your village. Why, I think that Running Fawn is the most beautiful woman I have ever seen. I'm surprised that you haven't noticed."

"I have noticed and I have stayed away from her purposely," Fire Thunder said, gazing down at her as she gave him a quick look. "She is trouble. And I even warn *you* to be wary of her and that which she might wish to pull you into doing. You have heard the gossip about her and her wanton behavior with Mexican men. When it is discovered to be true, she will be badly punished."

"But I do like her so much," Kaylene murmured. "She was so quick to befriend me when no other people of your village would."

"Just be wary of her is all that I can say," Fire Thunder warned again.

Kaylene eased from his arms. She smiled at him. "I

must know the full secret behind those blue eyes of your," she said. "They are so beautiful, yet I am surprised that you, being an Indian, would have such eyes. You earlier mentioned being part French. How much?"

"Only a fraction," Fire Thunder said. "It goes way back many, many winters, when one of my kin wed a Frenchman. But it is such a small portion of me that is French that I look to myself as full-blood Kickapoo."

Kaylene stretched out on her stomach beside Fire Thunder. She snuggled against him. "So often, since I have come to your village, the more I am around your people, I have felt a strange yearning," she whispered. "It is as though I am part Indian, myself. Do you think that perhaps, in my other lifetime, I was? What if it were true, Fire Thunder? Wouldn't that make your people look to me as someone worthy of their chief?"

"You are worthy because I say you are," Fire Thunder said, reaching a gentle hand to her cheek. "And, yes, just perhaps somewhere in time you *were* Indian. If it pleases you to think it, think it often. It would be good to see you enjoy this life that I have brought you to."

"You have adapted well to living in Mexico, haven't you?" Kaylene asked softly.

"Yes, it was made easy for us by the Mexicans," Fire Thunder said. "When we moved here, parcels of irrigatable farmland were allotted the heads of each household. These provided the families with crops of corn, beans, squash, watermelon, and melons. But as you know, our pride and joy are our longhorn cattle."

He shaped his body more fully into hers. "But, my beautiful woman, as for me, personally, the cattle now come second to the woman I love," he said huskily.

He cradled her in his arms and kissed her with a lazy warmth that left her weak.

How could she have ever hated him? she wondered to herself. How?

She had never felt as alive, as loved, as needed, as now, while with him.

She prayed that nothing would happen to give her cause to regret these wondrous moments with him.

15

Let us possess one world;
Each hath one,
And is one.
—JOHN DONNE

"Tell me why you look so different today," Running Fawn asked Kaylene as they walked through the village, on Kaylene's usual morning stroll with her panther. She stepped in Kaylene's way and smiled mischievously at her. "You look as radiant as someone who—"

Fearing what Running Fawn was about to say, that she had somehow surmised that Kaylene had been with Fire Thunder, Kaylene brushed past her.

How could she admit to having been with Fire Thunder not only once, but twice?

Last night, and this morning before Fire Thunder left to see to his chieftain duties.

Even *she* was in awe of herself for having gone to bed with him so easily.

Yes, she loved him. She adored him. But that did not give her cause to be a loose woman.

She was troubled now by her decision to stay with him. Perhaps it was a reckless one, having been blinded by her love for this wonderful Kickapoo chief.

How could she have ever lost sight of his being responsible for her father's death?

Surely she couldn't stay that easily with Fire Thunder, even though she knew that in his heart he had done the right thing about her father. He had avenged the honor of his beloved sister.

And, the many other children besides Little Sparrow who had unwillingly become slaves at the carnival.

Again the question about her parents came to mind, haunting her. She ignored Running Fawn's persistent questions, as she allowed her thoughts to stray to her childhood, and her life with the carnival, and the two people who had raised her. *Had* her life been nothing but a lie? Was the woman who had so lovingly held her as a child in her arms truly her mother?

"Kaylene, what is wrong with you today?" Running Fawn said, bringing Kaylene's thoughts back to the present.

Weary of the questions, finding them disturbing, Kaylene stopped suddenly and glared at Running Fawn. "What is wrong with *you* today?" she blurted out. "Why can't we have a pleasant walk without . . . without all of these questions?"

Running Fawn's lips parted in a soft gasp. Her dark eyes widened. "I am just being your friend," she murmured. "I am just trying to help you. First you look as though you are walking on clouds, your face pink and radiant, your green eyes gleaming. Then you look so troubled, as though you have doubts about something. Sometimes talking helps. But if you would rather walk and not talk, that is fine with me."

"Yes, that would be best," Kaylene said softly. "Please understand, Running Fawn. I do have a lot on my mind today. But it is best not spoken aloud. They are things that I must work out on my own."

"When you need someone to talk to, I will be there for you," Running Fawn said. She gave Kaylene a big hug. "Now let's go on and finish our walk. You still need to build up your strength."

"You are sweet for understanding so easily," Kaylene said, returning the hug.

As she eased from Running Fawn's arms, Kaylene suddenly felt ashamed for having spoken so sharply to her. Still only Running Fawn and Little Sparrow had offered their friendships to Kaylene. She did not want to lose either of them.

"Running Fawn, I'm sorry for having spoken so harshly," she apologized.

"If I were a captive, I would say and behave much worse," Running Fawn said.

Kaylene frowned as she continued walking silently beside Running Fawn.

Captive. That word! How it grated against her nerves.

She wondered if she insisted on going now, if Fire Thunder would even allow it? If he cared as much for her as he professed to, wouldn't he want her to do what made her happy?

But, of course, being with *him* made her happy. *He* was all that she wanted in life now and knew that she would not ask to be set free.

Yet she *did* plan to go to her mother and demand answers when she was strong enough for the journey.

The sun was warm. The wind was soft and sweet smelling as Kaylene walked farther through the village. She gazed around her and saw women working at their basketry and beading outside their lodges.

Earlier, Running Fawn had told Kaylene that the women made dyes from berry juices and roots to paint

designs upon their baskets, dwellings, and their husbands' hunting knives.

Red represented the sun, stone, and forms of animals. Blue represented heaven, winds, water, and
thunder. Yellow represented sunshine.

Again she experienced the same strange stirrings
that she had felt before while with these people—the
feelings of belonging to this culture, almost frightening her.

Why, oh, *why* did she feel this way? she wondered.
It was as though some large being had spread its arms
around her and told her she had come home.

Having walked farther than she had thought, her
mind straying too often to things that bothered her,
Kaylene suddenly found herself at the very edge of
the village, exactly opposite from where Fire Thunder's lodge sat.

She looked quickly around her and saw that she
had left all of the lodges behind, except for this one
that was isolated from the others. It was partially hidden by a cover of trees that stood like sentinels
around it.

It was a wigwam. The cattail mats that covered it
were aged and brittle. There were no windows, only
a door. An entrance flap made from an animal skin
hung over it, swaying gently in the breeze.

"Whose lodge is that?" Kaylene asked as she gave
Running Fawn an inquisitive stare. "It is so different
from the others. And it sits alone. Why, Running
Fawn?"

"The woman who lives here is Moon Glow," Running Fawn said, staring at the fluttering entrance flap.
"But most call her *muy-trote-adore*, 'trotter.' She has
had many husbands. Most have died mysteriously.
This is why she lives away from the others. People

have lost their trust in her. Men avoid her, fearing if
they marry her, they will also die strangely."

"Goodness," Kaylene murmured, finding this intriguing, to say the least.

"Come on," Running Fawn said, grabbing one of
Kaylene's hands. "I will introduce you to Moon Glow.
Rarely does anyone visit her. Only I do." She smiled
at Kaylene. "I have not visited with her since you
came to my village. You have taken the place of Moon
Glow. She was my confidante. Now *you* are."

Kaylene arched an eyebrow. "Confidante?" she
said. "How can you call me that? You have only confided in me once. Otherwise, you do not tell me where
you suddenly disappear to so often. Sometimes I go a
full day and evening without seeing you. If you have
not come here, then where do you go?"

Running Fawn shuffled her feet nervously. "Do you
remember a few moments ago when you did not wish
to respond to my questions?" she asked.

"Yes," Kaylene said, nodding.

"Well, it is the same for me now, Kaylene," Running Fawn said, almost hoarsely. "Please do not ask
questions about things I do not voluntarily tell you.
What I do, I do behind my father's back. If he ever
discovered the full truth about things I do when I am
away from him, he might, himself, banish me from
my tribe."

"Is what you do that terrible?" Kaylene could not
help but ask, knowing that Running Fawn was referring to being with Mexican men.

"Remember, I do not wish to talk about it," Running Fawn said thickly. Then she laughed softly.
"Come. Let us go and say hello to Moon Glow."

"What about Midnight?" Kaylene asked, giving her
panther a quick glance.

"Midnight will enjoy entering Moon Glow's lodge,"

Running Fawn said, tugging on Kaylene's hand. "Come. You will see why."

Kaylene sighed, then went with Running Fawn. Her fingers tightened on Midnight's leash, for something told her to never totally trust Running Fawn's judgment about things. Hadn't Fire Thunder warned her?

As Kaylene entered the small wigwam, she smelled such a horrible, vile smell, she doubted even more that she should have trusted Running Fawn enough to enter a lodge that the other people of the village avoided.

There was no fire in the fire pit, only glowing embers. And the only thing that Kaylene could see were many green eyes peering at her through the darkness.

When she heard Midnight emit a low snarling sound from the depths of his throat, she bent down beside him and stroked his back in an effort to calm him.

His eyes narrowed as he looked guardedly around him. When he sniffed, and his body stiffened, she knew it was not a reaction to the terrible stench that made Kaylene's nose curl up, and her throat burn.

It was something more.

When a cat leaped out of the semidarkness, and came sniffing at Midnight's feet, Kaylene then knew what the many green eyes belonged to in the lodge.

One by one, cats slunk from the dark shadows. They walked stealthily closer to Midnight. Some growled. Others were curious and friendly.

"Midnight, steady . . ." Kaylene whispered, her spine stiffening. "Remember that the cats are much smaller than you. Midnight, do not—"

Her words were cut off by a low, strange sort of cackling from the inner depths of the wigwam, causing chills to race up and down her spine as she peered more intently into the semidarkness.

She started when an elderly lady stepped fully into view, a cat curled in the crook of each of her arms.

Kaylene had never seen anyone as old as Moon Glow. Her copper face was a crater of wrinkles. Her dark, squinting eyes were set back deeply into her flesh. Her lips had narrowed from age into a straight, almost vanishing line.

Moon Glow's hair was wiry gray and hung almost to the floor. She wore a buckskin robe that was loose on her extremely thin body. Her hands were veined, the skin taut on her bones, like leather.

"My, my, but don't you have the greenest eyes," Moon Glow said, as she leaned closer to get a better look at Kaylene. "Green like my cats."

Moon Glow's gaze lowered to Midnight. "Pretty and sleek," she said, her head bobbing as though she could not control it.

Running Fawn took a step toward the elderly woman. She gestured with a hand toward Kaylene. "Moon Glow, this is my friend—"

Running Fawn got no further. She turned and gazed, startled and wide-eyed, at the entranceway, where Fire Thunder suddenly stood, his arms angrily folded across his chest. She swallowed hard and trembled as she took a slow step away from him.

Fire Thunder glared at Running Fawn. "You bring my woman here?" he shouted. "You know that you should not have." He doubled a fist at his side. "Running Fawn, you stay away from Kaylene. Today proves that I was not wrong not to trust you with her! You are a bad influence!"

Humble, hurt, *and* angry, Running Fawn swallowed back an embarrassing sob. Then she ran past Kaylene and by Fire Thunder as he stepped aside and allowed it, and outside.

"Fire Thunder, why did you do that?" Kaylene

asked, after getting over the initial shock of his severe scolding of Running Fawn. "She meant no harm." She took a bold step toward him, her eyes filled with fire. "Or is it because you wish to keep me all to yourself?"

Even more angry at Running Fawn now, for having caused Kaylene to be upset with him, Fire Thunder sighed heavily.

He then swept Kaylene up into his arms and carried her from the lodge. Midnight romped after them.

Kaylene struggled to get free from Fire Thunder. But his grip on her was too strong.

"Never go to that lodge again," Fire Thunder said as he stomped through the village, ignoring the eyes that stared at them.

"So now you are again going to tell me what I can and cannot do?" Kaylene fumed, her heart beating with her fury. "Perhaps that will work with Running Fawn. But not me. I am not your child, slave, *or* . . . or wife! You aren't my *chief*. I am my own person. I will do as I damn well please!"

The curse word brought Fire Thunder's eyes down to hers as she glared up at him. "It is not ladylike to say bad words that only bad white men speak!" he scolded. "Say them no more in my presence!"

"Again you are telling me what I can and cannot do?' she marveled. "Damn. Hell. Shit. And I shall go on with more if I wish." She laughed sarcastically. "What will you do? Wash my mouth out with soap?"

"Soap?" Fire Thunder said, forking an eyebrow. "I have never known of anyone who washes their mouths out with soap. Have you done this before?"

Seeing his innocence, and loving him so much she could not stay angry, she laughed softly and flung an arm around his neck.

Smiling, she gazed into his eyes. That same sensual warmth spread through her as she became mesmerized anew by him. She wanted to fight off the rapture, yet it felt too wonderful to brush it aside so easily.

She didn't *want* to argue with him. And she knew that he did not mean to order her around.

For some reason, he felt that she should not be in Moon Glow's lodge. He was only looking after Kaylene's best interest by scolding her so vehemently after having found her there.

"No," she murmured, "I've never washed my mouth out with soap, but perhaps I should. Those words I said are quite nasty. Cursing is not a normal thing for me to do. But ... you ... you ... riled me so by ordering me around. I'm sorry I got angry at you."

"*My* anger at finding you at the 'trotter's' house, and seeing you there with Running Fawn, was too quick," Fire Thunder said, as they went inside his lodge. "I apologize."

He placed Kaylene on her feet. She loosened the leash so that her panther would have freedom of the lodge.

Then she eased into Fire Thunder's arms as he reached out for her.

"Apology accepted," she murmured. She stood on tiptoe so that she could brush a soft kiss across his lips.

Then she eased from his arms and questioned him with her eyes as she gazed up at him. "That poor woman," she said, her voice drawn, "she is so alone. Why must she live in such total isolation?"

"That woman is a witch," Fire Thunder said. He bent to lift a heavy log onto the fire. "The fear of witchcraft, which *does* serve as an effective social control, pervades the life of every Kickapoo."

He looked over his shoulder at Kaylene. "Witchcraft is blamed for many mishaps. It is best that you, who will soon live the rest of your life as the wife of

a powerful Kickapoo chief, not associate yourself with
the lowest form of life."

"If this woman is so horrible, and hated by so many,
why is she allowed to stay in your village?" Kaylene
said, kneeling down beside him. She reached a hand to
his cheek. "She has not been totally banished. Why?"

"Any old person is considered a witch, whether they
are man or woman. They have lived many years and
are thought to have acquired the power to transform
themselves into anything they wish. Anyone whose
conduct is in the least deviant is considered a potential
witch. But as for Moon Glow? *She* is in my village,
still, for a purpose," Fire Thunder said.

He placed his hands at Kaylene's waist and yanked
her to him. He eased her down on the floor on her
back. He blanketed her with his body, a hand snaking
inside her blouse.

She closed her eyes and shivered in ecstasy when
his hand kneaded one of her breasts.

"What ... purpose ... ?" Kaylene managed to ask,
sucking in a breath of rapture as his other hand
smoothed its way up the inside of her skirt.

When he cupped the soft furry patch at the juncture
of her thighs, she closed her eyes and threw her head
back in a guttural sigh.

"Moon Glow absorbs the sins of others so that re-
spectability can be returned to them. Mainly the
young, who have a lifetime ahead of them that could
be useful to my people," Fire Thunder said huskily.

"That is a strange belief," Kaylene said, then recalled the elderly woman's many cats. "Would having
so many cats be looked on as something unnatural?"

"Yes, to some; no to others," Fire Thunder said.
"You see, cats are kept by some as pets, partly because of the belief that mice chew off human hair to
build their nests, causing the victim to lose his mind.

Moon Glow keeps the cats to prove that her mind is still vital, although knowing that most think her crazed. Let us speak no more of her," Fire Thunder whispered.

He kissed Kaylene's passion-moist lips. He found her mouth hot and sweet as she responded to his kiss.

He teased and stroked the satiny skin of her inner thighs, and then thrust a finger inside her.

She arched her hips as he moved his finger slowly in and out of her, his thumb grazing the core of her womanhood each time he withdrew his finger.

"I love you," she whispered as he kissed his way up her cheek and kissed her closed eyelids.

"Say you want me," Fire Thunder whispered, already pulling her skirt off.

"I want you," Kaylene whispered, opening her eyes to see the passion in his. "I need you."

Then she recalled what he had said earlier about her soon living the rest of her life with him as his wife.

She trembled with wondrous joy at the thought of being able to share these moments they were sharing now whenever they pleased, as often as they pleased, forever.

"I need you," Fire Thunder said, shoving his breeches down to his ankles. "I love you."

"Take me, for I am yours to love," Kaylene whispered, her face hot with a feverish fire of hungry need of him.

She lifted her blouse over her head. She reached for his hands and placed them on her breasts.

She closed her eyes and slowly tossed her head back and forth as he cupped her breasts and his tongue flicked from nipple to nipple.

She opened herself more fully to him when she felt the heat of his passion probing between her thighs.

She arched her hips upward and received him, softly

crying out with ecstasy as he began his rhythmic strokes within her.

He lay his cheek on hers. "I did not plan to do this," he said huskily, sweat pearling his brow as he did not miss a beat inside her. "We must leave soon to collect Solomon's seal for use in the New Year festival of my people."

"Solomon's . . . seal . . . ?" Kaylene faintly heard herself saying, yet truly unconcerned. She was only aware of the wonderful sensations floating through her like warm waves of sunshine.

She was only aware of her body responding to his, the pleasure building . . . building . . . building. . . .

White Wolf and Dawnmarie rode into San Carlos, glad to finally have reached the town where General Rocendo lived. If anyone could give them answers as to the whereabouts of the Kickapoo village, he could. He was in charge of this area of Mexico.

White Wolf and Dawnmarie had been told that he was fair to the Kickapoo, yet hated the Comanches.

They had been told that it was because of General Rocendo that the Kickapoo were in Mexico, under the best living conditions. He had been generous to them.

Perhaps he would be as generous to Dawnmarie and White Wolf when they asked him about Dawnmarie's kin, the Kickapoo.

White Wolf helped Dawnmarie down from her horse when they reached General Rocendo's villa on the outskirts of the city. They were in awe of his wealth. His villa spread out far on each side. There were many outbuildings. Cattle grazed in faraway pastures.

When a large, imposing man, dressed in brightly colored casual clothes, came outside and stood on the porch, Dawnmarie smiled up at him.

White Wolf stepped forward and offered a hand of friendship. "Are you General Rocendo?" he inquired, as he stepped up on the porch.

General Rocendo, his large mustache covering his upper lip, his dark eyes beady as they stared from White Wold to Dawnmarie, accepted White Wolf's handshake. "*Sí, sí, señor*," he said, nodding. "And you must be White Wolf? Your wife is *Señora* Dawnmarie?"

"Yes, I am White Wolf. My wife is Dawnmarie," White Wolf said, lowering his hand to his side.

"*Señor*, word was brought to me that you were questioning about me," General Rocendo said. He gestured toward the door. "I was told why. Come with me inside my villa. I will be glad to do what I can to help you in your search for your people, *señora*."

Smiling, relieved that her long journey was almost over, Dawnmarie went with the general and White Wolf into his vast, elaborate house.

She welcomed the soft, plush cushion of a chair as she sat down in his parlor. She feasted her eyes on the grand, rich paintings that hung on the walls in gilt frames. She had never seen such beautiful furnishings, carpets, and paintings. She could tell by all of this that the general was quite a wealthy man.

"And so now tell me about your journey to Mexico," General Rocendo said, nodding to a maid who brought in a pot of tea and colorful, dainty teacups.

Dawnmarie silently nodded a thank-you to the Mexican woman, then sipped the tea thirstily. Then she explained about her people, the Thunder Clan of Kickapoo.

She smiled happily when his eyes widened in recognition.

"*Señora*, your people live only a short distance from here in the mountains," General Rocendo said, stroking his long, lean fingers through his raven-black hair. "I will send soldier escorts with you tomorrow to Fire Thunder's village. You will spend the night? I have adequate bedding for overnight guests."

"Thank you," Dawnmarie was quick to say, recalling the many nights spent on straw in barns, or on the cold, hard ground between blankets that had not kept her warm enough.

"*Señora*, it is way past our supper hour," General Rocendo said, going to Dawnmarie, helping her from the chair as White Wolf rose from his. "Let me take you both to your room. Then food will be brought to you. And warm water will be brought to you in your room for a bath."

Dawnmarie gave the general a grateful smile.

After Dawnmarie and White Wolf were alone in their room, and had eaten, and bathed, she stood at the window and stared up at the mountain in the distance. She could see blazes of light. Surely she was seeing the Kickapoo's fires.

A shiver ran through her to know that she was finally close to her true people, her true destiny.

White Wolf came up behind her and wrapped his arms around her waist and drew her back against him. "My wife, my beautiful wife," he whispered, "are you happy?"

"Oh, so very, very happy," she murmured.

He turned her to face him, then swept her into his arms and carried her to the huge, plush bed.

When they made love, it was as though it was the first time.

16

Say thou lov'st me while you live,
I to thee my love will give.
                    —ANONYMOUS

"I'm not certain if I am well enough to ride a horse today, to go with you on your search for the "Solomon's seal plant," Kaylene said as she sat on the edge of the bed, slipping her foot into one moccasin, and then the other. She wore a long riding skirt made of calico, and a long-sleeved white blouse, her shoulder comfortably bandaged beneath it.

"Would you rather stay behind?" Fire Thunder said, tying a bandanna around his brow as a headband to keep his hair back from his face. He wore a hunting shirt and fringed pants made of calico.

"Do I have a choice?" Kaylene asked, surmising that he must think that if she was well enough to ride a horse, she was well enough to leave at her own will in his absence. "Dare you leave me alone?"

"I doubt that you would leave now, even if given the chance to," Fire Thunder said, reaching down and placing his hands to her waist. He drew her up before him and brushed her lips with feathery kisses.

"Now can you truly be that sure of me?" Kaylene teased. She twined her arms around his neck, her eyes twinkling into his.

"There is too much now that keeps you here," Fire Thunder said, his lips tugging into a slow smile.

"May I ask to what you are referring?" she asked, sending him a rueful, slow smile.

"*I* am why you would not leave," Fire Thunder said, chuckling low. "Surely you can't live without my lips, my hands, my *heat*."

Blushing, Kaylene cast her eyes downward.

He placed a gentle finger to her chin and lifted her face up to meet the passion in his. "My woman, is that not true?" he asked huskily.

She smiled shyly and nodded. Then he swung away from her.

She followed him into the living room, where Midnight was still stretched out asleep beside the fire.

"Tell me, Fire Thunder, more about this Solomon's seal," she said as she watched him lift a rifle from his store of weapons at the far side of the room.

He slipped a gun belt around his waist, a pistol heavy in one of the holsters. "Only clan leaders, the chief, can harvest Solomon's seal, the magical plant of my people," he said. He swung around and went and stood over her. "Although you do not see it, I carry some even now in a pouch in my breeches' pocket. All warriors carry a bit of the magical plant. It is a guarantee against most dangers, including witches."

He nodded toward the door. "See that small pouch scarcely visible above the door?" he said. "In it is some Solomon's seal. It prevents witches from entering."

"How intriguing," Kaylene said, eyes wide.

"Come," he said, reaching a hand out for her. "I will tell you more about it while we are searching for some in the forest at the far side of the mountain. Little Sparrow will be staying with Gentle Doe and her family while we are gone."

"I do believe that I am able to ride a horse today," she murmured. "I am scarcely aware anymore that my shoulder was injured."

She went to him and took his hand, then stopped and stared down at Midnight. "I'd best place my panther on a leash and secure him to a leg of the bed," she said, drawing her hand out of Fire Thunder's. "If he should awaken and find me gone, he might decide to come after me."

"Wake him and take him with us," Fire Thunder said, glancing over at Midnight.

"It's enough that you have me to burden your search for the magical plant," Kaylene said, laughing softly. "You don't also need my panther, who might tire from the search, or decide to go romping after a rabbit, or whatever else it might decide to do."

"Yes, I imagine you are right," Fire Thunder said. He stood beside the door as Kaylene gently awakened Midnight, then led him into the bedroom.

Smiling, radiantly happy to be leaving for a special outing with Fire Thunder, Kaylene came back to him and took his hand. "Finally I am ready," she said, smiling up at him.

Fire Thunder opened the door, just to find Little Sparrow running toward him, crying, her one hand covering one of her ears.

Fire Thunder lay his rifle aside and reached his arms out for his sister. "Little Sister, what it is?" he asked, as Little Sparrow flung herself into his arms.

Little Sparrow told her brother in quick sign language that a spider had crawled into her ear while she had been playing. Her body became racked with harsh sobs. She clutched at her ear again.

"Lord, no," Kaylene gasped, kneeling beside Fire Thunder to place a comforting hand on Little Sparrow's arm. "How did it happen, sweetie? How could a spider get in your ear?"

Little Sparrow gave Kaylene a tearful glance, then gazed up at Fire Thunder again and told him more details. She had been playing in the trees and she walked into a web. A spider in the web crawled into her ear before she was able to stop it.

She looked wild-eyed at Fire Thunder, her finger movements telling him that she knew the Kickapoo belief about never killing spiders. She had been taught that when *Wisaka* finished making the Indian world, he asked a spider to spin a strong web, with which he tied the world to the north so that it would not fall. Because of this, spiders were sacred. That was why she did not attempt to kill it before it crawled into her ear.

She tugged and scratched at her ear, begging with sign language for Fire Thunder to remove the spider. She was afraid that it was going to bite her.

Horrified by Little Sparrow's predicament, Kaylene recalled a way the spider might be removed. "Fire Thunder, one time during my performance at the carnival, a lady bug crawled into a small child's ear," she said. "I watched Mother remove it. I know what she did. I can do the same now for Little Sparrow."

"Do what you can," Fire Thunder said. He lifted Little Sparrow into his arms and carried her into the cabin.

Kaylene picked up his rifle and took it inside.

Then she hurried to the stove and heated some water in a teakettle. After it had just reached the tepid stage, she took the water and a small wooden basin to Fire Thunder.

Kaylene knelt down beside the bed where Little

Sparrow lay. She told the child that what she was going to do wouldn't hurt and when she was finished, Little Sparrow would be rid of the spider, and would, hopefully, be unharmed by it.

She glanced up at Fire Thunder. "Please hold the basin beneath Little Sparrow's ear," she said softly. "As I pour the water slowly in her ear, the spider should be washed out into the basin."

He nodded and held the basin out beside the bed as Kaylene turned the child so that she would be lying on her side, over the basin.

Scarcely breathing, Kaylene began slowly pouring the water into Little Sparrow's ear.

After only a few moments, the spider appeared in the water that flowed back from the ear. It was not a poisonous species. It seemed shaken itself from the experience.

Fire Thunder plucked the spider out of the water, took it outside, and placed it on the ground. Then he watched it crawl away in a sodden, clumsy motion.

He went back inside and stood at the door that led into the bedroom, touched by the gentle scene that lay before him. Kaylene had Little Sparrow on her lap, cuddling her close. She slowly rocked his sister as Little Sparrow clung to her, her cheek against Kaylene's bosom. It looked as though Little Sparrow had found a second mother in Kaylene. That gave Fire Thunder a choked-up feeling to know that he had chosen well in women.

Soon he would make her his wife.

He went and crouched before Kaylene. He placed a gentle hand on her arm. "*Tu medicina muy buen,*" he said thickly.

She looked quizzically at him. "What did you just say?" she asked, lifting an eyebrow.

"Your medicine very good," Fire Thunder said, in his eyes a silent, intense admiration.

Little Sparrow eased from Kaylene's arms and slipped from her lap. She thanked Kaylene in sign language, gave her another fierce hug, then ran from the cabin to play once again.

Fire Thunder drew Kaylene into his arms. He held her close and kissed her, then took her by the hand and led her to the door. He grabbed his rifle, that she had stood beside the door, then stepped outside.

Again they found someone there—but not just one person. *Many*.

Word had spread that quickly about what Kaylene had done for Little Sparrow. Little Sparrow had apparently run around the village, telling everyone that Kaylene had made her well.

People stood just outside the door, their eyes on Kaylene, smiling. Several came forth and embraced her and thanked her.

Kaylene was stunned to see how quickly they had accepted her. They saw her in a different light—as someone who cared, and someone who could be wholeheartedly accepted by them.

When they turned and left, Fire Thunder gave Kaylene a soft smile. "Now marrying you will be much easier," he said, chuckling. "My people will even dance at our wedding!"

So happy, so relieved that things had changed, and that she could walk around the village without the glares and looks of condemnation, Kaylene flung herself into Fire Thunder's arms.

"I'm so happy," she said. "I do wish to be a part of your people's lives. I wish to be your wife."

She closed her eyes and squeezed out thoughts of her father, and the wonder of whether her mother was, in truth, her mother.

This was *now*, and nothing would be allowed to spoil the moment. She had found her rightful place on this earth and it would never be taken from her!

Over Kaylene's shoulder, Fire Thunder saw Black Hair and several warriors leave on a *campanas*, hunting expedition, to get plenty of meat for the coming New Year celebration.

During this expedition, each warrior would be required to kill many deer, wild turkeys, and bears. The deer ribs and tongues, and bear ribs would be smoked. The brains would be spread on gunny sacks, dried, and saved later, for tanning hides. One- to two-inch layers of fat on the bears would be removed, rendered into oil, and stored in deer skins.

Fire Thunder's gaze shifted and he frowned when he found Running Fawn standing in the doorway of her lodge, also watching her father. He could not help but suspect that she was watching for all the wrong reasons. Surely after her father was gone, she would do as she pleased.

If Fire Thunder had not had plans of his own, he would follow Running Fawn and see what she did when she went absent from the village. If there *were* young men involved, she was breaking all the rules and she could be banished!

And even if she was his best friend's daughter, that would not stop Fire Thunder from sending her away. She had been nothing but trouble since the day of her mother's death.

For certain he would make sure that she kept her distance from Kaylene, unless Kaylene told him that she truly missed Running Fawn's companionship.

If he allowed them to be together, he would warn Kaylene not to be drawn into any of Running Fawn's mischief.

A young brave brought Fire Thunder his white mustang and handed Kaylene the reins of a gentle mare.

Fire Thunder thanked the child, then helped Kaylene onto the mare.

He swung himself into the saddle and rode slowly through the village with Kaylene at his side, as the children, including Little Sparrow, came and ran after them—laughing, giggling, and reaching up to touch him and Kaylene.

Kaylene smiled down at them. She felt blessed to be among such gentle, caring people, no matter how she had been brought there. The word "captive" was no longer a part of her vocabulary.

Her father and Chief Fire Thunder finally out of sight, Running Fawn left her lodge. She lifted the hem of her brightly flowered cotton skirt and ran around behind her cabin. She rushed into the shadows of many trees, where her three best friends waited for her on burros. A burro stood aside from the others, waiting for Running Fawn.

"It took you too long," Star Shine fussed at Running Fawn as she glowered at her. "Our boyfriends may have gotten too restless. What if they returned to San Carlos?"

Running Fawn mounted the burro and rode it bareback away from the village with her friends. "Pedro will wait for me," she said, lifting her chin confidently. "He loves me." She cast each of her friends a devilish grin. "But I am not sure about *your* boyfriends. Perhaps they do not care as much for you, as mine cares for me."

They rode on in silence down the mountainside until they came to a cabin snuggled beneath a thick covering of trees into the side of the mountain, halfway between San Carlos and the Kickapoo village.

Her heart beating soundly in her anxiousness to be with Pedro again, Running Fawn slid from the burro, secured its reins to a tree limb, then ran breathlessly to the cabin.

When she stepped inside, she found Pedro and his usual friends sitting around a table, drinking tequila and laughing drunkenly.

"*Señorita*!" the boys cried in unison when they found Running Fawn standing in the shadows of the doorway. "Finally you have come. Where are the others?"

"Outside," Running Fawn murmured as she stepped farther into the cabin. "They will be here shortly."

Pedro flashed her a wide grin. He scooted his chair back and left the table and went to her. A small-built Mexican man of eighteen years, dressed in red velvet breeches and a white, ruffled shirt that was unbuttoned halfway to the waist, his dark eyes devoured her as he drew her into his arms.

"My love," he whispered, his lips finding hers warm and eager as he kissed her.

Running Fawn felt her friends brush past her from behind. She heard the boys scoot their chairs back as the girls went to them, giggling.

Soon everything was quiet except for the moans, as everyone kissed and caressed.

Pedro was the first to speak. "Let us not be in such a hurry here," he said, laughing boisterously. "We brought cards. Do you not think it would be interesting to play some strip poker?"

The young men drew away from the Kickapoo girls. They shouted and laughed drunkenly.

Pedro took the cards from his breeches pocket. He let them tumble from his hands onto the floor, one by one.

"Bring the tequila!" he shouted merrily, as he

looked over at his best friend, Miguel. "Let's sit on the floor and see whose clothes will be removed first."

He winked at Running Fawn. "Hopefully yours, my very own sweet *señorita*," he said thickly.

Running Fawn felt the heat of a blush rush to her cheeks at the thought of unclothing in front of everyone. Thus far, only Pedro had seen her naked.

But that was all right, she thought. She planned to run away from home sometime in the near future and marry Pedro. His father was the rich, powerful General Rocendo, and Pedro could offer her, ah, so many riches.

She had seen his father's villa. Surely Pedro would inherit it. One day it could all be all hers and Pedro's, and their children's.

Giddy at the thought of the future, Running Fawn sat down beside Pedro. She didn't hesitate to drink from a jug of tequila as they proceeded with the card game.

One by one Running Fawn's clothes were removed as she lost at poker, more quickly than the others.

When it came time for her to remove her skirt, her breasts already bared to everyone's gawking eyes, she hesitated.

But, heady with tequila, and her love for Pedro, she stood up and looked around at everyone. She smiled wickedly as she slowly slipped her skirt down.

The young men gasped and gawked and whistled and cheered as they stared at her total nudity.

Jealous, not enjoying his friends taking such advantage of seeing Running Fawn nude, Pedro rose to his feet. Teetering from having consumed so much tequila himself, he took Running Fawn's hand.

"Come, my sweet *señorita*," he said, yanking on her hand. "We will go outside where we can be alone. We will make love while these others play their stupid game of poker."

His friends jeered him loudly. Pedro ignored it.

Running Fawn started to grab her clothes, but Pedro yanked her away from them. "You do not need clothes, *señorita*," he said, half dragging her out the door. He chuckled throatily. "No one but me and the sky will see you."

Lightheaded from the amount of tequila she had consumed, Running Fawn had no strength to fight back. She leaned into Pedro's embrace as he placed an arm around her waist and led her away from the cabin.

After he reached a place of privacy, where there were tall flowering bushes, Pedro lay Running Fawn on a thick bed of soft grass.

His eyes grew wide with a hungry intent as she lay there waiting for him, her arms extended toward him.

After dropping his breeches to the ground, he mounted her.

Running Fawn closed her eyes, thrilled by his nearness, by his hands, and his kiss, as his mouth covered hers. She lifted her hips to meet his every eager thrust, spiraling heavenward, it seemed, in the euphoria of the moment.

But suddenly the sound of horses' hooves from somewhere close by drew them apart.

"No," Running Fawn said, frantically trying to cover herself. "What if it is my father? He is hunting with his friends. They went a different direction, yet perhaps they circled around?"

His heart pounding, Pedro grabbed her by an arm and forced her into a thicker set of bushes, where they could now just barely see the path that led up the mountainside.

Breathlessly, eyes wide, they watched a slow procession of armed men.

Running Fawn was relieved that it was not her father. But what she saw made her insides run cold.

"Do you see how heavily armed they are?" she whispered harshly to Pedro. "And I do not know them. Do you, Pedro? Have you seen them in San Carlos?"

"None are familiar," he said, trying to focus his alcohol-hazed eyes.

"Only my people make their homes in these mountains," Running Fawn whispered, shivering from a sudden dread at realizing what these heavily armed men meant.

Surely they were headed for her village.

And they were not going there in peace. Their looks were too solemn—even angry.

She started crawling away through the brush. "I must go and warn my people," she cried softly.

Pedro panicked. He crawled on all fours after her and grabbed her by an ankle, hauling her to the ground on her stomach.

"No," he said, his voice a cold warning, "you are not going anywhere. You will place yourself in danger. Also, everyone would then know for certain that you were sneaking around with me. You know what could happen if anyone ever knew for certain about our trysts. You could be exiled from your village. Your people might come for me and hang me."

Tears splashed from Running Fawn's eyes. She yanked her ankle free and sat down and sobbed, her face within her hands. "I'm wicked," she cried. "Oh, so wicked! If I do not go and warn my people, what might happen?"

Seeing her distress, Pedro sat down beside Running

Fawn and drew her into his embrace. She cuddled against him as the tears ran in torrents from her eyes.

"You have no choice but *not* to tell," he whispered. "You have no choice."

Running Fawn closed her eyes and tried not to envision what might soon be happening in her village. Even their chief was gone. *And* many of their warriors.

Too many were there, as helpless as she was at this moment.

"You are doing the right thing for us," Pedro tried to reassure her. "If we are going to have a future together, this is the *only* thing that you can do."

Running Fawn wiped her eyes with the back of her hand. "Perhaps those men mean my people no harm," she whispered, yet knowing that she was only trying to fool herself into not feeling guilty.

17

In a field by the river,
My love and I did stand.
And on my leaning shoulder,
She laid her snow-white hand.
                —WM. BUTLER YEATS

Kaylene rode beside Fire Thunder up a gradual rise of land that led them farther up the mountainside away from his village. She could no longer look over her shoulder and see the valley below, where the long-horns grazed.

Now, whenever she took the time to look, all that she saw were jutting rocks and seas of pine trees standing below like columns, on both sides of her.

Occasionally she would hear and see long-tailed magpies.

But for the most part, she was alone with nature, and the man she could not help but love.

"How much farther?" Kaylene asked, giving Fire Thunder a questioning stare.

"We are almost there," he said, then gave her an easy smile. "You ride a horse well." His gaze swept slowly over her. Her back straight, she sat on the saddle of the mare as though she belonged there. She gripped the reins with ease with one hand, resting her other hand on her lap so that she could ease her injured shoulder.

His gaze slipped down to where her skirt was hiked up almost to her knees. He longed to place a hand between the angel-soft skin of her thighs.

His heart thumped erratically at the thought of what lay at the juncture of her thighs. He could feel it even now against the flesh of his palm, the soft tendrils of hair that led into the valley where the heat of her passion lay.

"I learned at a young age how to ride not only horses, but burros, as well," Kaylene said softly, blushing when she cast him a glance and caught him staring at her legs.

A thrill coursed through her when she recalled how it felt to have his hands there, stroking, petting, awakening her body to all sorts of new feelings.

She could never *not* love him.

She desired him so much, it made her insides ache.

"And your panther?" Fire Thunder said, now looking into her eyes, smiling. "Although I have never seen you on the panther, I can envision it. I can imagine how those who came and saw you felt. What a sight it must have been."

"I love Midnight so much," Kaylene said, sighing as she went back in time, to when she had found him, so small and motherless, wandering alone at the foot of a mountain. She had fallen instantly in love with him, and he with her.

"I never approved of training him to be a sideshow for the carnival," she went on. "Yet he accepted everything I did as though it was natural. I truly don't

believe he ever felt the humiliation that I felt for him
while we performed."

"In my culture, many animals are taboo for my people," Fire Thunder said, his eyes again forward, as
they approached the place where he would collect the
Solomon's seal plant. "Among them are the mountain
lion, coyote, prairie dog, and to the Buffalo clan, the
bison. Taboo animals must not be killed, except under
certain special circumstances. No snake may be killed,
and neither may the horned lizard. And as you know
already, the spider is taboo, as well as bumblebees."

He gave her a quick glance. "If the panther were a
taboo animal to my people," he said, his voice drawn,
"I would say to you that riding Midnight was
sacrilegious."

"And I would not argue that," Kaylene said solemnly. "I will never get on the back of my proud pet
again." She swallowed hard at the thought of her father. "There is no one now to force my beautiful Midnight into performing. I don't even wish to talk about
it. Please tell me more about how your people feel
about animals. I am in awe of your beliefs."

"We Kickapoo are observant of animals and their
activities," Fire Thunder said softly, touched to know
that she was being drawn more and more into the
mystique of his people.

He must make her hunger for even more knowledge. When she sat at his side as his wife, he wanted
his people to appreciate her for more than just being
the wife of their chief. He wanted them to admire
how much she knew about their culture.

"We depend on animals as forecasters, or augurs of
weather, death, or the presence of a witch," he continued. "Back in Wisconsin, the arrival of geese announced cold weather. When the cranes flew over the
river, we knew to expect rain. The arrival of the star-

lings and swallows announced the approach of warm weather."

He cast her a quick glance. "The cry of a fox presages a misfortune," he added solemnly.

Then he smiled and became lighthearted again. "When toads are seen in large numbers, it is a sign of rain," he said. "When rattlers climb trees, it is a forecast of heavy rains. And when an owl hoots, it tells us a witch is nearby."

He gave her a slow smile. "And let me tell you about the coyote," he said, his eyes dancing. "Besides his ability to pull down cornstalks, it is believed that the coyote is able to wipe off the thorns of the prickly pear fruit with his tail before eating it."

Unsure of whether he was being serious or not, Kaylene returned his smile and did not question whether or not he was jesting. Speaking of animals had catapulted her mind back to Moon Glow's wigwam. Kaylene had never seen so many cats in one place.

"Please tell me about cats," she murmured. "I still can't get over how many there were at Moon Glow's lodge."

When he didn't respond right away, Kaylene looked guardedly at Fire Thunder. She was not sure whether or not he would want to talk about the elderly lady, especially since he thought her a witch. Even now he carried bits of Solomon's seal in a small bundle of white cloth tied with a green ribbon in his pocket to ward off the evil of such witches.

"Cats are good scavengers," Fire Thunder finally said. "They keep mice and rats, the carriers of typhoid fever, away from our village. But cats are also the subject of several beliefs. Long ago, there was a woman who was caring for a setting hen. Her cat ate the chicks as they hatched. Understandably irked with the cat, the woman picked up a stick to kill it, but her uncle stayed her, saying that if she killed the cat, its spirit could return to harm her. Furthermore, he said to her, cats sometimes turn themselves into witches and witches into cats. The woman did not kill her cat, and this cat multiplied until it was many."

He frowned over at her. "The woman in my story was Moon Glow," he said solemnly. "And not only does she not kill her cats, no one else dares to. No one wishes to have their spirits live with them."

Kaylene's eyes were wide, stunned to know the extent to which the Kickapoo believed in, and feared, witches.

But her wonder was interrupted when Fire Thunder nudged the sides of his mustang with his knees and led his steed from the path on which they had been traveling.

They now rode through a thicket and trees toward a cliff.

"Come and let me show you the beauty of my land, and then I will collect sweet medicine," he said huskily.

"Sweet medicine?" Kaylene asked. She swung her horse to one side and again rode beside Fire Thunder.

"That is another term for Solomon's seal," Fire Thunder said, smiling over at her. "Other than tobacco, Solomon's seal is by far the most highly regarded and magical plant among the Kickapoo. It can only be harvested when the moon is full. That is when the plant's complete potency is assured."

When they got a few feet away from the cliff edge, Fire Thunder drew a tight rein.

Kaylene followed his lead, and before she could dismount, he was already there, his powerful hands at her waist, lifting her to the ground.

Hand in hand, they walked to the edge of the cliff

and stood on a prominent shelf that jutted out. He gestured in a slow, wide swing of his other hand toward that which lay below.

Kaylene gasped. Now that they were this high, and were standing out on this cliff, she could once again see, way in the distance below, as though they were no larger than ants, Fire Thunder's people's huge herd of longhorns.

Elsewhere, the land was rippled and dotted with plant life. She took in the grasses and pines, content to absorb the panorama.

"It is beautiful," she murmured.

She inhaled the sweet fragrance of the air. She closed her eyes, envisioning a perfect world while standing there with the man she loved.

She would not allow the circumstances that had brought them together to enter her mind.

She would not let anything spoil this moment, especially now, when Fire Thunder was placing his arms around her, drawing her close to his hard, perfect body.

"We have time before I collect the sweet medicine to do something my body hungers for," Fire Thunder whispered huskily.

He grazed her mouth with his, brushing teasingly soft kisses across her willing, parted lips.

"Tell me how I can feed your hunger," Kaylene whispered to him, her pulse racing.

"You tell me what *you* wish to do," Fire Thunder teased back, his fingers now on the hem of her blouse, lifting it slowly upward.

He nuzzled her, kissing the corner of her throat, flicking his tongue against the delicate column.

Kaylene felt the soft caress of the breeze touch her bared breasts as Fire Thunder continued to lift her blouse. When his trembling lips sucked on one of her nipples, her heart leaped with passion.

She closed her eyes, wove her fingers through his hair, then sighed languorously when he slipped his arms beneath her and lifted her and carried her away from the cliff edge.

"I need you so much my insides are aflame with the longing," Fire Thunder whispered as he lay her on a soft bed of grass. "My woman, I do not need you to tell me how much you desire me." He knelt down over her as she tossed her blouse aside. "I see it in your eyes and by the blush of your cheeks that you want Fire Thunder's heat."

"Don't you think that I might even want you more than you want me?" Kaylene asked, smiling devilishly up at him as she reached her arms out for him. "I feel wicked, yet deliciously so. All I want is you, Fire Thunder. My mind, my heart, my thoughts are full of you, only you. I cannot help but love you."

"You are in love with your enemy?" he whispered as he slowly raised her skirt up past her knees.

"Yes, and the most handsome enemy I have ever known," Kaylene said.

She smiled seductively up at him as she reached down and slowly shoved his breeches down past his hips.

She sucked in a wild breath of pleasure when she saw how ready he was for her.

It shocked her to realize just how much she desired this part of him, when until Fire Thunder, she had never even had a fleeting desire to see a man unclothed.

Now she did not only want to see this part of him, she wanted to touch him, to caress him.

Fire Thunder blanketed Kaylene with his body. He moved erotically against her.

And as he kissed her, his hands caressing her breasts, she reached down between them and gently clasped one of her hands around his heat.

Fire Thunder groaned with pleasure against her lips as she moved her hand on him, slowly up and down, until his whole body was moving with her, keeping rhythm with her strokes.

His kiss deepened. His fingers circled her nipples, softly pinching. And then he slipped his hands down her body and placed them beneath her.

"Part your legs," he whispered against her lips. "Open yourself widely to me. I want to fill you more deeply than ever before. Rock with me, my woman. Move with me. Let us travel the road to paradise again."

"Yes, yes," Kaylene whispered, her cheeks hot with anticipation.

She spread her legs and felt his hands beneath her hips, guiding her upward to meet the probing of his heat.

When he plunged into her with one insistent thrust, withdrew and plunged again in even deeper thrusts, she gasped with rapture.

Kaylene closed her eyes as once again he bent over her and pressed his lips softly against hers. Then he covered her mouth with his lips in a fiery kiss.

He cradled her close, his steel arms enfolding her as their bodies strained together in hungry motion.

Frantic with need of her, Fire Thunder's strokes speeded up, becoming deeper and deeper.

She clung and rocked with him, his fingers now caressing one of her breasts.

Kaylene sucked in a wild breath of rapture and a tremor went through her body when his mouth lowered and he rolled her nipple with his tongue.

Fire Thunder could not hold back the pleasure any

longer. His temples were pounding. His body was on
fire with the building rapture.

Again he kissed her.

His hands went beneath her and lifted her tightly
against him as waves of tremors went through his body
as Kaylene's body exploded in spasms of desire along
with his.

Afterward, they lay side by side, clinging. "Oh, what
you do to me," Kaylene whispered, cuddling closer.
"I wish we could stay here forever, in our own little
private world."

Fire Thunder started to respond, but his horse
neighing nervously and pawing the ground with a hoof
drew his quick attention.

His smile faded. His heart grew cold.

He leaped quickly to his feet and grabbed his
breeches, his eyes darting all around him. "My horse
might sense a mountain lion," he said. He gave
Kaylene a quick glance as she straightened her skirt,
then slipped the blouse over her head. "Stay close."

He moved stealthily to his horse and eased his rifle
from the gunboot on the saddle.

His eyes narrowed as again he looked around him,
into the dark-shadowed trees on one side, and into
the shade of the jutting rocks on the other.

The Kickapoo learned at a young age how to distin-
guish various animals in the dark shadows, by the
color of their eyes and the movement of their heads.

Fire Thunder knew that the deer's eyes lit up a
bright yellow. The coyote, whose eyes were blue,
moved their heads from side to side as though seeking
to escape. A cougar's eyes were small and red. When
it was detected, it lowered its head as though trying
to hide in the ground.

"I see nothing, nor hear anything," Kaylene whispered as she moved closer to Fire Thunder, staying protectively at his side.

"Nor do I," Fire Thunder whispered, puzzled when he saw no signs of any animals lurking close by.

And then his heart lurched. The Kickapoo believed that by an animal's behavior, they could perceive something was wrong.

And since there was nothing *here*, he had to think that it had to do with something at his village. Perhaps something was wrong *there*. They must return.

But first, he had to collect the Solomon's seal. He could not wait until the next full moon, for his supply had dwindled too much now, as it was. He had to have enough of the sweet medicine for the upcoming ceremonies.

"What is it?" Kaylene asked, seeing Fire Thunder's troubled expression, even though they knew there was nothing there to threaten them. "You look as though you may have seen a ghost."

"Not a ghost, but a premonition," Fire Thunder said, thrusting his rifle back inside its gunboot.

"Of what?" Kaylene asked. She hugged herself when the breeze grew damp and colder as it whipped through the pines.

Fire Thunder saw her discomfort. He took the time to reach into the parfleche bag at the side of his horse and take a blanket from it. "My horse is restless," he said as he gently slipped the blanket around her shoulders. "I fear that my horse has perceived danger. Perhaps back at my village."

"Then you won't be gathering the Solomon's seal, after all?" Kaylene asked softly.

"I *must* take time to gather sweet medicine," he said, grabbing a buckskin bag from the side of his horse. "Come with me. We are where I can find it quickly. Then we shall leave."

Kaylene followed Fire Thunder for a while, in and around the tall pines, and short, stubby shrubs, until she saw the most beautiful flowers growing from thick, tall, drooping stems. In the leaf axil of the plants were clusters of greenish-white flowers, surrounded by red berries. The leaves formed two rows along the upper part of the stem.

"Only I can gather the sweet medicine," Fire Thunder said over his shoulder at Kaylene. "I will not be long at doing it."

Kaylene sat down on a large boulder and watched him, taken anew by his customs, and the seriousness with which he went about things. He knelt on the ground before the Solomon's seal plants.

After taking a small pouch from his front right breeches pocket, and opening it, he sprinkled some tobacco on the plant closest to him. He asked the plant's permission to gather others in the area.

After placing the small pouch back inside his pocket, he wandered onward a few feet.

Kaylene stayed on the boulder and watched him meditatively gather the lovely flowers, as well as the leaves, and parts of the stems.

Then her stomach lurched and she saw his quick reaction, how he bolted suddenly to his feet, when somewhere in the distance a fox cried out three times.

Fire Thunder, carrying the bag of Solomon's seal in his right hand, went to Kaylene and took her hand and urged her in a brisk walk toward their horses.

"*Muy malo*, very bad," he said, obviously even more distressed than earlier. "The cry of the fox is very bad! Do you recall my telling you that the cry of a fox foretells a misfortune? Today the cry was three times! There is no doubt that trouble has come to my people!"

So caught up in everything, with being with Fire Thunder again sensually, and watching him as he gathered the sacred plants, Kaylene had not thought to become alarmed over the fox's cries. Nor had she noticed an approaching storm. She only now heard the low rumblings of distant thunder.

When she looked over her shoulder and up at the sky, a lurid streak of lightning suddenly raced across the dark heavens, causing her to flinch.

"It's going to storm," she said breathlessly, when they finally reached their horses. "Perhaps that is what unnerved your horse. Perhaps that is what caused the fox to cry."

"I cannot count on as simple a thing as that to be the cause," Fire Thunder said, tying his bag of Solomon's seal next to his saddle bag. "We must hurry back to my people."

The storm was racing closer by the minute. The thunder became large, deafening crashes as lightning bounced from one side of the sky to the other.

Kaylene slipped the blanket from around her shoulders and gave it back to Fire Thunder, quickly aware of her discomfort without it.

But she had to forget herself for the moment. She could see that Fire Thunder's concerns were mounting by the minute.

And although she did not see how his premonitions of doom could actually be real, she knew that his distress was.

The rain began in a slow drizzle. Kaylene huddled over her horse and rode beside Fire Thunder down the small mountain path.

Then the rain came down in heavy torrents, the drops so large, they felt like bee stings as they hit Kaylene's cheeks.

"We must find temporary shelter!" Fire Thunder shouted at her above the loud crashes of thunder.

He led her to a wall of stone, above which was a large overhang of rock. She quickly dismounted along with him. They held on to their horses' reins and huddled against the rock.

The wind was violent, snapping trees off at their trunks. Kaylene screamed and clutched Fire Thunder, welcoming his arm around her as a bolt of lightning downed another tree not that faraway.

Fire Thunder looked heavenward.

Kaylene stared disbelievingly at him when he pulled out a tiny buckskin pouch from his front breeches pocket, where he kept his Indian tobacco.

He sprinkled some of the tobacco in his left hand and offered it to the heavens.

"Go away!" he cried. "Grandfather, send the lightning and thunder away! Do not allow them to harm us!"

Kaylene was stunned to see that, as if by magic, the storm quickly abated. The clouds rolled away. The sun came out. The only sounds were the rivulets of rain running down the rock at their sides.

Her lips parted, her eyes wide, Kaylene stared at Fire Thunder.

A tremor ran up and down her spine. Was this man she had given her heart to bewitched? He had asked the storm to stop and it had, as though controlled by him.

She felt humble *and* afraid in his presence as they mounted their horses and rode onward.

18

O memory, ope thy mystic door;
O dream of youth return.
—DAVID GRAY

Chilled to the bone, shivering, and aching from being
on the galloping horse for longer than her weakened
body could stand, Kaylene saw Fire Thunder's village
a short distance away. Her heart lurched when she
saw several men on horseback approaching the village
on the opposite side from Kaylene and Fire Thunder.

"Do you see those men?" Kaylene shouted at Fire
Thunder as he was bent low over his mustang, determination etched on his sculpted face.

"Yes, and I also see the rifles that are in their hands
instead of in their gunboots!" Fire Thunder shouted
back. His eyes locked with Kaylene's. "You stay behind. I do not want you to enter the eye of danger."

"No!" Kaylene cried. "I can't just stay here and watch
your people get attacked. I can fire a gun. I want to help."

"Look at yourself!" Fire Thunder argued, his jaw
tight. "You are wet. You are cold. Surely you are
weakened by this hard ride on the horse."

He held on to the reins with one hand, while with his other he grabbed the blanket from his saddle bag.

He tossed it over to Kaylene.

She caught it clumsily.

"As I ride onward, you stop and stay here," he flatly ordered. "Warm yourself with this blanket. Only come into the village when you see that those men are gone."

Before Kaylene could say anything to him, he sank his heels into the flanks of his proud steed and thundered away from her, his rifle drawn.

Kaylene drew a tight rein. Her mare came to a shuddering halt, as she watched Fire Thunder as he drew closer and closer to the village. She then looked at the men as they almost reached the very outskirts of the Kickapoos' homes, where the Kickapoo thought they were safe from all intruders.

When gunfire broke out, she saw that it was from the assailants, not the Kickapoo. Kaylene's insides turned cold.

For a moment she watched the men randomly firing their weapons all about as the Kickapoos scattered in all directions away from them.

And then she caught sight of Fire Thunder again as he entered the far side of the village. She gasped when he raised his rifle and fired as he approached the men on horseback, then slid from his saddle and joined his warriors in a stand against the intruders.

Fear of Fire Thunder possibly dying grabbed Kaylene in the pit of her stomach. "I won't stay here and only watch!" she whispered harshly to herself. She tossed the blanket aside. "I must go and do what I can to help!"

She snapped her horse's reins, sank her heels into its flanks, then rode onward. She had to go to Fire Thunder's lodge and get a weapon. She felt lucky that, thus far, the main part of the fighting was on the other side of the village away from Fire Thunder's cabin. She hoped and prayed that Little Sparrow and Midnight would remain safe in the cabin. And Running Fawn! What about her? Her cabin was way too close to the battle scene.

She raised her eyes heavenward and whispered a prayer, asking the good Lord to, above all else, keep Fire Thunder safe!

As she rode into the village, she made a sharp left on the mare and rode only a short distance, then drew a tight rein before Fire Thunder's cabin.

Kaylene quickly dismounted. Breathing hard, panting, her wet clothes clinging to her flesh like a second skin, she ran into the lodge.

Frantically she searched for Little Sparrow, cold inside when she didn't find her. If she was outside, watching, she might be shot!

Then she breathed easier when she suddenly remembered that Little Sparrow was staying with a friend and her family. Their cabin was far from the gunfire. Surely she would be safe.

Kaylene went to Midnight. She could tell that the gunfire was affecting him. Although he was tied up, he was pacing nervously back and forth, straining on the leash when he could go no farther.

"I know that you are frightened, but I can't stay with you," Kaylene said, giving Midnight a quick, reassuring hug. "I must go and help Fire Thunder. Stay, Midnight. Whatever you do, don't break that leash and come outside where you might be shot."

Then she rushed to Fire Thunder's store of weapons. She grabbed a Smith & Wesson rifle. She smiled smugly. She knew this weapon well. She knew the power of this gun. Her father had taught her how to fire his. She would never forget his wicked laugh when she had been knocked to the ground upon firing it the first time by the kick of the firearm.

"Yes, this will do quite well for this occasion," Kaylene whispered. The rifle could throw its bullets with accuracy a distance of four hundred yards.

And Kaylene was a crack shot. She would scare the pants off those men who had come to wreak havoc on these innocent people.

She would show them that a woman could stand up against them as well as a man!

Her heart thumping with a fear she could not deny over what she was about to do—actually shoot at people instead of tin cans lined up on a fence—she rushed outside.

When she moved to Fire Thunder's side, his eyes narrowed angrily as he gazed down at her. There was such anger in his eyes at seeing her there, Kaylene recoiled somewhat.

Then she took a stubborn stand beside him, looked away from him, and raised the rifle to fire it.

But when she recognized who the invaders were, her finger seemed frozen to the trigger. As though in jerks, her eyes went from man to man, disbelieving that these were the men from her father's carnival.

She paled and almost dropped the rifle when she saw the face of a man among them that she had thought was dead!

"How can it be?" she whispered, stricken numb as she stared at her father, whose horse was suddenly rearing and balking from the Kickapoo's incessant spattering of gunfire. Kaylene wanted so badly to be glad that her father was alive. But his ruthless attack on the Kickapoo horrified her, even though she knew his reason for being there. He had come to rescue her.

But why? she despaired to herself. To rescue a daughter? Or someone who was nothing to him but a very valuable asset to his carnival? Everyone loved her act with the panther!

Still too shocked to fire the rifle, Kaylene gasped when his horse threw her father to the ground.

But that didn't stop his determination to kill many Kickapoo. He grabbed the horse's reins, steadied it, then used it as a cover as he began firing his rifle again.

A small brave ran from his lodge, panicking and crying, into the line of fire, and quickly fell to the ground, blood pouring from his wound. Kaylene snapped out of her frozen state. She began shouting her father's name as she shoved her way through the hardened line of defense of Kickapoo warriors.

She heard the startled cry of Fire Thunder when he realized what she was doing, but she kept on moving toward her father.

She was keenly aware that she was now halfway between both groups of men.

But she was also keenly aware that her presence had caused a ceasefire, as she had hoped it would do.

"Father, I'm all right!" Kaylene cried as she broke into a run toward him. "Please leave these people alone! They are my friends!"

John Shelton stepped slowly from behind his horse and stared at Kaylene. His face registered shock at what Kaylene had just said about the Kickapoo being her friends.

He looked over his shoulder at the men he had urged to come with him today, to launch this attack on the Kickapoo, and saw that they were also stunned by what she had said. They had lowered their firearms.

Some were edging their horses backward, as though they were ready to retreat and leave him there to fight his own battle over a daughter that had aligned herself with "savages." When a white woman took up with Indians, the white woman was scorned and ridiculed.

John looked desperately back at Kaylene as she kept moving toward him.

Then he looked past her as Fire Thunder stepped away from the others and started following her.

Anger came in hot flashes at this Indian having possibly turned Kaylene against her very own people. With wide, rigid nostrils and flaming eyes, Shelton slowly raised his rifle.

His gaze quickly shifted and he dropped his rifle when he saw a streak of black. He yelped with fear when Midnight leaped on him and knocked him to the ground, the panther's broken leash hanging loosely from around his neck.

"Get off me, you goddamn overgrown cat!" John screeched. He lay helpless beneath the full weight of Midnight's large paws.

Then he gasped with fright as the panther just barely sank its teeth into the flesh of his neck, as though John Shelton was another panther who was forced to submit and cower beneath Midnight's power and prowess.

Kaylene was stunned to see Midnight there. But she had been foolish to think that he would stay leashed when he sensed that she was in danger.

And hating the man who had taken a whip more than once to him, to force him into obedience, Midnight was obviously taking pleasure in what he was doing to John Shelton.

With John rendered helpless, the men who had accompanied him swung their horses around and fled in a tearing gallop.

Fire Thunder stepped up beside Kaylene and glared down at John.

Midnight's teeth were dangerously close to his jugular vein, so John lay perfectly quiet on his back, his eyes pleading up at Kaylene.

Kaylene stared down at him for a moment longer, her thoughts again filled with whether or not this man was her true father.

She tried to see some likeness of herself in his features and saw none. She tried to think of some of her features that might be her mother's. There were none.

"Kaylene, for Christ's sake, get Midnight off me," John managed to whisper. He scarcely breathed when the panther's teeth sank somewhat deeper into his flesh. He could feel a small trickle of blood flowing down his neck from a small puncture wound.

"Midnight, come here," Kaylene said, slapping her hands at him.

Obedient to her every whim, wish, and desire, Midnight swung around away from John, and went to Kaylene. He hissed and bared his fangs at John again when John glared at him.

Under any other circumstances, Kaylene would have leaped into her father's arms, so glad to know that he was alive.

But too much held her back. His attack on the Kickapoo. *And* her questions about her true parentage.

She looked past him, at those Kickapoo who were helping their wounded into their lodges. Tears sprang into her eyes when she saw Little Sparrow kneeling beside the wounded brave, holding his hand as his parents knelt over him, inspecting the wound.

She looked over at Running Fawn's lodge. Where was she? Even Black Hair wasn't there.

She suddenly recalled that Black Hair had gone on a hunting expedition. Surely Running Fawn had taken advantage of his absence and might even now be with her girlfriends, having fun with their Mexican boyfriends.

"White man, get on your feet," Fire Thunder demanded as he glared down at John, his rifle aimed at him. "You are lucky I do not send a bullet into your heart for what you have done today to my people."

John cowered beneath the threat of the rifle, then slowly rose to his feet. He glanced over at Kaylene. "Daughter, tell him to aim that firearm elsewhere," he pleaded. His hand went to the puncture wound at his throat. He wiped the blood from his flesh with his fingers, then lifted them before his eyes.

His gaze went to Midnight. "If that damn animal wasn't so important to me, I'd kill it right now with my bare hands," he said through clenched teeth.

First, his reference to Kaylene as his daughter made her wince, as doubt again filled her as to whether or not she was.

Secondly, how he spoke so threateningly to her panther, and then stated the reason why he wouldn't truly harm the animal—that Midnight was too important to him, made Kaylene once again wonder about her importance to him.

"You call me daughter," she blurted out, taking a bold step toward him, as two warriors came and grabbed each of his arms, to hold him steady between them. "Am I? Am I truly your daughter? Tell me the truth! I was stolen as a baby, wasn't I? You raised me only to use me, didn't you?"

Kaylene felt lightheaded and sick to her stomach when she saw his reaction to her questions.

19

I was young and foolish,
And now am full of tears.
—WILLIAM BUTLER YEATS

Seeing how her father paled at her question, as a child might do when caught stealing and by him not quickly saying that what she said was foolish! Hogwash! Untrue!, Kaylene knew without him speaking that he was not her father.

She fell back a step or two, as though she had been slapped.

John moved slowly toward her, his wavering eyes never leaving Kaylene. "Why did you ask such a thing?" he asked warily. "Why are you acting this way? What have the savages done ... said to you, to make you look at me as though I am a stranger? Why would you doubt that I am your father?"

He reached his arms out for her. "Aren't you glad to see that I'm alive?" he said sadly.

Kaylene swallowed hard, torn with feelings for this man. Although throughout her childhood she found him unaffectionate, still she had thought that he was her father, and that alone was the reason she had loved him. And now?

"How did you come out of this alive after being left at the pit?" she said, taking another step away from him when he took one toward her.

She now knew without a doubt that he wasn't her father. How could she ever forget that look in his eyes when she asked? A look that totally convicted him.

"A Texas rancher came by and found me," John said, again smoothing a trickle of blood away from his neck with his fingers. He wiped the blood on one of his trouser legs. "The snake? It fled without attacking me. The rancher took me back to the carnival campsite. After I was strong enough, I rounded up my men to come and rescue you."

His brows knitted into a dark frown. "And this is the thanks I get," he grumbled. "My very own daughter treating me as though I am a stranger."

"You know that I'm not your daughter," Kaylene said, her voice breaking. "I saw your first reaction to my question. Tell me the truth. You took me in only because you knew you had another child who would benefit you. Isn't that so? Please tell me the truth. Where are my true parents?"

"How could you know this?" John gasped out, again paling. He glared over at Fire Thunder. "Are he and his people psychics?"

Kaylene's knees grew weak. She gasped and covered her mouth with trembling fingers. Tears came to her eyes as she turned her face away from the man who had deceived her in the worst way possible.

Fire Thunder reached out for John and grabbed him roughly by an arm. He gave him a shove ahead of him. "You have hurt my woman for the last time," he grumbled out. "Go. I have a perfect place for you. You still have to pay for stealing my sister, and for, in part, being responsible for Good Bear's death. You must pay for what you did today to my people, and for what you have done to my woman all of her *life*."

"I ain't responsible for all those things!" John shouted. He stumbled as Fire Thunder gave him another shove when he tried to look at him. "I've come for Kaylene. I was going to release her from captivity! Now you, you damn savage, you've put all sorts of nonsense in her head! She sides with savages?" he laughed nervously. "Perhaps that's best. After seeing her today, and how she took your side against me, she ain't nothing better than a savage herself."

Fire Thunder reached out and grabbed John by the back of the neck. He stopped him and turned him slowly around to face him. "You listen well, white man, to what I say, or I will hand you over to my people to let them choose how you die," he hissed out. "It might be by removing your limbs, one by one. Or it might be instantly at the end of a rope. I would think you would prefer *my* sort of punishment. So, white man, close your mouth and stop saying things that get you deeper into trouble."

"You said a while ago that Kaylene was your woman," John said, eyes wide, and cowering beneath Fire Thunder's steely, dark, threatening stare. "What did you mean by that?"

"She is going to be my wife," Fire Thunder said, smiling smugly when he saw the look of utter horror in the depths of John's eyes.

Kaylene moved to Fire Thunder's side, Midnight beside her. Her eyes were red from crying.

It was the fact that she had been forced to live a lie that hurt. She doubted she would ever know her true parents.

"I am starting a new life here with Fire Thunder," she said, clasping Fire Thunder's arm possessively.

"But I would appreciate it if you would tell me the full truth about everything. My memory only holds you, Mother, and the carnival. Won't you tell me my true identity?"

"You are as crazy as him," John mumbled, nodding toward Fire Thunder. "You belong together."

"Then you still refuse to admit to the truth?" Kaylene asked, swallowing back another strong urge to cry.

"You're so smart, figure it out for yourself," John said, his lips tugging into a slow, mocking smile.

Kaylene turned her eyes away from him and closed them. A part of her cried out inside her, saying that surely this man was her father! Surely she had imagined the guilt in his eyes when she had first asked him whether he was or not? Surely she had only thought she had heard him ask if the Kickapoo were psychics? If he said that, he had condemned himself, twofold.

Yet now he seemed honestly hurt by her accusation. Oh, Lord above, was she wrong? Would she ever know?

Then the thought of her mother came to her. The woman she had called mother all of her life, who was as gentle as a spring breeze, surely would tell her the truth.

Kaylene would go and ask her. She would not rest now until she had all of the answers.

She composed herself and followed Fire Thunder, unsure of what his plans were for this man she despised, whether or not he was her father. He was a lowdown, evil man. He deserved the worst punishment for all that he had done throughout his life, to all of the children that he had enslaved at his carnival, and to her and Midnight.

She was surprised that Midnight had not killed him

when he had had the chance. He had hated John Shelton for as long as Kaylene could remember.

Ever since Midnight had taken that first whipping with John Shelton's sharp-tongued whip.

Kaylene's eyes widened when she finally realized just where Fire Thunder was taking John ... to the cage that she had been in, where Kaylene had spent the most horrible hours of her life.

Fire Thunder was going to make John know how it felt, also. *And* Fire Thunder was angry enough at this man that he just might leave him there, to die!

When they reached the cage, and John saw it, he let out a loud bellow like a cow being attacked by wolves. Shivers raced up and down Kaylene's flesh.

She took a quick step behind Fire Thunder when John turned horror-stricken eyes up at Fire Thunder.

She slowly peeked from around Fire Thunder, scarcely breathing when John began to beg not to be placed in the cage.

"I'll do anything!" he cried. He grabbed Fire Thunder by the arms. His fingers turned white in his iron-like grip. "Please don't place me in that cage. I'll do anything! Anything!"

His eyes cold and narrowed, Fire Thunder reached up and grabbed hold of John's wrists and yanked his fingers away from his arms. He doubled a fist and hit him in the jaw.

John fell to the ground. Rubbing his jaw and groaning, he looked sheepishly up at the Kickapoo who had come to watch his humiliation.

Little Sparrow ran to Kaylene and took her hand.

Kaylene stepped from behind Fire Thunder and gave Little Sparrow a forced, reassuring smile.

Then she once again stared at John as Fire Thunder grabbed him from the ground, to wobble on his feet. Blood poured from the corner of his mouth. His jaw was already swelling from the blow—a purplish-black hue of color spreading across his face beneath his thin stubble of beard.

"Unclothe yourself," Fire Thunder said, towering over John as the man cowered before him.

"What?" John gasped, his eyes staring up at Fire Thunder. "You are going to force me to strip?"

John glanced over at Kaylene, his eyes wavering. Then he looked up at Fire Thunder again. "I c-can't d-do that," he stammered.

"Then I will do it for you," Fire Thunder said darkly. He looked over his shoulder and searched the crowd for Black Hair.

When he didn't find him there, he realized that his friend and the others were still on their hunting expedition. He nodded toward another warrior. "Three Toes, come and hold the man while I unclothe him," he flatly ordered.

A good-sized warrior, dressed in only a loincloth, came away from the others. Limping on a foot that was scarred and had two toes missing, he went to John and grabbed him by the arms and held him while Fire Thunder first removed John's breeches.

John cried out and paled when Fire Thunder tossed the breeches aside and reached for the man's underpants. "I beg you not to do this!" he screeched. "You can't strip me naked! I won't let you!"

John struggled with the hefty man, only to exhaust himself as Fire Thunder patiently waited for him to stand still again.

Then he nodded to Three Toes.

The warrior nodded back and quickly shed John of his shirt.

Fire Thunder smiled as he took hold of John's cotton undershorts and ripped them from him, leaving him standing naked, all but for his shoes.

Kaylene swallowed hard. Her face flooded with color as John tried to hide his private parts behind his outstretched hands, his head hung shamefully.

She gasped and her fingers tightened around Little Swallow's hand when Fire Thunder shoved John into the cage and locked the door behind him.

"You Goddamn savage heathen!" John cried, sitting all scrunched up in the small space. He gripped the bars with trembling fingers. "I'll get you for this, savage. I'll find a way to escape and then I'll cut your throat! I'll cut your heart out! Savage! You demon savage!"

Fire Thunder grabbed a rifle from one of his warriors. Void of expression, he raised the butt of the rifle and hit John over the head, quickly silencing him as he fell, unconscious, to the floor of the cage.

Kaylene was stunned by everything. She stared down at John and tried to find a trace of remorse for this man she had always called "Father." But now, truly knowing the man and the worst of the deceits that he was capable of, she felt nothing but a sick loathing for him.

Kaylene stared at John for a moment longer, then turned to Fire Thunder. "What now?" she murmured. "What are you going to d-do . . . with—"

She stammered, not knowing what to call this man in the cage. She would no longer call him her father. He wasn't. To her now, he was nothing but a name.

"What am I going to do with this evil man?" Fire Thunder said, realizing that her awkwardness came from not knowing how to address this man now that she knew he was not her father.

"Yes, what is going to happen to him now?" Kaylene asked softly.

"He can die slowly in the cage, or he can be hanged and get it over quickly," Fire Thunder said sternly.

"Which do *you* prefer? You have been wronged the most by this evil man."

Kaylene turned her eyes away. She stifled a sob behind a hand for what this man had been to her for so long, a man she had never truly known.

So much came back to her, flooding her with memories of when she was a child.

Yes, this man had been cold and so often noncommunicative.

But she could remember times, although they were rare, when she had idolized him for being the man who made the carnival so pretty and fun. He had been a man of authority, someone everyone seemed to look up to.

But, of course, she knew now that those looks had not been admiration at all, but the false looks of masks, beneath which lay a seething hate for this man who had enslaved so many.

Even most of the men who came today to help free Kaylene had at one time been children raised at the carnival at John Shelton's mercy. Once grown, they had stayed on because they had nowhere else to go, or had no other skills than those they had learned at the carnival.

She had understood why they had turned and left him to fend for himself, that they had seen an opportunity to finally rid their lives of this tyrant!

But torn now by so many things, especially having been made a fool of all of her life by this man in the cage, Kaylene suddenly felt as though she were dying a slow death inside by not knowing who she truly was, or where her true roots may have been had she never been abducted as a child.

Roots! She had always hungered for roots. And this man had kept her from those who were truly hers.

Blinded by tears, Kaylene ran around the cage, and into the forest, Midnight quickly following.

She ran blindly onward until she tripped and fell on the root of a tree that had grown up from the ground in an arch.

Her body wracked with tears, she snuggled close to her panther as he lay down beside her.

Suddenly Fire Thunder was there. He reached down and lifted Kaylene into his arms and nestled her close to his chest. "My woman," he said, his voice drawn. "Things will be all right. You are loved. I love you. I will make life wonderful for you."

She clung around his neck. "I know," she said, sobbing. "But what of that part of my life that is lost to me? What have I missed by living with ... with total strangers?"

She looked desperately up at him. "I must find my true parents," she said, her eyes pleading with him. "Will you help me? Please? Will you?"

"You know that your father's carnival travels all over the country," Fire Thunder said thickly. "I would say that it is almost impossible for you to ever know your true parents."

"Mother—" she began, then broke into tears again to realize that the woman who had held her to her bosom as a child was truly not her mother.

"Anna ..." she stammered out, "she will surely tell me. Once she knows that I know everything, why wouldn't she?"

"She will deny everything," Fire Thunder said. "Are you prepared for that?"

Kaylene knew that he was right. She lowered her eyes. "I'm so sorry for John's part in the attack today against your people," she murmured. "I will find a way to make it up to you and your people."

"My woman, do you not know that you are not

required to do anything to make up for something you are not at all responsible for?" Fire Thunder said, carrying her toward his village. "Except, to—"

"Except to what?" Kaylene said, interrupting him. She was anxious to do anything for him. Anything!

"We must marry soon," Fire Thunder said, his eyes locked with hers. "We must face the future together as man and wife, as one heartbeat, one soul, one breath. Destiny has brought us together. One never questions destiny."

Kaylene suddenly recalled his powers to stop the storm, and her fright of it. "Fire Thunder, I witnessed something that I don't understand," she murmured. "You were able to stop the storm today by praying. Why is that? Such powers somewhat frighten me. It . . . doesn't seem natural."

"There is nothing to be frightened about," Fire Thunder said, hurt that she would be afraid of anything he did. "I was born during a fierce storm of fire, lightning, and thunder. That is how I got my name Fire Thunder. Ever since I was young, I've had special powers because of having been born during such a time, when the heavens were warring in battle. I have rarely used them. I do not want to be looked on as a witch by my people. Only a scarce few have seen my powers with the elements. You are now among those who know my whole, true self."

In awe of him, more than frightened, Kaylene gazed into his eyes.

"Are you frightened of the knowing?" he asked thickly.

"No, I'm not frightened," Kaylene murmured. "I love you. I admire you. I see you as a special man in so many ways." She reached her lips up to his and brushed his mouth with butterfly kisses. "And I shall never tell a soul what I witnessed."

He laughed throatily, placed a hand behind her head, and kissed her with fire, his tongue probing between her lips.

But knowing this was not the time to arouse so much between them, with so many injured, and with so many people to console, Fire Thunder drew his lips away and placed Kaylene on the ground.

When they entered the village, they discovered two Mexican soldiers escorting two people into the village on horseback.

One was a man. The other was a woman.

With Kaylene trailing behind him, her hand on Midnight, Fire Thunder went and met the strangers' approach. He stopped and waited for the man and woman to dismount.

White Wolf helped Dawnmarie from her horse, then slipped an arm around her waist and went to Fire Thunder, his gaze moving quickly to Kaylene, a white woman, as she stood beside Fire Thunder.

"I am White Wolf of the Fon du Lac band of Chippewa. I have traveled far with my wife from Wisconsin to find her true people, the Kickapoo," White Wolf said thickly. "General Rocendo appointed two of his soldiers to escort us here. He said that you are Kickapoo. Are you Chief Fire Thunder?"

"Yes, I am Chief Fire Thunder," Fire Thunder said, easing a hand of friendship out toward White Wolf. "You are welcome to my village." He cast a troubled glance over his shoulder. "You will have to overlook the condition of my people upon your first arrival here. We have just gone through an attack from white men."

"An attack?" Dawnmarie said, paling. She now recalled the men who had rode past her and White Wolf and the Mexican escorts. Some had been wounded.

"Yes, but let that not worry you," Fire Thunder reassured her. "They are now gone. The threat is over."

Fire Thunder reached a hand out for Dawnmarie. "And you are of Kickapoo descent?" he said, her hand soft as she twined her fingers through his in a handshake of friendship.

"Yes, in part, I am Kickapoo. My mother, Doe Eyes, was Kickapoo," Dawnmarie said softly. "My father was white. Long ago my mother told me the importance of making peace with my Kickapoo people. It is necessary for my afterlife. It is good to have finally found you."

"Many moons ago my mother and father lived in Wisconsin," Fire Thunder offered. "I was born there, but they moved often, sometimes to Illinois, sometimes to Indiana, wherever they could find peace with the white people. It was I who grew tired of broken treaties. That is why, upon the death of my chieftain father, I brought my people here."

He frowned. "Tonight was the first time my people have been attacked while on this mountain," he grumbled. "And it will be the last."

"My mother, Doe Eyes, was born among your people, and she was abducted by my father who was a trapper," Dawnmarie said softly. "She married the trapper. I was born. She was a devoted wife and mother. But all of her life she longed to be with her people. She died in sadness."

Suddenly Moon Glow came walking toward Dawnmarie, her many cats trailing behind her. She stepped up to Dawnmarie and looked at her through her squinting, aged eyes. "I knew a woman named Doe Eyes," she said huskily. "When we were both young and beautiful. It must be your mother I knew. She was dear to me. We . . . were . . . the best of friends."

A sudden strained silence fell on those who had gathered to see the woman who claimed to be, in part, Kickapoo.

20

They spoke as chords do from the string,
And blood burnt round my heart.
                    —JOHN CLARE

Dawnmarie gazed with parted lips at the woman. She
was so unkempt and wretched, so haggard. But that
didn't matter. Miracle of miracles! Dawnmarie had
found someone who remembered her beloved mother.
This woman who knew her mother was absolute proof
that Dawnmarie had found her true people!

Moon Glow moved closer to Dawnmarie. She
placed a bony hand on Dawnmarie's arm and leaned
close to her ear. "My name is Moon Glow," she said
in a soft whisper, because she knew not to speak her
name aloud. It was forbidden now that she had been
labeled a "Trotter," as well as the village witch. "I
gave your mother a friendship bag many years ago,
and then the very next day Doe Eyes disappeared."

Recalling the beautifully beaded friendship bag, the
very one that Dawnmarie's mother had given to her,
for her to give to a friend in turn, Dawnmarie choked
up with emotion. This was bringing her so close to

her mother. It was as though she were there with Dawnmarie, instead of in a dark, dank grave back in Wisconsin.

"You were her very best friend," Dawnmarie said, embracing Moon Glow, drawing gasps from the crowd who were gathered around them. "It is good to be with you. If only Mother could be here, as well."

"Your mother is now among our ancestors in the afterworld?" Moon Glow asked, easing from Dawnmarie's arms.

"Yes, and I am sure her spirit is here with us, feeling finally at peace because I have found my people, and her special friend," Dawnmarie said, wiping tears from her eyes.

Kaylene watched the emotional scene, of this woman of mixed blood meeting her people for the first time. Tears stung her eyes, to know that she herself had people out there somewhere whom she had never known, and more than likely never would.

But it looked as though Dawnmarie's persistence had worked.

Perhaps Kaylene would be even as persistent in searching for her parents.

Yet, she was not truly sure if that was wise. She had found a home here with Fire Thunder. Should she dare place it in jeopardy by leaving him, to search for answers that she would probably never find?

While with Fire Thunder, Kaylene felt as though she *had* the world. Surely she should be content enough with that. She had found roots with *him*.

She slipped an arm through his as she continued to watch Dawnmarie and Moon Glow, surprised that Moon Glow had been allowed to stay this long among the people.

"Tell me about your mother," Moon Glow murmured. "Where she went after she left our people.

Were there any more children besides you? Was she happy, truly happy, away from her people?"

"My mother was kidnapped by a trapper," Dawn-marie said, her voice breaking. "I was born of their union. I had no brothers or sisters. And, yes, for a while, my mother was happy. She loved my father. But she always pined for her people. She came looking for you. But she discovered that you had moved far-away. She gave up her search. She then even gave up her reason for living."

"That is sad," Moon Glow said, tears splashing from her eyes. "If we could have gotten together, perhaps both our lives would have been different."

"She would have been so happy to have seen you again," Dawnmarie said softly.

Moon Glow leaned close again. "I must return to my lodge," she said, looking guardedly around her. "It is forbidden for me to mix with the others, espe-cially guests. Before I am ordered back to my lodge, I will return."

Dawnmarie's lips parted to ask why, but before she could, Moon Glow had hurried back to her lodge, her cats trailing close behind her.

"I don't understand," Dawnmarie said, gazing at Fire Thunder.

"Do not question it," Fire Thunder said flatly. "Now tell me everything about your mother."

Dawnmarie looked with quiet sadness toward Moon Glow's lodge, then into Fire Thunder's eyes again. She told him about her mother's feelings about her true people, and again, this time, a more lengthy explana-tion about why she felt it was so important to be there herself.

Fire Thunder embraced her once she was finished. "You are welcome among my people and you are wel-come to stay as long as you wish," he said softly.

Dawnmarie hugged him back, then stepped away and stood beside White Wolf again. "You are very kind and generous," she answered. "But on my long journey from Wisconsin to Mexico, I have had time to think things through. I appreciate your invitation to stay, but once my mission is fulfilled, that of getting the Kickapoo to give their consent for me to enter the afterlife as a Kickapoo, I will most definitely return to Wisconsin, so that I can be with my children."

"If that is your decision, then so be it," Fire Thunder said. "We will all first celebrate the New Year, and then we will celebrate the Feast for the Dead, which should be enough for you to know that your hereafter life will be secured, as Kickapoo."

"Thank you," Dawnmarie said softly, still finding it hard to believe that she was there among her people. As she had told Moon Glow, she truly felt as though her mother's spirit had followed her from her resting place in Wisconsin and was happy for her daughter. Soon Dawnmarie would finally lay to rest her fears of her hereafter life.

"White Wolf, Dawnmarie, I would like for you to meet the woman who will soon be my wife," Fire Thunder said, placing an arm around Kaylene's waist, drawing her close to his side. "This is Kaylene." He then gestured down at Little Sparrow. "And this is my sister, Little Sparrow. She can speak only through sign language and she reads lips when one who speaks to her does not know the full art of signing."

Kaylene was thrilled at being introduced officially as his bride-to-be. She smiled half bashfully at White Wolf, and then Dawnmarie.

She felt Dawnmarie's eyes linger on her, and she knew why. Dawnmarie was part white and she had married an Indian.

Kaylene was anxious to talk alone with Dawnmarie

and question her about her life among Indians. It did appear, though, that her answers were there, in the way Dawnmarie clung to her husband's arm, and gave him an occasional adoring glance. She was happy, so intensely happy.

The introductions over, Fire Thunder looked nervously over his shoulder, at those who were still tending to the wounded before carrying them inside their lodges.

Troubled, he gave White Wolf a wavering gaze. "Kaylene will escort you to my home," he said thickly. "There we will shall later share food and conversation. But I must first see to my people. I must comfort and help those who need it."

"I shall go with you, if you do not mind," White Wolf said. "My wife can go with Kaylene. We can join them later."

"That is fine. I welcome you," Fire Thunder said. He placed gentle hands on Kaylene's shoulders. "This will give you time to become better acquainted with Dawnmarie, and she with you."

"I look forward to it," Kaylene murmured. She so badly wanted to give him a comforting kiss for his pain for his people and their wounds. "Again, I am so sorry about what happened today. I feel somewhat to blame. If—"

"No if's," Fire Thunder said, placing a gentle hand over her mouth. "Remember that it was I who brought you here."

She smiled as he eased his hand from her mouth.

Little Sparrow clung to Kaylene's hand as Kaylene and Dawnmarie walked toward Fire Thunder's cabin.

"The panther is beautiful," Dawnmarie said as she gazed down at Midnight as he strolled in his dignified fashion somewhat ahead of them. "I have never seen one that could be tamed enough to be a pet."

"His name is Midnight," Kaylene answered. "I found him when he was hardly larger than a house kitten. We became fast friends. Nothing could part us now. And whomever I choose as a friend, is his."

Dawnmarie gasped and paled. She stopped in mid-step when she saw John Shelton in the cage.

Kaylene gazed at John as he gave her a pleading look, while trying to keep that most private part of himself covered beneath his hands.

Every time Kaylene looked at him, she felt herself despising him more deeply. His presence there in the cage represented everything evil about him.

"Ignore him," Kaylene said icily. "He led the attack on the Kickapoo. He was captured. He is paying for his evil deeds."

"But who is he?" Dawnmarie asked, shuffling past him, embarrassed somewhat by his nudity.

"He once was my father," Kaylene said, her voice void of emotion.

Dawnmarie looked quickly over at Kaylene. "Your . . . father?" she gasped out.

"Only in pretense, it seems," Kaylene said, sighing heavily. She looked at Dawnmarie. "Please, let's not talk about him. Let's talk about other things that are more pleasant. I hope that you will tell me your feelings about living among Indians; about, oh, so many things. You seem to have experienced so much. Surely you can offer advice about that which is troubling me."

"And what is that?" Dawnmarie asked softly. "Tell me. I shall do whatever I can. You do seem troubled about so much."

"Yes, and life, in general, it seems," Kaylene said, again sighing. "But one thing is in my favor. I have Fire Thunder's love." She laughed awkwardly. "But

that did not come easy. He took me captive. I, at first
... hated him."

"Captive?" Dawnmarie asked, eyes wide. She
glanced over her shoulder at the cage, then paled as
she looked at Kaylene. "Do not tell me that you were
also placed in ... in ... that thing."

Kaylene smiled. "Yes, I know the miseries of that
hellish cage," she said softly.

"Yet, you are still going to marry Fire Thunder?"
Dawnmarie asked incredulously.

"My hate, my rage, for him, turned into something
more, something *beautiful*," Kaylene said, opening the
door to Fire Thunder's cabin. "We fell in love. I am
here now, because I wish to be."

Dawnmarie entered the lodge first. Kaylene and Little Sparrow followed, along with Midnight.

Midnight went and sprawled out before the roaring
fire in the fireplace, on the blanket he had claimed as
his own.

Kaylene offered Dawnmarie a chair, then sat down
opposite her, while Little Sparrow lay down on the
blanket with Midnight, soon cuddling against him,
asleep.

"Now, Dawnmarie, please tell me about yourself,
how you met White Wolf, and how you adjusted to
life with Indians," Kaylene began. She slipped her feet
beneath her, so glad that her dress and hair were finally dry after the drenching in the rainstorm.

"My life before I met White Wolf was pleasant
enough because my Kickapoo mother was so dear and
sweet to me," Dawnmarie said. "My father, until he
took to drinking, was kind and gentle. He was a trapper. Then he became the owner of a trading post. It
was there that I became acquainted with the different
tribes of Indians that lived in the Wisconsin area.

White Wolf stole my heart the moment I saw him. He
has had it ever since."

"And you married him," Kaylene said, raking her
fingers through her hair, drawing it back across her
shoulders. "Did his people accept you quickly?"

"I fit in like a hand snuggled into a tight glove,"
Dawnmarie said, laughing softly. Then her laughter
faded. "But for a time now, I have been too troubled
about things to enjoy being a wife to my husband, as
I have, in the past."

"And why is that?" Kaylene pressed. "If you don't
mind telling me, that is."

"It has been this constant need to find my true people," Dawnmarie said, her eyes taking on a faraway
look. "It has been so long now since the first time my
mother told me that I must seek out my people. But
life kept getting in the way. I now wish that I hadn't
waited so long. I could have had a lifetime of getting
to know them. Now it will be only brief, for I see the
importance of returning to my children, to enjoy *them*,
and my grandchildren. Life is sometimes cut off way
before one is ready. One must set things right as soon
as possible, or perhaps never get the chance."

She paused, reached over and placed a hand on
Kaylene's arm. "I was one of the lucky ones," she
said softly. "Although I waited so long to come to
Mexico, to be with my true people, it could have been
different. I might have waited too long."

"I am sure that Fire Thunder's people, *your* people,
are glad that you are here," Kaylene said as Dawnmarie eased her hand away and rested it on her lap.
"And perhaps you have told me enough for me to
know what *I* must do. Only recently have I discovered
that the man out in that cage is not my true father. I
have been living a lie. That man out there abducted
me when I was a child too small to even remember

my real parents. Now I must go and find them. What you have told me has helped my decision. Have I made the right decision? Should I seek the full truths about my parents?"

"I encourage you to," Dawnmarie said. "Please don't wait as long as I waited. Look at what I have missed by not knowing my people. The years, the love, the bond! Yes, follow your heart. Find those who unwillingly gave you up."

"But what if Fire Thunder gets impatient with my search and falls out of love with me by thinking that I care more for people I have never known than him," Kaylene said, her voice breaking.

"I saw the love that man has for you," Dawnmarie reassured her. "It matches the feelings my husband has for me. It is an eternal, deep love. He will stand by your decision, no matter the inconvenience it might bring him."

Kaylene left her chair and went to Dawnmarie. She knelt before her and reached her arms up. Dawnmarie leaned down and welcomed Kaylene's warm hug.

Kaylene then gazed intently into Dawnmarie's eyes. "I have failed to tell you how often I am puzzled by feelings that I belong to this way of life, as though I, in part, am Indian," she murmured. "Can it be because of a past life? Was I an Indian maiden in my past life?"

"Perhaps so," Dawnmarie said, gently smoothing a lock of hair back from Kaylene's brow. "I believe in reincarnation. I feel that I, too, have lived before. I wish I knew when, where, and who I was."

Then, when Kaylene heard the braying of a burro outside as it passed by, she thought of Running Fawn. This might be her returning. She jumped to her feet. She knew for almost certain now that Running Fawn had been with her gentleman friend. She wanted to warn Running Fawn that her father had not returned from the hunt just yet, and that it would be best if she hurry to her lodge in case he arrived soon. Although she felt that she was involving herself in some sort of conspiracy, she felt too much for Running Fawn now, and the depth of their friendship, to ignore her as she knew Fire Thunder wanted her to.

"Dawnmarie, will you excuse me for just one moment?" she said softly. "There's someone I must see."

"Go right ahead," Dawnmarie said, stretching her arms, yawning. "I will catch a moment of sleep before our men come back to us. The journey has been long. I am bone weary."

"Why not go and stretch out on the bed?" Kaylene said, nodding toward Fire Thunder's bedroom. "You will be much more comfortable than sleeping in the chair."

"I have learned to sleep while even riding on the *horse*," Dawnmarie said, laughing softly. "I can surely rest quite comfortably while sitting straight up in this comfortable chair."

Kaylene gave her a hug, then rushed from the lodge. When she stepped outside, she stopped and looked at Running Fawn as she slid from the burro's back, staring at John Shelton in the cage.

Then Kaylene rushed to Running Fawn's side. "Where have you been?" she whispered harshly. "Running Fawn, are you trying to get exiled? Or perhaps be placed in this cage? Where have you been? So much has happened."

"My father?" Running Fawn whispered. "Has he returned from the hunt?"

"No, but you know as well as I that he could at any moment," Kaylene said. "Why do you do these things, Running Fawn? It is as though you want to be caught."

"I love Pedro, that is why I go to him," Running Fawn said, leaning close into Kaylene's face. "As you love Fire Thunder, I love Pedro Rocendo!"

She turned slow eyes to John, then looked past him and paled when she saw the activity in the village: how some wounded people still lay outside their lodges, being nursed.

She implored Kaylene with wide eyes. "What has happened here?" she whispered, yet knowing, and dying a slow death inside over having been too cowardly to come home and warn her people of an attack after seeing the armed men.

"This man in the cage, who claimed to be my father throughout the years, came and attacked your village," Kaylene said solemnly. "He is the only one that was captured. The others got away."

Feeling sick inside for having failed her people, Running Fawn lowered her eyes. She sobbed. She grabbed Kaylene's hand. "I ... am ... responsible," she softly cried. She looked desperately up at Kaylene. "I saw them approaching with their firearms. Pedro encouraged me not to come and warn my people."

"You knew and still you did not tell?" Kaylene gasped out, paling. She stepped back from Running Fawn. "I doubt I shall ever understand you."

"Please do not tell my father or Fire Thunder," Running Fawn pleaded, suddenly clutching Kaylene's hands. "I had to tell someone. We are friends. I felt I could safely tell you. I had to get the burden out from inside me."

"Secrets like this are hideous," Kaylene said, shuddering uncontrollably.

Running Fawn pulled Kaylene into the dark shadows of the lodges. "Please swear to me that you will not tell!" she cried. "You are like a sister to me. Sisters look after each other. They confide. I have confided in you the worst of what I have done. Please promise that you will keep my secret."

Seeing how upset Running Fawn was, and how she seemed truly sorry for not having warned her people, Kaylene felt sympathy for this friend who seemed to have trouble knowing right from wrong. Kaylene drew Running Fawn into her arms and comforted her.

"I won't tell," she whispered, stroking her fingers through Running Fawn's thick hair.

"I wish I had met you sooner," Running Fawn murmured. "Friends like you are rare."

"I *am* your friend," Kaylene said. "But, please, Running Fawn, try to change your ways. No man is worth losing everything over, is he?"

"Would you give up Fire Thunder for any reason?" Running Fawn asked, leaning away from Kaylene, their eyes locking. "You love him heart and soul, do you not?"

"He is my world," Kaylene conceded.

"And so Pedro is the world to me," Running Fawn said.

Running Fawn turned with a start when she heard horses entering the village. She swallowed hard when she recognized her father in the lead. Horses dragged many travois behind them, heavy laden with meat.

"Father!" Running Fawn gasped.

Without another word, she turned and fled into the darkness.

Kaylene took a last look at John, then turned, and walked back toward Fire Thunder's lodge. Just as she got there, a woman arrived, carrying two pots of food into the cabin.

Kaylene went inside. She thanked the woman as she waddled past her, to leave.

Absently, Kaylene peered into the pots. Venison ribs filled one of them. Purple corn the other.

And even though it had been a while since she had eaten, she felt no hunger.

There were too many things on her mind. Most prominent of all, her wish that Fire Thunder loved her enough to understand her need to find answers to the questions that were eating away at her insides.

"He has to understand," she whispered. "God above, if not, what shall I do? I can't bear the thought of possibly losing him! Yet, how can I forget what Dawnmarie told me about not waiting too long? One never knows if they will see tomorrow!"

When Fire Thunder entered the lodge with White Wolf, she gazed at him with a sadness she did not want to feel.

When he came and embraced her, it was sheer heaven. No, she could never do anything that might cause her to lose him.

And yes, she understood Running Fawn's reason for risking all by meeting the man she loved!

21

The hours I spent with thee, dear heart,
Are as a string of pearls to me.
—ROBERT CAMERON ROGERS

It was now the fourth day of the Kickapoo's New Year Clan Festival. Kaylene had learned that it never occurred on a fixed date. Before the New Year could be celebrated, certain phenomena had to be observed.

The wild black cherry had to be flowering. The constellation of the Pleiades was observed, and when it approached the zenith, approximately at sunset, the New Year was imminent.

And the Kickapoo spent their nights watching for lightning from the four directions. This was the last sign sent by the grandfathers, the thunderers, to notify them that the day had arrived to celebrate the New Year.

And they had gotten the first sign they had waited for. The thunderer from the north was the first to be seen as he flashed across the sky. It was a good omen for the Kickapoo. But the new year would not arrive until lightning from the other three directions was also sighted.

Fire Thunder and his people felt uniquely blessed this year, for a heavy rain, with much lightning, fell over the village on the first day of the festival. This signified that the thunderers had taken special pains to notify them. It was as though they themselves had come to tell the people.

As soon as the lightning from the four directions had been seen, the warriors, following Fire Thunder's lead, had gone into the *monte* to chant and offer Indian tobacco to the thunderers, thanking them for the message that the New Year had arrived.

On this fourth day of the festival, everyone was gathered in the Thunder Bundle House, a building made of split logs, with a tree-bark roof. The music from many drums and gourd rattles was rhythmically soft. The people sat around a great fire in the firepit, quiet and meditative.

Kaylene was proud to be among them. She wore a low-swept cotton blouse and fully gathered skirt that Running Fawn had loaned her for the special occasion. She wore flowers in her hair.

Kaylene gazed at Fire Thunder as he sat with the other warriors, and saw how handsome he was today—even more so than usual. He wore a spanking-new buckskin outfit and beautifully beaded moccasins that a distant cousin had made for him for this special occasion.

Kaylene sat with Dawnmarie on a bench. Little Sparrow sat with the children, all eyes, as she watched the continuing activity of the New Year festival.

Kaylene looked slowly around the group of people, her heart sinking when she realized that Running Fawn wasn't there. To add insult to injury, as far as her people were concerned, she had slipped out and was not observing the special ceremonies.

It was apparent to Kaylene that Running Fawn had

felt that her father would be too involved in the festival to notice her absence.

Thus far, Kaylene felt that perhaps Running Fawn had been right. At this moment Black Hair seemed all absorbed in the rituals of the day.

"I find this all so wonderfully interesting," Dawnmarie whispered as she leaned closer to Kaylene. "It is wonderful to be among my people in this way."

"Do you understand the meaning behind what the warriors are doing?" Kaylene whispered back to her.

"Some," Dawnmarie said, gazing at Kaylene. "My mother told me much about my people when I was growing up. She hoped that I would one day be among them. She felt it important that I know as much about their customs as possible."

"It is a miracle that you happened to arrive at such an important time," Kaylene murmured, silently admiring Dawnmarie's snow-white doeskin dress embellished with lovely beadwork.

And she could not help but be taken by the color of Dawnmarie's eyes. She understood why White Wolf called her Violet Eyes. Never had Kaylene seen eyes so violet in color.

"It was the work of *Kitzhiat*, the Kickapoo great spirit, that led me and my husband here at this moment in time," Dawnmarie said, smiling warmly at Kaylene.

"I hope to understand everything about your people one day," Kaylene said. "One thing in particular has been on my mind that I would like to know."

"What is it?" Dawnmarie said softly.

"I have seen Fire Thunder praying, and during his prayers, he calls out to 'Grandfather.' To whom is he referring?"

"The four corners, or directions, the four winds, and the sky that watches from the heavens, are all *ma-*

nitou, and are called *grandfather*," Dawnmarie explained. "They are vigilantes and messengers who notify the *manitou*. The Kickapoo speak of the *grandfathers* as *those who walk above*."

"How interesting," Dawnmarie said, now looking at Fire Thunder again, and at what he was doing. He had told her earlier that all the fires in the village would be extinguished. Now the large lodge fire was being covered with dirt, to extinguish it. He was responsible for making a new fire with his bow drill in the Thunder Bundle House, and then he would be the one who would distribute fire to all of the homes of the village.

Several young men came and took away the dead ash. Fresh wood was placed in the firepit. Everyone was quiet as Fire Thunder started the new fire with his bow drill.

As they waited for the fire to take hold, a new buckskin was placed on the ground, and pieces of the rhizome of Solomon's seal were laid on it. Pieces of Solomon's seal were also added to the tobacco in a large, long-stemmed pipe. Before the pipe was sent around the circle of men to be smoked, they prayed and sang three songs.

The pipe was then taken by each warrior. They took long puffs from it and blew the smoke in the four directions—east, west, south and north—always in the same order.

After the pipe was passed around the full circle, another prayer was said to *Kitzihiat*.

When the new flames leaped high in the fire pit, Fire Thunder lifted many pieces of the burning wood with tongs and placed them in large copper tubs that young braves brought to him.

Once the tubs were filled with burning wood, warriors carried them from the council house. Fire Thunder accompanied them. He would go inside each lodge and place one of the burning pieces of lumber in the fireplaces or fire pits. The new fire meant a new beginning. The new year would have truly begun for the Kickapoo.

Kaylene watched several women come forth. They placed large trays of food around the lodge fire. There were braids of thinly sliced squash and pumpkin that had been dried in the sun. There were huge piles of venison, bear ribs, tongues, turkey, and white corn. Everything smelled delicious.

Sassafras tea was brought in large wooden pitchers, as well as many wooden cups.

But Kaylene's thoughts strayed from the food. She thought of John Shelton. Although she knew that he deserved to be punished, she was glad that Fire Thunder had taken him from the cage, out of view of his people and herself. She was glad to have him where she couldn't see him every time she went outside. Just the sight of him sent her mind into a tailspin of despair and doubt.

This man who had claimed to be her father was now being kept a prisoner in a lodge at the far edge of the village. She was not sure yet what his fate would be.

But as for herself, she was greatly disappointed that he had not yet told her her true birthright. The smirk on his face each time she asked him proved to her, over and over again, that she was right about him, that he most definitely was not her father.

Again she thought of Running Fawn to whom she had vowed secrecy. Although Running Fawn was a friend, Kaylene could not help but regret having become her confidante. She feared Running Fawn's final fate. She might one day be raped, or she might be killed by a jealous suitor!

Or, she might be banished by the tribe.

Kaylene felt helpless to help her. As long as Running Fawn would not listen to reason, and continued to be disobedient to her father and chief, and her people, there was nothing Kaylene could do to help her.

"We are having our own New Year's Festival," Running Fawn said, laughing softly as she poured herself another glass of tequila.

She would not allow herself to recall how it affected her the other times, especially that one time she had fainted and had awakened to find herself at the edge of the village. Had her father found her in a drunken stupor, that would have been the end for her.

Her three girlfriends sat with their young lovers, laughing, giggling, and drinking tequila. Pedro sat beside Running Fawn, frowning.

"It was not wise to meet today," he grumbled, his dark eyes flashing angrily into Running Fawn's. "Had I known your people were celebrating their New Year festival, I would have never come. It is dangerous. Should you be missed, Running Fawn, it could be the end for all of us."

"Will you stop worrying?" Running Fawn said, snuggling close to him as they sat beneath the shade of a tree. "Father is thinking of nothing else but the festival and his part in it. A daughter is the farthest thing from his mind."

Running Fawn set her empty glass aside. She moved to her knees before Pedro. She framed his dark face between her hands. "Do you not remember why you came today?" she said, her eyes dancing. "My sweet Mexican lover, you did not come only to see me. You are to get a tattoo on your leg to match the one I have on mine. Will that not truly bond us as lovers?"

"I do not like tattoos," Pedro growled, taking her hands from his face. He looked over at his friends. "*Señorita* Running Fawn, we should go. We have stayed too long as it is."

"Coward," Running Fawn hissed out, her eyes narrowed. She rose to her feet in a huff and placed her hands on her hips. "How could I have fallen in love with such a coward?"

Pedro rushed to his feet. He took her by the wrists and yanked her close. He glared down at her. "I am no coward," he said tightly. "I just do not like tattoos."

"If you do not allow me to place a matching tattoo on your leg, then you will not see me ever again," Running Fawn said, lifting her chin haughtily.

"Coward!" the three other girls chimed in. "Pedro is a coward!"

His eyes wavering, feeling as though he was quickly losing face with these beautiful *señoritas*, Pedro stepped away from Running Fawn. "All right," he said, idly shrugging, "to prove that I am no coward, you can tattoo me."

Running Fawn's eyes lit up. She grabbed Pedro and hugged him. "I knew that you would let me," she said, snuggling her body against his. "After I have tattooed you, then we can make love."

"That is my reward for proving I am no coward?" Pedro said, chuckling.

"Something like that, my handsome Mexican lover," Running Fawn said, inching from his arms.

"Let's get it over with," Pedro mumbled.

"Sit down and roll up your pants leg as I gather the poison ivy," Running Fawn said, giggling when she saw how the words "poison ivy" made Pedro grimace. She leaned into his face. "Are you going to change your mind? Are you too cowardly to let me touch you with the poison ivy?"

"Poison ivy," Pedro grumbled. "Whoever heard of using poison ivy for a tattoo? Only Indians would think up such nonsense as that."

He nodded toward Running Fawn. "Get on with it, *Señorita* Running Fawn," he grumbled. "Or I just might decide you are not worth all the worries you put me through."

He sat down and rolled up his pants leg as he watched Running Fawn go to a thicket and pluck several twigs of poison ivy. He scarcely breathed when she came to him and began squeezing the juice of the poison ivy carefully along his flesh in the design of a dog.

After Running Fawn was finished, she tossed the poison ivy aside. "Now when the sores are gone, and the scarring is left behind, you will have yourself a tattoo just like mine," she said, smiling at him.

Her smile faded when Pedro started to gasp for breath, his eyes wide with terror. She backed away from him when he began clawing at his throat.

"I . . . can't . . . breathe!" he choked out. "My heart! It is racing so much I feel I might pass out!"

"Why?" Running Fawn cried. Fear circled her heart as Pedro crumpled to his knees, his hand now clutching at his swollen leg where the tattoo was inflamed. "What is happening, Pedro?"

"He is having some sort of a reaction to the poison ivy," Miguel shouted. He went to Pedro and held him. "We must get help for him. Running Fawn, your village is closer than San Carlos. Go for help. Surely your people will have something to counteract the reaction. Go! Find out! Pedro might be dying!"

Running Fawn felt as though she was being squeezed from both sides. She was torn with what to do. If she went to her village and let them know about Pedro, then she would forever be condemned in their eyes! Oh, surely she would be banished, a shamed person forever in the eyes of *Kitzhiat*.

"Running Fawn...." Pedro managed to say in a whisper as he reached a hand out toward her. "*Señorita*, I'm ... dying."

"But, Pedro, if I go to my village—" she began, but stopped when he began choking again, his eyes wild as he stared up at her.

"I will get you help," Running Fawn said, knowing that she had no choice. She loved Pedro. She would sacrifice anything if it meant that he would live. "I will bring my shaman to you."

"No, there is not time," Miguel said. "We will take Pedro *there*. We will follow you, Running Fawn. Lead the way."

"But, my people are celebrating the New Year," Running Fawn cried. "I cannot interrupt the celebration. Let me just tell Bull Shield. Is that not enough?"

"Look at Pedro!" Miguel cried. "He is now unconscious. He may not have long to live. We must take him to your village."

Tears flooding her eyes, her heart pounding with fear of her father's *and* her chief's reaction when they saw her and her three friends enter the village with the four Mexican men, Running Fawn broke into a mad run through the forest.

She could hear the harsh breathing of Miguel as he followed closely behind, Pedro in his arms.

She glanced over at her friends whose faces were pale with fear.

They all knew what the result of today would be—banishment!

22

I will not let thee go,
Ends all our month-long love in this?
Can it be summed up so?
Quit in a single kiss?
I will not let thee go.
—ROBERT BRIDGES

Now at the end of the festival, as food and drink were being shared by all, Kaylene felt a delicious warmth inside herself, to know that she was being accepted by these people who would soon be truly a part of her life by marriage.

As she sat beside Fire Thunder, eating the delicious venison and corn, and listening to the gay laughter all around her, Kaylene felt strange longings inside herself again, which made her feel as though she was already a part of the Indians' lives, as though somewhere in time she had been an Indian.

She scooted her empty wooden platter aside, confused anew about these feelings which would suddenly come upon her like a mighty embrace. She reached over and took Fire Thunder's hand.

Fire Thunder looked at her and saw something new

in the shadows of Kaylene's eyes. "What is it?" he asked, placing his own empty bowl aside. "There is something mystical about the way you are looking at me."

Kaylene was distracted for a moment by Dawnmarie's quiet, sweet laughter as she sat amidst the other Kickapoo women. She glanced over at her, seeing the radiance that seemed to glow around her in her happiness to be there with her true people.

Kaylene glanced then at White Wolf, as he sat by his wife, watching her. She could see the adoration he felt for her, and hoped that Fire Thunder would still love *her* as much, after they had been married for many years.

"Kaylene?" Fire Thunder said, placing a finger to her chin, bringing her eyes back around to meet the question in his. "Moments ago you seemed filled with laughter. Now? I sense there is something troubling you."

"I . . ." Kaylene began, as she felt it would be good to inform him of her sudden strange feelings, but stopped when a commotion outside the lodge drew her eyes to the door.

Running Fawn suddenly appeared, her eyes fearful, her face flushed with color. Kaylene's insides turned cold. Something had to be terribly wrong for Running Fawn to just suddenly appear like that, and let everyone know that she had not been among them all along, enjoying the festivities. Until now, no one had questioned her absence. Now, everyone would.

Kaylene started to rise to her feet, but Fire Thunder's firm grip was too quickly around her wrist, stopping her.

She turned questioning eyes to Fire Thunder.

His response was a sullen glare and a slow shake of his head.

Swallowing hard, Kaylene nodded and stayed beside him as Black Hair rose and went to his daughter.

Cold with fear, Running Fawn gazed up at her father. She could see his anger by the way his jaw was so tightly set and by the way his eyes seemed to brim with fire. She wanted to retreat to the forest, to hide, but Miguel's voice behind her, urging her onward, caused her to grab her father's hand.

"Father, please come outside with me," she asked softly. She looked past him and felt the eyes of everyone on her. Her presence had even stopped the soft thumping of the drum, and the rhythmic shake of the rattles.

Everything seemed stopped in time, except her rapid heartbeat and the fear that was building inside her.

Black Hair didn't budge. He doubled his hands into tight fists at his sides as he looked past her and saw the other three Kickapoo women, and then the young Mexican men, one of them carrying General Rocendo's son, Pedro.

He then glared down at Running Fawn. "You are a disgrace," he hissed out. He ignored Pedro's groan as it wafted through the air toward him. He flailed a frustrated hand in the air as he leaned his face down into his daughter's. "Where have you been? Did you not know that you were expected to be here as we brought the New Year in for our people? You and your friends were, instead, with Mexicans?"

Running Fawn lowered her eyes. "Yes, and I am sorry, Father," she whispered. Then she lifted fearful eyes up to him again. "But, Father, now is not the time to scold me." She turned to Pedro, wincing when she saw how his face was now so swollen, his eyes hidden in the deep folds.

She turned back to her father. "Pedro is ill," she

blurted out. "Please let our shaman see to him. If you do not, I fear Pedro will die."

"Let him die," Black Hair growled. "He has sinned with you. He deserves not to live!"

Having heard everything, and deciding that it was not best after all to let Black Hair handle this awkward situation that had become a show for all of his people to view, Fire Thunder rose quickly to his feet and hurried to Black Hair's side.

Worried about Running Fawn, and her father's anger, Kaylene hurried after Fire Thunder and stood at his side as he intervened.

Kaylene gave Running Fawn a sympathetic look. Although she knew that Running Fawn had been wrong to go against her father's wishes, she saw that her fears were confirmed about Running Fawn's trysts bringing her trouble. Kaylene looked outside and saw the young man being held in the arms of another young Mexican man. His face was swollen grotesquely. He lay limp and unconscious in the arms of his friend, perhaps near death.

Panic seized Kaylene at the thought of the young man dying. Running Fawn would not only be in trouble with her people, but also with the Mexicans.

Things had gone beyond trysts. Way beyond.

"Black Hair, let us deal with your daughter later," Fire Thunder interceded. "Look at the young man. He is in trouble. Our shaman must take a look at him."

Black Hair gave Fire Thunder a sullen stare, then nodded. He went to Bull Shield, who sat quietly among the other men.

After hearing about Pedro, Bull Shield left the lodge with them to take a look at Pedro.

"What happened to send the young man into an unconscious state?" Bull Shield asked, looking from one young Mexican man to the other, then glaring at the girls who stood there, their eyes downcast.

"Poison ivy, I believe!" Running Fawn cried. "I . . . I . . . made a tattoo on his leg with poison ivy. Soon after he became ill."

"I see," Bull Shield said, kneading his chin thoughtfully. "He has reacted badly to the poison ivy. I have seen this before. I have a remedy—a medicine that will counteract it."

He gave Miguel a quick glance. "Young man, come," he said flatly. "Follow me. Bring the ailing one to my lodge. Leave him there. I will do what I can to make him well."

Pedro was taken there. After he was stretched out on a pallet of furs beside the lodge fire, the Mexican boys were made to stand outside.

Fire Thunder, Kaylene, Black Hair, and Running Fawn were allowed to stay, silently watching as Bull Shield concocted his medicine from several small vials of liquid.

Once the concoction was poured down Pedro's throat, and Bull Shield shook his rattle over him and chanted, it was only a short while afterward that Pedro came to.

His breathing was even again. The flush to his face had softened into something more normal. He was awake enough to see Running Fawn, and then her father, standing over him.

He gasped. His eyes grew wide with fear.

"Do not allow yourself to get upset by anything right now," Bull Shield said, as he noticed Pedro's reaction to seeing Black Hair glaring down at him. "Young man, you are not well enough to make the trip down the mountainside to San Carlos. You will spend the night in Bull Shield's lodge. I will keep watch on you. Tomorrow, perhaps, you can return home. But not until then. Do you understand?"

Pedro nodded and turned his eyes away from Black Hair.

Kaylene clung to Fire Thunder's arm as she watched Black Hair grab Running Fawn by the arm and take her outside.

She gazed up at Fire Thunder. "What's going to happen to her?" she asked softly, not wanting Pedro to hear.

"Now is not the time to discuss that," Fire Thunder said. He thanked Bull Shield for giving of his time and medicine to cure the young man, then stared down at Pedro for a moment. Fire Thunder felt lucky that he and General Rocendo were close friends, or this incident with his son might have caused war between the Mexicans and Kickapoo.

As it was, Fire Thunder would have only explanations to make, and then he would have the perpetrator daughter to reprimand. He knew almost for certain the punishment he was going to hand down to her and her friends. He had hardly any choice in the matter since they were grossly disobedient, not only to their families, but also their chief.

"Come, we will go to my lodge," Fire Thunder said, taking Kaylene gently by an elbow. "I no longer wish to join the festival activities. I need to be alone with you. My heart is weary for that which lays before me."

"You are speaking of Running Fawn's punishment?" Kaylene asked, fearing his answer.

"Yes, I must make the decision," Fire Thunder grumbled. "Being chief is many things to me. I am rewarded often by my people for my tendering to them. Then there are times like this, when I am faced with the bad side of chieftainship . . . when the fate of four beautiful young women lies in my hands."

"Fire Thunder, can't you be lenient this time?" Kaylene asked, her eyes wavering from his when he turned her way.

"And what is lenience when it comes to more than one of our young people being so blatantly disobedient?" he said, his voice drawn. "That young man could have died. Those young girls could have been taken by the Mexicans and tried for murder. What I will do will be way less harsh."

Kaylene felt that she had said enough for now. She could tell that he was heavily burdened by his decision. She did not want to make it worse by being a nag. She had to put his feelings before those she felt for Running Fawn.

She followed Fire Thunder into their cabin. She stood over the fire as he closed the door. She watched him as he knelt before the hearth and shoved more firewood into the fire.

Then he rose to his feet before Kaylene. He framed her face between his hands and drew her lips gently to his. "I need you," he said huskily. "My woman, help me forget for the moment the chore that lies before me."

Her knees weak with desire for Fire Thunder, Kaylene didn't have to be asked twice. Her fingers trembled with anxiousness as she undid his breeches and put her hands down the front of them.

She could feel his breath quicken when she circled her fingers around his throbbing member.

When she began moving her hand on him, and he gyrated himself against her hand, she felt the heat rise within herself, as her own needs blossomed within her.

Their kiss deepened as he ran his hand up the inside of her leg. He splayed his fingers across her buttocks and shoved her against his hardness as she slid her hand free of his breeches.

"I need you," she whispered huskily as his lips slid down and he nibbled at her neck. "Now, my darling. Please make love to me."

He swept his arms beneath her and carried her to the bed, where Midnight lay beside it in a deep snooze.

Afraid that someone might come in his lodge before they were through, Fire Thunder kicked the bedroom door closed.

His passion-filled eyes smiling down at Kaylene, he quickly disrobed.

Then he knelt down beside her and hurriedly took off her clothes.

Silkenly naked, Kaylene ran her hands across Fire Thunder's muscular chest, then down lower, across his flat belly.

She then wove her fingers through the shock of hair between his thighs, where his manhood thrust out away from it, powerful, thick, and long.

"Come to me," Kaylene whispered, guiding him over her, so that he straddled her.

She opened her legs to him and closed her eyes in ecstasy when, with one powerful shove, he was inside her.

Kaylene wrapped her legs around his waist and moved rhythmically with him. She twined her fingers through his hair and brought his lips down to one of her breasts.

She sucked in a wild breath of rapture when his tongue circled the nipple. Then his teeth nipped at it until she felt as though she would die with pleasure.

He licked her breasts with his tongue. He licked and sucked every inch of them.

Then he caught her throat in his teeth, groaning as she lifted her body to meet the rhythm of his thrusts.

She responded to him, heart and soul, his lovemaking leaving her breathless when it was over.

"Why must it end so quickly?" she whispered as she cuddled close to him.

"So that we will leave some for tomorrow and all the tomorrows after that," Fire Thunder said, stroking her tender flesh between her legs, where she still throbbed from the aftermath of having flown with him to paradise.

Then she giggled when she felt something else on the bed with them. Midnight leapt at her feet and stretched out, purring.

"I fear someone feels neglected of late," Kaylene said, glancing down at Midnight whose green eyes were watching her. She moved to her knees and crawled to Midnight. "My sweet pet, I hope you aren't missing the cheer of the carnival crowds. Never again will I ride you."

"Why not just one performance?" Fire Thunder said, sitting up in bed, resting his back against the headboard. "For me? In this room? No one but us will be the wiser."

Kaylene looked from Midnight back to Fire Thunder. "I don't know," she murmured.

"Just this once, Kaylene, so that I can see the beauty of it," Fire Thunder said, giving her a look she could not say no to.

"Oh, all right," she said, sighing. "But only this once, mind you. My pet is now just that, nothing more. He deserves to be loved only for himself, not for the money he earned for my fath—for John Shelton's carnival."

She went to a chair, over which hung Midnight's leash. She urged Midnight to the floor. She talked to him soothingly and sweetly as she put the leash in place around his neck.

"This is the last time, sweetie," she whispered in Midnight's ear. "But since it is, let's give him a show to remember!"

Having never rode naked on Midnight before, Kaylene felt wicked climbing on his back now without a stitch of clothes on.

But knowing that Fire Thunder's eyes were on her, and no longer at all bashful in front of him without clothes, she took the leash, straightened her back, and gave Midnight a slight nudge in the sides with her knees and rode him proudly up and down the full length of the room.

She closed her eyes, shivering inside when she suddenly realized that *she* missed the limelight. She could not help but remember the applause, the cheers, and the looks of admiration, as she and Midnight had rode around the circle of people.

She now realized just how much she had loved the attention. Truly loved it. Yes, only now, did she know for certain just how much.

Tears streamed down her cheeks. She lowered her eyes and climbed from Midnight's back. She went to Fire Thunder and flung herself into his arms. "My Lord, how I do miss it," she cried. "I didn't think that I would but, Fire Thunder, I do. What am I to do? I could even feel Midnight's response. He loved it as much as me!"

"Too often in life one has to give up that which they love, to have something they love more," he whispered, stroking her back. "Tell me you love me more than anything, Kaylene. I need to hear it."

Kaylene sniffled, swallowed back a sob that became lodged in her throat, then looked him in the eye. "Oh, I do love you so much," she whispered. "Way more than anything else in my life, ever."

"So you see?" Fire Thunder said, laughing softly. "That wasn't so hard to figure out, was it?"

She giggled and leaned into his tender embrace. "You are everything to me, and more," she murmured.

When Midnight came and placed a paw on her leg,

she reached over and stroked it. He, too, would learn to take from life the best part of it, and Kaylene knew now, that for them both, it was to be with the Kickapoo.

Then her heart sank when she again thought of Running Fawn. She eased from Fire Thunder's embrace. "What of Running Fawn?" she asked softly. "What is going to happen to her?"

"That is not a part of your happiness, Kaylene, to worry yourself about matters that truly do not concern you," Fire Thunder said, yet in a gentle way so as not to be offensive.

"But she is my friend," Kaylene protested. "I can't help but be concerned about her."

"Should you have never met me, nor known her, things would be no different than what they are now," he tried to explain. "She was having trysts with Pedro long before you knew her. As chief, I shall hand out my punishment to her and the three other young women, as though you were never here to forge a friendship with Running Fawn. And everyone, you as well, will have to accept my decision."

"I do feel so very sorry for her," Kaylene persisted.

"And so you should, because I fear her punishment is going to be severe enough to make everyone's feelings to be the same as yours," Fire Thunder said. "Yet it must be done. And tomorrow I shall see that it is."

"What of Pedro? What of the young men that were with him?"

"The three young men are staying the night because they fear returning to San Carlos without Pedro," Fire Thunder said, rising to get dressed. Kaylene moved from the bed and started dressing, also. "Tomorrow we will take Pedro home on a travois. That is when the other young men will also return to San Carlos. They will all have to face the general together."

"And what about Running Fawn's father?" Kaylene asked solemnly. "Black Hair was furious with her."

"I imagine at this very moment Black Hair is shaming his daughter," Fire Thunder said, placing his headband around his brow.

"Fire Thunder, I just thought of something," Kaylene said, her eyes wide. She went to him and grabbed a hand. "Darling, didn't you tell me once that the 'Trotter' absorbs sins for others so that those who have sinned are free to make a life again among your people? Why can't the Trotter absorb Running Fawn's sins? Then Running Fawn could start anew. Surely she would behave after coming this close to being so severely punished."

"I will not allow the Trotter to absorb any of those four young women's sins," Fire Thunder said, his eyes narrowing. "Their sins are too great. No one will pay for them, except themselves."

"And what of John Shelton?" Kaylene asked. "You haven't yet told me what your plans are for him?"

"I do have a set plan for him, but I will tell you later," Fire Thunder said, easing her hand from his. He went to the door and opened it. "White Wolf and Dawnmarie, and Little Sparrow should be here soon. Let us wait for them out by the fire."

Kaylene went to the living room with him. She sat down on a blanket before the hearth and stared into the rolling flames.

Yes, she adored this man, this handsome Kickapoo chief.

But she knew that there would be times when he left her out of his life, when he was being a chief who was burdened with decisions.

It might be hard to learn when, and when not, to step aside and be his silent partner.

23

If so I meditate alone,
He will be partner of my moan.
—THOMAS LODGE

The morning sun splashed its orange glow along the horizon as the slow procession of horses and burros made their way down the mountainside. Pedro had been too ill to place on a travois. Instead, a wagon was being used to transport him home.

Kaylene was on the floor at the back of the wagon, cradling the young lad's head on her lap. As she caressed his feverish brow with a damp cloth she gazed down at him. She was glad to see him sleeping peacefully enough.

Kaylene was also glad to see that the swelling of his face was almost gone.

Her gaze moved down to his leg, where Running Fawn had so foolishly rubbed on the poison ivy. The blisters were large, oozing, and red. She shivered to think that he just might lose his leg. She recalled one of her mother's friends, long ago, whose arm had been amputated after having been exposed to the smoke of burning poison ivy. It had grown twice its size with infection. It had filled with pus. Nothing they did helped it.

Kaylene lifted her eyes to the blue heaven above and said a soft prayer that this young man would not lose his leg over something that Running Fawn had done. For certain, if he did, hate would run rampant through the Mexicans toward the Kickapoo.

Her thoughts dwelled on Running Fawn. Kaylene hadn't been allowed to see her since she had been sent into isolation in her lodge. And Kaylene still had no idea what Running Fawn's punishment was going to be.

Her thoughts shifted to Black Hair. Although it was his daughter, not himself, whom had done this to the young man, he was carrying the burden on his shoulders as though it were he. Black Hair had shut himself inside his lodge with his daughter after telling Fire Thunder that he felt as though he was a part of his daughter's betrayal to their chief, since he had not been able to teach her the true meaning of respect for a father's wishes.

Kaylene swallowed hard, feeling as though she were a part of this betrayal, since she had sworn herself to secrecy to Running Fawn.

Yet, she knew that she was not truly to blame for anything that Running Fawn did. She had just chosen not to get involved, which made the secret pact with Running Fawn seem even somewhat logical. It was not her place to interfere in these people's lives. Until only a short while ago even, she had been a captive whose word meant nothing to anyone.

To get her mind off these worries, Kaylene looked around her, at those who were accompanying Fire Thunder down the mountainside to San Carlos.

Pedro's three Mexican friends were on burros at the head of the procession, their heads hanging.

Several warriors rode just behind them, their rifles in their gunboots, their holstered pistols at their hips.

Another warrior held the reins of the wagon in which Kaylene traveled.

Dressed in a buckskin jacket and leggings that fit him snugly, Fire Thunder rode to the left of the wagon, giving Pedro occasional worried glances.

Yes, Kaylene thought to herself, it was very obvious how concerned Fire Thunder was over the welfare of this young man. If Pedro died ... ?

When Fire Thunder cast Kaylene a glance, she smiled at him. "I'm almost certain Pedro is going to be all right," she offered as some encouragement to him. "His brow isn't as hot and he's resting better now."

"Foolish, *foolish* Running Fawn," Fire Thunder growled out between clenched teeth. "How could it have happened that she could be this wild hearted? Her mother was as tame as a lamb. She was sweet. She was considerate. Running Fawn seems driven by demons!"

"Yes, and that is so sad," Kaylene murmured. "Otherwise, she is so kind; so generous."

"Yes, I know there is much good in Running Fawn," Fire Thunder said, nodding. "But the bad too often outweighs the good."

He turned his eyes from her and watched the trail ahead of him again.

Kaylene wanted to ask him again what his plans were for Running Fawn, but she knew, by the way that he had become so quiet, that he did not wish to speak of it any further at this time. His eyes were on the city that was now in view at the foot of the moun-

tain, spread out along the valley, its villas snuggled
closely together at the edge.

Kaylene's heartbeat quickened as she looked anxiously past the city to the far side, where she remembered the carnival tents had been set up. Oh, but how
memories flooded her, of her performance with Midnight, and the applause and cheers of those who
watched.

That was the wonderful side of her memory.

The black side was when she had discovered that
Little Sparrow had been abducted while the carnival
had been set up in San Carlos.

And then the horrifying moment when she had seen
Little Sparrow in the cage when they had pitched their
tents again after leaving San Carlos behind.

How could her father have done that to the innocent child? she despaired again to herself, as she had
done so many countless times before since Little Sparrow's abduction. How could he have done so much
evil against so many?

Little Sparrow had begged to come with them
today. But not only had Kaylene's memories of seeing
Little Sparrow in the cage been powerful, so had Fire
Thunder's. He had adamantly told Little Sparrow that
she had to stay behind this time. It would be a while
before he would let her go anywhere. With many warriors surrounding and protecting the Kickapoo village,
which was now necessary since the white man's recent
attack, Little Sparrow's safety was secured.

Dawnmarie and White Wolf had offered to stay
with her. Kaylene had also left Midnight behind for
safekeeping.

And now Kaylene was filled with curiosity as to
where the carnival might be. Surely her father had
seen that it was moved elsewhere before launching his
attack on the Kickapoo village. He would not want

the Kickapoo to find them so easily in case he left survivors.

Therefore, Kaylene herself knew not where to find the woman she needed to question about her birthright.

But this was not the time to think about things concerning herself. Fire Thunder's plight was of the utmost importance.

She stiffened as they entered the outskirts of San Carlos. She looked guardedly around her as people stopped and stared at the three young Mexican men who rode slowly down the dirt road on burros, their heads still hanging, and then at Pedro as he still lay asleep in the wagon, his head on Kaylene's lap.

To avoid any eye contact with any of the Mexican people, Kaylene looked straight ahead. She grew tense when she saw the protective walls ahead that circled the land and villa owned by General Rocendo. Well-armed *vaqueros*, guards, stood at the wide, closed gate.

Kaylene watched Fire Thunder as he nudged his horse with his knees and rode on ahead and stopped a few yards from the guards.

"*Captain* Fire Thunder, what has happened?" one of the guards asked. His gaze moved slowly from one of the Mexicans to the other. Then he strained his neck to look into the wagon.

"I must see General Rocendo," Fire Thunder said thickly. He gestured toward the young men whose eyes were wide with fright. "As you can see, I have escorted these young men to San Carlos." He looked over his shoulder and frowned as he stared at Pedro. "Also, Pedro, the general's son."

"Is Pedro injured?" one of the guards asked, walking quickly past Fire Thunder, to gaze in concern at Pedro. He gasped when he saw Pedro's leg.

Then his gaze moved slowly up, to look at Kaylene. "What is the meaning of this?" he hissed out. "And do I not know you, *señorita*? Did I not see you when the carnival people were here? Did you not ride a panther?"

"Yes, that was me," Kaylene said, scarcely breathing when the other guard came and looked in horror at Pedro, then looked with recognition at her.

"You are the panther *señorita*," he said, a white flash of teeth showing when he smiled at her.

"Yes, I was," she murmured, yet puzzled that he showed more attention to her, than to the ailing son of his general.

Then one of the guards returned to Fire Thunder. "*Capitan*, you can explain what happened to General Rocendo," he said, the other guard opening the gate. "I will ride ahead and tell him that you are coming." He untied the reins that secured his horse to a hitching rail, then mounted and rode into the courtyard.

Fire Thunder rode through the gate and stiffened when he saw General Rocendo step out onto the porch of his huge, widespread villa. He was shirtless. His hair was mussed, as though he had just left his bed.

Fire Thunder watched the general's expression as the guard explained why Fire Thunder was there, and about the general's son not being well.

General Rocendo left the porch in his bare feet and met Fire Thunder's approach.

Fire Thunder dismounted and shook the general's hand, then walked with him back to the wagon, where Pedro was just awakening.

"And, *Capitan*, how did this happen to my son?" the general growled out, toying with his thick, black mustache as he slowly looked up at Kaylene. "And Jose told me that the panther lady from the carnival is the one on whose lap my son's head lies. *Señorita,* I missed your performance when your carnival was here. I hope to one day see you ride the panther." His eyebrows forked. "But what are you doing away from your people? I do not understand."

Again Kaylene was amazed at how little anyone seemed disturbed by Pedro's illness. She was in the limelight, which unnerved her.

"She is soon to be my wife," Fire Thunder said, intervening. "Now, General Rocendo, about your son. I apologize for the carelessness of one of my Kickapoo young women. She tattooed your son's leg with the juice of poison ivy. He had a bad reaction. But he is much better than he was last night."

"A tattoo?" General Rocendo said, leaning over the side of the wagon, inspecting his son's leg. He looked up at Pedro who was watching him guardedly. "Pedro, did I not tell you that sneaking around with Kickapoo *señoritas* could get you into trouble?" he chuckled. "I never expected it to be *this* sort of trouble. I would have thought it might be more like you coming to me with a complaint that a beautiful Indian *señorita* was heavy with child ... *yours.*"

"Father, do not blame Running Fawn for any of this," Pedro managed weakly. He looked with panic at Fire Thunder. "*Capitan* Fire Thunder, do not punish Running Fawn. This was all in fun. It just got out of hand."

"It is good to see that you are well enough to talk, but what you say is wasted breath about Running Fawn," Fire Thunder said tersely. He glowered at the general. "And do you not recall my having come to you, asking you to talk to your young men about coming and sneaking around with our Kickapoo girls? We need to work together on problems like this or things like what happened yesterday to Pedro might happen again." He narrowed his eyes. "And I do not take lightly to how you find even the thought of one of our young women becoming heavy with child from trysts with your young men amusing."

General Rocendo toyed with his mustache for a moment as he gazed intently up at Fire Thunder, being much shorter than the Kickapoo chief. "*Capitan*, if you must know," he then said, much more seriously, "I *did* warn my son and his friends not to come anywhere near your village or your *señoritas*. It seems they do not have ears that hear too well. When my son did not return home last night, I did not think that he would be with any of your girls. I thought he might be spending the night with women from our brothels. I have grown accustomed to my son's adventures with the local *señoras*, so often staying the night with them."

"Your son is young," Fire Thunder challenged. "How can you approve of him bedding up with women of your village as though he were a man?"

General Rocendo's shoulders tightened. He glared up at Fire Thunder. "*Capitan*, do not speak of my son in such a way, or how I choose to raise him," he spat out. "I admire a son whose prowess is so well developed at his young age. I see my son being with older women at the brothels as a way to make a true man out of him!"

The general turned glaring eyes to Pedro. "I cannot be angry at the Kickapoo girl who administered the near fatal poison to my son's leg, as I must apologize for a son who goes behind his father's back to do as he was told not to, for I did tell him to bed Mexican *señoritas*, while he is practicing to be a man!" he said, his voice drawn and icy.

General Rocendo then reached toward Pedro and clasped one of his arms. "Leave the wagon, Pedro," he said tightly. "*Now*. And do not whine about not being strong enough. You chose to behave like a man. *Act* like one."

Kaylene paled. "But, sir, he—"

"This is my son," the general hissed, sending a glare Kaylene's way. "I make decisions for him. *Not* a panther lady *señorita*. He has humiliated me enough by what he has done, let alone now, by lying his head like a child on the lap of a woman!"

"Father, I do not believe I have the strength," Pedro said, groaning as he tried to raise himself to a sitting position. He cried out when he put his full weight on his leg. "My leg! Father, I cannot stand on my leg!"

General Rocendo's eyes wavered. He turned and backoned to his guard, Jose. "Jose, come and get Pedro," he shouted.

Kaylene breathed more easily as she saw the more tender side of the general surface. She gave Pedro a hug, then sat back from him as Jose came and gently took him into his arms.

"*Capitan* Fire Thunder," General Rocendo said, clasping his hands together behind him, "my son and his friends will never interfere in the lives of the Kickapoo again. You have my word. They will stay in the perimeters of their city, or pay for their disobedience."

"As far as Running Fawn and her three friends are concerned, it is too late now for such promises," Fire Thunder said tightly. "The girls' reputations are already ruined. They will be exiled from my village! And I forbid them to come here, to be a part of the lives of Mexicans, the very people who have caused their shame."

Kaylene was stunned to hear this. Fire Thunder had ignored her pleas. Running Fawn and her friends were going to pay the full price for their sins after all.

Kaylene so badly wanted to understand. People made mistakes. They learned from their mistakes! She couldn't understand why Fire Thunder couldn't give these girls a second chance.

Pedro paled when he heard what Fire Thunder had planned for Running Fawn. "No!" he cried. "Do not banish her. But if you must, do not keep her from coming to me. Although we are only children in your eyes, we are in love. I want to marry her!"

"Running Fawn and her friends' punishments must be real," Fire Thunder growled. "It must be truly felt. You will never see Running Fawn again!"

"I love her!" Pedro cried, tears flooding his eyes. He reached out for his father. "Tell him, Father, that you will allow her in our house as my wife. Tell him, Father. I love Running Fawn! Please, Father? Please?"

"Pedro, your fever is causing you to talk out of your head," General Rocendo shouted. "Jose, take him away. I don't want to hear any more of his lunacy!"

"I will go now," Fire Thunder said, swinging himself back into his saddle. "But be warned, keep your young men away from our girls, or there will be hell to pay."

Kaylene sucked in a wild breath when she saw the sudden anger flash in the general's eyes.

She was glad when the wagon made a wide turn and they were soon out of the general's courtyard, and on the road that led up the mountainside.

She scrabbled from the back of the wagon and sat down on the seat beside the silent warrior.

She cast Fire Thunder occasional glances as he rode his horse beside the wagon. He was quiet and brooding as he kept his eyes forward, away from hers.

Then he slid his eyes slowly her way.

She grabbed the opportunity to speak.

"Are you certain you wish to be so harsh on the girls?" she murmured, her eyes defiant. "There is such a thing as forgiveness for sins. Would it be so hard to give them a second chance? Why punish them so severely?"

"I have made up my mind and will not change it," Fire Thunder said, his jaw tight. "It is an example for the other young girls who might chance filling their stomachs with a child at age fifteen! And such behavior tempts warring between my people and the Mexicans. Did you not see how close General Rocendo and I came to words that could cause a bitter hatred between us? No. I cannot. I will not change my mind."

Feeling unnerved by Fire Thunder's harsh decision, Kaylene grew silent.

Yet she knew that the Kickapoo had their customs; she had hers.

She would just have to accept what they did, or forget her plans to marry Fire Thunder. And loving him so much, she could not forsake Fire Thunder. Not for anyone, or for any reason.

When they arrived at their village, Kaylene watched Fire Thunder dismount and give the reins to a young brave. He did not look her way as she climbed from the wagon.

Her insides grew cold when she saw the determination in his steps as he walked toward Black Hair's lodge.

Knowing what he was about to do, and fearing for Running Fawn, Kaylene followed him, but kept far enough back so that he would not know that she was there. She did not want to give him the opportunity to turn and scold her, and send her to his lodge.

Hearing whispers on all sides of her, Kaylene looked over her shoulder and noticed that everyone had heard the arrival of their chief. They had come from their lodges and were watching Fire Thunder.

When Fire Thunder stepped up to Black Hair's lodge, he did not have to announce his presence. Black Hair had also heard Fire Thunder's arrival. He came outside, a firm grip on one of Running Fawn's wrists as he half-dragged her with him.

Kaylene moved closer as Fire Thunder and Black Hair stood eye to eye.

"My decision is made," Fire Thunder said, his eyes locked with Black Hair's. "My friend, I must send your daughter and her friends away from the village, to live in exile. You know, as I, that I have no other choice."

Running Fawn screamed and wrenched herself free from her father's steely grip. She ran to Kaylene and grabbed her hands. "Tell Fire Thunder not to do this!" she cried. "He loves you. He will listen to you. Please, Kaylene, tell him not to send me and my friends away!"

Fire Thunder went to Running Fawn. Gently, he took her by an arm. "Do not bring my woman into this," he said softly. "Running Fawn, go and gather up your belongings. This is the time to prove that you are strong, that you have the brave heart of a Kickapoo."

"Fire Thunder, are you sure you must do this?" Kaylene asked, her voice breaking.

"All people need authority," Fire Thunder said, his voice thick with regret of what he was forced to do to four of his people. "I am my people's voice. Never must I falter in my decisions that affect my people's future. The youth, the children *are* my people's future. They must lead clean, respectable lives. Making love loosely, unwed, at such a young age, and with young men not of our culture, soils the bodies and futures of those who commit such sins. I will not have children walking around my village heavy with child to display their disobedience, their sins. Our youth, as they grow into adulthood, must set good examples. Running Fawn and her friends were given many chances to prove they were good at heart; clean in spirit. I have come to the very end of my patience. What must be done, will be done."

Kaylene stifled a sob behind a hand.

When she felt a gentle hand on her arm, she turned and gazed into violet eyes.

Dawnmarie slipped an arm around her waist. "Come with me," she murmured. "Let Fire Thunder do his duty as chief, as I often had to step aside to let White Wolf do what he must do as chief. You will learn in time to accept that what your beloved does is for the betterment of his people."

Kaylene gave Fire Thunder a soft gaze, smiled a quiet apology for having spoken out of turn, then turned and walked away with Dawnmarie toward Fire Thunder's lodge.

When Little Sparrow came and took her other hand, Kaylene was able to put what was happening behind her, to the farthest recesses of her mind.

Fire Thunder went and got the other three young women and waited for them to get their belongings.

Then when all four girls were huddled together, Fire Thunder embraced them each and said a soft prayer over them.

"Go in peace," Fire Thunder said softly. "*Kitzhiat*, our Great Spirit, will always be with you."

Downcast, tears silvering their eyes, the girls left together.

Solemn and heavy hearted, Black Hair watched his one and only child leave the village. His gaze shifted to the mothers of the other three girls. In their grief, they were chanting, crying, and pulling at their hair.

He looked again at the girls as they walked farther and farther from the village. And although he knew that their expulsion was the fate of those who lived reckless, shameful lives, he could hardly bear to live with the decision, or without Running Fawn.

Although he was trying to be strong, he hung his head. He was so tormented, he was not sure if he could make it another day with the guilt lying heavy on his heart.

His own daughter! How could she have done this? She betrayed *his* loyalty to their chief by her wrongful behavior.

He turned to say something to Fire Thunder, to apologize again, but Fire Thunder was almost at his cabin.

Everyone turning their backs on him, Black Hair walked through the village until he got to the corral. He saddled his horse then swung himself into the saddle and rode away in a different direction from the path that took Running Fawn away from him.

He had to get away, to think, to plan his future which no longer included a daughter.

He had to plan a future that surely no longer held the full respect of his best friend, his *chief*.

24

It smites my soul with sudden sickening;
It binds my being with a wreath of rue—
This want of you.
                                    —Ivan Leonard Wright

Two days had passed and the Kickapoo were involved
in another celebration—the first of three Feasts for
the Dead ceremonies, which always followed the New
Year. No children were allowed. Only the adult men
and women participated in this solemn ritual.

It was midmorning. Fire Thunder sat on the west
bench, with Kaylene at his left side, while the other
Kickapoo men and women, among them Dawnmarie
and White Wolf, sat on the north and south benches,
all facing the fire. A ladle rested on everyone's lap,
which would be used during the ceremony.

Ten copper kettles of food were cooking over the
fire. This was the ideal amount for this particular feast.

But only one type of food simmered in these pots—
ne-pupe, stew, the ceremonial meal.

The stew was made up of venison ribs, squash, and
Indian corn. Fried bread also lay in large heaps on

platters, as well as small cakes made from wild berries harvested in the forest.

Earlier in the day, Fire Thunder had explained this special, *necessary*, ceremony to Kaylene. He had told her that the spirits of the Kickapoo dead must eat three times a year, as the living were required to eat three meals a day. Otherwise the spirits would become hungry and be forced to eat foam off the water in the mountain streams.

He had further explained to Kaylene that the spirits did not look kindly upon their Kickapoo relatives when this negligence occurred, and might bring them harm. Therefore, after the death of a relative, it was incumbent that someone in the family assume the life-long responsibility of attending the three annual feasts.

The hosts were many today, for all adults attending the ceremony had lost a loved one during their lifetimes.

The feast meant more than one certainty to Kaylene. Soon after, when the sun rose tomorrow, she would be saying a final farewell to Dawnmarie.

And that made her sad. Kaylene hated to see Dawn-marie leave, because Dawnmarie had become a sort of mother figure to her. Theirs was a genuine sharing. Unlike what Kaylene had found with Running Fawn, there was a trust between herself and Dawnmarie.

Also, tomorrow, John Shelton was going to be released from his captivity—not so much to give him his freedom, but to give him the chance to unknowingly lead Kaylene to the carnival, so that she could question the woman she now knew was not her mother.

Fire Thunder was responsive to Kaylene's troubled heart, to her *needs*, and had volunteered to help her find her true mother after procuring the needed information from Anna Shelton.

Of course it went against Fire Thunder's grain to

release a guilty man from imprisonment before he had received his full punishment.

But Kaylene had convinced him that John had suffered much already while being caged in total isolation. Surely just sitting there pondering his fate from day to day had put the fear of God in him, perhaps causing him to change his ways.

Yet deep down inside where Kaylene's memories were sharpest of John's mental, and sometimes physical abuse to Anna Shelton, she had to wonder whether or not she should help him return to be a part of Anna's life again. Kaylene's only hope was that the captivity *had* changed John Shelton.

Yet she had not fully trusted that enough to ask John to willingly lead her to the carnival. Knowing the mean side of him so well, Kaylene dared not depend on him changing so much so quickly.

Therefore, they would follow him without him being aware of their presence on the trail.

Kaylene gazed over at Dawnmarie, where she sat opposite the fire from her on the bench. She smiled when she saw Dawnmarie's radiance, and the peace she outwardly showed as she sat among her true people, participating in the ceremony that would bond her with them for eternity.

Dawnmarie surely had to know now, for certain, that she had a place in the hereafter with those who had passed on before her. A place was being reserved in the heavens, where she would one day walk hand in hand again with her dearly departed mother, Doe Eyes.

Kaylene frowned when she looked among the warriors who sat around the fire. Black Hair wasn't there. No one had seen him since Running Fawn had left the village.

Sighing, Kaylene realized that the celebration today

was tarnished somewhat by the girls being sent into exile, and from those who loved Black Hair, wondering where he might be. He hadn't told anyone he was leaving, yet he had gone without a trace.

Everything was keenly quiet in the council house. There were no musical instruments playing. All that could be heard above the popping and hissing of fire in the firepit, were the breaths of the people.

All waited for Fire Thunder to begin the ceremony. It would not last long, but it meant very much to everyone who was in attendance today.

Fire Thunder stepped down from his bench. He withdrew a small pouch from his front right breeches pocket. He held it in the palm of his left hand as he rose his eyes upward, his voice low and husky as he prayed and chanted.

He stopped long enough to open the pouch and sprinkle some tobacco into the fire. This was his offering to the spirits.

He again prayed, notifying the other *manitou* to carry the message to the spirits of the deceased who dwelled in the West with *Pepazce*. The spirits were urged to attend the feast.

Goosebumps rose on Kaylene's flesh as Fire Thunder continued to pray, asking for blessings and long life for all those present. He prayed for Dawnmarie, asking the spirits to accept her as one with them.

When Fire Thunder's prayers ceased and he sat down again beside Kaylene, an elderly man stepped forth who was called the "waiter" today. With a trembling hand, he dipped his ladle into one of the pots of stew and took a bit of the food from the brass kettle. He slowly poured the food on the ground to the west of the fire, this also a gift for the spirits.

After he had served the spirits, he emptied the contents of the kettle into large pans and placed several in front of the benches where the people sat, quietly waiting to do what was required of them next.

He then passed everyone broken pieces of fried bread, and then bits of the sweet berry cakes.

Before everyone began to eat, Fire Thunder rose from the bench again and sprinkled a bit of Indian tobacco near the food for the spirits and invited them to join them for this occasion.

"Your sons and daughters are giving you tobacco and a feast," Fire Thunder said, his eyes lifted heavenward. "Surely come and join us in this occasion."

He sat back down and joined the others as they quietly partook of the food.

While eating, and being a part of this spiritual ritual, Kaylene felt the same strange feelings overwhelm her that she had felt countless times since she had arrived at this Indian village.

She did not feel awkward or strange partaking in this ceremony. She felt as though she had done it before, somewhere in time, through the eyes of someone else, yet in truth, whose eyes were now her own.

A shiver raced through her when she felt as though someone's breath was touching her cheek in a soft, caressing kiss. But Fire Thunder was the only one near her, and he was meditatively eating the food, not even offering her a quick glance, much less a kiss.

The strangeness of these feelings somewhat frightened her. Would she ever know why it was happening? How would anyone even know how to explain it?

The food now gone from the pans and large copper pots, Fire Thunder rose to his feet again and prayed. "Spirits who are here today, who have been honored with this feast and caring, please be kindly disposed toward my people, look after them. Remember always they have not forgotten *you*. Hear the words of the hearts of those people assembled here today. The smoke of tobacco rises. Give attention to our words as they rise to you in the smoke."

When the prayer was over, everyone rose and left quietly through the door at the north side of the lodge.

The last to leave, Kaylene walked beside Fire Thunder toward the north door.

A sound behind her caused her to look over her shoulder just as the waiter took a burned end of a log and carefully raked the food and tobacco that had been offered to the spirits into the fire.

Fire Thunder caught her looking at what the waiter was doing. "The fire will be allowed to burn until morning," he explained. "Before breakfast tomorrow the ashes will be gathered and taken outside, to the west side of the council house, in a place specifically reserved for this purpose."

"You told me that there are three such ceremonies like the one that was performed today," Kaylene said as she walked with Fire Thunder. "When will the next one be held?"

"The second Feast of the Dead will be held in the summer when cantaloupe and watermelon will be the main foods served," he said, smiling at White Wolf as he and Dawnmarie waited outside for them.

"And so do you think our wives can do without us for a while?" White Wolf said, clasping a gentle hand on Fire Thunder's right shoulder.

"I think they would not mind if we leave for a while as I show you my longhorn cattle, and the land that I am so proud of in this beautiful mountain valley," Fire Thunder said, smiling at Kaylene. "I believe my woman wants time alone with your wife, anyway. They have good-byes of their own to say."

"Please do go on," Kaylene murmured. "Dawnmarie and I do have much to say before she leaves tomorrow."

"And you, Violet Eyes?" White Wolf asked as he dropped his hand from Fire Thunder's shoulder, to take his wife's hands in his. "Do you mind?"

"It is not as though we won't be together day and night these next several weeks as we travel back to our Wisconsin homeland," she said, laughing softly. She stood on tiptoe and gave White Wolf a kiss on his cheek. "Go on, darling. Enjoy."

Kaylene and Dawnmarie stood back and watched their men ride off on their horses.

Kaylene sighed. "Aren't they both so handsome?" she murmured.

"Yes, and my husband is as handsome as the day I first laid eyes on him at my father's trading post those many years ago," Dawnmarie said, for a moment going back in time.

She fondly recalled that day when she had stood at the doorway of the trading post, so bashful, so in love, as she had watched White Wolf walk up the path toward her from the river.

When their eyes had met and held, she had felt such a strange, wondrous melting at the pit of her stomach.

Dawnmarie had loved White Wolf instantly. Completely.

And now it was so many years later and she still loved him as much.

"It shows," Kaylene said, placing a gentle hand to Dawnmarie's cheek.

"What shows?" Dawnmarie said, her eyes gleaming with wonderful memories.

"How much you love him," Kaylene murmured.

"As I see it in the way you look at Fire Thunder how much you love him," Dawnmarie said, drawing Kaylene into her arms, gently hugging her.

"He may hate me after what I do today," Kaylene

said, her voice breaking. "Yet I feel I must, to help *you*."

Dawnmarie stepped away from Kaylene. "You do not have to go into her lodge," she murmured. "I shall encourage her to step outside. We can talk as well there, as inside."

"But if I am seen outside with Moon Glow, even that might enrage Fire Thunder enough into thinking that he can't trust me," Kaylene demurred.

"Then I encourage you not to go with me," Dawnmarie said softly. "I want to do nothing that might cause a strain between you and Fire Thunder."

"Perhaps I *had* best wait for you in Fire Thunder's cabin," Kaylene said, never wanting to do anything to upset Fire Thunder. The Kickapoo rules were rigidly obeyed. If she broke just one of their rules now, she might lose fire Thunder forever.

"I won't be long," Dawnmarie said, lifting the skirt of her white doeskin dress and walking away.

Kaylene watched, then turned and walked toward Fire Thunder's cabin. She smiled when she saw Little Sparrow standing in the door with Midnight at her side.

She ran to them. She knelt and embraced Little Sparrow, then Midnight.

Then she leaned away from them both and spoke in the sign language that she was learning to use more skillfully each day, and told Little Sparrow that she had missed her during the ceremony.

Little Sparrow told her that soon she would be old enough to participate in all the activities of their people. A soft color of pink flooded her cheeks when she told Kaylene that she now had a boyfriend. He even overlooked her inability to speak. She was teaching him her sign language. He enjoyed learning.

Kaylene told her that she was glad, then hugged

Little Sparrow again as her thoughts were filled with
how Moon Glow would react to Dawnmarie's question, a question spoken from the depths of Dawnmarie's heart.

"Moon Glow," Dawnmarie said, as she stood just
outside the Trotter's small wigwam. "It is I, Dawnmarie. Please come out and talk with me. I am leaving
tomorrow. I have something to ask you."

She waited patiently in the deep, dark shadows of
the trees that surrounded Moon Glow's lodge. The
coolness of the forest interior wafted by and touched
Dawnmarie's cheeks. She felt a chill run slowly up and
down her spine the longer she waited. She hugged
herself, her eyes wavering, thinking that Moon Glow
did not want to see her.

She started to turn and leave when suddenly the
entrance flap was swept aside and Moon Glow was
there, a cat in the crook of her left arm, the others
slinking around her ankles, looking up at Dawnmarie
with their luminous eyes.

"I knew you would not leave without saying good-
bye," Moon Glow said in her raspy, old voice.

"I thought you perhaps didn't want to, since you
did not come out right away," Dawnmarie said, her
gaze moving slowly over Moon Glow.

Her gray, thinning hair touched the ground in awkward wisps. She wore a shabby robe of white rabbit
fur which she had surely had way back when she knew
Dawnmarie's mother. Her eyes were weary, their dark
brown color now almost gray. But in them Dawnmarie
saw a warmth and love.

"I was not sure if I should come out when you
called my name," Moon Glow said, looking quickly
past Dawnmarie, to see if anyone saw them standing
there, talking. "I was not sure if Fire Thunder would

approve. I waited to see if he came to whisk you away." She cackled as her eyes moved back to Dawnmarie. "Since he did not come, I had to believe that you succeeded at coming without him seeing you."

"He is with my husband on horseback, enjoying the last hours he has with him as he shows him his land and longhorns," Dawnmarie murmured.

"Yes, I have seen the longhorns and I have seen the land, but only in my dreams," Moon Glow said, her voice taking on a melancholy hollowness. "I have only glimpsed the longhorns as they have been driven on the outskirts of the village toward their pasture. That was enough to give me cause to dream of them. I, before I became labeled the Trotter, knew the land as well as anyone. I, too, enjoyed taking walks, looking at and feeling the peacefulness of everything. It is so much different than Wisconsin, Illinois, or Indiana. Even Texas. I like this place. It is good that Fire Thunder's leadership was strong enough to settle our people here."

"Then you would not leave, even if it meant that you would no longer be forced to live in isolation?" Dawnmarie said, watching Moon Glow's expression change to that of wonder.

"I have never been given the chance to leave," Moon Glow said softly. "Even when I gave my people cause to label me as different than they, I was not banished. I was able to stay."

"Then would you leave if given the chance since you have been forced into a life of isolation?" Dawnmarie asked, her voice and eyes anxious.

"Daughter of my friend Doe Eyes, what are you saying?" Moon Glow said warily.

The cat on Moon Glow's arm leaped, hissing, when Dawnmarie reached for Moon Glow's hands and took them.

"Moon Glow, come with me and White Wolf," Dawn-marie blurted out, aware of the boniness of Moon Glow's hands. "Live with us in our village many suns' ride from here, in Wisconsin. There you will live a life free of disgrace. No one there will know of your past. You can begin life anew. Surely you can be happier there than here, where you are, in a sense, a prisoner."

"You are your mother's daughter," Moon Glow said, her voice breaking. "Like Doe Eyes, you are a woman of a kind and generous heart. But I cannot go with you."

"I don't understand," Dawnmarie said, stunned that Moon Glow would refuse this chance to leave her life of seclusion. "How could you want to stay here, where no one is allowed to talk to you?"

"Although I am living a sort of exiled life among my people here in the Mexican mountains, in truth I feel important," Moon Glow tried to explain. "I have the power to absorb the sins of others so that those who have sinned can begin life anew, as though born again. If I leave, who then would my people look to for help?"

Dawnmarie choked back a sob to see this elderly woman who was once her mother's very best friend think only of others. Her mother had been the same. She always put other people before herself. Dawn-marie had never wanted for anything that her mother could possibly get for her.

Dawnmarie took the frail, elderly woman within her gentle arms. "I will not say any more to you about leaving," she murmured. "But even though I am leav-ing you behind, I will take a part of you with me inside my heart."

"As your mother did those long years ago when she was stolen from her people," Moon Glow said, her voice breaking. "I never forgot your mother, nor her goodness." She cackled as she leaned away from

Dawnmarie. "She and I differed in one respect. I could not love just one man. I loved them all."

Dawnmarie laughed softly when she saw that that thought brought a look of satisfaction to Moon Glow's eyes, as well as enough memories perhaps to content her until she walked the road to the hereafter.

"I imagine you were beautiful, so beautiful the men could not stay away from you," Dawnmarie said, her eyes dancing.

"Your mother was as beautiful, but *she* knew how to turn her back on temptation," Moon Glow said, cackling again. Then she grew somber. "And dear, sweet Running Fawn has the same restlessness as I did. But it was whose arms she chose to fill that was the difference. I never looked for loving elsewhere. The men I bedded were always Kickapoo!"

Then Dawnmarie heard horses arriving at the village, and thinking it might be Fire Thunder and White Wolf returning, she grabbed Moon Glow in her arms and gave her a last hug. "I truly must go now," she whispered. She clung to Moon Glow, the same as she might her mother were she still alive. "I will never forget you."

"Nor shall I you," Moon Glow said, then broke away and hurried back inside her wigwam, her cats trailing along behind her.

Dawnmarie wiped tears from her eyes. She felt as though she was saying another good-bye to her mother. She then rushed away from the small wigwam nestled amidst the thick stand of trees.

When she stepped out into the sunshine, she smiled, for everything was finished and she had the rest of her life to fill with her children, and . . . grandchildren! Tomorrow she would begin her journey home, her *true* home.

25

Brightest truth, purest truth in the universe,
All were for me
In the kiss of one girl.
—ROBERT BROWNING

The procession was slow as it made its way down the mountainside. They stayed far enough back from John Shelton so that he was not aware of being followed. Fire Thunder had released him from captivity and handed him the reins of a burro, and John had realized that he was free to go. Kaylene had stood stiffly at Fire Thunder's side watching John's reaction. She could tell that he was suspicious of the release.

And he had the right to be, for although released, he was still somewhat a captive. If he did not lead Fire Thunder and Kaylene to the carnival, Fire Thunder would quickly confront him. If John Shelton suspected why he had been released, and refused to lead Kaylene to Anna Shelton, so that she could question her, John Shelton's freedom would be shortlived. As it was, he was lucky enough to get a second chance at life again, once his use to Kaylene was over.

The sun was moving toward the zenith, as noon approached. Kaylene realized how long she had been on horseback. Eight hours.

They had risen and left before dawn.

And they might have to travel until the moon was high in the sky to finally reach the carnival. Several warriors had stayed behind to guard the Kickapoo village in Fire Thunder's absence. Several more warriors were traveling with Fire Thunder, Kaylene, White Wolf, and Dawnmarie.

Kaylene was already weary from the journey, San Carlos having been left behind long ago. They had crossed the Rio Grande, and were now riding along its shore in Texas.

"We are almost at the departure point," Dawnmarie said as she sidled her horse closer to Kaylene's gentle mare. "It is sad that we have only met and become friends to then so soon say good-bye."

"You said that you are going to return to Fire Thunder's village from time to time to be with your people again," Kaylene said, smiling softly at Dawnmarie. "Our friendship will strengthen with each of your visits."

"Yes, we will return, should our health hold up and allow it," Dawnmarie said, glancing at White Wolf, who was riding beside Fire Thunder, talking. She looked at Kaylene again. "You are getting a good man when you marry Fire Thunder. When do you think the marriage ceremony will be held?"

"Soon, so says Fire Thunder," Kaylene said, thrilled at the thought of being with him forever. "I can hardly wait."

"But you are smart to first seek the truth about your parents' identities," Dawnmarie said, becoming somewhat somber. "My life would have been more fulfilled had I found my true people sooner. Although

I do not see how, since White Wolf has been so good to me, I am certain that I would have been happier had I made peace with my people long ago. Perhaps soon you will be able to make peace with your troubled heart."

"But what if the names of my parents are never known?" Kaylene murmured. "What if my . . . if Anna cannot remember? What if she won't tell me? What if my parents are *dead*?"

"Do not burden your heart with such concerns until you are given cause to," Dawnmarie said, reaching over to gently touch Kaylene's arm. "Have faith, much as I, and your wishes will come true. You will know your parents. You will then have cause to rejoice."

Fire Thunder drew a tight rein. He wheeled his horse around and rode back to Kaylene and Dawnmarie, White Wolf beside him.

White Wolf edged his horse up closer to Dawnmarie's. He reached over and gave her a soft kiss on her cheek. "Violet Eyes, this is where we must head homeward," he said, gesturing toward the east. He then gave Kaylene a warm smile. "Kaylene, this is where we must say a farewell, but not a final one. As long as our bodies are able, I will bring my wife to Mexico to be with her people. Soon you will be Fire Thunder's wife. When Violet Eyes and I return, you might even have a child to share with us."

"Yes, I shall act as grandmother to the child," Dawnmarie said, laughing softly.

"That would be wonderful," Kaylene said, her insides glowing at the thought of having children with Fire Thunder, and of giving the child a true home.

Dawnmarie reached over and hugged Kaylene. "Be happy," she whispered.

"Please be careful on the long journey that lies ahead of you," Kaylene said, returning the hug.

Dawnmarie led her horse to one side while White Wolf came and gave Kaylene a hug, then clasped hands of friendship with Fire Thunder.

"May the Great Spirit follow you forever and keep you safe," Fire Thunder said, his voice drawn.

Kaylene and Fire Thunder's horses moved closer. They waved at Dawnmarie and White Wolf as they rode away.

They continued on their own journey, a scout having gone ahead to keep track of John Shelton.

They rode in silence for a while longer. Then in the distance, Kaylene caught her first sight of several tents, and many wagons that were spread out along the river.

"They have made camp, it seems, not knowing where to go, or what to do, without the leadership of your father," Fire Thunder said. He nodded. "See now how your father is so close? Soon they will know that he has been released unharmed."

"Surely the carnival men will become suspicious of his release," Kaylene said, drawing a tight rein alongside Fire Thunder. They were far enough back, with several trees obscuring the view of the carnival tents, yet close enough to watch what was happening there.

Soon there was a flurry of activity as John was spied riding toward the campsite. Men, women, and children ran out to meet him.

Kaylene swallowed hard. Tears of regret filled her eyes when she saw the familiar figure of Anne Shelton come into view, hesitant, not appearing all that happy to see that her husband was alive.

And Kaylene understood. Surely being separated from him, had given Anna a peaceful heart if only for a short time.

Guilt spread throughout Kaylene, that she was, in part, responsible for John's reappearance in Anna's life. Now she wondered if it had been right to sacrifice Anna's happiness to ensure her own.

John slid from his burro and walked it on toward the camp, Anna walking a short distance behind him, now seemingly hesitant at how to react in his presence. He even ignored *her*.

Fire Thunder yanked his rifle from its gunboot. "Are you sure you want to do this?" he asked, giving Kaylene a wavering stare.

"I was, until I was reminded of John's cruelty to Anna," Kaylene murmured. "But now?" Her jaw tightened and her eyes flared with a renewed anger over what had been kept from her all those years, and by whom.

"Yes, I'm quite positive I want to do this," she said. She took a small derringer from her front skirt pocket and clutched its handle tightly.

"We will not use the firearms unless our lives are threatened," Fire Thunder reassured her. "If gunfire breaks out, go into hiding. Kaylene, I do not want to lose you while I am trying to make life right for you."

"I'll be all right," Kaylene said, swallowing hard.

Fire Thunder raised his rifle into the air as his men swarmed around him, their own firearms drawn.

Kaylene rode off with them. She kept close to Fire Thunder's side. She scarcely breathed, she was so afraid. And in a matter of minutes she found herself with the Kickapoo warriors and Fire Thunder in a wide circle around the camp, the men in the camp rendered helpless beneath the aim of so many firearms.

John Shelton sent a seething glare at Fire Thunder, and then Kaylene. "I should have known that you weren't letting me go just from the goodness of your hearts," he said, his voice a low, angry hiss.

Ignoring him, Kaylene dismounted, her eyes locked

with Anna's. Her heart thundered wildly as she moved toward this woman she had loved from childhood, yet now was hesitant to embrace.

This woman had deceived her. How could she ever have any feelings for her again?

"Kaylene, darling," Anna said, running toward her. Kaylene eased her derringer to her side as Anna came closer. She took a step away from Anna, not able to embrace her as they came face-to-face.

"Kaylene, what's the matter?" Anna asked, tears filling her eyes. She gazed at the small gun in Kaylene's hand, then questioned her again with her eyes. "Why are you behaving like this? Why was your father released, and then the Indians have come and surrounded us, their firearms drawn?" Again she looked at the derringer and stifled a sob behind her hand. "And, Lord, Kaylene, even *you* are armed."

Kaylene could hardly stand there so cold and impersonal in the presence of this lady. Her very heart seemed to be wrenched from inside her. For no matter how much Anna had deceived her, Kaylene knew now, as she stood so close to her, that a part of her would always love her.

And pity overwhelmed Kaylene, pity for a woman who had always been forced to bend to the will of her husband.

Yet Kaylene still didn't embrace her, even though she wanted to with every fiber of her being.

"I know that you are not my mother," Kaylene finally blurted out. Anna's whole body lurched as though she had been slapped.

In order to trick this woman into being truthful to her, Kaylene chose to use a tactic that might draw a quick reaction from Anna and, inevitably, the truth. "John Shelton, the man who professed to being my father as far back as I can remember, told me that you aren't my parents," Kaylene said, her voice drawn as she watched Anna cover a wild, disbelieving gasp behind one of her hands.

John stepped up next to Anna, his eyes wide.

Then he looked slowly down at Anna, whose eyes were on him, condemning him for having told such a truth. "I d-didn't tell her," John stammered out. "Anna, I swear it. I never told her anything of the kind. I have no idea where she got the idea!"

A dark scowl covered John's face and he turned glaring eyes toward Fire Thunder. He started to say that this was all Fire Thunder's fault, but stumbled over the words, knowing that anything he said now could mean life or death to him. John's fate was all up to Fire Thunder. So not to antagonize him, he stopped in midsentence and gave his wife a wavering, apologetic stare.

Then what happened next was so fast, no one had any chance to stop it.

Anna grabbed the derringer from Kaylene's hand. She aimed it at John. She pulled the trigger and shot John. Then she cried softly when he clutched his chest and fell to the ground, writhing at her feet.

As he gazed wildly up at Anna, she dropped the derringer and covered her mouth with a hand. "Why did you have to tell her?" she sobbed. "She'd have never known! She ... was ... all I had in life. I lost you long ago. All I was to you was something to beat on and berate when you were angry. Well, John Shelton, I've just changed that. Die then! Rot in hell!"

John shifted his gaze toward Kaylene. He reached a hand out for her, his eyes pleading. Then he rolled over in spasms, and lay quietly in his own pool of blood.

"Lord ..." Kaylene said, numb from what had happened. She looked quickly over at Anna. "You . . . killed . . . him."

"Yes, and I should have done it long ago," Anna cried. She turned and ran from Kaylene, then fell in a heap as she fainted just outside her personal tent.

"I'm so stunned by all of this," Kaylene murmured as Fire Thunder placed a gentle, comforting arm around her waist. "I never thought my tricking my mother into telling me the truth, herself, would cause this. She killed him, Fire Thunder. She actually killed him."

"Her rage has built up inside her through the years against this man who was cruel to her," Fire Thunder said. "A person can take just so much abuse, so much badgering. Then when she thought that he had told you the truth about your birthright, that was all it needed to make her snap. This man had taken from her something precious. You were all that she had left. And now she doesn't even have you."

"It's so sad," Kaylene said, wiping tears from her eyes. Her tears were not for John, but for the way it had turned out. It had started the day they had taken her to raise as theirs.

"Go to your mother," Fire Thunder said thickly.

"Mother . . . ?" Kaylene said, giving him a startled, questioning glance.

"In a sense she is," Fire Thunder said. "She loves you, Kaylene. She has sacrificed for you. Go to her. She is a woman in need."

"But she is also a murderess," Kaylene said, an involuntary shiver racing across her flesh.

Fire Thunder clasped her shoulders with his hands. "She has done everyone a good deed by ridding the world of that vile man," he said. "Go to her. Hold her. Then question her. Perhaps now she will tell you the full truth."

Kaylene gave Fire Thunder a soft kiss on his lips, then turned and went to Anna.

Several women were caring for her, wiping her brow with a cloth, trying to awaken her. Kaylene nodded to the women and they stepped aside.

She knelt down beside Anna and she placed a gentle hand to her brow. "Mother," she murmured, "please wake up. I'm sorry if I hurt you. I do love you, but . . . but . . . I want to know my true mother."

Anna slowly opened her eyes. Tears filled them again when she found Kaylene there, being so sweet, so gentle, so caring. As she had awakened, she had heard Kaylene call her mother.

She reached a hand out for Kaylene. "I do love you so," she murmured. "Kaylene, you are my life."

"And I love you," Kaylene said, trying desperately to brush aside the fact that this woman had deceived her for so long. "But that doesn't keep me from wanting to know my true mother. Please tell me. It's not fair keeping it from me any longer."

Trembling, Anna moved to a sitting position. She hugged herself as she gazed at Kaylene. "Yes, I will tell you," she murmured. "Then you will know that it is not as bad as it seems, your being here, raised as my child."

"Please tell me everything," Kaylene said, as Fire Thunder came and stood over her and Anna, listening.

"One day, long ago, while giving a show at Laredo, an ailing lady named Eloisa Soriano, came to me with her six-month-old baby," Anna said, her voice drawn. "The woman explained that she was ill and that she was unwed. She was from Gypsy stock, but had been cast away when it was discovered that she was in the first stages of leprosy."

Kaylene paled and gasped. "Leprosy?" she said, in barely a whisper.

"With my husband's consent, I took the child, a precious tiny girl," Anna said softly. "Before the woman left, she told me that if I ever wanted to bring the child by on occasions, for her to see from a distance, so as not to give the child leprosy, she would be living in Laredo."

"Did you?" Kaylene asked, her eyes wide, her heart thumping wildly to know the truth, troubling though it was. And it was wonderful, it was a relief, to know that she hadn't been stolen, and that she had been taken in to raise as a daughter, not as a slave. Knowing that meant a lot to her.

"No," Anna said, slowly shaking her head. "Never. I feared the leprosy. And I feared that she might change her mind and want you back."

"Do you think she is alive?" Kaylene asked, hardly able to envision what the lady might look like with the leprosy. She knew little about the disease. It terribly disfigured a person. And no one would go near anyone with it. They were usually outcast from the community.

"I'm not certain if she is or isn't," Anna said, then reached over and placed a gentle hand on Kaylene's face. "Through the years, Kaylene, John for the most part behaved kindly toward you. When he became greedy and loved tequila too much, he totally changed. He beat me whenever he chose to. And he saw you as a draw for the carnival, especially when you found the baby panther and raised it into a tame adult. That's when John started seeing you more as an object for making money, than as a daughter."

Anna hung her head in her hands. "You don't know how often I begged him not to treat you like the other children he stole and placed into slavery," she cried. "But he would never listen. He was blinded by so many things. I'm ... glad that I shot him."

"So Father *did* abduct other children," Kaylene

said, shivering at the thought of how many she had seen working in the carnival.

"Yes, they were abducted," Anna said, lifting desperate eyes to Kaylene. "That is why we had to keep on moving so often, from town to town, from state to state. He was always afraid of being caught. In the end, he became too smug ... too careless."

Anna flung herself into Kaylene's arms. "I have always loved you," she cried. "I love you now, as though you are my true child. Do not forsake me, Kaylene. Not now, not when I need you so much."

Kaylene looked up at Fire Thunder. "Can she go back to the village with us?" she asked hoarsely. "Fire Thunder, I just can't abandon her. Please? Can I take her with me?"

Fire Thunder hesitated, then nodded. "Yes, if that is what you wish," he said, clasping his hands tightly behind him.

Kaylene framed her mother's face between her hands. "Mother, will you take me to my true mother?" she asked warily.

"Kaylene, is it not enough that you know who your true mother was?" Fire Thunder said, bending to a knee beside her. "Leprosy. It is a bad disease. Do not chance getting it."

"I will keep my distance, Fire Thunder," she said in a rush of words. "I have come this close to knowing my true mother. How can you expect me not to go all of the way?"

Then a thought came to Kaylene. "Mother, who is my true father?" she asked softly.

"I have no idea," Anna murmured. "Your mother would not confess such a truth to me. Perhaps she doesn't even know herself who impregnated her."

"I must find out everything I can," Kaylene said determinedly.

She looked up at Fire Thunder again. "You *will* take me to search for my true mother in Laredo, won't you?" she asked softly. "It is important for me to see her at least just this once. And to allow her to see me, the daughter she gave away. I want her to see the man I am going to marry!"

Fire Thunder rose to his full height. He took Kaylene's hands and urged her to her feet. He wrapped his arms around her waist and drew her into his embrace. "My woman, I will do anything for you, you know that," he said thickly. "Yes, we will go to Laredo. But if your mother is no longer there, the search stops there. Do you agree?"

"Yes," Kaylene murmured, hugging him. "Thank you, darling. Thank you for giving me this chance."

"But we must leave now," Fire Thunder said, easing her from his arms. He turned to Anna. "If you are going with us, you must leave now. You must leave all of this behind you. You will start a new life among my people." He glanced over at John. "And you cannot stay even long enough to bury your husband."

Anna looked down at John, shuddered, then reached a hand out for Kaylene. "I am ready," she said, proudly lifting her chin.

Kaylene took Anna's hand. She squeezed it affectionately, then walked away forever from the life that she had known since she was a child.

A horse was brought for Anna. She mounted it. She looked around her at the men, women, and children who stared up at her. "This is all yours," she said softly. "Do with it what you wish. I gladly rid my life of it."

Kaylene smiled, then rode off with her mother at her left side, Fire Thunder at her right.

She looked straight ahead, her heart anxious for what lay waiting in Laredo.

26

Her lovely yielding form I pressed,
Sweet maddening kisses stole.
—ROBERT DODSLEY

They had made camp for one night and headed out
again for Laredo the next day. It was growing dusk
when they saw Laredo not that far ahead in the
distance.

Fire Thunder drew a tight rein. He wheeled his horse
around and faced his faithful warriors. "Make camp
here," he said. "Only Kaylene and I will ride on into
Laredo. We shall return after our mission is complete."

Kaylene turned to Anna, whose shoulders were
slumped with weariness from the long travel on horseback. "Mother," she said softly. It did still seem right
to call Anna mother. She had been Kaylene's mother
for too long now, to address her by anything else. It
would seem disrespectful, somehow. "You will be safe
here with the Kickapoo warriors. Rest. Eat. Then
sleep. I am not certain if we will even return tonight.
It's according to what we find out about . . . about my
true mother."

Tears filled Anna's eyes. "I wish you hadn't found out," she murmured.

"Knowing isn't going to change all that much in my life now," Kaylene tried to reassure her. "I am going to marry Fire Thunder. No matter whether or not I had found out the truth about my parents, I would have still stayed with Fire Thunder as his wife."

Anna cast Fire Thunder a shy glance, then looked over at Kaylene. "I will never understand how you could fall in love with a man who took you captive," she said softly, so that Fire Thunder wouldn't hear.

"You will soon understand why I could have never hated him," Kaylene said. She gazed at Fire Thunder, as taken now with him as the first time she had seen him on his horse with his warriors as they had passed by the carnival. She smiled at her mother. "I would wager a bet that you will soon be as smitten with Fire Thunder as I," she said, laughing softly.

Fire Thunder rode up next to Kaylene. He eyed Anna, seeing her weariness, then dismounted. He went to her and placed gentle hands to her waist and lifted her from the saddle. "You need rest," he said. "Take advantage of my and Kaylene's absence. When Kaylene and I are through with our mission, we will have a long travel ahead of us again to reach my mountain."

Anna gave him a nervous smile as she stepped away from him. She stared up at him, his height so much more than most men she had ever known. "Thank you," she murmured, "I do appreciate your kindness."

Kaylene's insides warmed when Fire Thunder gave Anna a gentle hug, so glad that he was showing Anna the sort of man that he was. She could tell by Anna's expression that she was surprised by Fire Thunder's gentleness. Her eyes were wide and her cheeks flushed pink as he turned and went back to his horse.

"Wish me luck, Mother?" Kaylene said, her voice breaking when Anna came quickly to her and reached her arms up for her.

"May God be with you," Anna said, hugging Kaylene as Kaylene leaned down low enough for the embrace.

Swallowing back the urge to cry, Kaylene gave her mother one last hug, brushed a kiss across her cheek. Then she sat straight in the saddle and rode off with Fire Thunder.

As the sunset splashed Laredo the color of sin, the brilliant red color reflecting from the windows, Fire Thunder and Kaylene rode slowly down the main street. The town had a reputation for scenes of violence, Indian wars, border banditry, and rowdyism.

Kaylene now recalled having been to Laredo one time, when the carnival had set their tents on the far edge of town. She had been frightened by the gunmen who came and saw her show. It was so vivid in her memory that it was as though she were there now, performing on her panther. She could hear their bawdy talk as they shouted at her and tormented her with lewd teasings. If ever she had been afraid in her life, it had been then.

Even now, she tensed as she looked on both sides of her. The street was a solid block of buildings with wooden canopied sidewalks. There were mainly saloons and bawdy houses. She could hear the drunken laughter wafting from the saloons, the bat-wing doors swinging in the haze as drunks staggered from the establishments. She could hear the tinkling of pianos, the clink of coins, and she could smell whiskey and cigarette smoke.

Standing just outside the doors were men in leather chaps, buckskins, and some wore denim breeches and shirts. Cigarettes hung from the corners of most of their mouths.

But their eyes were the most prominent features as they stared at Fire Thunder and Kaylene on horseback among the other horsemen and buggies and carriages.

A covered wagon rode past Kaylene, upon which were painted several advertisements. One stated PRATT'S HEALING OINTMENT FOR MAN AND BEAST. Another: CHILL TONIC WHICH MAKES CHILDREN AND ADULTS AS FAT AS PIGS.

She laughed at these promises, knowing that most medicines sold by these men were little more than alcohol and a few pungent herbs.

The voice of a barker for a street show, inviting cowhands to see the freak pig or watch the performance of "The Armless Lady," caused Kaylene's thoughts to return to her years at the carnival. Oh, she was so relieved to no longer be a part of that life.

She breathed more easily when they left that part of town and rode past adobe houses, church buildings, and plazas.

Kaylene glanced over at Fire Thunder. He seemed to know where he was going, as though he had been in Laredo many times before.

"You are familiar with this town?" Kaylene blurted out.

"Yes, I have been here many times to speak with the sheriff when my people lived close by, on land we never truly felt comfortable on," Fire Thunder said, his voice drawn. "When our cattle were stolen, I reported it." He gave her a half glance. "But the white sheriff scoffed and did nothing about it."

"Then do you truly feel comfortable being here now?" Kaylene asked, seeing out of the corner of her eye a large adobe building that Fire Thunder was now directing his horse toward.

"That was many years ago," Fire Thunder said, drawing a tight rein beside a hitching rail. "There will be a different sheriff. Let us go and inquire about this woman named Eloisa Soriano, your mother."

"Part of this town is lovely," Kaylene said, dismounting. "The other part is ugly in its unpleasantness."

"This town that sits on the Rio Grande, across from Nuevo Laredo, Mexico, has had many faces," Fire Thunder said, slinging his reins about the hitching rail. "It was established as a ferry crossing to Mexico. It was named for Laredo, Spain."

"You know so much about Laredo," Kaylene said, flipping her horse's reins around the rail, beside Fire Thunder's. Her heart pounded to know she was in the very town where she might find her true mother. This small talk that she was making with Fire Thunder was helping her keep down her excitement.

"Living near it, as my people did, its history became familiar to us," Fire Thunder said. He glanced over his shoulder as two horsemen rode past, their eyes on him and Kaylene. "After the revolt against Mexico in 1836, Laredo was in a no-man's land and became the seat of the shortlived 'Republic of the Rio Grande.' Now it is just another town, fighting to be a place of respect."

Fire Thunder nodded toward the large adobe building, where above the door hung a plaque on which was painted in bold black letters the word JAIL. "Let us go inside and speak with the sheriff," he said. "Perhaps he can direct us to your mother."

"What if he can't?" Kaylene said, stepping up on the wide porch beside Fire Thunder.

"Then we will go elsewhere in town for answers," Fire Thunder said. He gave Kaylene a wavering glance. "But, Kaylene, if we do not find your mother in or near Laredo, we must give up the search. I have been gone from my village much longer than I had planned."

"I understand," Kaylene said softly, nodding. She said a prayer to herself that she would be given this one chance to see her true mother. If not, she despaired, what in life was fair?

Fire Thunder held the swinging door open for Kaylene.

She gave him a weak smile, then stepped inside.

She was glad when he was at her side again when she found herself suddenly face to face with a short, yet burly, aging man, whose dark eyes bore into her as he stared up at her. He then looked slowly over at Fire Thunder.

His gray hair hung to his collar. His face was lined with craters of wrinkles. He wore a buckskin outfit, a sheriff's badge pinned to the shirt, with heavy pistols at both his hips.

Recognizing the man to be a much older Sheriff Adams than he had dealt with in the past, Fire Thunder stiffened.

"Fire Thunder?" Sheriff Adams said, taking a slow step toward him, away from the bulletin board where he had been pinning wanted posters. "Is that truly you?"

"Sheriff Adams, it has been many moons since we last talked," Fire Thunder said, not taking the hand that the sheriff extended toward him. He had too many memories of this man that grated at his nerves.

"You are making your residence in Mexico now, I hear," Sheriff Adams said, slowly easing his hand to his side.

"Yes, and now no Kickapoo are threatened by white rustlers," Fire Thunder grumbled.

Kaylene gave him an uneasy glance, fearing that if

bad feelings erupted between these two men who seemed to have had an uneasy past, the sheriff might not be willing to supply them with the information she so terribly wanted.

"Fire Thunder, ask him," she blurted out. "Please ask him if he knows my mother."

Fire Thunder gave her a slow gaze, then knew that with her astuteness, she was aware of the tension between him and the sheriff, and concerned about it.

"Mother?" Sheriff Adams said, idly scratching his wrinkled brow. "Miss, what's her name? I know everyone in these parts who deserves bein' known."

"Eloisa Soriano," Fire Thunder answered for Kaylene.

Kaylene paled when she saw the quick reaction of the sheriff—how his jaw tightened and his beady eyes narrowed even more.

"Eloisa Soriano . . . is . . . your . . . mother?" he questioned warily. Forking an eyebrow, he looked Kaylene slowly up and down.

Then he looked up at Fire Thunder. "This woman you are looking for is a leper," he said, his voice tight.

"Yes, we know that," Fire Thunder said. He reached a hand out for one of Kaylene's and squeezed it reassuringly.

"Then you do know her," Kaylene said anxiously. "You do know where she lives."

"Everyone knows of Eloisa Soriano," Sheriff Adams grumbled. "And everyone knows not to go near her."

"I must see her," Kaylene said, her voice breaking. "I have never known her. I have never seen her. I must, this once, see my mother."

"She is not pleasant to look at," Sheriff Adams said, visibly shuddering. "And I warn you not to get near her. She is cursed!"

Kaylene paled. She turned her eyes away from him, then gazed intently at him again. "Tell me how to find her," she said, her voice grim.

"If you must know, she lives far into the hills, alone," Sheriff Adams said. He then took them outside onto the porch and pointed out the direction they should take to get to Eloisa Soriano's cabin.

"Thank you," Kaylene said softly.

"Fire Thunder, it was good to see you again," Sheriff Adams said as he walked them to their horses. "Come again. All past differences are forgotten, are they not?"

Fire Thunder glowered at the sheriff as he untied the reins of his and Kaylene's horses.

He then helped Kaylene onto her horse, swung himself into his saddle, and rode away with Kaylene without even a nod to the sheriff.

"You haven't changed a bit, you damn savage!" Sheriff Adams shouted after them. "You're like all redskins. You don't have an ounce of appreciation in you! You just take, take, take!"

Fire Thunder rode onward in the direction of the hills. He looked heavenward, and saw how the sky was darkening. "We will make camp, then go to your mother tomorrow," he said, giving Kaylene a soft gaze. "We are unfamiliar with the terrain. It would not be safe to travel up the hillside in the dark."

"Whatever you think is best," Kaylene said, glad to be out of the town of Laredo, now where the countryside seemed less threatening. The scent of spring was in the air as the wildflowers which dotted the landscape sent off their spicy fragrance.

When the moon was full overhead, and a thick stand of trees for the cover for their camp was found, they quickly built a small fire within a circle of rocks.

Kaylene ate the beef jerky and slices of dried pumpkin that Fire Thunder had taken from his store of food in his parfleche bag. She kept looking toward the hillside which housed her mother, somewhere among the trees.

"I will soon know my true mother," she whispered as she took the last bite of the jerky. She drank big gulps of water from the canteen, then crawled over to Fire Thunder and sat down on his lap, straddling him with her legs.

She eased the last tiny piece of jerky from his hand and tossed it aside, then twined her arms around his neck and drew his lips to hers.

"I love you so," she whispered against his lips. "You are so good to me."

"You would not have said that a few weeks ago," Fire Thunder said with a low, throaty chuckle as his hands crept up inside her blouse. "I was a vicious savage in your eyes."

"I never saw you as a savage," she whispered. "And please, *please* never say that word again to me. It is white men like my ... like John Shelton, and even perhaps that sheriff in Laredo, who are the true savages of our world."

"You are a woman who fills my heart with so much joy," Fire Thunder said, then kissed her with a tenderness that grew slowly into a surge of passion.

When he cupped her breasts, she moaned softly into his mouth. Her skin was warm and smooth against the flesh of his fingers. Her lips were moist and hot against his mouth.

She pulled her lips away. She gazed at him in the moonlight, his eyes shining with passion.

"Tell me what is in your heart," Fire Thunder whispered huskily.

"I want you," Kaylene whispered. She reached her

hands to the tail end of his shirt and lifted it slowly up his powerful chest, and then over his head.

Fire Thunder placed his hands at her waist and lifted her from him. He drew her to her feet before him. Methodically, slowly, meditatively, he undressed her.

She, in turn, slowly finished undressing him, until they were both standing nude in the soft night air, hardly aware of the rustling of leaves overhead as the breeze sang through them.

Fire Thunder gazed at Kaylene, his pulse racing as he once again became in awe of her gentle curves. He ran his fingers over her breasts, then lower across her flat stomach. He splayed them over that shock of hair that framed that part of her that he hungered for.

When he thrust a finger inside her, he watched Kaylene's expression turn to ecstasy as she closed her eyes, sighing. He stroked her woman's center.

He leaned low over her and flicked his tongue over one of her breasts, the nipple hardening.

"Take me, darling," Kaylene whispered, as she reached down and touched his thick, long shaft. Her voice quivered emotionally in her excitement. "Fill me."

He sucked in a breath of passion when she came to him and leaned her soft body against the hardness of his. He placed his hands at her buttocks, and when she lifted a leg around one of his, she guided him inside her pulsing cleft. She threw her head back in a guttural sigh of pleasure when he began his eager thrusts.

He drove inside her as he held her in place against him, then withdrew from her and lay her down on the blanket that he had spread beside the fire.

He moved over her and parted her thighs. His warm breath mingled with hers as he kissed her, then shoved himself deeply inside her.

When he entered her she shuddered sensually. She rode with him as he began his rhythmic strokes.

Fire Thunder reverently breathed her name against her neck as his lips slid from her mouth. Then again he kissed her long and deep and moved slowly, powerfully within her.

His mouth slid from her lips and showered her with feathery kisses along her throat until he reached a breast. With exquisite tenderness he chewed on the nipple.

They made love until they were exhausted.

Then they drew blankets around their shoulders and sat beside the fire, their eyes heavenward. "It is such a beautiful night," Kaylene murmured. She giggled as she gazed over at him. "In many ways, my love."

Suddenly there was a meteor shower overhead.

Fire Thunder jumped to his feet as though he had been shot as he watched the falling stars.

Kaylene dropped the blanket from around her and rose quickly to her feet beside Fire Thunder. She stared at him, seeing terror in the depths of his eyes for the first time, ever.

"What is it?" she gasped. "You look so frightened?"

"Do you see what is happening in the heavens tonight?" he said, his voice drawn.

"Yes, it is a meteor shower," Kaylene said warily. "I . . . I think it is quite lovely."

"There is nothing lovely or good about it," Fire Thunder cursed as he gave Kaylene a quick frown.

"Why not?" Kaylene asked softly. "Or is it something in your customs that causes your reactions? Do meteor showers mean something bad to the Kickapoo?"

"It forewarns disaster," Fire Thunder said in a tone of voice that sent splays of icy fingers across Kaylene's flesh.

Kaylene recalled the one other time when Fire Thunder had been away from his village and he had been forewarned of a disaster. He had been right to be alarmed then.

Was he also this time? she despaired to herself.

27

We met on roads of laughter;—
Now wistful roads depart,
For I must hurry after
To overtake my heart.
— CHARLES DEVINE

At first Kaylene and Fire Thunder followed a creek in the tall woods. The path was so narrow, sometimes they snapped off the branches on either side of them.

When Kaylene saw a lone cabin through a break in the trees, only a short distance away, she scarcely breathed. Could it be? she wondered, her pulse racing.

As she and Fire Thunder rode closer, her heart did a flip-flop and her fingers tightened around the horse's reins as she saw an old bent woman sitting on a chair outside the door of the cabin.

A soft spray of sunshine broke through the umbrella of trees overhead, giving Kaylene a better view of the elderly lady.

Yet to her disappointment, she could not see the woman's face. She was bending low over an animal that lay dutifully at her right side on the ground, gently stroking its gray fur.

"My mother," Kaylene said in a timorous whisper. "That has to be my mother."

Her gaze shifted. She studied the animal, gasping when she discovered that it was a wolf. This choked Kaylene up with emotion, knowing that her mother had the same sort of bond with animals as herself. Kaylene now knew where she got the deep feelings she had for animals. *From* her mother.

Kaylene looked quickly at Fire Thunder. "Surely that's her," she said, her voice anxious. "Don't you believe so, Fire Thunder? This is the only cabin we've seen. It *is* so isolated. Don't you believe that's my mother?"

Fire Thunder's gaze moved slowly over the elderly woman who wore a faded cotton dress and whose gray hair was wrapped in a tight bun atop her head.

"Yes, I believe it is your mother. But until we see her face, and see whether or not she is a leper, we shall not be certain," Fire Thunder said, drawing a tight rein. "Let us leave our horses here and go the rest of the way on foot. We do not want to alarm the woman. And thus far I do not think she has heard the approach of our horses." His gaze shifted. "Nor has the wolf."

Kaylene drew a tight rein and slid out of the saddle. "Do you think the wolf could be a threat?" she asked. "What if he attacks us as we approach?"

"Most wolves are not as prone to attack as a dog might be when strangers approach," Fire Thunder said, tying his reins to a low tree limb. "Although most people think of wolves as vicious and mean, for the most part, they are gentle. They tend to cower from strangers, not pursue them."

Kaylene laughed nervously. "I hope you're right," she said, but doubted he was so sure of what he said when he grabbed his rifle from the gunboot on his saddle.

"Come," Fire Thunder said, nodding toward her. "Let us go now and introduce ourselves to the woman. My *main* concern is that she will flee back inside her lodge when she sees us. Surely she has grown to fear strangers since those who know she is a leper would not go near her. She would have to believe that those who *do* approach her cabin would only do so out of ignorance and might be someone with evil on their minds."

"Oh, how I hope she will give us a chance to speak with her," Kaylene said, falling into step beside Fire Thunder as they slowly walked toward the cabin. "I have to tell her who I am. I *must* ask her who my father was. Surely he is someone I can go to without the fear of such a dreaded disease as leprosy."

"Do not count on too much, Kaylene," Fire Thunder said, giving her an uneasy glance. "If you do, you might be disappointed."

When they got close enough to the cabin for the wolf to sense their presence, his steely-gray eyes raised and he saw them. He immediately showed his fangs and growled, causing the elderly woman to lift her head in a panic.

Kaylene's insides swam with emotion when she saw the lady's face, now for certain that she was gazing upon her mother's. She was shocked and saddened by her appearance. Pain for her mother shot through Kaylene's heart when she saw the layer after layer of scales, like those of a fish, on her face. Her eyes were sunk deeply into the scaly flesh, allowing her only to see in a squint.

She wanted so badly to reach out to her, to explain who she was. Yet she feared the wolf as it crept closer with a steady, low growl in the depth of its throat.

Kaylene looked at her mother, then at the approaching wolf, then at her mother again.

Her heart leaped with panic when the woman picked up a cane from the ground and leaned against it as she rose slowly to her feet and started backing away, the door only inches behind her.

Kaylene raised a hand and gestured toward her. "Please don't go inside," she cried. "We haven't come to harm you. I need to speak with you. Please listen to what I have to say. I have waited a lifetime to know you. Please, oh, please allow it."

The old woman stopped and stared at Kaylene. "Who are you?" she asked in a raspy voice. She gazed sharply at Fire Thunder. "What do you and that Indian want of me? I've got nothing of value here. I'm a leper. Don't you know that? No one comes close to a leper. No one cares about a leper. What brings you here?"

"Long ago you gave a child up to carnival people," Kaylene said, half watching the wolf as it slunk closer. Kaylene could feel Fire Thunder's readiness beside her. Should the wolf leap toward them, Fire Thunder would get a shot off quickly to stop it.

Kaylene's eyes widened in surprise when the wolf, instead, crept up to her and knelt, its teeth no longer bared, its gray eyes looking trustingly up at her. Her heart went out to him, for he was treating her as though they were long-lost friends.

"How would you know about me giving up my baby?" Eloisa asked, her voice breaking. She took a shaky step forward, peering more intently at Kaylene through her small eyes.

"How would I know?" Kaylene said, choking back a sob that was threatening to surface. "I am that child."

When she saw Eloisa's reaction, and how she sud-

denly swayed, as though she might faint, Kaylene
started to rush to her and hold her.

But Fire Thunder's hand moved like a streak of
lightning as he grabbed her arm and held her back.

"You cannot approach her any closer than this," he
said flatly. "You cannot chance it, Kaylene. You must
control your strong desire to hold her, to embrace her.
She is unembraceable, Kaylene."

Tears flowed from Kaylene's eyes. "Yes, I know
that," she murmured. "But for a moment I forgot."

"Emotions make one forget," Fire Thunder said,
easing his hand back to his side. "And she will understand why you cannot come to her. She would not
even want you to. She would not want to condemn
you to the same sort of life she has been forced to
live."

"You are my daughter?" Eloisa finally said, sobbing
as tears rushed from her eyes.

"Yes, I am your daughter," Kaylene said, wiping
tears from her cheeks. "My name is Kaylene."

"How did you know how to find me?" Eloisa asked,
her eyes taking in every inch of Kaylene.

"I only knew recently that I had been raised by
people who were not my true parents," Kaylene said.
"When I discovered that I had been taken as a child,
and raised by someone other than my mother, I demanded to know who my real mother was. As soon
as I knew, I came looking for you."

"I would have never given you up had I not been
forced to by circumstances," Eloisa said, her voice
breaking. "Have you been happy?"

Kaylene hesitated, for she was not quite sure how
to answer that. Except for John Shelton, for the most
part, she had done well enough in the carnival. So it
would not be so much a lie when she told her mother
that, yes, she had been happy enough.

"And I soon will be married," Kaylene said, reaching a hand out to Fire Thunder, twining her fingers through his. "Mother, this is Fire Thunder. He is a Kickapoo chief. I so badly wanted you not to only know me, your daughter, but also the man I will soon marry, who will then be your son-in-law."

Kaylene noticed how her mother suddenly flinched. She wasn't sure what had caused her reaction. It surely had to do, though, with whom Kaylene was marrying. Perhaps she disliked Indians, as so many white people did.

One thing for certain, Kaylene was not going to ask her. She did not want to know that her mother was prejudiced toward Indians.

Fire Thunder nodded a silent hello to Eloisa, and she to him. Then Eloisa's eyes brimmed with tears again as she took the time to again slowly look her daughter over.

"You are so beautiful," she then said. "And you are a woman of kind heart for having come to talk to me."

"I so badly wish to embrace you," Kaylene said, stifling a sob behind a hand.

"As do I you," Eloisa murmured. She used the loose sleeve of her dress to wipe the torrent of tears from her eyes and face. "But it is enough for me just to get to see you and talk with you. Never had I thought it possible to see my daughter again. And now here you are, a grown woman who is soon to marry."

"And soon I hope to also be a mother," Kaylene said, feeling Fire Thunder's grip tighten on her hand at the mention of children. She knew that what she said pleased him. "I will bring your grandchildren and let you see them also."

"You would do that?" Eloisa said, her voice breaking again.

"Yes, I promise you that I shall," Kaylene said, again wiping tears from her eyes.

"Where do you live?" Eloisa asked, glancing over at Fire Thunder, then back at Kaylene.

"I live with Fire Thunder now at his Kickapoo village not that far from San Carlos, Mexico," Kaylene answered. "Yes, it isn't all that close to your home, but I will still manage to come from time to time to have such chats as we are having today." She swallowed hard. "That is, if you wish me to."

"I have been quite lonely," Eloisa said softly. "Yes, do come whenever you can." She glanced down at the wolf. "Wolf is my best friend. He does not fear my scaly body."

Kaylene started to kneel down to embrace the wolf, but again Fire Thunder stopped her.

"Who is to say the disease of your mother would not be carried on the fur of the wolf?" Fire Thunder said thickly. "Do not chance it, Kaylene."

Eloisa whistled for the wolf.

He turned toward her and ran quickly to her.

She reached out and patted him, then guided him to her side.

"I was told, Mother, that you traveled with Gypsies," Kaylene went on. "Could you tell me something about yourself and your Gypsy people? Where are they? Can you tell me who my true father is?"

Eloisa smiled slowly. "Yes, I can tell you about your father," she said. "But until now I have told no one. I kept the secret, so that when he was alive, he wouldn't have to be embarrassed by people knowing that he had loved a woman such as I, who was truly never pretty, but instead someone who knew well the art of loving a man."

Kaylene's heart sank when she realized that by her

mother's words—"when her father *was* alive"—that he was now surely dead.

She paled and gasped when her mother told her that her father was a great Comanche war chief. That meant that she, in part, was Indian!

"He is dead now for many winters," Eloisa said solemnly. She gave Fire Thunder a frown. "He was killed in a battle with the Kickapoo."

Everything became suddenly quiet between them. As for Kaylene, she was afraid to ask any more about her father, fearing that she might discover that her betrothed might have killed him.

She was glad when her mother broke the silence and told her at length about her Gypsy family, that they were now faraway, never staying put in any one place for any length of time.

"They will never return this way ever again because they do not want to associate themselves with this old woman whose body has betrayed her," Eloisa said sullenly.

They talked awhile longer, until Kaylene saw how weary her mother was becoming. And she knew that Fire Thunder was eager to return home.

And that was all right with Kaylene. She had succeeded in her mission to find her mother.

Now perhaps she could rest at night and proceed with the rest of her life with the man of her midnight dreams, and make a life with him that would be wonderful.

They said their good-byes and tears spilling from her eyes, Kaylene went back to her gentle mare.

Fire Thunder kissed her softly, then lifted her into the saddle.

For a while they rode down the hillside in silence, beneath the umbrella of the trees, and then through vast fields of wild flowers.

"How do you feel about my father being a Comanche war chief?" Kaylene finally blurted out, unable to hold it inside her any longer.

"How do you think I should feel?" Fire Thunder said, giving her a slow gaze.

"I'm not certain," Kaylene said, sighing deeply. "It's just that I know now that he died while battling the Kickapoo. Could it have been you?"

"Not all Comanche are my enemy," Fire Thunder said solemnly. "Only those who crossed the border into Mexican territory, to raid and steal from those I promised to keep safe when a treaty was reached between myself and General Rocendo."

He paused, then said, "There was only one Comanche war chief that I have actually gone to war against. And that was Chief Panther Crow."

Kaylene stiffened at the name, reminded of her pet panther and how it had seemed to have come to her out of nowhere the day she had found it.

Could her father have been Panther Crow? Could he have been reincarnated into the panther and have come to her?

She didn't voice this thought aloud to Fire Thunder. She would keep it close to her heart, the only secret she would ever keep from her beloved Kickapoo chief, her wondrous lover.

Then another thought came to her that shook her innermost being. She suddenly remembered those strange stirrings that she had felt after she had arrived at Fire Thunder's village, while mingling with his people. So often she had felt as though she might have been an Indian in another life. Now she understood those stirrings!

It was wonderful to know that she *was* part Indian in *this* life!

It would be something she would carry proudly with her while she lived among Indians.

Yes, now she understood why she had so quickly felt as though she belonged with the Kickapoo.

Yet she could not help but feel as though she had been deprived of something precious in her life by finding out just now that she was part Indian. But she would make up for it now that she knew. She would learn everything Indian. She would live it.

The one thing that took away from this wonderful moment was the sadness she felt over the illness of her mother.

She vowed to herself that this woman would never forget her. She would go as often as possible to talk with her. Her true mother would no longer be alone in the world.

Then a thought came to Kaylene that excited her at the possibility of being able to do it. She looked quickly over at Fire Thunder.

"Fire Thunder, why must my true mother be forced to live in such total isolation so far from me, her only family?" she blurted out. "Could she come and live on your mountain, where I could go and see her more often, than if she should stay where she lives now? And, when we have children, we could share them with her." Her eyes pleaded. "What do you think?" she asked, her voice trembling in her anxiety.

Fire Thunder thought for a while, then gave Kaylene a soft smile. "Yes, we can work that out," he said. "We will go soon and tell her the news. We will give her the opportunity to be a part of our lives, if she wishes to be."

"Oh, she will," Kaylene said, sighing contentedly. "I just know that she will."

"But still, you can only talk with her from a distance," Fire Thunder said. "Will that be enough?"

"Yes, oh, yes," Kaylene said, nodding. "You are so kind, Fire Thunder. So sweet, so caring. How am I so lucky to have met you?"

"I am the lucky one," Fire Thunder said, again smiling.

They rode onward until they reached the others they had left behind at the campsite.

Then everyone rode together back toward Fire Thunder's village.

They traveled until evening came, but they still went on. They crossed the Rio Grande, rode past the outskirts of San Carlos, then proceeded up the mountainside.

Halfway up the mountain, Fire Thunder's insides turned cold and he drew his horse's reins tight and stopped. His eyes could not leave the horrendous sight of Black Hair as he hung from a tree in the moonlight, a rope tied securely around his neck. His head lay limply to one side.

Kaylene's eyes followed Fire Thunder's.

She felt faint when she saw Black Hair's body swaying in the gentle night breeze, his horse grazing close by, as though it was dutifully waiting for him.

The other warriors circled around, staring, low chants beginning from the depths of their throats in plaintive, sad wails.

Kaylene gave Anna a quick glance, who had turned her eyes from the grisly sight.

Fire Thunder rode over to Black Hair. He waited for two warriors to stand beneath the body and reach up and take hold of its legs.

Then Fire Thunder slipped a knife from the sheath at his left side and cut the rope in half, loosing Black Hair.

Black Hair's body fell clumsily downward. The two warriors caught him, then lay him on the ground and stood over him.

Fire Thunder dismounted.

Kaylene followed his lead and hurried to his side as he went and stood over his departed friend.

"How do you think this happened?" Kaylene asked softly, turning her eyes away from Black Hair.

"His appearance tells me that he has been dead for some time," Fire Thunder said. "I am remembering now how sullen Black Hair was after his daughter humiliated him by her shameful behavior that last time in front of the whole village."

"You . . . think . . . he killed himself?" Kaylene asked, gazing up at Fire Thunder, seeing his anguish.

Fire Thunder held his face in his hands. "No," he said, his voice choking. "I will not believe that he killed himself. The Kickapoo think suicide an unforgivable, mortal sin."

He flung his hands from his face and looked heavenward. "Who could have done this thing?" he cried. "This man. This brave warrior! He was so much to me! He was my closest friend, to whom I gave the right hand of my heart!"

He looked down at Black Hair again. "There are many possibilities," he growled out between clenched teeth. "The Texas ranchers. They could have discovered that we Kickapoo are responsible for the recent thefts of their cattle, not the Comanche. They could have come across Black Hair as he traveled alone. As a mark of vengeance against our whole tribe, they could have killed Black Hair, one of our most valiant warriors."

He looked over his shoulder, in the direction of San Carlos. "It might have been some of General Rocendo's soldiers," he hissed out. "The general might have ordered this done, making Black Hair pay for Black Hair's daughter's sin of consorting with his son Pedro, and for Running Fawn being responsible for his son being so ill from having made the tattoo on his leg."

He turned glowering eyes toward Anna. "Or it could have been carnival people from John Shelton's troupe who came and avenged John Shelton's death," he said sullenly.

"No, it surely wasn't them," Kaylene cried, knowing the importance of keeping Fire Thunder and his people from resenting Anna for any reason. "His men did not care for him that much. They only tolerated him because they had no choice. They were raised to know only one thing—carnival life. And don't you remember? Mother gave the carnival to them. They would be too happy for that good fortune, to come and kill one of your men. They have cause to thank you, not resent you."

"I will never know who is truly responsible," Fire Thunder said, his voice breaking.

He glanced over at Black Hair's horse. He nodded toward a warrior. "Get his horse," he said softly. "Place Black Hair across the saddle. Let us take him home. Soon Black Hair will be riding the spirit of a horse long since gone from this earth on his trip heavenward."

Kaylene watched solemnly, thinking how complicated life was. Only a short while ago she had felt so blessed and happy to have been able to talk and be with her true mother.

Only moments ago she had been content to know that her very own mother might soon live near her, so that they could talk whenever they chose to.

And now, it was the worst of times, when the man she loved was filled with such despair over the loss of a loved one.

It always seemed that it was hard to keep a good, hard grip on true happiness, for there was always someone, or something there, to tear it all down again.

28

She walks among the loveliness she made.
—VITA SACKVILLE-WEST

Several weeks had passed. The mourning period was now over for Black Hair. Fire Thunder no longer wore narrow strips of braided buckskin around his neck and waist to show his mourning. Nor was his entire face covered in the black ash of mourning.

As Fire Thunder had said, Black Hair's storms of life were over. He was at peace.

And so Fire Thunder was now at peace with Black Hair's death, yet would forever miss him.

Kaylene was all aflutter inside because this was the day when Fire Thunder was going to make his formal announcement to his people about his upcoming marriage to her.

She sat before a roaring fire in Anna's cabin as Anna brushed her hair for the coming ceremony. Although Kaylene had lived among the Kickapoo for many weeks now, the formality of the ceremony was required so that she would be living by the rules set down by them. She would be practicing their customs.

"You have so many things to learn about Fire Thunder's people," Anna said softly, as though she had read Kaylene's thoughts. "Take this for example—that I could not brush your hair in Fire Thunder's cabin. I shall never understand, Kaylene. It seems so wrong. Soon his cabin will be yours. Is he going to force you to step outside every time you want to brush or comb your hair? You can't tell me that he tends to his own long hair outside his lodge."

"Yes, he does," Kaylene murmured. "It is taboo for anyone to brush or comb their hair in a Kickapoo lodge. Now I will be the first to admit that I find that strange, also. But it is just one of those things I must accept. I am hellbent on learning everything Kickapoo and living among them as one with them."

"I am grateful, oh, so grateful to Fire Thunder for allowing me to live here, and for giving me this fine cabin. But I too often feel as though I am an intrusion in your lives," Anna said, her voice breaking.

Kaylene looked over her shoulder at Anna. "I understand that so much has changed in your life," she said thickly, "And I can see how you might feel as though you are intruding ... as though you don't *belong*. Please listen when I say that I am so happy that you are here."

Kaylene rose from the chair and turned toward Anna. "And one day you will feel as though you belong," she softly encouraged her. "You are so much the same as I, in how we never had roots until now. It is a difference I love. But you were with the carnival for much longer than me. It will take longer for you to adjust."

Anna laid the brush aside as Kaylene stepped closer. She drew Kaylene into her arms. "You could hate me, yet you don't," she whispered, stroking

Kaylene's back. "Thank you, darling, for caring . . . for taking me in when I felt I had lost everything."

"I'm glad to be able to give you something back after all that you did for me," Kaylene murmured.

She swallowed hard when she recalled how she had felt hate for Anna the first time she realized that Anna had deceived her by making her believe that she was her own daughter.

Kaylene was happy to know that she hadn't been abducted like the others. She had been taken in to raise as a *daughter*. How could she hate Anna when she had taken pity on her as an infant?

If Anna had not done this, Kaylene shivered at the thought of what might have happened to her. For certainly, she would never have met Fire Thunder.

A shadow filling the open doorway brought Kaylene from her mother's arms. She smiled as Fire Thunder stepped into the room with the grace of a deer, his gaze roving over her.

Kaylene squared her shoulders and straightened her back as she allowed him a longer look before going to him to fling herself into his wonderfully strong arms.

She ran her fingers down the front of the dress that she had purchased in San Carlos on her last shopping spree with Anna and Little Sparrow. It was blue silk, with puffed sleeves and a fully gathered waist. White lace trimmed the low bodice and the edges of her long sleeves. She wore dainty slippers.

All but for the flowers that her mother had not yet placed in her hair for the ceremony, Kaylene was ready to go out and face Fire Thunder's people.

Kaylene looked at Fire Thunder and the way he was dressed in a neat suit of buckskin, with fringe on the sleeves, across the shoulders, and down the trouser legs. He wore high moccasins made of the softest, cream-colored skins. His hair trailed down his back, braided and decorated with artificial roaches of dyed bristles of deer hair and shells.

Kaylene was taken anew by his handsomeness, by his gentle smile, and by the shine in his blue eyes. She had never thought that love could be this strong between any man and woman, especially after being raised in a family where man and wife scarcely ever embraced. Even smiles were vague between them. It seemed to have been a business transaction between John and Anna Shelton. Nothing more; nothing less.

With Kaylene and Fire Thunder, it was going to be a sharing of hearts until they took their last breaths on this earth. Theirs was a special loving, a special, mutual admiration between them. And she felt so very, very blessed!

"I have come for you," Fire Thunder said, reaching a hand out for Kaylene. "Come. My people are waiting."

"The flowers," Anna said, rushing to Kaylene with a handful of pink roses, their thorns removed from the stems. "Let me put the flowers in Kaylene's hair."

Fire Thunder's eyes danced at Kaylene's. "Yes, make my woman special today," he said huskily. "A surprise awaits her this morning."

"Surprise?" Kaylene said, her eyes widening. She stood perfectly still as her mother pinned the roses in her hair above each ear. "What sort?"

"Now if I told you, it would not be a surprise, would it?" Fire Thunder said. He turned to Little Sparrow as she came into the cabin with Midnight at her side, on a new red leash.

The way Little Sparrow smiled so devilishly up at her, Kaylene's curiosity increased.

With her hands she spoke to Little Sparrow, shaping the word *surprise* on her lips in a question.

Little Sparrow giggled and shook her head, refusing to tell Kaylene what the surprise was.

"Well, I guess I'll just have to wait and see," Kaylene said, letting out a frustrated sigh, then laughed softly.

"There, darling, the roses are beautiful," Anna said, stepping back to admire her daughter.

Anna wore a new dress, also, one that she had purchased at San Carlos. To her surprise, only one week ago, several carnival men came to the village and handed her an envelope in which she found several hundreds of dollars.

The men had sold the carnival. They had brought Anna her share of the money, having kept only enough to tide them over until they got established elsewhere, doing other work.

Anna had been deeply touched by their generosity. She felt rich, not only money-wise, but also mentally, as well, for never had she been as happy as now.

Fire Thunder went to Kaylene. He gently framed her face between his hands. He gazed at her, at her flawless features. He had never seen her so vibrant and glowing as now. He so badly wished to cover her moist lips with his mouth, but held back until later, when they would be alone and free to do as they pleased.

The soft glimmer of her hair spilled over her bare, fair shoulders and tumbled down her back in thick waves.

The bodice of her dress was low, and he gazed down the front of it, his heart leaping with desire at the sight of her tantalizing cleavage.

He ran his thumbs over the exquisite, creamy flesh of her cheeks.

Then his hands rediscovered the delicate contours

of her face as she gazed up at him with eyes darkening with the depths of her emotion.

Again Fire Thunder cradled Kaylene's face in his hands and brushed a soft kiss across her lips. "Are you ready?" he whispered.

"I'm somewhat frightened," Kaylene whispered against his lips. "Should I be?"

"There is no reason to be," Fire Thunder said. He eased away from her and took one of her hands. He gave her a smile of reassurance, then left the cabin, with her mother and Little Sparrow following close behind them.

When Kaylene stepped outside, her breath was stolen away as she looked at what awaited her. While she had been inside Anna's cabin, getting ready for this special day, a great outdoor fire had been built. Large platters of various types of food had been placed around it. Wild flowers lay strewn along the ground that led to a platform that was also covered with flowers.

Fire Thunder's people were all there, smiling, and watching her.

Something else drew Kaylene's attention. She gasped when she saw the large pile of gifts that were scattered before the platform, among them everything that she could ever imagine that a woman might need for housekeeping, or to wear.

She turned joyous eyes to Fire Thunder. "This is a wonderful surprise," she said, tears filling her eyes. "Everything is beautiful."

"My woman, this is not the surprise I was referring to," Fire Thunder said, his eyes flashing devilishly into hers, with almost the same expression that Kaylene had seen when she had tried to urge Little Sparrow into telling her what the surprise was.

"Then . . . *what*?" Kaylene said, her eyes widening. "How could anything else be as wonderful as this?"

"Come and you will see," Fire Thunder said, placing his hand at one of her elbows.

He led her through the crowd.

She was touched by how some of them reached out and gently touched her, as though she were a fragile doll.

She could tell by their smiles and gentle expressions that she had been accepted as she had wanted to be accepted. She was one with them in her heart, soul, and being. She was so touched by this, she could hardly keep from crying.

And her knees were so weak from emotion, she could hardly step onto the flower-strewn platform.

Once there, with Fire Thunder beside her, she turned and faced the crowd.

Anna was standing with Little Sparrow among them, Midnight lying at Little Sparrow's feet, his green eyes on Kaylene.

Suddenly a young brave, the one that Little Sparrow had pointed out to her one day, as being the one whom she had special feelings for, came to Kaylene.

Dressed in a buckskin outfit, and smiling broadly up at Kaylene, he handed her a small bird's nest filled with wild daisies.

Touched deeply by the sweetness of it, Kaylene reached her hands out and took the nest of flowers. "Thank you," she murmured, seeing how the young brave's eyes shifted quickly to Little Sparrow as she moved to his side, smiling.

Then the young brave lifted his eyes back to Kaylene. He smiled at her again, then stepped back with Little Sparrow into the crowd.

One by one the people came to the platform, each taking Kaylene's hand, then telling her which gift that

lay beside the platform was theirs. Before it was all
over, Kaylene's jaws ached from smiling so much.

Then it came to her that something seemed amiss
here. No one had yet even mentioned the marriage
today. It was as though she and Fire Thunder were
already married. It was as though the announcement
had already been made. Surely it had not been done
in her absence. He had always talked about it as
though it was something they would do together.

Kaylene sent a quick questioning look Fire Thunder's way. "When will you make the announcement?"
she whispered as she leaned next to him. "When are
we going to be married? It is as though your people
think we are already. Why is that, Fire Thunder?
Where is the surprise that you mentioned? I don't
understand."

"That *is* the surprise. We *are* married," he said,
smiling mischievously at her when he saw her stunned
reaction. "My woman, all there is to a Kickapoo
'marriage ceremony' is 'to bind,' for the formal announcement comes after the marriage has been con-
summated, which it was, the first time we made
love."

"What . . . ?" Kaylene softly gasped. "Why didn't
you explain this to me earlier? Why would you not
tell me?"

"Did it truly matter?" Fire Thunder said, taking her
hand, squeezing it affectionately. "Do you not recall
all of the traumas we have been faced with since we
first met? It did not seem important to sit you down
and explain to you what does or does not compose a
marriage ceremony. What was important was getting
to a point where we could celebrate our union with
nothing else on our minds that would take away from
the joy of it. Today is the right day, the right time for
such a celebration for us. So much bad and ugly is

behind us, a part of our past. Our future is what we should be concentrating on. And *now*, when we are among my people, showing them our devotion to one another."

"I love you so," Kaylene murmured, beaming.

He placed an arm around her waist and drew her close to his side. "Today I make the formal announcement that this woman is my wife!" he shouted, his voice reverberating skyward, reaching the far sides of the mountain, the trees, the streams, and the land that belonged to the Kickapoo.

The people showed their feelings about his choice by raising their voices in loud cheers.

Fire Thunder led Kaylene from the platform and once again his people floated past them, each of them taking turns embracing Kaylene and Fire Thunder.

When Anna came to Kaylene, Kaylene looked deeply into her eyes and saw the intense love this lady felt for her. She drew Anna into her embrace. "I shall always love you," she whispered. "Mother, thank you for giving me your love as I was growing up, which gave me the ability to love."

"I'm glad that you are happy," Anna murmured. "Your happiness is all I ever wanted out of life. My own never meant all that much to me."

"And that is what makes you so special," Kaylene said, stepping back from Anna. Her eyes blinked. "I was wrong to allow hate for you to enter my heart those few days when I was so confused about so many things. Do you forgive me?"

"You have done nothing to be forgiven for," Anna said, again slowly drawing Kaylene into her arms. "Child, child, I just wish I could have spared you so many things. It is I who should be asking forgiveness of you."

Kaylene clung to Anna, yet her thoughts strayed to

someone else—her true mother. She had gone earlier in the day and had sat and talked with Eloisa from the short distance they now allowed themselves, where Fire Thunder himself had built Eloisa a cabin not all that far from his village. Kaylene had shared her happiness with Eloisa then, and her adoptive mother now.

"Wife?" Fire Thunder said, taking Kaylene by the hand. "Are you through talking with Anna?"

"Yes, I believe we've said all that needs be said for now," Kaylene said, smiling from Fire Thunder to Anna.

"I have one more thing that I would like to say," Anna said. "My darling Kaylene, you don't know how it thrills me, clean into my soul that you still call me mother. I thought I lost all rights to that when you discovered that your true mother was alive."

"Mother, do you not know that that makes me doubly blessed?" Kaylene said softly. "Just how many can boast of having two mothers?"

Fire Thunder swept Kaylene up into his arms. He started walking away from the crowd, toward his cabin.

Kaylene looked over her shoulder at all of the people watching them, and then at all of the food that still lay untouched on the platters. "Darling, aren't we going to join the feast?" she asked, gazing at him. His blue eyes melted her insides as they locked with hers.

"Who needs food?" he said huskily. "At least for now, my wife, food is the last thing on my mind."

Kaylene rested her cheek against his chest, a sensual warmth already swimming through her body. "Yes, who needs food," she whispered, so contented, she quivered from the intensity of it.

After they were in their cabin, standing before the fire on a large, outspread bear pelt, Kaylene was the first to initiate undressing. As her eyes locked with

Fire Thunder's, his face a mask of naked desire, she slowly disrobed, teasingly at first, and then more quickly when her desire for him became too strong.

Her last garment now tossed aside, and her shoes kicked off, Kaylene watched with a feverish heart as he disrobed until he was standing perfectly nude before her.

Her gaze burned over his naked flesh, greedily absorbing the sight of his muscled limbs, the sleekness of his copper skin, and ... and that part of him that was already aroused and ready to take her to paradise and back.

She sucked in a breath of wild rapture. The air was filled with anticipation when he came to her, and his hands moved slowly over her, teasing, stroking, loving the supple lines of her body.

She closed her eyes and threw her head back in ecstasy when he bent closer and his tongue slowly worshipped her body, beginning with her breasts. His tongue was wet and warm as he licked every inch of her breasts, stopping long enough to pull her taut nipples between his teeth.

Then when his lips, hands, and tongue moved lower on her body, and he reached her throbbing center, Kaylene swooned from the intense pleasure when he knelt before her and kissed her where she so unmercifully throbbed.

The kiss was wonderful in itself. But he did something else that made her cry out as though she were in pain. In truth, what he was doing was making her head spin so crazily with pleasure, she could hardly bear it.

She wove her fingers through his hair and drew his mouth closer, trembling from head to toe with rapture when his tongue flicked and licked rhythmically across her woman's center.

"I . . . don't . . . think I can last much longer," she managed to say in a husky whisper. She looked wildly down at Fire Thunder. "Please, Fire Thunder, please . . ."

Seeing her distress, that she was almost over the edge with total ecstasy, and wanting to join her on the journey as though on wings flying to the heavens, Fire Thunder rose to his feet.

He drew her into his embrace and kissed her. He held her against his hard body as he slowly lowered her to the softness of the bear pelt.

And when she was spread out below him, he stretched out over her and braced himself with his arms, his hands catching hers. His fingers intertwined with hers, and he held them slightly above her head and entered her in one deep thrust.

They made love, his hands now beneath her buttocks, lifting her closer as he moved rhythmically within her.

He touched his tongue to hers, then feverishly kissed her again, his mouth urgent and eager.

His hands found the soft swells of her breasts. His mouth lowered and his lips fastened on a soft, pink nub, gently sucking.

The ecstasy building, Kaylene strained her body upward. She drew him even more deeply inside her as he plunged over and over again into her willing, hot flesh.

Her gasps of pleasure became long, soft whimpers. She felt the pleasure growing again inside her, spreading, filling her with such bliss she wanted it to never end. She clung around his neck. She felt his body trembling, knowing that his ecstasy matched her own.

Fire Thunder was fighting off reaching the end, wanting it to last forever. He pressed endlessly deeper into her moist channel. He felt the need rising within him, burning with a fierce heat. It was both agony and bliss, these last moments before giving in to the intensity of the final sensual abandonment.

He slithered his lips down her neck.

He breathed her name against her flesh.

His head reeled.

His lips brushed the smooth, glossy skin of her breasts.

And then he let it spill forth from within him, this sensual shock that came with the great bursts of passion. He felt it growing, growing, and the final bursting point came when he cried out after finding total fulfillment, his body quivering into hers, hers answering as it rocked and swayed against his.

And then they lay quietly together for a moment longer, clinging, listening to the laughter and merriment outside their lodge.

"My people are now dancing," Fire Thunder said, hearing the rhythmic beat of the drums, and the shuffling of the feet in time with the music. "Shall we join them?"

"Don't you mean to say *our* people are dancing?" Kaylene said, laughing softly when he smiled at her, showing that he understood her meaning.

"Yes, our people," he said, chuckling.

He took her hands and drew her to her feet. Slowly he dressed her, but not in the silk clothing she had worn during the ceremony. Right before Dawnmarie had left for Wisconsin, she had given Fire Thunder a beautiful, white doeskin dress, with the bead designs of the forest flowers sewn on the front.

"This is a gift from Dawnmarie," he softly explained. "It was a dress worn by her for special functions. She wanted you to have it. She said that when you wear it, you will remember her, and the friendship that you found together."

Kaylene gazed down at the dress, recognizing it, remembering when she had seen Dawnmarie wear it. She grew warm inside at the thought. "She is so special," she said, choking back a sob. "I hope one day to be able to thank her for this wonderful gift."

When it was on her, she ran her fingers over the beautiful beads. "How lovely," she said, touched deeply by the gift.

"You are lovelier," Fire Thunder said, then left the room for a moment.

When he came back to Kaylene, he held something behind him. "Close your eyes," he said softly. "Stand still and do not open your eyes until I tell you to."

"Another surprise?" Kaylene said, giggling as she closed her eyes. She grew quiet when she felt Fire Thunder pin something to the bodice of the dress.

"Look now and see," Fire Thunder said, watching Kaylene's expression as she gazed down at the brooch. Her eyes were wide. Her lips were parted in a pleased gasp.

"It's beautiful," she murmured, running her fingers over the small, elaborately etched brooch.

"My woman, this has been in my family for many generations," Fire Thunder said thickly. "It is a German silver brooch. It has been used in conjunction with rhizome to enamor the person one desired. It has the power to catch. It has worked, has it not? I have you, the light of my heart."

"Does the brooch still have the power to 'catch' someone?" Kaylene asked teasingly.

"Yes, always," Fire Thunder said, chuckling. "Have you not noticed the two little claws which serve to catch the one desired?"

"I will wear it proudly to *keep* the man of *my* desire," Kaylene said, her eyes dancing.

"You have me forever," Fire Thunder said, stepping into his breeches.

Again he gazed at length at her. "You are ever so beautiful," he said huskily.

"Yes, I must admit that I *feel* beautiful," Kaylene said. Her laughter rippled as she looked up at him. "And those gifts, Fire Thunder, that your people gave us. I am so very touched by everything and everyone."

"They are all gifts from the heart," he said, pulling his shirt over his head.

"The bird's nest filled with daisies was so sweet," she murmured, as she ran her fingers through her hair in an effort to remove the tangles that lovemaking had created.

She realized the roses were gone. She gazed down at the bear pelt and found them there, scattered across the pelt, as though they had been purposely placed there for their lovemaking.

"That gift that you thought was so sweet could have gotten the young brave in trouble," Fire Thunder said, his eyes twinkling into Kaylene's.

"How could it have?" Kaylene asked, her eyes wide.

"Children are taught not to disturb bird's nests," Fire Thunder said, stepping into a moccasin. "But if they find them on the ground, abandoned, that is the difference. When I saw the young brave with the nest, I questioned him. He said that he had found it beneath a tree. No birds or eggs were anywhere near it."

"I understand why a bird's nest shouldn't be disturbed in a tree, but a child might, in innocence, take one down," she murmured. "Would the child even still be, as you say, in trouble?"

"Sanctions for killing or disturbing taboo animals are administered early to Kickapoo children," Fire Thunder said, gently placing his fingers on her shoulders. "I will tell you one example. One day a very young brave of five winters, while cutting firewood, came upon the tiny nest of a hummingbird, in which lay a newly hatched bird. Elated over his find and wishing to make a present of it to his grandmother, and foolishly having forgotten his teachings about the sanctions for killing or disturbing taboo animals, he proudly carried it home. On seeing what the young boy had done, the grandmother cut off a switch and punished him until the blood ran from his legs. Crying with pain, the young boy was directed to take the nest to the exact branch where he had found it and told never again to molest this bird, as it was sacred to our clan."

"That seemed too severe a punishment," Kaylene said, shuddering at the thought of a young boy's legs bleeding from a whipping.

"The switching that the young man received was mild compared to the sanctions imposed by the supernatural on adults who molest or kill taboo animals," Fire Thunder said thickly. "Let me tell you another tale as an example. There was a young man who once killed a chicken hawk by a shot through the head. An older brother who accompanied him on the hunt was indignant and alarmed and reprimanded him, saying 'Younger brother, you have indeed done a grave thing and you will be punished; perhaps not immediately, but eventually.' Sometime later the young man was thrown off a horse and hit a rock in the same spot where he had shot the bird. He died from the blow."

"Why, that is even worse than the tale of the young boy," Kaylene said, again shuddering.

"The child of my story, who stole the bird nest, was me," Fire Thunder said somberly. "The young man who died was Black Hair's brother."

"You . . . were that little boy who was so unmercifully whipped?" Kaylene said, glancing down at his legs, not remembering any scars.

"Yes, and I do not resent it," Fire Thunder said, drawing her into his embrace. "One must learn by doing, even if sometimes what one does is wrong." He got a faraway look on his face as he gazed into the fire. "And so did Grey Thunder who was Black Hair's brother. I ... miss both very much."

The laughter and singing outside drew them. "Let us go outside and join the merriment," Fire Thunder said, taking her hand, leading her toward the door. "I should not have told you depressing tales, especially not on our special day."

When they stepped outside, they discovered that day had turned to night. The moon was full and bewitching overhead. "My wife, do you see the moon tonight?" Fire Thunder said, gesturing toward it.

"Yes, and I don't think I have ever seen it look so beautiful," she murmured, watching it.

Fire Thunder turned to Kaylene. He lifted her chin with a finger so that their eyes met. "The moon herself is a woman," he said softly. "Tonight she shines brightly just for you, my *wife*."

Again he looked heavenward, drawing her eyes there also. "Black Hair is up there in the heavens, perhaps one of the stars that twinkles the brightest tonight," he said, his voice somewhat shaky. "Or he might be riding a horse spirit and gazing down at us, wishing us well!"

"And we won't disappoint him, will we, darling?" Kaylene murmured. "Our marriage is going to be the envy of all who know us."

Fire Thunder turned to her. "I am the envy of all who know me for having won you as my wife," he said thickly, then kissed her, leaving her weak in the knees as though it were their very first kiss.

29

Loved you when the summer deepened into June,
And those fair, wild, ideal dreams of youth
Were there, yet dangerous and half unreal.
As when Endymion kissed the mateless moon.
—VITA SACKVILLE-WEST

Five Years Later—

Her fingers sore and split from having been cattailing
with the rest of the Kickapoo women these past two
days, Kaylene walked homeward with several heavy
bundles of cattail leaves secured on the back of her
burro.

She smiled, to know that she was now a part of the
Kickapoo's lives, blending in well with their customs
because of her eagerness to learn them.

But today, now that her cattailing was complete, she
was anxious to return home, to her family. She never
liked being gone from her two children for any length
of time.

And then there was Fire Thunder. How she ached
for him in his absence. Theirs was a love affair that
was neverending.

Family, she sighed to herself, thinking of the others
who were an intricate part of her life.

Anna, ah, sweet Anna, who was always eager to care for her two grandchildren, Kaylene and Fire Thunder's lovely daughter and handsome son.

Eloisa, her true mother, cherished the moments when Kaylene took her children close enough for her to see them—her grandchildren—and marvel over.

And pretty and delicate Little Sparrow! How she always brightened up a room when she entered.

But Little Sparrow's being there, in their home, would soon end. When she reached her sixteenth birthday, she would marry Wolf Fire, a young man she had fallen in love with only a few weeks ago, leaving her puppy love for the other young brave behind her.

Wolf Fire was a patient man. He was willing to wait for Little Sparrow to become sixteen. He himself was twenty, and had become a fast friend of Fire Thunder's. He was Fire Thunder's sidekick, a brave young warrior who hardly left Fire Thunder's side when there were things to be done for their people.

Kaylene's smile faded when she thought of Midnight. Her beloved panther was not at all well. He scarcely ate anymore and he spent most of his time sleeping.

But it comforted Kaylene to know that they had had the best of times together. He had been her salvation during her years of feeling so alone, and dreaming of a day she might find "roots" in her life.

Yes, she would mourn him, as though he were a person. But one could not change one's destiny. They had lived theirs out, it seemed, and soon it would be time to say a final, sad farewell.

She thought back to the Kickapoo women, with whom she now traveled down the mountainside, and how they had spent their time away from their families these past days. When they had arrived at a distant stream, farther up the mountain than their village, they had immediately built a flimsy camp of saplings, over which they had spread a canvas. They had taken their bedding, cooking utensils, and enough food to last for two to three days.

In two days, they had cut enough cattail leaves to supply them with several months of work. When they had first entered the stream, where the cattails stood majestically tall, each woman had said a prayer and offered a bit of Indian tobacco to the snakes who owned the water and cattails. They had asked permission to cut only what they needed and asked the snakes not to molest them.

Only the leaves ten feet high or more had been cut, just above the rhizome. A companion had held the leaves for the cutter and tied them into manageable bundles with split pita, which they had brought for the purpose.

Each woman worked until she had at least fifteen bundles for making bed and household mats. Those who lived in wigwams needed more, for repairing the roofs and sides of their lodges.

When the women returned home, the bundles would be propped up against their lodges, to dry. When a woman found time from her many daily chores, she would take one bundle at a time, sit outdoors, and with a sharp knife, begin to clean the cattails. She would separate each leaf from the others, cut off the pithy bottom and the tapering end, and save only those leaves which were nine feet long.

The cleaned leaves would be soaked in hot water to make them pliable and give them a tawny-green color.

As Kaylene moved onward, having encouraged the women to take this different route down the mountainside this time, thinking it might be shorter, she gazed around her at the difference in the foliage.

Nothing of nature seemed disturbed. The trees were thick. Flowering vines ran up the trunks of each, sending off a sweet and spicy fragrance.

As she looked up into the trees, Kaylene saw birds she had never seen before as they flitted from limb to limb.

Yes, this way was different than the other side of the mountain, and she remembered now that Fire Thunder had said that this one side was not frequented by his warriors when they went on a hunt, mainly because of the thickness of the trees and bushes.

Kaylene regretted having come this way. It was hard to squeeze the burros through the denseness of the trees. And she had rips and tears on her skirt caused by the thorny bushes.

Suddenly her heart leaped with surprise and she stopped to listen. Up ahead, through the trees, she thought she had heard someone laughing softly.

She turned to the woman beside her. "Did you hear laughter?" she asked, seeing that the other women had also stopped, and seemed to be scarcely breathing as they also listened.

"Yes, I heard it, but who could it be?" Blue Cloud said. "No one else but we Kickapoo live on this mountain."

Kaylene turned her head in the direction where she once again heard the laughter. "Someone *is* here," she said, her eyes widening in curiosity.

She turned to the women again. "Let's go and see who it is," she said, and was surprised to see that none of them seemed willing to.

She gave Blue Cloud a long stare. "Even you are afraid to go with me?" she said, having made a strong bond with this woman, almost the same as she had formed with Running Fawn when they had first become acquainted.

"I shall hold the reins to your burro," Blue Cloud said, taking them from Kaylene. "I shall stay behind with the others. But do not go too close, yourself, until you see who it is and if they are alone."

Kaylene inhaled a nervous breath, then turned toward the sound of the laughter again. She *had* to see who was there. Curiosity was killing her.

She moved stealthily, her hand slipping her cutting knife from the sheath at her left side. When she came to a clearing and she could see more easily what lay ahead of her, her eyes widened in surprise.

She saw a cabin, and outside the cabin there was a beautiful lady sitting on the ground, playing with a small child, a boy who was surely four or five years old.

The woman's back was to Kaylene.

Then suddenly the woman turned and revealed her face, causing Kaylene's knees to suddenly weaken with the surprise and shock of the discovery.

"Running Fawn!" she gasped. "It's Running Fawn!"

Her gaze swept down to the small boy. He was adorable, with his long black hair flowing down his bare back to his waist. His skin was copper, his eyes pitch black. And when he laughed, it sent a warmth through Kaylene.

She then realized that Running Fawn must have been pregnant with Pedro's son when she had been exiled from the village. That had to mean that Running Fawn had given birth to this child and had raised him alone.

Unless . . . ?

Kaylene looked around and saw no signs of a man living there with Running Fawn.

She took a step closer, stepping on a twig and snapping it with a loud noise. Her presence had been revealed.

She slipped her knife back inside its sheath and quickly stepped out into the clearing for Running Fawn to see.

She reached a hand out for Running Fawn, to stop her, when she grabbed her son in her arms and started backing toward her door.

"Running Fawn, it is me, Kaylene," Kaylene said, reaching a hand out for her friend. "It is so good to see you."

When Running Fawn backed up closer to her door, panic seized Kaylene. "No, Running Fawn, don't go inside. Please let's talk."

"Go away!" Running Fawn cried. "My son and I do not want you here. Leave us alone!"

"Running Fawn, please let me talk to you," Kaylene pleaded, inching closer. "Tell me how you've been. Tell me about your son."

"No!" Running Fawn cried, tears springing into her eyes. "It is useless! Do not break my heart by coming and then leaving. I do not want to feel the pain again that I felt when I was banished."

"Things have changed, Running Fawn," Kaylene cried. "Had we known you were here you would have been invited back to live among your people. Fire Thunder has softened in his mood about the young women of his village and who they do or do not wish to become involved with. Times are slowly changing this particular custom among them."

"Fire Thunder would never change his mind about me," Running Fawn said, taking another step toward her door. "I do not want to hear anything you have to say! Little Pedro and I have done quite well on our own! Before he was born I went to San Carlos and managed to steal all that I needed to make life comfortable for me and my son. The seeds I stole give me food each year in my garden. I have never gone back to San Carlos again. We are happy and safe here. We need no one!"

Kaylene suddenly recalled that Pedro had never married. He still loved Running Fawn. "Your son is Pedro Rocendo's son, is he not?" Kaylene asked. "Pedro would still marry you. I know he would. He has never married. He has even broken ties with his father. Pedro manages a general store. He pines for you, Running Fawn. He has told me this, himself! Come with me now, Running Fawn. Let's go back to the village. Make peace with your people. Then you can go on to San Carlos. Pedro will give you and your son a good life!"

"You are saying things you do not know are true," Running Fawn cried. "Why make my life complicated when now it is so simple for me and my son? Surely Pedro has forgotten me."

"No, he hasn't," Kaylene said, moving toward Running Fawn. "I'm telling you the truth when I say that he told me how he still feels about you. He misses you. He is only half a man without you."

"Kaylene, please stop!" Running Fawn shouted, then turned and ran inside her cabin and slammed the door behind her.

Kaylene was not going to give up that easily. She went to the cabin and opened the door and stepped inside. A fire was burning in the fireplace. The cabin was immaculately clean, but scarce of furniture. Yet it had many comfortable mats everywhere, making Kaylene realize that Running Fawn also frequented the streams to do the cattailing.

"Kaylene, you are not welcome here," Running Fawn said as she backed away from her, her child held tightly within her arms. "Please leave!"

"Not unless you leave with me," Kaylene said softly. She moved toward Running Fawn, backing her up against a wall.

When Running Fawn couldn't move away from her, Kaylene reached a hand out to the child and gently touched his soft, copper face. "I also have a son," she murmured. "His name is Little Thunder. And I also have a daughter. Her name is Snow Bird. I would love for you to see them, Running Fawn."

Running Fawn offered no response.

"Do you remember how close we were?" Kaylene said, now reaching to Running Fawn's hair, and stroking it. "Do you remember brushing my hair, and how you refused to let me comb it in Fire Thunder's lodge? I couldn't understand. I didn't know then that it was a taboo thing to do. Now I know so much about your people and their customs. I love being among them. Please come back with me. If Fire Thunder had known that you were this close, living alone with your child, he would have come for you, himself."

"As he would my other three friends?" Running Fawn said sarcastically.

"Where are they. Do you know?" Kaylene asked softly.

"No, I have not seen them since they left with me that day from our village," Running Fawn said. She laughed sarcastically. "They are probably even dead, and what would our chief care if they were?"

"He cares," Kaylene admonished her. "And he regrets many things and has made changes that suit his heart more than before. Always before, he followed the strict teachings of the Kickapoo. But now, as times change so has he. He is still a great leader, but much more lenient than before."

"I would not believe it, even if I saw it," Running Fawn spat out.

Then Running Fawn's eyes blinked. "I would so much like for my father to see his grandson," she said, her voice breaking. "How is my father, Kaylene? Has he ever married, to fill the void left there by so many things in his life?"

The sudden realization that Running Fawn wasn't aware of her father's death made Kaylene's insides tighten and grow cold. Oh, how she dreaded having to tell her, but she must. Running Fawn had been deprived already of too much. She should not be deprived of knowing about her father's death any longer.

"Your father, Running Fawn, is—"

She didn't get the rest of the words out before Running Fawn gasped and paled. "I see it in your eyes and hear it in your voice that you have no good news about my father," she said, a sob lodging in her throat. "He is dead. My father is dead!"

"Yes, Black Hair is dead," Kaylene said, her voice drawn.

Running Fawn began sobbing. She turned her eyes away from Kaylene, then turned slowly toward her again. "How?" she said, composing herself for the sake of her son. "How did my father die?"

Kaylene knew that telling her how Black Hair had died might even be worse than telling her that he was dead. "You don't want to know," she blurted out.

"I deserve to know," Running Fawn said flatly. "I want to know."

"He died shortly after you left the village," Kaylene said softly. "No one knows who is truly responsible. They found him . . . hanging . . . from a tree. Someone hung him."

Running Fawn was dying a slow death inside, but again for her child, kept her feelings to herself. "Please leave, Kaylene," she said, her voice void of emotion. "I want to be alone with my son."

"I'll leave now, but I will be back," Kaylene said, leaving a soft kiss on the child's cheek. Her eyes looked into Running Fawn's. "I've seen your son. Now I so badly want you to see mine."

Running Fawn stared silently at Kaylene as she drifted toward the door.

"I *will* be back," Kaylene said, then turned and ran from the cabin.

When she got outside, she broke into tears for the heartache that she had brought to Running Fawn. Now she regretted having found them. They seemed to have been living a life of peace and harmony.

"Now what should I truly do?" Kaylene whispered to herself as she turned and gave the cabin one last look before joining the other women. "Should I leave her alone? Or come back for her?"

30

With tongues all sweet and low,
Like a pleasant rhyme,
They tell how much I owe
To thee and Time!
—BARRY CORNWALL

"Then you will allow Running Fawn to return from exile?" Kaylene asked, looking anxiously at Fire Thunder.

She had just told him about having found Running Fawn, and her son. She had pleaded Running Fawn's case and now awaited his response.

"You said that you told her about her father," Fire Thunder said, turning to look down at the flames stroking the logs in the fireplace.

Everything was quiet in the lodge. Midnight was sleeping on the hearth, close to the warmth of the fire.

Both of Kaylene and Fire Thunder's children were asleep in the bedroom they shared with Little Sparrow.

Little Sparrow was away from the village, riding horseback with her betrothed.

"Yes, I told her, and she became very distraught," Kaylene said as Fire Thunder turned slowly to face her again. "It's cruel to leave her there alone, not only because of her torment over having lost a father, but also because of little Pedro. He needs to know more people than his mother to grow up and be a normal child."

"She could have gone into San Carlos long ago and made a life for herself," Fire Thunder argued. "No one was there stopping her."

"But she was doing as you told her to do," Kaylene murmured, keeping to herself the secret that Running Fawn *had* gone into San Carlos, if only that one time. "You forbade her to see Pedro again. If she had gone into San Carlos to live, she would have seen him."

"Yes, I forbade her to see him again, and here you are asking me not to only allow her to return to her people, but also to go to the very man who took part in turning her away from what was right for her, a Kickapoo," Fire Thunder said.

Then he drew Kaylene into his arms. "Yet, I do see the need for the boy to be raised around people," he said thickly. "And, yes, he does need his father, a man we both know has never married because of his love for Running Fawn."

When Kaylene realized that Fire Thunder was weakening in his decision about Running Fawn, her heart began to pound with an excitement she had to keep from him, until he gave her the answer she so badly wanted.

"What are you saying?" Kaylene asked softly, leaning away from him, looking up at him.

"I have something to do," Fire Thunder said as he broke away from her. "I will be only a minute."

Kaylene nodded and watched him leave.

Sighing, she began to pace back and forth. She

started to clasp her hands nervously behind her back but the cuts from cattailing pained her, and she quickly drew them apart again.

She turned and stared at Fire Thunder as he came back into the lodge.

"Where did you go?" she asked warily.

"I sent a warrior to San Carlos with the news about Running Fawn," he said, gently framing Kaylene's face between his hands. He bent a soft kiss to her lips, then smiled into her eyes. "And I asked Anna if she would mind coming to babysit for a while, while you and I go and get Running Fawn and her child."

So excited, so happy, so relieved, Kaylene flung herself into his arms. "I knew that you would!" she cried. She gave him frenzied kisses across his lips. "Thank you, darling. Oh, thank you, thank you."

When Anna came into the cabin, Kaylene gave her a quick embrace, and even though she was bone tired from the days of gathering cattail leaves, and from the long journey down the mountainside, Kaylene had renewed energy at the thought of making things right for Running Fawn and little Pedro.

Hand in hand she left the cabin with Fire Thunder.

Two horses were waiting for them. Fire Thunder lifted Kaylene into her saddle on her mare, then swung himself into his own saddle. They rode off as the sun crept lower in the sky. They left the village and made their way up a narrow path on the mountainside.

"The route I took from cattailing took me by the burial grounds of your people," Kaylene said, giving Fire Thunder a glance. "That is the only way I will know how to find Running Fawn's cabin again."

They swung their horses right and moved onward.

When the burial grounds came into sight, Kaylene gasped and gave Fire Thunder a quick look.

"She's there at her father's grave," she said in a rush of words. "That's Running Fawn kneeling over her father's grave. She came and found it."

"I did not think she would stay long at her cabin once she knew her father was dead," Fire Thunder said, looking satisfied. "She is Kickapoo after all, for no Kickapoo could ever not want to see the grave of their dearly beloved departed."

His gaze shifted just as little Pedro stepped from behind his mother and knelt beside her over Black Hair's grave. "And so there is Black Hair's grandson," Fire Thunder said, his eyes devouring the child, making him feel as though in the child, he might have a part of his friend back again. "We will wait until she is finished praying and then go to her and tell her that all is forgiven," Fire Thunder said thickly.

"You never disappoint me," Kaylene said, reaching out a hand and taking one of his.

Back in their cabin, freshly bathed, and having eaten a delicious meal that her mother had prepared for Kaylene's family in her absence, Kaylene snuggled close to Fire Thunder as they stood over the beds of their children.

"Don't our children look content in their sleep?" Kaylene murmured, first gazing at her four-year-old son, Little Thunder, and then looking over at their two-year-old daughter, Snow Bird.

"They have a good home where there is much shared love," Fire Thunder said.

He placed gentle hands on Kaylene's shoulders and turned her to face him. Little Sparrow was still with Wolf Fire, giving Fire Thunder and Kaylene all the privacy they needed.

"And now that Running Fawn has gone with Pedro

to his home," he said softly, "even that home will be filled with love."

"Thank you, darling, for welcoming Running Fawn into the lives of the Kickapoo again," Kaylene said, her voice breaking. "Thank you for forgiving her. Who knows what the future holds for *our* daughter? She might grow up with the same sort of wild streak that has always plagued Running Fawn. It is good to know that you no longer send young girls into exile for bad behavior, for I could not stand to see our own daughter forced to live alone, as Running Fawn has these past five years."

"You need not concern yourself about such things," Fire Thunder said.

He swept her up into his arms. She clung about his neck as he carried her from the children's room.

"With such a mother as you," he said, "no daughter born of your womb could be anything but sweet, caring, and gentle."

As Kaylene laughed lightly and teasingly, Fire Thunder carried her into their bedroom and kicked the door closed with his foot. Then he placed Kaylene on their bed. He stood over her and began to undress.

With soft, wondering eyes, Kaylene watched her husband, never getting enough of seeing him.

His body had long sinewy muscles. He was slender and thin of flank, his arms rippling bands of muscles.

Unclothed, he crawled on the bed beside her. "Are you too tired to make love?" he asked, his hand already sneaking up the inside of her skirt.

When he found her woman's center and began his slow caresses with his fingertips, he knew by her gasps of pleasure, and by how she spread her legs open to him, that she need not speak an answer out loud.

He moved over her and flipped her skirt up to her waist.

His mouth covered hers in a fiery kiss as he, with one heaving thrust, entered her.

Over and over again their wild whispers filled the dark, midnight air of their love haven.

"Everything is beautiful and, oh, so perfect," Kaylene whispered against his lips, his heat becoming hers.

"Had I not taken you captive—" he began, her soft finger against his lips stopping him.

"But you did, my sweet," she whispered back. "You *did*."

He chuckled, then again kissed her with fire, his body's rhythm sweeping her away on wings of rapture.

Letter to the reader:

I hope that you have enjoyed reading *Wild Whispers*. I put my heart and soul into each of my books. My next book for Topaz, *Comanche Dawn*, is filled with much adventure, Native American lore, and passionate, hot romance! It will be in the stores approximately six months from the release date of *Wild Whispers*.

I love to hear from my readers. For my latest newsletter, and for information about The Cassie Edwards International Fan Club, please send a self-addressed, stamped, legal-size envelope with your letter to me at:

Cassie Edwards
R#3 Box 60
Mattoon, IL 61938
Always,

Cassie Edwards

◆✦◆ TOPAZ

UNTAMED DESIRE
FROM CASSIE EDWARDS

☐ **WILD WHISPERS** Kaylene Shelton had no one to talk to in her father's carnival except for the black panther she raised from a cub. But she knew that somewhere love was waiting. Then, she was abducted by Chief Fire Thunder in revenge for her father having put his sister in a sideshow. Now could tantalizing passion and irresistible powers bring two strangers together?   (406796—$5.99)

☐ **WILD THUNDER** For Strong Wolf, Hanna was supposed to be the enemy, allied not only to the settlers he distrusted but to a man who coveted his land, the brutal foreman of her brother's ranch. He felt only sorrow could come of their love until the day Hannah rode to his lodge, fell into his arms, and began their hearts' journey to a glorious place where neither betrayal nor tragedy could follow.
                                                                          (405862—$5.99)

☐ **WILD BLISS** When a band of renegade Sioux kill Dawnmarie Garrett's English father in a raid of terror, she is forced to flee for her life, not knowing what has become of her gentle Indian mother. In a world of great spirituality and darkest savagery, fate could make Dawnmarie a slave to the Sioux's cruel desire ... or join her very soul to the chief of the Chippewa, her warrior lover, protector of native magic, fiery rapture, and ... wild bliss.   (405854—$5.99)

☐ **WILD SPLENDOR** Headstrong Leonida Branson isn't about to let her youth dry up in a duty-bound marriage to the pompous General Porter.... When she first sees Sage, the fierce Navaho chieftain her fiancé has sworn to crush, she knows that the comforts of civilization are no match for the adventurous passion the copper-skinned brave awakens in her.   (404041—$4.99)

*Prices slightly higher in Canada

Buy them at your local bookstore or use this convenient coupon for ordering.

PENGUIN USA
P.O. Box 999 — Dept. #17109
Bergenfield, New Jersey 07621

Please send me the books I have checked above.
I am enclosing $_____ (please add $2.00 to cover postage and handling). Send check or money order (no cash or C.O.D.'s) or charge by Mastercard or VISA (with a $15.00 minimum). Prices and numbers are subject to change without notice.

Card #_____ Exp. Date _____
Signature_____
Name_____
Address_____
City _____ State _____ Zip Code _____

For faster service when ordering by credit card call **1-800-253-6476**

Allow a minimum of 4-6 weeks for delivery. This offer is subject to change without notice.

◈ TOPAZ

SIZZLING ROMANCES
BY CASSIE EDWARDS

☐ **WILD EMBRACE** Exquisite Elizabeth Easton discovers the real wilderness when the noble Indian brave, Strong Heart, forces her to go with him in a fight back to his Suquamish people. Here both of them are free of all the pride and prejudice that kept them apart in the white world . . . as this superbly handsome, strong and sensitive man becomes her guide on passion's path to unfettered joy and love. (403614—$4.99)

☐ **WILD DESIRE** Stephanie Helton contrasted starkly with the famous "white Indian," Runner, adopted by the Navaho as a child and destined to be their leader. Tall, lithe, and darkly sensual, Runner immediately recognized Stephanie as the fire that set his blood blazing . . . and his sworn enemy. Runner felt his soul driven by conflict—he could not both lead his people and join his destiny with this woman. (404645—$4.99)

☐ **WILD ABANDON** Lauralee Johnston must place her trust in the handsome Cherokee brave, Joe Dancing Cloud as he teaches her about the kind of passion they have in common. But the bond forged between this bronzed, proud man and shy, beautiful woman becomes rattled with the prejudice and hate swirling around them . . . as a red-haired Yankee villain threatens to tear their union asunder. (404653—$4.99)

*Prices slightly higher in Canada

Buy them at your local bookstore or use this convenient coupon for ordering.

PENGUIN USA
P.O. Box 999 — Dept. #17109
Bergenfield, New Jersey 07621

Please send me the books I have checked above.
I am enclosing $_____ (please add $2.00 to cover postage and handling). Send check or money order (no cash or C.O.D.'s) or charge by Mastercard or VISA (with a $15.00 minimum). Prices and numbers are subject to change without notice.

Card #_____ Exp. Date _____
Signature_____
Name_____
Address_____
City _____ State _____ Zip Code _____

For faster service when ordering by credit card call **1-800-253-6476**

Allow a minimum of 4-6 weeks for delivery. This offer is subject to change without notice.

◆I◆ TOPAZ

TALES OF THE HEART

☐ **CAPTIVE by Heather Graham.** When sheltered Virginia belle Teela Warren gets a taste of the lush, exotic Florida Territory, her senses are dazzled. But when she glimpses halfbreed James McKenzie, the most attractive man she's ever seen, her heart is in danger. (406877—$6.50)

☐ **A TASTE OF HEAVEN by Alexis Harrington.** Libby Ross came to Heavenly, Montana, hoping for a new start, a family, children and a good place to raise them. What she found was terrible. The cowboy who duped her into being his mail-order bride had died, leaving her penniless with nowhere to go. That's when she heard about Lodestar Ranch and its owner, Tyler Hollins. (406532—$5.50)

☐ **ANGEL OF SKYE by May McGoldrick.** Alec Machpherson, famed warrior chief of the Highlands, has served King James IV of Scotland with his sword. Now he would give his very soul to protect Fiona, the spirited, red-haired lass from the Isle of Skye. But it will take Alec's Highland strengths pitted against a foe's cruel ambitions to prove, through blood and battle, which will reign—an army's might or the powerful passions of two lovers. (406745—$5.50)

☐ **PRINCE OF THE NIGHT by Jasmine Cresswell.** The Count of Albion, sequestered in an Italian villa, hid his secrets well—until the beautiful Englishwoman, Miss Cordelia Hope arrived. Irresistibly drawn to this cloaked, commanding count, Cordelia sensed his pain and, in all her innocence, craved his touch. He would become her destiny—the vampire whose love she was dying to possess. (405668—$4.99)

*Prices slightly higher in Canada

Buy them at your local bookstore or use this convenient coupon for ordering.

PENGUIN USA
P.O. Box 999 — Dept. #17109
Bergenfield, New Jersey 07621

Please send me the books I have checked above.
I am enclosing $_____ (please add $2.00 to cover postage and handling). Send check or money order (no cash or C.O.D.'s) or charge by Mastercard or VISA (with a $15.00 minimum). Prices and numbers are subject to change without notice.

Card #_____ Exp. Date _____
Signature_____
Name_____
Address_____
City _____ State _____ Zip Code _____

For faster service when ordering by credit card call **1-800-253-6476**

Allow a minimum of 4-6 weeks for delivery. This offer is subject to change without notice.

BREATHTAKING ROMANCES YOU WON'T WANT TO MISS

☐ **Wild Bliss** by Cassie Edwards   (405854—$5.99)

☐ **The Duke** by Catherine Coulter   (406176—$6.99)

☐ **Whisper My Name** by Raine Cantrell   (406052—$4.99)

☐ **A Taste Of Heaven** by Alexis Harrington   (406532—$5.50)

☐ **Falcon's Fire** by Patricia Ryan   (406354—$4.99)

☐ **Touch Of Lightning** by Carin Rafferty   (406133—$4.99)

☐ **Petticoats And Pistols** by Margaret Brownley

(406184—$4.99)

☐ **The Thistle And The Rose** by May McGoldrick

(406265—$4.99)

☐ **Bed Of Roses** by Suzanne Simmons   (405196—$4.99)

☐ **Stormswept** by Deborah Martin   (405293—$4.99)

☐ **Moonspun Dreams** by Elizabeth Gregg   (405730—$4.99)

☐ **Stolen Hearts** by Melinda McRae   (406117—$5.50)

from **TOPAZ**

Buy them at your local bookstore or use this convenient coupon for ordering.

PENGUIN USA
P.O. Box 999 — Dept. #17109
Bergenfield, New Jersey 07621

Please send me the books I have checked above.
I am enclosing $_____ (please add $2.00 to cover postage and handling). Send check or money order (no cash or C.O.D.'s) or charge by Mastercard or VISA (with a $15.00 minimum). Prices and numbers are subject to change without notice.

Card #_____ Exp. Date _____
Signature_____
Name_____
Address_____
City _____ State _____ Zip Code _____

For faster service when ordering by credit card call **1-800-253-6476**

Allow a minimum of 4-6 weeks for delivery. This offer is subject to change without notice.

WE NEED YOUR HELP
To continue to bring you quality romance
that meets your personal expectations,
we at TOPAZ books want to hear from you.
Help us by filling out this questionnaire, and in exchange
we will give you a **free gift** as a token of our gratitude.

- Is this the first TOPAZ book you've purchased? (circle one)
  YES   NO
  The title and author of this book is: _____

- If this was not the first TOPAZ book you've purchased, how many have
  you bought in the past year?
  a: 0 - 5   b 6 - 10   c: more than 10   d: more than 20

- How many romances in total did you buy in the past year?
  a: 0 - 5   b: 6 - 10   c: more than 10   d: more than 20 ___

- How would you rate your overall satisfaction with this book?
  a: Excellent   b: Good   c: Fair   d: Poor

- What was the main reason you bought this book?
  a: It is a TOPAZ novel, and I know that TOPAZ stands
     for quality romance fiction
  b: I liked the cover
  c: The story-line intrigued me
  d: I love this author
  e: I really liked the setting
  f: I love the cover models
  g: Other: _____

- Where did you buy this TOPAZ novel?
  a: Bookstore   b: Airport   c: Warehouse Club
  d: Department Store   e: Supermarket   f: Drugstore
  g: Other: _____

- Did you pay the full cover price for this TOPAZ novel? (circle one)
  YES   NO
  If you did not, what price did you pay? _____

- Who are your favorite TOPAZ authors? (Please list)

- How did you first hear about TOPAZ books?
  a: I saw the books in a bookstore
  b: I saw the TOPAZ Man on TV or at a signing
  c: A friend told me about TOPAZ
  d: I saw an advertisement in_____magazine
  e: Other: _____

- What type of romance do you generally prefer?
  a: Historical   b: Contemporary
  c: Romantic Suspense   d: Paranormal (time travel,
     futuristic, vampires, ghosts, warlocks, etc.)
  d: Regency   e: Other: _____

- What historical settings do you prefer?
  a: England   b: Regency England   c: Scotland
  e: Ireland   f: America   g: Western Americana
  h: American Indian   i: Other: _____

- What type of story do you prefer?

  a: Very sexy
  b: Sweet, less explicit
  c: Light and humorous
  d: More emotionally intense
  e: Dealing with darker issues
  f: Other

- What kind of covers do you prefer?

  a: Illustrating both hero and heroine
  b: Hero alone
  c: No people (art only)
  d: Other_____

- What other genres do you like to read (circle all that apply)

  Mystery   Medical Thrillers   Science Fiction
  Suspense   Fantasy   Self-help
  Classics   General Fiction   Legal Thrillers
  Historical Fiction

- Who is your favorite author, and why?_____
  _____

- What magazines do you like to read? (circle all that apply)

  a: *People*
  b: *Time/Newsweek*
  c: *Entertainment Weekly*
  d: *Romantic Times*
  e: *Star*
  f: *National Enquirer*
  g: *Cosmopolitan*
  h: *Woman's Day*
  i: *Ladies' Home Journal*
  j: *Redbook*
  k: Other:_____

- In which region of the United States do you reside?

  a: Northeast   b: Midatlantic   c: South
  d: Midwest   e: Mountain   f: Southwest
  g: Pacific Coast

- What is your age group/sex?   a: Female   b: Male

  a: under 18   b: 19-25   c: 26-30   d: 31-35   e: 56-60
  f: 41-45   g: 46-50   h: 51-55   i: 56-60   j: Over 60

- What is your marital status?

  a: Married   b: Single   c: No longer married

- What is your current level of education?

  a: High school   b: College Degree
  c: Graduate Degree   d: Other:_____

- Do you receive the TOPAZ *Romantic Liaisons* newsletter, a quarterly newsletter with the latest information on Topaz books and authors?

       YES   NO

  If not, would you like to?   YES   NO

  Fill in the address where you would like your free gift to be sent:

  Name:_____
  Address:_____
  City:_____Zip Code:_____

  You should receive your free gift in 6 to 8 weeks.
  Please send the completed survey to:

  Penguin USA•Mass Market
  Dept. TS
  375 Hudson St.
  New York, NY 10014